THE VINYL DETECTIVE

LOW ACTION

Also by Andrew Cartmel and available from Titan Books

Written in Dead Wax
The Run-Out Groove
Victory Disc
Flip Back

THE VINYL DETECTIVE

LOW ACTION

ANDREW CARTMEL

TITAN BOOKS

The Vinyl Detective: Low Action
Print edition ISBN: 9781785659003
E-book edition ISBN: 9781785659010

Published by Titan Books
A division of Titan Publishing Group Ltd.
144 Southwark Street, London SE1 0UP

First Titan edition: May 2020
10 9 8 7 6 5 4 3 2 1

A CIP catalogue record for this title is available from the British Library.

Printed and bound by CPI Group Ltd, Croydon CR0 4YY.

For Linda Kissick, most astute of readers.

1: NEW GIRLFRIEND

"I'd like you to meet my new girlfriend," said Erik. "Someone's trying to kill her."

He offered this remark in such a casual, offhand, everyday manner that I had to repress the urge to reply, "That's nice."

Erik Make Loud—less pretentiously, Eric McCloud—was a former rock star, comfortably wealthy and, if you stretched a point, our neighbour. I'd never got along very well with him. Erik was self-regarding and superior, to commence a long list. But one muffled grey afternoon in a recent winter we'd undergone a very horrible near-death experience together.

And I suppose that *had* bonded us.

Perhaps even made us friends.

At least, friends to the extent that he'd generally now make eye contact when he spoke to me. Which is what he was doing right now as he loomed in my doorway, emanating a cloud of expensive aftershave.

I said, "Come in, Erik." Before I shut the door behind him, I looked around outside to make sure the new girlfriend whose life was putatively in danger wasn't actually standing there, waiting to shake hands.

Erik didn't bother with shaking hands. He was content to slap me on the shoulder in what would have been a comradely fashion, if it hadn't been so heavy-handedly hard, as I led him into our sitting room where our cats looked up at our guest and regarded him with suspicion. As well they might.

For a start, Erik was wearing a cap that looked like it had been looted off a dead Confederate soldier, along with an elaborately fringed and brightly beaded buckskin jacket that might have been looted off the Comanche brave who had just killed the Confederate. Plus, of course, very skinny black jeans and very expensive black sneakers. Turk took one look at this apparition then sensibly darted out the cat flap just as Nevada came hurrying in from the kitchen.

"Did I hear that correctly?" she said. She looked at Erik with shock in her mesmerising big blue eyes. "Did you actually say…?"

"Yes, dear," said Erik, gazing at her fondly. Erik had always liked Nevada. Who wouldn't?

"You've got a girlfriend?"

"He also said someone was trying to kill her."

"One thing at a time. One earth-shattering revelation at a time. You mean a real, seeing-her-on-a-regular-basis girlfriend? Not one of your usual…" Nevada waved her hand in the air in a manner which Erik and I both understood to mean *inappropriately nubile and fleeting, celebrity-besotted one-night stands.*

"Yeah, going steady. We've been seeing each other for a few months now."

"*Mein Gott.* Who is this girlfriend?"

"She's called Helene—"

"Lovely name," said Nevada. "It means light."

"Does it?" said Erik. "All I know is that she plays a mean guitar."

"Ah, so she's a musician, too." Nevada looked at me. "The extraordinary longevity of their relationship begins to make sense."

Erik chuckled. "Well, yeah, it is nice to be able to connect on a musical level, you know, as well as everything else. Very good guitarist, she is. Plays big chunky phrases. Reminds me a bit of Blood Ulmer."

"Well, I'm delighted for you," said Nevada. She took my hand. "We're *both* delighted for you. Now, what's all this business about someone trying to kill her?"

Nevada sat down with Erik in full charm mode while I made coffee. I used the good stuff—the serious nature of the impending discussion seemed to merit it, even if it was only *attempted* murder. When the coffee was ready I carried the mugs through on a tray featuring a black-and-white picture of Marilyn Monroe. It was a gift from our friend Tinkler and, to those in the know, continued the murder theme.

Nevada and Erik were sitting at the dining table with our cat Fanny lying at the centre where other people might have situated an elegant vase of flowers. As if to emphasise the contrast, she was unconcernedly and shamelessly licking her private parts.

But Erik hadn't noticed. He was studying a record he'd picked up from the pile in the armchair beside him, where I tended to keep my current listening selection. It was John Mellencamp's *Uh-huh*, the British edition with the different and much superior cover art. As I came into the room he looked up from the album and regarded me with mild surprise—and perhaps even something resembling respect. Erik had me down as a jazz nut, which I am.

But I listen to other stuff, too.

I put the tray down on the table. Nevada glanced at it and gave me a droll look; she got the reference, all right. Then she passed Erik his mug. Fanny stopped washing herself and looked up at us attentively. Nevada peered directly into her eyes and said, "Our friend Erik is going to tell us about something terrible that has happened to his girlfriend."

In response to this declaration Fanny yawned luxuriantly, her mouth gaping wide to reveal tiny fangs while her small ears folded neatly back, flat on her head. Then she jumped down from the table and disappeared under the nearest armchair.

Erik didn't seem offended. He said, "The first attempt—"

"*First?*" said Nevada. "How many have there been?"

"Uh, let me think."

I saw a familiar stoned-rock-star vagueness drift into Erik's eyes. So I said, "Let's just let him tell us the story in his own way, honey."

"Of course," agreed Nevada. She was all business now, perched on her chair, hands hugging one knee, listening politely and giving Erik the big eye. But he was shaking his head ruefully.

"I suppose it would be easiest to get her to tell you all about it herself," he said. "To let Helene tell you all about it."

"All right," I said. "When would you like to arrange that?"

Erik shrugged. "Now, I guess."

"Now?"

"Yeah, she's out there in the car."

"*Out there in the car?*" said Nevada, scandalised. "Don't you think she might like to come in?"

"Yeah. Probably. All right."

Five minutes later Erik came back with a tallish woman. Other than that it was hard to immediately discern much about her because she was wearing an ankle-length dove-grey coat and a black hat. The coat was an upmarket, and no doubt eye-wateringly expensive, version of a Spaghetti Western duster. Her hat, thankfully, was not a cowboy one but what they call a porkpie hat, as affected by the late, great Lester Young.

I wondered if she and Erik had both been bilked by the same eccentric headwear emporium. By way of illustrating the point, they hung their hats up side by side on the multicoloured Eames coat rack in our hallway.

"This is Helene," said Erik. "Helene Hilditch." He was rather touchingly proud.

Helene's age was hard to determine. There was no chance of detecting lines on her face because she'd applied a swathe of striking black make-up around her pale grey eyes, suggestive of a raccoon or indeed a bandit's mask. Set deep in those dramatic black circles, her eyes peered out at us quite shyly.

Under this theatrical disguise, Helene was clearly at least ten years younger than Erik. Which still made her, under normal circumstances, about thirty years too old to be acceptable rock-star-girlfriend material.

We all shook hands, and Nevada helped Helene take off her coat and hang it up. Removal of the duster revealed a white silk blouse so sheer it was almost transparent, disclosing an emphatically black bra underneath. The blouse was tucked into skinny black jeans, which were identical to Erik's. But rather than sneakers Helene wore very high-heeled and pointy-toed black leather boots. Fanny crept over and sniffed these carefully. She seemed quite intrigued by our visitor.

I saw that Helene was blonde, so we could tick that rock-star-girlfriend box, at least. A rather fetching shade of platinum blonde. If it was dye, Nevada would no doubt enthusiastically brief me later. As Helene turned around to go into the sitting room, I saw there was a jagged pink streak in her hair, which even I could identify as dye. Very rock and roll.

I'd used the time lag between Erik's departure and return to conjure up a fourth mug of coffee, which Helene now picked up gratefully. She sipped while Erik cleared his throat and, despite having said that he wanted her to tell her own story, he resumed his solo account.

"So, right, the first attempt—although of course we didn't know it was an attempt at the time, an attempt at anything…" He lost his thread for a moment, then manfully recaptured it. "But it was. It was an attempted hit and run."

Apparently a car had almost smashed Helene down as she was stepping off the kerb to cross the street near her flat in Muswell Hill, heading to the local park for her morning run. "I had my earbuds in," she said. "But fortunately I hadn't started playing my music yet. So I heard it coming."

And she had excellent reflexes. She'd dodged back onto the pavement just in time. "It passed so close that the side of the car bashed the toe of my running shoe. If they'd been driving an electric car I would have been done for. I would never have heard them."

The car had smoked-glass windows and Helene hadn't been able to see who was inside—or even to tell if it was a man or a woman. Or indeed if there had been more than one person in the car. But she had got her phone out in time to take a photo of the fast-vanishing vehicle.

Again with the excellent reflexes.

And she'd caught the licence number.

"I suppose I should have just forgotten it, put it out of my mind. I mean there was no harm done."

"No physical harm," said Erik fervently. "But what about the psychological, *the psychological* harm?"

Helene nodded. "Anyway, I was really angry about it." She didn't strike me as someone who had been psychologically scarred by the experience. She struck me as someone you didn't particularly want angry with you.

As if to confirm this, Erik said, "You don't want to get in Hel's way when she's cross." He shook his head with an *it's just not worth it* expression on his face.

"So I went to the police," said Helene. "But of course they just thought it was an accident. Not even an accident, because there wasn't any damage or injury. They didn't know why I kept pestering them, or what all the fuss was about. After all, I was fine, wasn't I? But I did keep pestering them. And finally they told me the car had been stolen."

"It had been stolen by someone about half an hour before they tried to run her over," said Erik. "And they abandoned it immediately afterwards." He glared at me as if I'd been at the wheel. "Pretty suspicious, eh?"

"It could just have been joyriders," I said.

"That's what the police think," said Erik with contempt. "If it was, they didn't get much joy. Or do much riding."

The second attempt took place when Helene had returned to her flat in the early hours one morning. "I smelled gas as soon as I stepped in the front door. So I opened all the windows and went to look in the kitchen. One of the burners on the stove top had been turned on, but not lit."

"You couldn't have left it on yourself?"

"No." Helene was thin-lipped and adamant.

"But it's not just that," said Erik. "It's the day it happened."

"The day?" said Nevada.

"Yeah, you see, we've got into the habit of Helene coming to stay at my place on the weekend and also on Tuesday and Thursday nights."

I could see that Nevada was impressed. Sleeping over

four nights a week: this was a serious relationship.

"Because, you see, Tuesdays and Thursdays are Bong Cha's regular nights off." Erik looked at us to see if we were following. We were; in Nevada's case, avidly. "But on this particular week, Bong moved her nights off around, because her sister was down from Birmingham and... Anyway, she took Wednesday night off. So Helene came over on Wednesday instead."

"And it was the following morning, when I came home, that I found the gas on," said Helene.

"You see what we're getting at?" said Erik.

"Yes," I said. "Normally on a Wednesday night Helene could be expected to be at home."

"That's right." She nodded. "At home sleeping in my own bed. So someone came in, in the middle of the night, and switched on the gas. Making sure, they thought, that I wouldn't wake up."

"So you see what *that* means," said Erik. "It has to be someone who knew our regular routine well enough to expect Helene to be at home that night."

"And it was just sheer luck that I wasn't. It's a small flat and it was a cold night, so I would've had the windows shut. I would have suffocated. I never would have woken up."

"Or if you had woken up," said Erik, "you might well have lit up a roll-up." He mimed rolling a cigarette with his fingers. "Like you usually do. And then... boom."

"That's right," said Helene. "Either way I would have been dead."

Not to mention the neighbours, I thought.

"That's right," said Erik, looking at Helene. "Someone is trying to kill my girl."

Helene reached over and fiercely grabbed his hand. They squeezed their hands together, gazing into each other's eyes. Nevada gave me a quick and amused *these two should get a room* look. Helene seemed to sense it, because she turned back to us, eyes staring out from that black bandit's mask. "And then there was the third attempt," she said.

Their account of what they called the third murder attempt involved Erik disclosing his use of illegal drugs.

If they expected either Nevada or myself to be deeply shocked and upset by this revelation, and possibly flee the room in horror, they were disappointed. Nevertheless, Erik seemed at pains to justify his behaviour.

"We don't indulge that much. Just generally on Friday nights, when we watch Graham Norton. Isn't that right, babes?"

Helene nodded. "We like us some Graham on a Friday night. Putting the cares of the working week aside." I wondered when was the last time that either of these two had been required to concern themselves with the working week. But I forced myself to concentrate on the story.

It seemed that Erik had a habit of keeping his cocaine in 'wraps'—folded pieces of paper. For this purpose he used pages torn from a high-class skin magazine—photographs of nude models. "And I have a particular way of folding them, ah…" He glanced at Nevada with embarrassment. It was interesting that he wasn't bothered at all by Helene hearing this, but then she'd probably got to know Erik and his quirky habits intimately by now.

"You see, I fold them so that, uh…"

"So that his favourite girl is on top," said Helene.

Erik nodded, thankful for this no doubt euphemistic intervention. "And one night we took out one of the wraps of cocaine and it wasn't quite folded right." Erik began to enlarge on this ritual of porno origami applied to drug storage, rather drifting off the point. I wondered if he was high right now.

"So," I said, cutting to the chase, "you thought someone had tampered with it."

"Someone *had* tampered with it," said Erik, giving a knowing nod. "We didn't take any—thank god. I was going to taste it—you know, dip my fingertip and lick it. But I changed my mind."

Indeed Erik had shown great restraint. Not to mention acuteness and caution that I wouldn't have attributed to him in his pre-Helene days. So he'd sealed up the packet of cocaine again, untouched. "And then I sent it off for analysis. To this bloke I know."

"You know someone who analyses drugs?" Again, not surprising.

"I know someone who *synthesises* them. Knows a bit about molecules, does Mr Tetlock. Interesting bloke. Big fan of Valerian." Valerian was the famed band Erik had played in when he was young. "Anyway, he analysed it. And guess what?"

"It was poisoned," said Nevada. "Spiked with something."

"Right. Fentanyl."

"Jesus," said Nevada. As well she might.

"Exactly. Never mind coke. That stuff is fifty times stronger than *heroin*. If Helene had snorted it she would have been dead before she hit the floor." He looked at us. "And me, too," he added diffidently.

"So whoever is doing this isn't worried about collateral casualties," I said.

"And they might have got Bong Cha, too," said Nevada. "Or doesn't she partake?"

"Of course she doesn't partake," said Erik testily, as though everyone should be expected to know this. It was a measure of how on edge he was that he'd snapped at Nevada, whom he normally revered.

Bong Cha was Erik's housekeeper. She lived with him, and this had led some people, Nevada and our friend Agatha particularly, to speculate that she was his mistress. Nothing could be further from the truth. She did share one passion with Erik, but that was the history of the Second World War.

I said, "So someone tampered with your stash."

"But how could they get at your stash?" said Nevada. "That means they would have to be able to get into your house."

Erik shook his head and explained how he kept the drugs outside—in a fake boulder in his garden—all the better to fool the police if they ever searched his premises.

My attention drifted away during this explanation. Partly because I already knew about the boulder, and partly because, despite myself, I was beginning to believe their story. It looked like someone actually might be trying to kill Helene.

And all of the attempts they'd described had one thing

in common: they were dangerously plausible. The very thing that made them seem innocuous—how many times a day was someone in London almost run over? How many people forgot they'd left a gas ring on?—made them exemplary murder methods.

Admittedly, adding Fentanyl to cocaine was a bit more esoteric. But if they had succeeded in killing Helene in this manner, and indeed Erik into the bargain, no one would have suspected a thing.

It would have been another tragic rock-star overdose.

It would have been a perfect murder.

Just then the doorbell rang.

The sudden noise caused Fanny to flee to the bedroom. Indeed, everyone jumped. Without our realising it, the rambling story from Erik and his sweetheart had gradually thrown a dark mood over the room.

So much so that I felt a twinge of wariness as I went down the hallway to the front door and opened it.

Standing outside was my old friend Jordon Tinkler.

He was surprisingly well dressed—particularly by Tinkler standards—in items of high-end menswear that someone had bought cheap in a charity shop and sold to him at less than her usual cut-throat markup. To wit, Nevada.

"Not interrupting anything, am I?" he said, smiling his lopsided smile. He sounded hopeful—hopeful that he *was* interrupting something. And that, combined with the smart clothes, told me exactly what he had in mind.

"As a matter of fact," I said, "we have some people around." His face immediately lit up and I added hastily, "Not Clean Head, though."

Tinkler's face fell and I couldn't help but sympathise. He'd probably even had a shower, just in case. "But come in anyway."

These last words were drowned out as Tinkler, peering over my shoulder, caught sight of Erik and the two men exchanged glad cries of greeting. Tinkler hurried into the living room—it wasn't Clean Head, but it would do for now—and Erik rose from the table and the two men embraced.

"Mate!"

"Mate!"

Helene watched indulgently. She'd evidently met Tinkler before.

Erik pounded Tinkler on the shoulder, rather too hard; I was glad it wasn't just me. "You've been midnight toking, mate," he said, sniffing. "And it's not even five o'clock."

"How did you know?" said Tinkler.

"Because you smell like someone torched Bob Marley's compost bin."

With the arrival of our dear old friend we were now officially short of coffee, so I went into the kitchen to make another pot.

Tinkler followed a moment later and began tugging frantically at my sleeve while I tried to pursue my preparations, for all the world like one of our cats who wanted to be fed.

"Erik's got his girlfriend with him," he hissed, looking back over his shoulder towards the sitting room.

"Yes, I know," I said as I selected a coffee filter. We had plenty of these now that I'd upgraded my record cleaning regime from the good old Knosti Disco Antistat. "We've been chatting with her for quite some time."

"Okay, so you know who she is, don't you?"

"Yes. Helene something." I searched for her last name. "Hilditch. Like a hill and a ditch."

"Yes, that's her *real* name. But it's not the name everyone knows her by."

Nevada came into the kitchen and joined us. She was ostensibly here to bring the mugs out for refills, but in fact I knew she'd heard Tinkler whispering. Nevada was not one to be left out of an intrigue.

"What do you mean?" I said.

Tinkler nodded towards the sitting room again. "The name everyone knows her by is Howlin' Hellbitch."

"Now, that's just not nice, Tinkler," said Nevada.

"No, seriously. That was her *nom de guerre*."

It's a brave man who essays a phrase in French in front of Nevada. The risk of having your pronunciation corrected is the least of it. But this time she contented herself with merely asking, "What war was she in?"

"Well, not a war but a punk band. One of the all-time great punk bands."

"Helene was in a punk band?" Nevada seemed surprised, but personally nothing would surprise me after those eye make-up tips courtesy of *Blade Runner*. Or was it *The Girl in the Spider's Web*?

"Maybe the greatest all-girl punk band," said Tinkler. He was grinning with pride. Apparently the glamour of Helene's history extended its aura over him, as a friend of her boyfriend. "Hey, isn't that the tray I gave you?"

"Yes it is," said Nevada. "You know it is. Now stop fishing for compliments. It's a very tasteless tray anyway."

"Why?"

"Because of the associations."

"It's not tasteless," said Tinkler, fondly inspecting the tray with its black-and-white photo of Marilyn Monroe varnished on it. "The child's coffin I had made into a cocktail cabinet—now *that's* tasteless."

He went back to hang out with the happy couple and I continued fixing the coffee while Nevada set about looking for suitably posh biscuits to feed our honoured guests. The sound of her opening and shutting food cupboards brought Fanny in at a dead run from the bedroom, followed a moment later by Turk from the back garden. Further evidence of the acuity of feline hearing.

Indeed they'd managed to detect our activity despite the loud music now issuing from the sitting room. Tinkler had evidently found my copy of the Mellencamp album and decided to put it on. It had to be Tinkler, because putting a record on a turntable was too much like manual labour for Erik.

With the arrival of the cats Nevada had suspended her search for suitable biscuits and instead commenced feeding the pair their main meal of the day.

Finally the cats were fed, the biscuits located and the coffee ready. We rejoined Helene and Erik at the table. Tinkler was sitting on the other side of the room on the sofa listening to the music, bending forward to get his head in the sweet spot between the Quad speakers like a happy dog leaning out the car window to savour the breeze.

Helene thanked us for the coffee and biscuits and Erik hurriedly followed suit after she shot him a glance. I was impressed at the level of domestication she'd achieved with him in just a few short months.

Erik took a biscuit off the plate and broke it in two, inspecting it thoughtfully, as if expecting to find a slip of paper with his fortune printed on it. *They're not those sort of biscuits, mate*, I thought. He looked at me and said, "So, what do you think?"

"I believe you."

"Say what?"

"I believe you. It sounds like someone is trying to kill Helene."

"Well of course they are," said Erik impatiently. "Haven't you been listening? What have I been trying to tell you?" While he was still working his way through a long list of pugnacious and rhetorical questions, Nevada drew her chair closer to the table, sitting upright now and looking very alert.

We were getting down to business.

"But here's the thing," I said. "I don't know what I can do to help you. I'm not actually a real detective. I don't investigate crimes. I look for records."

Not for the first time I felt a weary regret that I'd ever saddled myself with such a troublesome moniker.

Erik nodded happily.

"Your missus said you'd say that. That's why we've got you a record to look for."

2: EEK!

I turned to my 'missus', who was doing her best innocent look.

I said, "You already knew about this?"

"No details," said Nevada quickly. "Erik phoned last night, but he just said he might want to hire you."

I thought she had been in an exceptionally good mood this morning. Nothing cheered Nevada up more than the thought of money coming in. In this case, potentially large sums of money, fleeced from a wealthy semi-retired rock god and sort-of friend.

"He didn't give me any details," repeated Nevada, now turning to Erik and wagging her finger at him in playful reprimand. "And no mention of any new girlfriend." She smiled at Helene.

They all turned and looked at me. Obviously I was supposed to say something.

What I said was, "You should go to the police."

This didn't go down well.

Nevada looked crestfallen; Tinkler flinched—a reflex

brought on by any mention of law enforcement—and left the table. Then Erik and Helene immediately launched into a diatribe so well organised that they might have rehearsed it earlier.

Perhaps they had.

"Number one," said Erik, "the police won't believe us."

"Number two," said Helene, "even if they did, there's virtually nothing they can do."

"Because we have no idea who's behind it all," said Erik.

"They could find out who's behind it all," I said. "That's what the police are for."

"To do that, basically they'd have to look into virtually everyone I know." This was Helene again. I was impressed with the way they were tag-teaming me. "And they simply don't have the resources for that."

"Bone idle bastards," said Erik, who was never too fond of the police.

Helene shook her head emphatically. "Government cuts, doll."

"So…" I said. "So, you expect *me* to look into virtually everyone you know?" Their logic didn't impress me as much as their teamwork. "Like I told you, I am not actually a real detective of any kind."

"Yes, you are," said Nevada hastily. She'd been showing remarkable restraint by not entering the conversation up to now, though she'd been hanging on every word. "You are a *vinyl* detective." She looked at our guests. "And he's a very good one."

I said, "Yes, but—"

"Which brings us back to that record," said Erik. "That record we want you to find." He was grinning like we were playing a game of chess and my last move had just put me into his carefully constructed trap.

"That's right," said Helene. "And in the course of finding that record for us, you will have to look into virtually everyone I know."

There was a moment of silence while this sunk in.

"We really do want this record," said Erik. "And we would have hired you to find a copy anyhow. But this way, you can have a proper nose around while you're doing it. So it's a two-for-one."

Helene smiled sweetly. "Plus it gives you a perfect cover story. No one will know that you're also looking for my assailant. So their guard will be down."

"Yeah," said Erik, "even if we could get the cops to investigate, everyone would see them coming from a mile off, and clam up."

"Perhaps a private investigator…" I said. I could feel Nevada's gaze boring into the side of my head as I tried to talk myself out of a job.

"We discussed that," said Helene quickly. "But if we did hire a private investigator, they'd have to invent some kind of cover story to put people off their guard. And how likely are they to pull that off successfully? Whereas *you* come with a *built-in* cover story. And it's flawless. Because it's the truth."

"Plus we're willing to pay you a big fat fee," added Erik, delivering the *coup de grâce*.

Nevada smiled her most angelic smile when he said this. A big fat fee. That was her kind of fee.

Checkmate, I thought.

They started to tell me about the record they wanted me to find. Or they tried to. But it involved first telling me about Helene's career in a punk band. This discussion drew Tinkler, who'd been busy rifling my record collection, back to the table to join us.

Even Fanny came sauntering in from the bedroom, where she'd been digesting her diced veal, and lay down at my feet as though interested in the unfolding narrative.

"It was the summer of 1977," said Helene. "The first summer of punk."

This occasioned an immediate discussion—or, less politely but more accurately, an argument—about the exact dates of punk's origins, between Erik and Tinkler. It was interesting that, despite Helene being the only true punk in the room, neither of the men seemed interested in her opinion on the subject. Helene herself didn't seem put out. She watched with a serene smile as the blokes thrashed it out between them.

This suggested that she really did like Erik. Maybe even more than 'like'. Though why she should cut Tinkler so much slack, god only knew.

Finally the boys agreed that although the Sex Pistols' appearance at the Free Trade Hall in Manchester in June 1976 had been a seminal event—"Without that gig, you could kiss the Hacienda goodbye," said Erik; Tinkler nodded in sage agreement—the real beginning of the movement was the two-day 100 Club Punk Special event in September 1976. "And it was all over by January 1978," said Tinkler, shaking his head sadly, as if he'd ever owned, or indeed even listened to, a punk album. Erik glossed this for us, explaining that January 1978 was when Johnny Rotten quit the Sex Pistols, stalking offstage at the Winterland Ballroom in San Francisco.

Now that the lads had set the parameters of the discussion, Helene was allowed to continue.

"So, as I was saying, it was summer. The end of the school term. Myself and a bunch of friends were in our last year at school. And instead of going on to university, we thought it would be fun to start our very own punk band."

Oh, the heady spirit of '77.

"So we decided to call ourselves Blue Tits." At this statement Nevada shot Helene an odd look. I would almost say she looked shocked, which was weird because my darling is one of the most unshockable people you could ever wish to meet.

"And we chose names for ourselves, inspired by the likes of Sid Vicious and Johnny Rotten and Poly Styrene. Or, wait a minute, was Poly even around at that point? Or did she come on the scene a bit later?" I could see that Tinkler was eager to answer this question. He'd evidently boned up on the history of punk as a tribute to his buddy's new girlfriend. He was bursting with more facts than a week of pub quizzes could exhaust. And, indeed, later he would insist on telling Nevada and me about Marianne Joan Elliot-Said and how her first record was a reggae single.

But thankfully, right now Helene wouldn't give him an opening. She just kept on talking. "Well, whatever, we reckoned we could come up with names that were at least *that* good. So we got a couple of bottles of cider—we didn't have access to anything stronger at the time, though that was definitely about to change—and we got pissed and had a brainstorming session to come up with names for the lot of us."

Thus Helene Hilditch became 'Howlin' Hellbitch'. And her chum Tania Strack became 'Tongue Strap'. "We never were entirely satisfied with that one. It wasn't emphatically *obscene* enough. I mean, what is a tongue strap, anyway?" I could see that Tinkler was eager to offer some suggestions on this too, no doubt plenty obscene enough.

But Helene kept on talking, holding the floor with admirable firmness. "We called Dylis Lispector 'Dildo Inspector'. Now, *that* was a good one. And then Ophelia— Ophelia Brydent—became 'Feel Up Rodent', which was our absolute favourite. We pissed ourselves laughing when we thought of that one. And once we had the names we divided up the tasks in the band. Tania became the singer. She had never been good enough for the school choir. All the rest of us had got into the choir, and none of us were even particularly good singers, so as you'll gather she really wasn't a great vocalist. In other words, she was perfect."

"Because she was so imperfect," I said.

Helene nodded. "Precisely for that reason. And what's more, it was her revenge, indeed all of our revenge, for them not letting her in the choir. Two fingers up to the school. She was the perfect vocalist: one who couldn't sing. Very punk indeed. And then, since anybody can play the drums, we decided Ophelia would do that. Sorry, I mean Feel Up Rodent could do that."

I thought 'anybody can play the drums' was a bit harsh. But it did bring to mind Chet Baker's adage that you had to be a pretty good drummer to be better than no drummer at all.

"And then, because we needed a bass player, we decided Dylis would do that. Not because she could play bass, you understand. She couldn't."

"But you could play guitar, couldn't you, doll?" said Erik. "And play it bloody well, too." He turned to me. "Do you know who she reminds me of?"

I braced myself for the boredom of him repeating his James Ulmer comparison, but to my surprise he said, "Bo Diddley. Early Bo Diddley. Bo Diddley in his prime."

"Prime Diddley," said Tinkler, managing to give the phrase an indecent connotation. Which, come to think of it, was his specialty. Everybody ignored him. Especially the lovebirds, who were holding hands again and gazing into each other's eyes.

"Thank you, doll," said Helene.

"It's true, doll," said Erik. "You've got that raw, chunky thing going on. The irregular beat." He looked at me. "She plays low action guitar. A very mean low action guitar. Do you know what that means?"

"No," I said, and waited for Tinkler to rush in and fill the vacuum of my ignorance. But he remained startlingly silent. The pub quiz research had evidently been exhausted.

So Erik drew in his breath, gearing up for a lecture. But before he could get started, Nevada leaned over to Helene and said in a quiet aside, "By the way. When you say you got together at school, do you mean a private school?"

I thought this was a very odd question, and not just because there aren't too many kids called Helene at state schools. Not to mention Ophelia. It also stopped Erik in midstride, which isn't an easy thing to do when he gets talking about guitar technique.

But Helene wasn't taken aback. She just nodded. "Yes. We were all posh girls."

"Did you by any chance go to Eek?"

At this point it was Helene's turn to look shocked. But only for a moment. Then she shrieked, released Erik's hand and seized Nevada's instead, grinning. "Did *you* go there?"

"Oh yes," said Nevada. She too was smiling. "And I suppose you were in Blue Tits?"

This was an even odder question, since Helene had just spent a fair chunk of the afternoon establishing exactly that. But Helene wasn't fazed by the question. "Yes, I was. Were you?"

Nevada nodded. "I was dehoused."

"Rehoused?" said Tinkler, who was as baffled as I had initially been by the turn this conversation had taken.

"*Dehoused*," said Nevada.

"Deloused?" suggested Tinkler.

"Stop pissing about, Tinkler. I was booted out of my school house for bad behaviour. They call that being dehoused."

"Do they now?"

"And consequently I was put in the house where they put all the troublemakers."

"Blue Tits," said Helene, her head bobbing in happy agreement. "All the school houses were named after birds. There was Golden Eagles, which was for the sporty girls, the athletes. White Owls for the swots, the academically gifted. Grey Doves, they were the debs. And…"

"And Green Woodpeckers," said Nevada.

"That's right!" Helene frowned. "The girls in that house weren't really distinctive in any particular way. Not that I can recall, anyway."

"But you can imagine how they had the piss taken out of them," said Nevada. "The Green Woodpeckers."

"Because of the word 'peckers'," said Tinkler.

"Yes."

"And green."

"Yes."

"So it was like a green penis!"

"Yes, Tinkler."

"A diseased penis."

"Yes."

"And one that was made of wood, at that."

"That's right," said Nevada. "Non-stop mockery for the poor girls in Green Woodpecker."

"Non-stop," agreed Helene.

"So Eek is the name of the school?" I said, managing to jump into the conversation at last.

"Nickname," said Helene.

"Emily Kelso," said Nevada.

"EK for short," said Helene. "Hence Eek."

"The Emily Kelso Academy for Young Ladies," said Nevada, nodding fondly.

"You went to an all-girls school?" said Tinkler.

Nevada nodded. "That's right. And we were all going down on each other in the dormitory every night."

Tinkler's eyes widened. "Jesus! Were you?"

"Of course not, you fucking fool. The last thing you're interested in, or at least the last thing that *I* was interested in, when you're cooped up with a bunch of girls all the time is girls. Anyway, that's how it was for me."

Helene was nodding and smiling.

"Which is why I kept going over the wall into town," said Nevada. "Which is why I got dehoused. And anyway, we didn't have dormitories. We had little cottages for each house."

"Shared cottages?" said Tinkler hopefully. "Where you slept together?"

"Tinkler, I refuse to provide you with girls' school masturbation fantasy fodder."

"They're strictly sixteen-plus fantasies," said Tinkler. "All totally legit."

"So you guys were both in the same house at school?" I said. Helene was no longer holding Nevada's hand, but nonetheless they looked like they'd bonded for life. Nice work, Nevada.

They nodded in unison. "Albeit in different years," said Nevada.

"Different decades," said Helene.

"I love it," said Erik. He was certainly grinning as if he loved something. "Punk was a genuinely working-class movement… for about thirty seconds before the rich kids moved in." Despite his devotion to Helene, he clearly hadn't been won over by punk as a genre of music. The thought of its purity being diluted by gentrification seemed to delight him no end.

"We weren't rich," said Helene. "Well, not all of us. But we were all at least middle class. Which was sort of the point."

"You mean the point of your rebellion," I said.

Helene looked at me with her raccoon eyes. "That's right. Rebellion was exactly the point. Rebellion against middle-class values. Against our parents sending us to that school thinking it would give us a massive head start for university. Because there we were saying that we wouldn't go to uni at all. We were going to form a band. Again, two fingers up."

Personally, I felt a bit sorry for the parents in question. But I kept my mouth shut.

"Anyway we formed our band, naming it Blue Tits after our house."

"More fingers up?" I suggested.

"That's right. A big fuck off to the school. To Eek." Helene glanced hurriedly at Nevada. "Sorry—I mean, if you were *fond* of the place…"

"Oh no," said Nevada. "Hated the dump. Absolutely hated it."

Helene grinned a foxy grin. "There speaks the true Eek old girl. Anyway, we just started the band. Began gigging right away, while most of us were still learning to play our instruments. Of course, some of us never did learn to play them. Not naming any names, but Dylis was always useless. Not that it mattered. We just got in there and *did it*. Blue Tits were go."

This was the famed punk do-it-yourself ethos. It was another reason the Sex Pistols had proved so influential, if you wanted to be uncharitable about it. A lot of people heard them and thought, *If they can do it, anybody can.*

But what was preoccupying me was the name they'd chosen for the band. It was a very clever choice. On the one hand it sounded rude, not to mention slightly painful. While, on the other, it was utterly innocuous, since in the UK at least a blue tit was a beloved small bird that frequented back gardens everywhere, including ours. Although in ours they were wary of the resident felines—especially Turk, who was a ruthless hunter.

In America it didn't have the same plausible deniability, though. "That name got us into a lot of trouble," said Helene, grinning. She was obviously very proud of it.

But back here in Britain, no one could complain about it because the band could always play the bird card. So to speak. If they wanted to. Not that they necessarily ever did want to, since confrontation and controversy seemed to be their main aim.

"Do you remember that time we were on television?" said Helene. She had begun to emanate a happy glow of nostalgia. "The Bill Bridenstine show? No, of course you wouldn't. You're too young."

"I'm not, dolly girl," said Erik, grinning toothily. "I'm not too young. And I remember." He turned to us—the youths—and said, "You can see it on YouTube. Famous, it was. Their appearance. What a fucking uproar it caused!"

Helene's happy glow increased.

So controversy was indeed the objective. Still, the double meaning of the band's name was clever. The combination of the innocuous and the far-from-innocuous reminded me of something. I had to think for a moment about what this was... while Helene continued happily reminiscing, talking about the Blue Tits' North American tour. ("It ended in a complete shambles in Winnipeg. They love heavy metal in Winnipeg. It turns out, punk... not so much.")

Then I got it. The duality of the name reminded me of the methods of attempted murder—viciously calculated mayhem clad in an innocent guise.

This realisation gave me a cold shock.

Could it be the same mind at work in each case?

"Anyway, we made quite a splash, if I say so myself," said Helene. We weren't the first all-girl punk band on the scene, but we were one of the first. And we got a recording deal almost right away." She looked at me. "Which was when the problems began."

3: ACID, MAN

The Blue Tits had no idea how to go about making a record. But that didn't matter. Again, the anybody-can-do-it spirit of 1977 was in the air. "So we just went into town," said Helene. "We hopped on a train to London and found a record shop where they sold a lot of punk music and asked *them*. And it turned out it couldn't have been easier, and we couldn't have gone to a better place, because Lenny said he actually had just started a record label upstairs. Over his shop."

"Lenny?" I said. Alarm bells had started to ring. "This record shop was run by a guy called Lenny?"

"Yes."

"What was the shop called?"

"The Vinyl Crypt."

"Jesus," I said.

"What's the matter?" said Helene.

"Nothing," I said. "It's just that I think I know this guy. Did he have a tendency to wear berets?"

"You know, thinking about it, I believe he did."

"Is this the same Lenny who serves the Chablis and is always proffering vacations to a Greek island?" said Nevada.

"That's the one," I said. "Proffering them to you, anyway."

Nevada turned to our guests. "He's always trying to hit on me," she declared contentedly.

"Of course he is," said Erik, with a note of gallantry.

"But he never gets anywhere, of course," added Nevada.

"You know what?" Helene was frowning with thought. "He hit on us, too. And I think he actually got somewhere with one or two of us."

Well, there's no accounting for taste. And Lenny would have been a hell of a lot younger then, of course. Not that that would have made the berets any more acceptable.

I made another note, to have a chat with Lenny. He might provide some useful background, even if he wasn't a suspect. Then the thought struck me.

"Could Lenny be behind this?"

"What?" Helene seemed genuinely startled. "You mean behind the attempts?"

I shrugged. "Why not?"

"Why would he?"

"Were you one of the girls that he hit on? And did you succumb? Either way, there might be grounds for a grudge. If you slept with him he might never have got over it…"

"Well, I like that idea," said Helene cheerfully.

"And I like the use of the word 'succumb'," said Nevada. "Full marks, love."

They were both chuckling, but I persisted. "And if you *didn't* sleep with him he might have an even stronger motive. Resentment."

Nevada and Helene both suddenly looked more serious. "Do you really think Lenny could be a killer?" said Nevada. "Beret and Chablis and all? And even if he was, do you think he would still be bearing a grudge after all these years?"

"To be frank," I said, "no, I don't. But I've been wrong about these things before."

"Amen to that," said Nevada.

Helene was shaking her head. "I just don't see it. I mean, feel free to explore the possibility. But if you're looking for someone who didn't get to sleep with me and who resented it, I have a much better candidate. Much better."

"Okay," I said, "fire away."

Helene took a deep breath. "So there we were at the Vinyl Crypt, back in the summer of 1977. In those days it was a little shop on King Street in Hammersmith, up the Chiswick end by the cinema. Of course, all that's gone now. The shop and the cinema and everything. All luxury flats. Anyway, we rocked up at the shop and declared that we were a band and we wanted to make a record." A wicked grin twitched her lips and deepened her eyes in their black mask. "At this point we'd had about three rehearsals, mind. But we looked the part. We didn't have our instruments with us, though I might have had my guitar, but we *had* dressed for the occasion. For our London debut, so to speak. Leather jackets and bin liners were very much in evidence. And, ahem, modified school uniforms. Plus some highly creative use of make-up."

Unconsciously, her hand drifted up to her face and touched the bandit mask around her eyes. Suddenly both the middle-aged woman and the teenage girl seemed to be sitting at our table.

She cleared her throat. "Lenny was suitably impressed. He took us upstairs."

"To his boudoir?" suggested Tinkler hopefully.

"Lenny wouldn't know from a boudoir. He took us up to the offices of his newly formed record company."

Erik nodded. "It was called Crypt Kicks, except it was spelled with an 'x', 'Kix', because they thought it was more hip or something."

This disdain was amusing coming from a man who'd gone from Eric to Erik for much the same reason.

"We went upstairs to his office, and then across the road to the pub where we all drank ourselves legless and then we signed with Crypt Kix records, without having played them a note. Three weeks later we'd played a lot of notes. We'd cut our first album and it was on sale in the shop." Helene said this with a certain quiet pride. But then the look of satisfaction faded from her face. "Which was when the shit hit the fan."

Erik leaned over and rubbed her shoulder. "Ah, babes, it's just the music business. Happens to everyone. Happens to us all. Happens to the best of us." He was trying eagerly to make eye contact. Helene finally looked at him and they both relaxed.

I felt moved despite myself. These two were good for each other.

I said, "What happened, exactly?"

"Okay, so the album came out," said Erik. He had taken over the story, as if it was too painful for Helene to continue. "Here you go. This is what you're after." He was holding up his phone with a picture of an album cover on it. It was a square of shocking pink, Day-Glo pink, with black high-contrast photographs of four faces on it.

Four teenage girls in savage haircuts and garish make-up. I tried to single out Helene, but couldn't at this size. The title *Blue Tits* was in bold marker pen style scrawl—it might actually have been hand lettered straight onto the cover—with the word *Blue* in black and the word *Tits* in blue. Imaginative.

"That's the record you want me to find?" I said.

"Yeah," said Erik. "The first pressing."

"I imagine they didn't manufacture many copies," I said. An unknown band on a small, fledgling label like this, I would be surprised if they'd made more than five hundred of them.

"You're right," said Erik. "But that ain't the difficulty."

"What is the difficulty?"

"They were pulled from the shelves," said Helene sullenly. After all these years this still clearly hurt.

"Why?"

"Because it was too good," said Erik.

"Because it wasn't punk enough," said Helene. She managed to put an impressive payload of bitterness into the word 'punk'.

"It was too good," repeated Erik firmly.

"I wasn't punk enough."

"You were too good, doll." Erik turned to me. "Her guitar playing—"

"That's what the problem was," said Helene.

"It was too high quality," said Erik, his eyes locked on mine. He seemed determined that I understand. "For the situation. You see, Helene was playing solos."

"That's right, I was," said Helene, nodding.

"Punk bands didn't play guitar solos. Not then anyway." Erik, in contrast to his honey, was shaking his head. They made an interesting pair like this, and indeed in general. "The fucking idiots didn't appreciate it. I've heard those solos. They're terrific." He glanced at Helene. "Go on, hon."

"What else is there to say? They pulled our album, took it off the market. And made us rerecord it."

"Playing worse guitar solos?" said Nevada.

"Playing no guitar solos," said Helene.

"Still," I said. "Lenny must have had a lot of faith in you, in the band." I was reluctant to say 'Blue Tits'. For some reason it was just plain embarrassing to say it to her face. "I mean, for him to remaster the album and release it again, to give it a second chance…"

"It wasn't Lenny," said Helene. "Lenny had nothing to do with it."

"I thought you said—"

"Lenny *signed* us. He handled the business end of things. But the recording, the artistic side, the production side…"

"The production and A and R side," said Erik.

"That was all handled by Saxon," said Helene.

"Saxon?"

"Saxon Ghost."

The ludicrous name caused us all to shut up for a moment. The only sound was Fanny scratching the underside of the armchair. She emerged gradually from underneath it, doing a sort of sideways swimming motion, sliding across the floor, and peered up at us.

"Saxon Ghost," I said. "Is that a person?"

"Not really," said Helene. "But you should put him at the top of your list."

"My list?" I said. "Of suspects?"

"Exactly."

"You think he might be trying to kill you? Because of what happened with the album?" It seemed a pretty tenuous motive.

"No," said Helene. "Because of what you said earlier."

"What did I say earlier?"

"Not sleeping with him. Saxon fancied himself as our Svengali. Thought he could manipulate our career. Like Malcolm McLaren and the Pistols. He thought he could make us a brilliant success."

"And that's why he suppressed your first record?"

"Yes. Because my guitar playing wasn't crap enough." Helene shrugged. "The problem was, he was right. The second version of the album was a hit. And on the back of that he got us onto Bill Bridenstine's TV show." She fell silent. For a moment memories threatened to overwhelm her, but she mastered them. "The point is, Saxon wanted to sleep with us; with each, any and all of us," she said. "He was very pissed off that he never did. With any of us. I mean, *very* pissed off. Never forgave us."

"Did he particularly want to sleep with you? More than the others, I mean."

"Perhaps I ought to be insulted, but I don't believe he did." She paused for a long moment, and then said in a quiet voice, "And there was something else."

"Another reason why he might want to kill you?"

"Yeah."

"Well, what is it?"

Helene seemed to shrink into herself, her shoulders hunching. Her gaze skittered away from mine. "What's the time, doll?" she said.

Erik hastily glanced at his phone. "Oh, yeah, we've been here for ages." He looked at Nevada. "We're taking up all your time."

"No, no," said Nevada. "No problem at all. I was just going to suggest we could open a bottle of wine." She glanced at me. "And put out some nibbles." This was my cue. I immediately began mentally inventorying what we had in the fridge that could be swiftly turned into snacks of a suitably high standard for our esteemed guests and potential clients.

"Wine?" chirped Tinkler. "Nibbles? Now we're talking."

But Helene was shaking her head. "No thanks. We've got to be going. After we tell you about the fourth attempt."

"You know how I do a regular gig at the Bull's Head?" said Erik. "You know, in that new room they have, at the back?" I nodded. I knew it well.

"It's not a bad space," said Erik. "The piano's in a bit of a funny position, but it's not a bad space. And it's handy for me." Handy was understating it; Erik lived virtually next door to the pub. "I play there about once a month, usually on a Sunday. Me and some of the lads from Valerian. A few others sometimes, the line-up always changes. It's just a bit of a jam session. It's good to keep your hand in, playing to a live audience." He looked over at Helene, who sat listening, sombre and tense, as though she was in court waiting for her verdict to be read out.

"I thought Helene would enjoy it, so I invited her along one Sunday. Introduced her to the lads. Our routine is, we set up our gear, then we go into the bar for a quick drink and a bite to eat, and then we go back to the music room to get ready." He paused and looked at Helene. She was staring off into space, her expression unreadable.

"So we have a bite of lunch and take our time, wander back in to the music room. We're just about to get up on the bandstand and pick up our instruments when I notice something. I'm looking at Helene's amp. My amp. It's actually my amp. I lent it to her for the gig, so I want to make sure it's behaving itself. And I see something..."

Erik looked at me. His gaze was hardening, and he was getting an edge to his voice. I wasn't sure if he was angry or scared—and perhaps neither was he. "It was the cord. The power cord attached to it. I always use a black one because it matches my black Fender Hot Rod amp."

"Of course," I said, with a straight face.

"But the fuse on the plug blew, and Bong Cha was too

lazy to replace it, so she borrowed a cord from the kitchen. And this thing was bright red."

"Looked quite nice," said Helene. "I quite liked that red cord with the black amp. It really popped."

"I know you liked it, love, but…"

But it wasn't sufficiently rock and roll, I thought.

What he actually said was, "But then Bong Cha finally got off her arse and replaced the fuse, so I put the black cable back on it." He gave a savage little chuckle. "So imagine my surprise when we came back from the bar and I saw that the cord on the Fender had miraculously changed colour. From black to red."

I nodded. "Someone was operating on slightly out-of-date information."

"Exactly. I wouldn't let Helene anywhere near it, and I told everybody to stand back. We told the people in the audience to go back outside. They were pissed off. The people who run the gig were pissed off. The lads in the band thought I was out of my mind. Making all this fuss about the colour of a power cord."

"I didn't think you were out of your mind," said Helene softly. She was gazing at him adoringly.

Erik was gazing adoringly right back at her. "After everything you'd been through, I wasn't taking any chances."

"You saved my life, love," said Helene. They looked into each other's eyes for a long moment. I wondered if they were going to hold hands again, but evidently they didn't need to.

"I told everyone to keep their distance," said Erik, "and I cut the power, to all of our kit, not just the amp. Then I went for a closer look. A very, very careful closer look. For all I knew this fucking thing was a bomb. And that's when I saw that it wasn't my amp at all. My amp had a mark on it where I gave it a bash loading it in a van one time. On the top right between the presence control and the reverb control. And the mark wasn't there. So this wasn't my amp. It was the right make and the right model, the Deluxe IV. But it wasn't mine."

I stated the obvious. "So someone took your amp and substituted this one."

"That's right. Substituted a very special deluxe modified version. Which they must have had all ready, waiting to go. Complete with the red cord."

"But why not swap the cord?" I said. "Take the black cord off your amp and switch it over."

"Maybe they didn't notice," said Tinkler. "I don't think I would have noticed."

"I'll tell you why they didn't switch it over," said Erik. "Because later when we looked at that red cord, someone had taken out the fuse and bypassed it with some wire which they'd soldered in."

"Jesus," I said.

"That's right," said Erik.

Nevada was looking at me. "So what does that mean?" she said.

"It means that someone didn't want to spoil their fun by having the fuse blow and cutting off the power to Helene's amp."

"That's right," said Erik. "The fucking fuckers didn't want it spoiling their fucking fun. So there I was looking at my amp, or rather this thing that definitely wasn't my amp, wondering what the hell to do about it, wondering if I should call the bomb squad. And then suddenly..."

"There was this smell," said Helene.

"Yeah, we smelled this smell. And we saw a puddle on the floor, spreading out from under the amp."

"It was acid," said Helene.

"Acid?"

Erik nodded. "Seems that amongst the other modifications, someone put acid in an acid-resistant reservoir inside the amp. And when a switch was tripped..."

"When the power went off," I said.

"That's right. The acid flowed out and destroyed everything in the amp. Well, almost everything. All the modified components."

"So there was nothing left?" I said.

"Oh, there was plenty left, but it was a complete mess. As soon as we worked out what was happening, as soon as we sussed it was acid, we went across to Sainsbury's and bought a load of baking soda."

That was smart.

"We poured it all over the amp—and into it—and salvaged what we could. I had an electrical engineer mate of mine look at what was left. He was the one who spotted the hard wiring in the plug. As far as he could tell, if Hel had picked up her guitar she would have been electrocuted and that would have been that." He looked at Helene. "That would have been that," he repeated softly.

"And then, presumably, you would have cut the power,"

I said. "Which means the acid in the amp would have been triggered and it would have self-destructed."

"Like *Mission: Impossible*," said Tinkler. "Cool."

Everyone ignored him.

"And all the evidence would have been destroyed," said Erik. "All the evidence *was* destroyed."

"They very nearly got me that time, love," said Helene softly. It was almost as if she didn't want the rest of us to hear. This was just between the two of them. "If it hadn't been for you, they would have got me."

Erik nodded. His eyes were glistening with tears.

"And that's not all," said Tinkler. Everyone looked at him. "They also stole your amp."

Erik's nodding transformed into a spasmodic bobbing of the chin and after a moment of worried puzzlement I realised he'd begun to laugh.

Helene started laughing too.

"That's right," sputtered Erik. "That's the main thing." He could hardly get the words out, he was laughing so hard. He was now weeping with laughter. "Never mind nearly topping Helene. The main thing is that the bastards made off with my Fender Hot Rod Deluxe IV!" He and Helene collapsed into each other's arms, shaking with laughter.

Tinkler gave us a smug look, as if to say, *See my power at work?*

The slightly hysterical bout of mirth was certainly a release for Erik and Helene. It made me realise that it must have been tough, a little traumatic even, for them to have to relive all these experiences as they told us about them.

And any doubts I had about the reality of the threat to Helene's life were absolutely gone.

They were replaced, however, with a wide range of difficult and stubborn questions. I started ranking them in order of urgency.

Erik wiped his eyes and turned to Nevada. "So, we're on, are we?" He shot a sideways glance at me. "He's going to find it for us, is he?"

"Yes, he is," she said confidently.

Erik leaned over and slapped me on the shoulder. Hard. We were back to where he came in. "The second pressing has a different cover," he said. "So you won't have any trouble knowing when you've found a copy of the first pressing." He stood up, and Helene rose from the table with him.

"I'll get you a list," she said. "Of people who might have a copy. And then you can start looking for it."

Erik paused in the act of putting on his Confederate cap and buckskin jacket. "And, if you happen to work out who's trying to kill Helene along the way, then you'll tell us, won't you?"

"Of course he will," said Nevada firmly. "He's very good like that."

4: NIGHT VISITOR

I woke up in the middle of the night to the sound of furry little bodies violently crashing through the cat flap.

I realised Nevada was sitting up in bed beside me. It's odd; she can sleep through music at the level of an artillery barrage, but the tiniest of sounds can wake her—if it's the right kind of sound.

Or, perhaps I should say, the wrong kind of sound.

She was instantly and fully awake and she reached out to grab my shoulder, arresting me in the process of getting out of bed.

"The cats just came bursting in and—"

"I know," she said. "There's someone in the garden."

I looked at her. She stared back at me, her dark eyes steady and serious.

We both got up, pulled on some clothes and hurried into the sitting room. Or at least I hurried into the sitting room. Behind me I heard the word "*Wait*" and I turned back to see Nevada rummaging in one of the cabinets in the kitchen.

"What are you looking for?" For some idiotic reason I was whispering. In my own house, in the middle of the night.

"You know where we put all the wine that people bring when they come to our parties? The wine we don't want to drink, the rubbish wine…"

I said, "You're looking for rubbish wine?"

She turned to me, now holding a bottle by the neck. "Well, we wouldn't want to use *good* wine in the event we need a weapon."

We pulled on our shoes and went to the back door, me holding the keys, Nevada with the wine bottle. Through the glass panel in the door we could see the garden lights slicing up the darkness. These were on a timer, turning on more or less at sunset and off at four o'clock in the morning. So it wasn't yet four.

There were three lights. One was pointed at the sycamore, another at the honeysuckle and the acer and the third at the big potted Japanese rose bush against the centre rear wall of the garden. Between them they gave an effect that was both decorative and served to illuminate pretty much all the garden. There was, however, a block of fairly impenetrable shadow between the acer and the rose bush.

It was in this block of shadow that our visitor had contrived to stand.

There was very little we could see of this intruder. They were human. They were bulky. And they were very intimidating indeed. A slab of watchful, unmoving shadow.

I unlocked the door as quietly as possible—I wasn't quite sure why—and we stepped tentatively out into the garden.

Nevada was holding the wine bottle out to her side where it was in an ideal position either to be thrown—for example at someone's head—or swung like a club.

The figure must have seen us approaching, but did not move. This person had let themselves in through the garden gate (supposedly locked, by the way), and now here they were, simply standing silently in the shadows, looking big and forbidding, staring at our house in a spooky fashion.

As we drew closer, the shadow's head moved, indicating that they were staring at us now instead of the house, though in an equally spooky fashion. And there was something unsettlingly odd and rather aggressive about the shape of that head.

There was also a powerful smell of booze—beer, to be specific—coming from the bulky figure. This was in no way a good sign and it caused Nevada and me to stop even further back than we might otherwise have done.

So the three of us stood there, all now motionless, in the dark, quiet garden. The only sound was the wind rustling the leaves in the trees.

I cleared my throat, suddenly not having a clue what to say. I wasn't sure of the etiquette for this particular social situation. As it turned out, I didn't need to say anything, because the person in the shadows beat me to it.

"Help me," she said.

The fact that it was a woman was our first surprise, but far from our last.

"Please," she said. "I came to beg you for your help. I know it's late. I know I woke you up. I know I shouldn't have let myself in."

"How did you let yourself in, by the way?" said Nevada. "That gate's locked."

"Oh, anyone can get in *that*," said the woman, momentarily losing the beseeching note in her voice and becoming almost chipper. "I just stood on my toolbox, reached over and turned the latch."

"Your toolbox?" said Nevada.

"Yeah, I got it out of my van. Never go anywhere in the van without the toolbox. At least not my van. The thing's going to fall apart at any minute." She was starting to sound downright chatty and, now that the initial surge of fear had passed, I was getting a little pissed off.

"Who are you?" I said.

"Monika," she said, sounding a trifle surprised by the question.

"Monika?"

"Monika with a 'k'," she said. "Monika Dunkley." She now actually sounded a little annoyed, this intruder in our garden in the middle of the night. *Surely you've heard of me*, her tone implied.

I was about to ask her who the hell she was, or who the hell she thought she was, when she added, "You've heard of the Blue Tits?"

At my side I felt Nevada relax fractionally for the first time since we'd been woken up. The mention of Helene's band suddenly and vastly reduced the odds of this being a random dangerous nutter in our back yard.

"You know the Blue Tits?" I said.

"Know them?" Monika was now officially deeply

affronted. "I'm one of them."

Nevada tensed again. 'Dangerous nutter' was immediately back on the menu, though intriguingly 'random' could no longer apply.

"You're one of the band?" I said, mentally running through the four names I knew—Helene, Ophelia, Somebody Strack and Dylis something.

"Well, not exactly one of the band. I mean sort of. I mean, of course I was. I just didn't play an instrument."

"You were in the band but you didn't play an instrument?"

"Yeah. I was the roadie."

This time I felt Nevada relax definitively. We knew our guest couldn't have been one of the players in the band, but roadie was entirely plausible.

"I drove the van," said Monika, "I lugged the equipment, I set everything up for the gigs. I carried everything back after the gigs. I carried *them* back after the gigs, when they were too drunk or stoned…" It was beginning to sound like a potentially endless list of grievances from the under-appreciated.

"Excuse me, Monika," I said, "but what are you doing in our garden?" *In the middle of the fucking night*, I didn't add.

"Oh." She was caught off guard for a moment. "Didn't I say?"

"No, you didn't say," said Nevada sweetly.

"Someone is trying to murder my friend," said Monika. "And I want you to find out who it is… and stop them." She took a step forward into the beam of one of the garden lights, revealing that she had a classic mohawk cut—a thick slice of bristling hair sticking up from her otherwise shaved skull. Well, that explained the odd look of her head in the shadows. She looked from one of us to the other. The beseeching note was back in her voice, and her face was suddenly that of an anxious child.

I said, "Would this friend be Helene Hilditch, by any chance?"

"Howlin' Helene, yes. How did you know?"

"Because her boyfriend Erik beat you to the punch, I'm afraid," said Nevada.

"Beat me to the punch?" It wasn't clear whether she didn't understand the expression, or was merely baffled by its application here.

Nevada put a hand on my shoulder. "Erik has already hired him to look into the case." The obvious pride in her voice gave me a warm feeling deep in my stomach, though I wasn't wild about her calling it a case.

"Oh," said Monika. Now it was suddenly her turn to not have a clue what to say. Her shoulders dropped visibly as she relaxed, then she smiled and said, "Well, that was easy." She looked at Nevada. "Were you going to offer me a drink?"

Nevada looked at the bottle of wine she was still brandishing in her hand. "Well, that was one option," she said.

We took Monika into the house, where the cats cautiously emerged from the bedroom to study the interloper who had caused them to flee from their own garden. After a quick glance they seemed to come to the same conclusion we had—possibly completely bananas, but apparently harmless—and left to go about their feline pursuits: Turk back out the cat flap to resume terrorising the neighbourhood; Fanny back into the bedroom to claim the most comfortable spot on the bed.

Despite Monika's willingness, indeed eagerness, for us to open the bottle of wine Nevada had been brandishing and get properly stuck into it, we decided that coffee was a much better way to go. Indoors, Monika smelled even more strongly of beer.

As we put the lights on, we got our first proper look at her.

Monika was broad-shouldered and stocky, with a bland, chubby, pleasant face under that rather aggressive mohawk. She was wearing torn blue jeans and a black leather biker jacket—the standard uniform of punk, come to think of it— and what at first I thought was a red and black kilt—another approved punk accoutrement—protruding from the bottom of the biker jacket and extending halfway to her knees. But then I realised it was just the tails of a long tartan shirt.

She was wearing black lipstick and her eyebrows were sharp, narrow black crescents. She had a ruby-red Soviet star earring in one ear and a red hammer and sickle in the other. *At least it isn't a swastika*, I thought. It was interesting how thoroughly she seemed caught up in a punk time warp, though.

I made the coffee in short order and got a mug of it into Monika's hand. She clutched it and peered at it with a mixture of fascination and bafflement, showing no inclination to drink the stuff. It was instant, but it wasn't that bad.

Admittedly, neither Nevada nor I were drinking ours either, not feeling the need to pour caffeine onto our already jangled woken-up-in-the-middle-of-the-night nervous systems. Monika watched rather wistfully as Nevada put the bottle of rubbish wine, formerly her cudgel, back in the rubbish wine cabinet.

"I was their roadie," she said dejectedly. "I was the Blue Tits' roadie." Had she forgotten she'd already told us this? She looked at me. "Didn't she mention me?" She turned to Nevada. "Didn't Helene say anything about me?"

She looked so forlorn that Nevada said, "I'm sure she did. But there was such a welter of names, you know…"

"Oh. I see." She bought it so totally that I felt a bit bad about deceiving her, as a big smile creased her plump, childish face. But since we'd trooped in from the garden I'd had a chance to come up with a question of my own.

I said, "How did you know who I was?"

Monika swivelled her head to look at me with sudden alarm. "What? Sorry?"

"How did you know that I was someone who might be able to help Helene with… her situation?"

"Oh, yeah… Do you know Erik's maid?"

"Do you mean Bong Cha?"

"Yes, his housekeeper or cook or whatever. I met her when I was taking Helene's gear over there. Well, anyway, she recommended you. She recommended that I come and talk to you."

"Did she now?"

"Yes. She knew I was really worried about Helene and I wanted to do something to help her. So she said I should try you." A frown deepened the crease between her eyebrows.

"But she didn't tell me that Erik was going to ask you to look into it himself." She blinked her eyes at me in deep puzzlement. "That doesn't make any sense at all."

"It does if you know Bong Cha," I said. "She's a belt and braces kind of gal."

More blinking and puzzlement. "What, you mean like bondage?"

Nevada smiled a patient smile. "No, he means that Bong Cha likes to make doubly sure that something is going to happen. She likes to be absolutely certain."

"Oh, I see. So she knew Erik was going to ask you. But she wanted me to ask you, too. As a sort of backup."

"Exactly."

"Well, that was clever," said Monika.

Was it? I thought. The lights in the garden suddenly went out, throwing the space beyond the windows into complete, inky blackness. It was abruptly four in the morning and here we were, wide awake and full of adrenalin, any chance of a good night's sleep shot to hell, wasting our time talking nonsense to a total stranger.

Thank you, Bong Cha.

Monika glanced once more at the cup of coffee in her hand, and then hunched forward with such a sudden lunging motion that I thought she was going to throw it across the room. The thought, *it's instant but it's not that bad*, flashed through my mind again. But instead Monika jerked the cup up to her mouth and proceeded to drain it in one long swallow, as if to confirm that it really wasn't that bad. I was glad I'd added some cold water to it, though, as she glugged it all down.

Monika set the now empty cup aside and wiped her mouth daintily with the sleeve of her leather jacket. Then she looked up at us and said, rather shyly, "I suppose I'd better be going." She stood up and turned towards the back door, studying it with alert interest as if it presented an intriguing and novel enigma.

Cue enormous relief from Nevada and myself. We'd both been wondering how long we'd have to spend entertaining our guest. Heavy quotation marks around entertaining and guest.

This relief was replaced almost immediately, however, by a brand new worry.

"Please don't drive," said Nevada, beating me to it by a fraction of a second.

Monika turned from her contemplation of the door and looked at us in surprise. "Why not?"

"You've been drinking."

"Have I?" She frowned as she gave this question serious and nuanced consideration. "Have I? Yes, I have. I think I have. I reckon you're right. I have. Been drinking. A bit. I think." She did some more blinking. Her eyes were actually rather large and beautiful. "How did you know?"

Nevada opened her mouth to reply, shut it again, perhaps to prevent inhaling any more than she absolutely had to of the vastly potent beer fumes pouring off our guest, and turned to me helplessly.

"She's really good at spotting the signs," I said.

"Ah," said Monika, apparently deeply satisfied with my reply. "Well, I'd better be off."

"But you're not going to drive," said Nevada.

"No, of course not," said Monika. "I'll just curl up in the back of the van and go to sleep until I sober up. It won't be the first time. Or, I expect, the last."

I turned to Nevada. I was wondering if we should perhaps offer her our sofa instead of the back of the van. Nevada had no trouble following my line of thought and she gave a tiny, almost imperceptible shake of her head. *No way.*

Fair enough.

So we said our goodnights and Monika went out the back door, back through our garden and out the garden gate. There was a thump and a metallic clatter at that point as Monika apparently collided with something. After a brief pause, a scraping sound and some soft cursing from Monika, I realised that she was picking up the toolbox which she'd used to stand on and reach over the gate to get into our garden during her break-in. She'd apparently just left it lying there. The gate finally slammed shut, somewhat petulantly, and there was the sound of a car door opening. Or rather a van door. Then the rattle and clatter of the toolbox apparently being thrown inside the vehicle, even more petulantly.

And then the sound of the van starting and pulling away.

"So much for sleeping it off in the back," said Nevada.

The Vinyl Crypt, known to the cognoscenti simply as Lenny's, had for many years resided happily, if that was the word, in a former bus garage in the hinterland between Highgate and Hampstead in north London. I'd had no idea that before that a shop of the same name—and indeed an associated record label—had been situated in Hammersmith.

But ever since Helene had mentioned it the other day I'd been itching to pay Lenny a visit.

He and his shop had continued their peregrinations and were now located in Notting Hill, on one of the side streets off the famed Portobello Road. This latest iteration of the Vinyl Crypt was a basement establishment, apparently never heated at any time of the year. Perhaps in homage to its name; it certainly was in keeping with the freezing conditions that had prevailed at the one-time bus garage, an icy warehouse of a place which I was glad to see the back of.

It wasn't freezing today, though. It was a glorious spring morning and I savoured the walk to the shop after Nevada and Agatha had dropped me off in Agatha's taxi. Agatha DuBois-Kanes, sometimes known as Clean Head, was tall, slender, elegant and one of London's fleet of expert black-cab drivers. Although Agatha was also a black cab-driver. As well as quite obviously being a woman. Which were both fairly unusual in that profession.

We, or rather Nevada, had hired her as soon as the first payment from Erik hit our PayPal account. "If a sudden windfall of money isn't to be spread around to one's friends, I don't know what it's for," she opined.

She was particularly pleased because she'd begun to fret about Agatha's ability to earn a living since Uber and its like had started making inroads on the official cab business in London.

It has to be said, Agatha herself didn't seem as worried. Nonetheless, Nevada had immediately booked her and sent through a deposit on her services. And then, top priority attended to, she'd set about assembling an order from the Wine Society and searching online for treats for the cats. "And don't forget to get something nice for yourself," she'd said to me, grinning.

"I think I'll nab that Liberty pressing of *Idle Moments* I've had my eye on," I said. "It's got Van Gelder metalwork."

"I should hope so."

So it was that a fully paid-up and cheerful Agatha had driven an equally cheerful Nevada and myself across Chiswick Bridge—Hammersmith Bridge being currently subject to one of its intermittent closures—and over the strange, angular, somewhat homemade-looking flyover past the Tesla showroom and up towards Hammersmith, Brook Green and points north. They'd dropped me off on the far side of Holland Park and backtracked in the rumbling black cab so Nevada could ransack every charity shop in the vicinity of Shepherd's Bush.

I was somewhat less cheerful than the women, because now that we'd accepted money from Erik there was no way I could refuse to take this job on. And I foresaw problems with it. Finding the record being the least of them.

Because, despite the apparent robust confidence of virtually everyone involved, I was far from sure I could find Helene's would-be killer. And certainly not before they made another attempt.

Possibly a successful one.

And then whose fault would it be?

On the other hand, if I *did* dredge up the identity of the killer…

I just wished that they'd handed the whole mess over to the police.

These were the thoughts weighing on me as I walked towards Lenny's shop. But I tried not to dwell on them as I sauntered down a street lined with cherry trees, all thick with pink blossom. It was a warm day, with a definite smell of spring and fresh growth and renewal in the air.

All of which didn't stop Lenny wearing a coat indoors. He also, as advertised, had a beret, of dusty blue rather than the raspberry one he often wore, possibly in tribute to one of Prince's finest songs. Lenny listened to classical and opera, but surely even he admired Prince?

But it was the coat that was the real showstopper. It was a vicuña coat. I knew this because it was almost the first thing he said when I came through the door of his shop.

"Do you know what a vicuña is?" he demanded, looking up at me from the stool where he perched behind the counter.

As Nevada had mentioned, Lenny had made numerous attempts in the past to try and go out with her, despite him knowing full well that she was living full time with me. And 'go out with her' was a staggering euphemism. So we were certainly owed some form of payback for all that.

Which is why I decided to have some fun with him and said, "Some kind of cheap synthetic fibre, isn't it? Like polyester?"

But I regretted it immediately because his face, normally a creepily perfect baby-pink in colour, deepened several shades and his mouth, always downturned even at the best of times, tightened sharply in a grimace that revealed narrow yellow teeth in need of an expert dentist. As it happened, I knew a terrific one just up the road. But there seemed to be more pressing medical matters at hand as Lenny sucked in a series of sharp, shallow breaths.

I found myself trying to remember how to spell the word apoplectic. Also, what was the essential first aid you were supposed to provide to someone having a seizure? Nevada would know, but I didn't.

So I hurriedly added, "Just kidding. It's like merino, isn't it?"

"It is *not* like merino," he snarled. But his colour improved sharply. "Merino is the wool of a variety of sheep. Vicuña is also technically designated a specialty 'wool', but it is actually taken from one of only two varieties of South American camelid living in the high alpine Andes."

I wondered how these high alpine critters felt about their wool being 'taken' from them, but Lenny was in full swing. He touched upon the Peruvian government's strict limitations on how much of the stuff was allowed to be harvested and exported, and the unsurpassed fineness and softness of the fabric. As he delivered this lecture he pulled at his wispy grey beard. It was such an unusual shape that I wondered if it was intended to evoke the facial hair of a noble South American camelid.

"And it sells for about three grand per metre," he concluded, pausing to fondle the lapel of his coat, as if to check that I hadn't somehow slipped it off him.

I said, "Aren't you worried about being mugged on the way home, wearing that?"

He snorted. "They're such idiots around here they'll probably think it's some kind of cheap synthetic fibre, like polyester." He gave me a low, gimlet look to make sure I didn't miss the reference.

Opening pleasantries concluded, I said, "I'm looking for a record."

This put a big smile on Lenny's face, as he prepared either to tell me with lip-smacking satisfaction that my quest was impossible, or alternatively, that he knew of a copy but he could only part with it for a price that was way north of extortionate.

I wrong-footed him by adding, "But first I'd like some information."

He sighed and turned to the mini-fridge he kept behind the counter. It contained a variety of deluxe refreshments, but solely for Lenny, never for the customers. Unless, of course, Nevada dropped by. "Information?" he said wearily, popping the door of the fridge open and peering inside, his beret, beard and disgusted visage all now dramatically illuminated by the glow of the bulb within.

With his face thus pointed about as far from my direction as it could be, he asked, "What do you want to know?"

"Somebody told me that you used to have a shop in Hammersmith."

"Everybody knows that," he said, rummaging in the fridge. "Didn't you know that?"

"And apparently you used to run a record label."

Lenny's head and shoulders popped back out of the fridge. He looked at me for the first time with something resembling interest. "That's right. Crypt Kix. Spelled with an—"

"X. Right. Yes. So I understand."

"A short-lived but highly influential label," said Lenny, grinning with satisfaction. He reached back into the refrigerator and pulled out a half-empty bottle of white wine and a long-stemmed glass, chilled and attractively frosted. He kicked the fridge door shut with the toe of a well-polished shoe and poured a glass of the wine. Then he looked up at me. "Some classic punk rock was released on Crypt Kix."

"And if I was looking for one of those albums?"

"Forget it. For. Get. It. I wish I'd kept some myself. I could have retired by now. Rare as hen's teeth. Haven't seen one for donkey's years." He paused, apparently straining to think of a third animal cliché to add to his menagerie. *You don't stand a cat's chance of finding one*, I thought, but didn't say.

He contented himself with declaring, "No way. Forget it," and shaking his head.

I said, "I understand you ran the label with someone else."

"Well, I wouldn't say he *ran* it with me. He worked with me. Worked *for* me, actually, if you think about it." Apparently Lenny had thought about it, quite a lot.

"This is the guy with the weird name?" I said.

"That's right. Saxon Ghost." Lenny chuckled. "Do you know what his real name was? Finbury Stott. Finbury Stott! Can you imagine staggering around saddled with that?"

I thought a little more forbearance should be forthcoming from someone called Lenny Nettleford. "No," I said.

"Do you know how he came up with his name? His replacement name?"

"I have absolutely no idea."

"It was because he wanted to be the master manipulator manager, the behind-the-scenes A&R and production genius who nurtures artists and makes them rich and famous and, much more importantly, makes himself rich and famous in the bargain."

I remembered what Helene had said. "Like Svengali."

"Precisely." Lenny nodded with satisfaction and sipped his wine. He didn't offer me any, and indeed I would have been shocked if he had. "And young Finbury Stott decided he should have a name to match his ambitions. So he took the names of two of his idols, two of the great rock impresarios—Phil Spector and that execrable McLaren person who managed the Sex Pistols—and he combined them."

He waited to see if I got it. I didn't.

So he sighed and said, "Spector? Spectre? Ghost?"

"And the Saxon bit?"

"Well, Norman McLaren. Get it? Saxon, Norman. There's a sort of association there. People who've conquered this sceptred isle."

"But the Sex Pistols' manager was *Malcolm* McLaren."

"I know!" Lenny began to croak with laughter. "The dumb bugger got it wrong. The putrid maggot-brained dolt got it wrong and didn't even realise." He laughed heartily, sniffed hard, and croaked, "Norman McLaren actually being—"

"A famous Canadian animator," I said, spoiling Lenny's fun.

I saw his face beginning to shut down with sulkiness so I added, "He's a favourite of Nevada's. She's a bit of a film buff."

This meretricious use of my beloved's name got Lenny talking again, all right. And the wine must have helped, because he was waxing downright voluble.

"So he set himself up as Saxon Ghost and helped me launch the Crypt Kix label. Right above my little shop in King Street. Used to be a kebab joint. Not the office upstairs. That used to be a bucket shop. Do you remember bucket shops? They used to sell cheap airline tickets. It went bust and I snapped it up. We ran the label up there, sold the records in the record shop downstairs and distributed them all over London, in the van. I used to have a van."

"I take it you're not still in business with him, Saxon Ghost?"

"What? Christ, no. Jesus Christ, no way. That wanker? That absolute tosser? The record label only lasted about three years, and that was it. I mean it. That was absolutely that. Never again. I'd sooner get a blood transfusion from a syphilitic leper than go into business with Saxon Ghost again. I'd sooner stick my face into a ceiling fan. I'd sooner..." He struggled to think of something else he'd rather do, but failed, shrugged and drank some more wine.

"I take it you wouldn't know how I could get in touch with him, then?"

"Oh, sure. I had supper with him just the other night."

At first I thought he was joking, but he took out a pen and wrote down a number. "Here you go. Give him my love."

I took the number then had a quick look around the shop. It had originally been a residential basement, and quite a large one, with seven or eight rooms. These were all now stacked with records, including in the erstwhile bathroom. I found the punk section, but it consisted solely of 180-gram reissues of The Clash.

That done, I rifled through the jazz with a clear conscience, finding a British stereo Vogue issue of *For Real!* by Hampton Hawes, with Harold Land on tenor sax. Since it was the British release it hadn't been pressed from the original Roy DuNann metal, but I trusted the Decca engineers to have done a good job. The heavy LP slid smoothly out of the poly-lined sleeve and I held it up to the light. The immaculate microgroove vinyl contrasted beautifully with the pale green label.

And Lenny had seriously under-priced it, as he confirmed with a purse-lipped frown when I paid.

As I left the shop he shouted after me, "There's a tilde over the 'n' in vicuña!"

5: RICHMOND PARK

I used the number Lenny had scribbled down for me. To my relief, indeed to my astonishment, it had the correct number of digits, it rang, and someone actually answered. A male voice.

"Saxon Ghost."

He pronounced the name with no apparent self-consciousness. But then he'd had many years to get used to it.

I'd thought carefully about what approach I should take and finally I gave him a variation on the cover story I'd used in the past. I told him I was researching Crypt Kix records, which was true enough, for an article I was working on, which wasn't.

This could scarcely have been more vague. But in our age of the Internet and self-styled bloggers, when even real honest-to-goodness journalists were writing pieces which would never appear in a physical magazine or newspaper, the line between authentic practitioners and madcap amateurs had been hopelessly and probably permanently blurred.

In any case, I needn't have worried. He agreed immediately to see me, which was a refreshing change.

We arranged a time and I took down his address and hung up with a feeling that this had been all too easy. But then, it was about time something was.

I checked his location online and discovered he lived just outside the Richmond Gate exit from Richmond Park, on Star and Garter Hill, shortly before you reached the RSPCA Monument. This latter was a lovely elegant black and gold piece of decorative Victorian wrought iron that had once been a fountain. Nevada and I had always admired it, and we were delighted when it turned out to be dedicated to the Royal Society for the Prevention of Cruelty to Animals— preventing cruelty to animals being one of the few things that the Victorians had got right.

Saxon Ghost, crazy name and all, lived just down the hill from the former fountain, in the Royal Star and Garter development—'stunning apartments in a meticulously refurbished Grade II listed landmark overlooking the magnificent green lungs of London'.

The easiest way for me to get there, and by far the most pleasant, would be to travel directly through those green lungs. Which was to say, Richmond Park. It was a bit too far to walk, but it was perfect for a trip by bicycle.

Nevada and I didn't own bicycles, but we knew someone who did.

I set about making arrangements.

* * *

Nevada would have come with me; indeed it would have made for an ideal excursion on a spring afternoon. But she and Agatha had already planned a girls' afternoon out— for which read more driving around in Agatha's cab and plundering charity shops all over London, thus serving the twin purposes of topping up Nevada's stock of vintage clothing while simultaneously topping up our friend's bank account, all thanks to the recent munificence of Erik Make Loud.

I waved the two of them off and then went next door to Ginnie and Sue's, with the bottle of wine Nevada had selected for them. It was the Duo des Mers Sauvignon-Viognier with the cute cartoon fish on the label. Not the most expensive bottle from our wine rack, but certainly not any of the random ones left over from parties and now considered useful only as blunt weapons. Anyway, Ginnie accepted it gratefully. She'd received identical bribes in the past.

"You two really need to get bikes of your own," she said, stashing the bottle in her refrigerator.

"I know, I know."

She closed the refrigerator and paused for a moment, looking at me with an uncharacteristically serious expression. "There was someone prowling around in your back garden the other night."

"I know. Sorry about that. Did it wake you up?"

"It woke Sue up. She heard them open your gate. She was thinking about calling the police. So she woke me up. I sleep like a hog, or—wait a minute—is it a log? A log. And so that took a while. And by then we heard you guys talking to whoever it was in the back garden. So we figured it was all right. It was all right, wasn't it?"

"As it happens, it was. But in the future, in a situation like that, don't hesitate to call the police."

"That's what I told Sue."

"If it's a false alarm we can always sort it out later."

"Exactly. That's what I told Sue. That's what the police are for."

"Exactly."

"So that's what we'll do."

"Thanks." Having established this procedure as a matter of standard policy I felt a slight easing of the generalised iron grip of apprehension that had locked around me ever since I'd been cornered into helping out Erik and Helene.

"Who was it, by the way? The person in your back garden?"

"Friend of a friend." This was true enough.

"Was she drunk?"

"Drunk really isn't a strong enough word for it."

We went out to Ginnie's back garden and chatted while she unlocked one of their bikes from the steel anti-theft bracket I'd helped them fix to their wall. In our own garden next door Turk heard my voice and set up a piteous cry. She hated to be left out of anything.

"She won't try and follow you, will she?" said Ginnie.

"I hope not."

"I'll keep an eye out and make sure she doesn't."

"Thanks, Ginnie."

"Can I put some cat treats over the garden wall for her?"

"Only if they're organic, hand-made and really expensive."

Ginnie laughed and held the garden gate open for me as I wheeled the bike out onto the narrow stretch of road that separated our houses from the Abbey. I thanked her and she called, "Take care," as I pedalled out into Abbey Avenue, turning right and heading for the park. I entered through Roehampton Gate, sped past tall trees in full leaf, fallen trunks lying among them in the grass, and across Beverley Brook, heading west towards Richmond.

For a long stretch there were no cars on the road and I was the only cyclist. Sunlight poured down on me from the vast blue expanse of the sky and herds of deer paused and peered at me from where they were sheltering in the shade of the big trees.

The trees in Richmond Park are fascinating. They are all oaks and chestnuts, but they have a distinctly Japanese look to them, all neat and uniform and apparently all carefully pruned, with their clean-cut foliage beginning at a standardised height above the ground.

That height being about the maximum distance a deer can reach, when stretching up on its hind legs to feed. As if to demonstrate the principle, a deer stood up as I went by, rearing on its hind legs to rip at the lowest hanging leaves on a branch.

There were lots of deer. I saw a stag standing alert and erect, watching a woman and her tiny dog walk past.

Deeper in the shadowed woods were the bleached, contorted forms of fallen trees, like carefully planted modernist sculptures. The only other humans I saw were on foot, like the lady dog walker.

Clean air, silence, sunshine, endless green vistas.

As I often felt at such times, I wondered why I didn't get on a bike more often.

As it happened, that question would soon be answered.

While I rode along I had time to think.

I'd mentioned Lenny when setting up the appointment with Saxon Ghost—I still couldn't quite take that name seriously, though now I knew its origin it had begun to seem somewhat touchingly human. And if I was Saxon... Mr Ghost... I would have checked back with Lenny to confirm my visitor's credentials. And Lenny wouldn't have had any hesitation in telling him everything he knew about me. So I decided to come clean about hunting for the record, as soon as I could comfortably do so after I arrived.

I handed Saxon Ghost my card. He studied it carefully, then looked up at me and grinned. "The Vinyl Detective, eh?" I was right, he'd definitely been talking to Lenny, because I no longer printed that title on my business cards.

He ushered me into his apartment. It was a big, open-plan space with thick white carpeting on the floor—our cats would have sunk luxuriously into it—and a leather sofa and armchairs upholstered in a black and white zebra-striped pattern. These, along with a wide assortment of rampantly healthy-looking green plants, suggested something of a jungle vibe. But if so, it was a jungle on another planet. The entire place had been decorated with what looked like props from *Barbarella*, exotic and retro-futuristic.

The glass dining table, which was a strange, irregular fan shape, had a full cutlery set spread out on it: gold knives, forks and spoons with pale blue handles, and a variety of streamlined decanters with different brightly coloured fluids in them, like the potions in a mad scientist's lab. I wasn't going to be accepting a drink from one of those any time soon.

Floor-to-ceiling windows provided views which no doubt were referred to in the property prospectus as stunning—in this case, no lie—and let in a great deal of cheerful daylight. On the high white walls were huge canvases in silver metal frames that gleamed; someone was doing a lot of dusting in here on a regular basis.

The man standing amidst all this dubious splendour was dressed in a pricey-looking yellow tracksuit with lavender trim, and immaculate white sneakers that blended imperceptibly into the pile of the carpet. He managed the impressive trick of looking both fat and toned—like a muscular Buddha.

His big blunt head was carefully shaved, as was his face. Unless he was suffering from some unusual condition, his eyebrows had been meticulously plucked until they were almost non-existent. He had an earring, but it was small, gold and unobtrusive.

This all had the effect of focusing attention on his otherwise nondescript eyes, which were small and pale blue.

Despite the extravagant campness of his surroundings and his clothes, the man himself seemed down to earth and oddly unpretentious, his accent that of an unreconstructed East London lad. "Is your bike locked up okay?" he said. I realised he must have watched me arrive from his window. How long had he been keeping vigil, awaiting his visitor? That suggested a lonely and rather empty existence. Or maybe he'd just been walking past the window and had spotted me. It would be hard to walk past a window in this place and not spot things.

"Yes," I said. Ginnie had provided me with a solid-looking bike lock. "It should be fine. Especially around here."

"Don't count on it, mate. Rich people are even more likely to be thieving bastards than anyone else." He grinned at me, revealing synthetically white and regular teeth. "Would you like something to drink?"

My mind moved in a panicked flash to the mad scientist decanters. "Just water, please. Tap water is fine."

We walked back to the living room area with my drink of water and he indicated that I should sit on the zebra-striped leather sofa. I sank down into it—and it really did involve quite a lot of sinking, being somewhat too soft for comfort—as he settled into a zebra-striped armchair opposite me.

From where I was sitting I found myself looking at a section of the wall adorned with musical memorabilia. Framed award certificates, gold discs and publicity photographs of music stars, some of them with a younger and slimmer but equally badly dressed Saxon Ghost featured in them. I hadn't really registered this display before because it had blended in with the general kitsch brightness of the place. Especially those gold discs. There were an impressive number of these, and also award certificates, which I noticed were mostly for high sales rather than artistic achievement.

All of which went a long way to explaining how Mr Ghost could afford to be spending his later years in this luxury dwelling.

"You looking at my hall of shame?" he said.

"It's an impressive array."

"Thanks."

"Nothing there from the Crypt Kix days, though," I said.

He pointed with a lazy finger at another wall and I turned to see, sure enough, an assortment of punk rock images in black and white or shocking Day-Glo shades, including a photo of him standing with his arms around the shoulders of the Blue Tits, two girls on either side of him. It was at the centre of the collection, in the place of honour, so to speak, and it was a big picture. So big that Helene was identifiable even at this distance, short spiky black hair and a heavy slash of black eye make-up. That, at least, hadn't changed.

"She's not in the picture," I said.

"Who?"

"Monika Dunkley."

I didn't think he'd get it, but he roared with laughter. "You are so right, mate. You are so right. She always thought she was a member of the band, Monika. Like the fifth Beatle or something. Fifth wheel, more like. You've really got her number. You've been speaking to her, then? Mohawk Monika?"

"Yes, but not getting a lot of sense out of her."

"That sounds like Monika, all right. So what's the thrust of this article you're writing? What's your angle?"

I took the plunge. "Well, to tell the truth, I'm not really writing an article. I am researching the label, but it's more because I'm looking for a record."

"The Vinyl Detective, eh?"

"Yes."

"So basically you blagged your way in here under false pretences?"

"Yes, you could certainly say that."

He was giving me a cold, hard stare. But then his face softened and he chuckled. "Relax, son. Don't sweat it. That's what I've been doing all my life, blagging my way into places I didn't belong. That's how I got where I am now." He stared around contentedly at the cheesy opulence of his nest, his gaze finally returning to me. "So you're looking for something on the Crypt Kix label?"

"That's right."

"Got to be the Blue Tits' first album, hasn't it?" I wasn't quite able to conceal my surprise and he smiled with satisfaction. "Well, it couldn't really be anything else, could it? All of those Crypt Kix releases are rare, but only one is really sought after." He studied me shrewdly. "And it's worth a few bob now, isn't it?"

"I'll be happy to pay a fair price for a copy, providing it's in good shape."

He chuckled. "There speaks the true professional at work. Sorry to disappoint you, son, but I don't have one."

"That's a pity," I said.

"Can you believe that once upon a time I had boxes of that LP? *Boxes* of them."

"Yes," I said. I could easily believe it. "You withdrew it from sale, didn't you?"

"That's right. And we just got rid of them, you know. Just dumped the records. Just threw them away."

Despite myself, I felt a pang when he said this. The music wasn't my cup of tea, but all the same, what a waste. Poor little records.

"I saved a few, though," said Saxon Ghost.

"You saved a few copies of the record?"

"I saved a few *boxes* of the record."

We looked at each other. The room suddenly seemed very quiet. I said, "What happened to those?"

"I put them aside because I thought one day some idiot might pay a lot of money for them."

I said, "So, what happened?"

"One day some idiot paid a lot of money for them."

"You wouldn't happen to know the name of that idiot?"

"As it happens, I would." Saxon Ghost paused. "Well, sort of."

"Sort of?"

He shrugged. "It was Fanzine Frank. I don't know his real name. I mean, his real name was Frank, but I don't know his last name."

"Who was he?"

"Well, as his name suggests, he used to publish a fanzine. All right, 'publish' is a bit of an exaggeration. Used to put it together in his bedroom and get it photocopied somewhere. No doubt for nothing, if I know Frank. Then he'd staple it together, very crookedly, with the help of his mum, and bring copies up to our shop."

"The one in King Street?"

"Right. He'd drop off new copies and collect any money for the last issue if that had sold, which amazingly it generally had, and then he'd go away again and come back with the next issue, and so on."

"Go away where?" I said.

He frowned. "Sorry. I don't know. Croydon maybe. Somewhere south, I think. I can't really remember."

"Don't worry, it's not a big deal," I said, lying. "It was a punk music fanzine, I take it?"

"It was at first. General punk fanzine. But it very rapidly became just about the Blue Tits. Very taken by the Blue Tits, was Frank."

"And you sold him all the surviving boxes of their first album?"

"Yeah, years later this was. He shelled out a hefty price for them."

"So you were still in touch with him years later?"

"I was, but I'm not anymore. Sorry, mate."

Dead end. I sensed our meeting drawing to a conclusion. And not a conclusive one.

I took one last shot. "Are you still in touch with anyone else from those days, from that circle?"

He didn't pause to give it much thought. "No, not really."

Well, that was that. I began to compose my exit line, and then he said, "If you find a copy of the record, are you going to keep it for yourself or sell it on?"

"I've already got a buyer."

He nodded. "Not your kind of music, then?"

"Not really, no."

"It's a pretty good album."

"So I understand," I said.

"Musically it's miles better than any of the other stuff we released."

I wasn't going to let him get away with this. "But you're the one who ordered it withdrawn, aren't you?"

He nodded placidly. "Yeah. For exactly that reason. It was way too good."

"I understand Helene Hilditch's guitar playing was particularly outstanding."

"Yeah, that was pretty much the whole problem. She played a hell of a guitar for a little teenage girl. It broke her heart when we scrapped everything she did and rerecorded it all. Did it all over again, the same but worse. If you know what I mean. It was a crying shame." He looked at me. "Don't get me wrong. If I had to make the same decision today I wouldn't do anything different. It was the right decision, business-wise."

"But not music-wise?"

He shook his head. "No. Even I could hear that she was something special. I hated that stuff, but even I could tell."

"You hated punk rock?" I was startled by this disclosure.

He shrugged. "I could see its appeal. And I could tell the authentic stuff from the fake stuff. You know, like when someone just phones it in. But I didn't enjoy it."

"What kind of music do you enjoy?"

He looked at me for the first time with a gleam of real interest in his small eyes. Instead of replying, he reached for a remote control and pressed a button.

A section of what I had thought was solid wall slid upwards with a faint humming sound and disappeared into the ceiling, revealing an alcove. When I saw what was in the alcove I almost jumped off the sofa. It was a hi-fi system, and quite an extraordinary one.

The turntable was a John Michell GyroDec. Its design, which looked like a space station, was entirely in keeping with the science fiction vibe of this pad, but it was also a hell of a piece of kit. On either side of the turntable were B&W Nautilus loudspeakers. These were the ones that resembled giant snails on an alien planet, quite possibly hostile giant snails. Saxon Ghost had gone for the bright blue models, which I thought showed considerable restraint since they also came in red. These beauties cost over fifty grand a pair. There was also a rack of McIntosh amplifiers, which probably cost the same or more.

More importantly, there was a shelving unit full of LPs. I was on my feet and heading over to them before I remembered my manners. "Do you mind?" I said.

"Be my guest."

I made a quick survey. "Jesus Christ," I said.

"What is it?"

"These are all Decca SXLs and Mercury Living Presences."

"Of course they are."

I carefully extracted a Decca Stravinsky *Firebird*. It had the colour printing on the back cover. "And first pressings."

"Naturally."

"Are they all classical music?"

"Nothing but the best for Saxon Ghost," he said smugly. He was grinning broadly now.

I began to slip the inner sleeve out of the cover. "May I?"

"Help yourself."

I took out the inner sleeve. It was an original Decca one, of course, and I carefully drew the record out of it. It was perfect. Nothing but the best indeed.

I put the record back and came and sat on the sofa again. "Nice collection," I said.

"Thank you."

"Just one thing," I said.

He was instantly wary. "What?"

"Some of those vintage inner sleeves with poly liners have a nasty tendency to bond with the playing surface of the record."

"What do you mean, bond?"

"Stick to it, creating a residue on the vinyl that you can't remove and which makes a lot of noise when you play the LP."

"Fucking hell." It was his turn to shoot to his feet. "Are you serious?"

"Absolutely. You often find it with a collection where the records haven't been played for years. They should be perfect, untouched, but the plastic sleeves have been slowly merging with the vinyl. It's tragic."

"Fuck, fuck, fuck." He was over by the hi-fi now, staring at the shelves of records. "What do I do?"

"Replace them with Japanese Nagaoka-style sleeves. Or don't even replace them. Keep the old ones and just stick the new sleeves inside them. They'll be fine."

He was gazing at his record collection like a worried parent watching for a playground accident. "Where do I get these sleeves?"

"I've got a load of them. I can send some over to you."

He turned to me. "How much?" Even in the midst of his anxiety, he was always the businessman.

"No charge," I said.

"Are you sure?"

"Consider it a thank you for your time," I said.

"All right, all right, thank you, mate." He turned back to his records. "I'll send a courier over to your place to pick them up."

"Perfect," I said.

He ran his hand over the spines of the records. "Is there anything I can do in the meantime?"

"Sure. Just take the records out of the sleeves and put them back."

"Put them back?"

I nodded. "Once you've taken them out you'll have interrupted any adhesion process that's begun and they'll be fine again for a while."

"Okay, excellent, thanks." He began to take records off the shelf.

"Do you want me to give you a hand?" I offered. I would have, too. When a brother in vinyl needs help, you don't hesitate.

"No, that's all right, mate. Cheers, though. Much appreciated." He came out of the alcove to face me as I got up from the sofa, ready to go.

"Listen," he said. "There actually is one person I'm still in touch with from the old days. Tania Strack. You know, Tongue Strap as was. I'll give you her number and set up a meeting if you like?"

"I'd really appreciate that, thanks."

"No problem. No problem at all. I don't think she's that likely to have a copy of the LP. But she was always very shrewd with investments, so she just might have one salted away."

"Okay, great."

"And if I can think of anyone else who might be helpful, I'll let you know."

"Thank you," I said.

He shook my hand warmly as I left. Never mind the poly sleeves and the vinyl, it looked like Saxon Ghost and I had bonded.

The glorious weather had, if anything, improved by the time I took my leave of Mr Ghost, pedalling through the gate and into Richmond Park. If I exerted myself mildly I could be home in fifteen minutes, listening to music and fending off the cats while I started to get supper ready. I wondered if Agatha would be joining us and I started to plan a contingency menu as I cycled briskly along.

I was so deep in culinary scheming that I didn't hear

a car pull up behind me. But all at once I felt its presence, looming at my back. The car was moving fast, far too fast for this strip of park road where the speed of vehicles was rigorously restricted to protect the wildlife.

And, in theory, the cyclists.

But this joker wasn't having any of it. I glanced quickly over my shoulder and glimpsed a low-slung yellow sports car, moving fast and closing in on me inexorably. The person driving was wearing sunglasses and through the tinted windows I couldn't even determine if it was a man or a woman before the car was upon me. I was now pedalling as fast as I could, veering hastily towards my right.

Not hastily enough for the yellow car. It ploughed past me, nudging my rear wheel with its right bumper. It was the merest of contact, but it was enough to send me flying. I found myself instantly airborne, separated from the bike as we tumbled through the air.

The bike and I landed in a ditch along the side of the road. I hit the ground hard enough to have the wind knocked out of me and lay there for a moment, shocked, hurt and somewhat stunned, but not appreciably injured. The bike clattered down beside me like an afterthought.

I rose shakily to my feet. The yellow car was buzzing swiftly away in the direction of Roehampton. I thought of Helene Hilditch and her own close encounter, and that made me think of taking a picture of the car. I reached for my phone, but by now my assailant was just a dwindling yellow spot in the distance. I turned my attention to the bicycle lying beside me. Once I'd determined that I hadn't suffered any serious harm, my main concern was that Ginnie's bike might be damaged. But as far as I could tell, it was okay.

From the shade of a nearby tree a group of deer watched warily as I got on the bike and set off on the road again. My knees were trembling so much that pedalling was a challenge, but I gradually back got into the rhythm of it.

I couldn't stop myself glancing back over my shoulder every few seconds, though.

6: SLEDGEHAMMER

As I emerged out of the park into Abbey Avenue my body began to ache in earnest and I realised that I hadn't got off as unscathed as I'd imagined. Some extensive bruising, at the very least, was clearly on the cards. By the time I reached our road and turned into it, an enormous weariness had settled over me to accompany the aching.

I got Ginnie to inspect the bike while I told her what had happened.

"Some people drive like maniacs through there," she said. "They're supposed to proceed at a crawl, not just because of cyclists but because it disturbs the deer." I reflected that the deer hadn't seemed too disturbed as they watched my near demise.

Ginnie shook her head. "Some bastards are just too impatient," she said.

Nevada had a different theory when I told her about the incident. After cursing fluently in several languages she said, "Maybe someone doesn't want us looking into Helene's situation."

"That thought had crossed my mind. But it could just be like Ginnie said. Some inconsiderate idiot driving too fast."

She put her arm around me. "Is that really the way to bet?"

"I don't know. I do know that I'm not entirely delighted to be involved in this situation."

"I know, love," said Nevada. "So from now on we stick close together. When you go somewhere, I go along. Next time something like this happens, I'm going to be there."

"That's one reason I'm not delighted with this situation. I want you in danger even less than me."

She kissed me. "But I can take care of myself. More importantly, I can take care of us." This was undeniably true. "I don't suppose you took a picture of the car?"

"You know what, I didn't even think of it until they were well out of range."

"Not like Helene when she was almost run over."

"Not like her at all," I said.

Nevada nodded thoughtfully. "She showed surprising presence of mind in that situation, don't you think?"

"I do think. What are *you* thinking?"

"That maybe she wasn't entirely surprised when that happened."

I said, "You think she might have been expecting it?"

"It or something like it."

"Which would mean…"

"Which would mean that there's more to this whole situation than she's telling us. That maybe she knows more than she's letting on."

It was my turn to lean over and plant a kiss. "You have no idea what a relief it is to hear that," I said.

"Because you had your own doubts about Helene?"

"Well, mostly because I thought you two had bonded so firmly, what with being old school chums and all, that you might be a little bit blind to her flaws and shortcomings."

"Oh no," said Nevada. "I know where my loyalties lie." She took my hand. "With you. Well, with you and the cats. Well, you and the cats and Tinkler and Clean Head. Speaking of Agatha, would you mind if she joined us for supper?"

"I suspected she might. There should be plenty of food."

"Excellent," said Nevada. "That's the kind of food we like. Plenty. She should be here soon. She just popped home to change. And when she arrives she's going to swing for her supper."

"Sing for her supper?"

"*Swing*." Nevada went out into the hall and came back proudly holding a brand-new sledgehammer.

Our local supermarket has had its ups and downs with Nevada. When it ceased stocking her favourite budget wine, the fabled Jaboulet Parallèle 45, she'd come close to enacting a total boycott—or perhaps just a blood feud. But lately it had been back in her favour, not least thanks to the rich assortment of cat-related treats which could be found there. The store also provided free newspapers when you spent over ten quid.

And it was in such a free newspaper, a copy of *The Guardian*, that she had found the ad for stylish garden furniture, which had led to a complete revamping of our lifestyle. Once we'd acquired an outdoor sofa and chair set, we'd begun to sit out in the back garden on a regular basis. And while sitting out there, sipping wine, Nevada had started actively scheming on further ways to renovate our garden.

The latest of these strategies was to remove the unsightly slab of concrete that ran from the garden gate to the door of our shed. Nevada correctly reasoned that if we smashed up the concrete and exposed the earth underneath we would magically have the wherewithal for a large and handsome flowerbed.

First, though, we had to smash the concrete.

Which is where the sledgehammer came in.

The sledgehammer and Agatha.

Agatha turned up half an hour later, coming in through our garden gate wearing jeggings, sneakers and a large white T-shirt with bold black lettering that read I WENT TO CANTERBURY AND ALL I ROBBED WAS THIS LOUSY GRAVE.

I'd seen this garment before, indeed I owned a similar one myself, and it brought back a lot of memories, not all of them good. Nevada greeted Agatha holding the sledgehammer, an iron pry bar and two pairs of industrial goggles.

"Do you want the hammer or the bar?"

"The hammer, of course," said Agatha.

"Okay. Well, get your eye protection on. We don't want any ocular tragedies as a result of flying chips."

"Speaking of chips..." said Agatha, putting on her goggles.

Nevada was already wearing hers. "You'll get your supper when we've wrought sufficient mayhem on this concrete, young lady."

"Can I help with anything?" I said.

"You just get in the kitchen and get cooking," said Agatha. "And make it good. Now stand back." She grabbed the waist of her T-shirt and peeled it off over her head, revealing a black sports bra.

At that exact moment the front doorbell rang. I went back inside the house as Nevada handed Agatha the sledgehammer.

I opened the front door to find Tinkler standing there. His timing really was genuinely extraordinary, since he was deeply and hopelessly besotted with Agatha. "Hey there," he said. "What's happening?"

"Not much. Clean Head is in the back garden taking off her clothes."

"Oh yeah. Ha-ha. Very funny, I— Holy fucking mother of god!" He dashed through the house to the open back door, from which the sound of metal impacting on concrete had begun to ring. I showed him out into the garden, or rather followed him as he charged into it.

"Look who's here," I called.

"Tell him to stand well back, especially when I'm swinging this thing," said Agatha, bringing the sledgehammer down again on the concrete, which had already begun to crack under the impact. As soon as any crack was sufficiently big, Nevada got in there with her pry bar and began to enlarge it. Not to be outdone, she too had stripped down to her bra.

The two young women, semi-topless, wearing goggles and wielding heavy-duty tools, looked like they were posing for a particularly niche fetish calendar. Tinkler's eyes were just about out on stalks as he watched them.

I was in the odd position of finding this both creepy and totally understandable.

We stood in the doorway, watching the women smashing the concrete. Fanny and Turk came and joined us, observing the spectacle with embarrassed astonishment at such foolish human behaviour—indulging in physical labour, and for an abstract, future purpose, too. It was as baffling as eating vegetables.

Tinkler murmured in my ear, "They don't expect us to help, do they?"

"No. As a matter of fact I've been relegated to the kitchen."

"Excellent. Can I come and help you?"

"I wonder. Can you?"

"Well, I can drink wine and offer unwanted criticism."

"Sounds like a winning formula," I said. "Come on."

But I'd hardly got started on supper—salmon fillets with courgette and turmeric sauce—when the doorbell rang again. "Christ," I said. "Who is it this time?"

"Well, it's not me," said Tinkler. "So you're safe." He moved to the window and looked out. "Holy shit," he muttered. I went over and looked out with him. It was Helene Hilditch.

"And no Erik," said Tinkler forlornly.

I left him in the kitchen—since there was no Erik he wasn't particularly interested—and went to let Helene in.

Tonight she had red eyeliner instead of black, no hat, faded blue jeans and a black leather jacket instead of the duster. The jacket reminded me of something and I tried to remember what it was as we exchanged standardised greetings.

"Sorry to just drop in on you like this," she said.

"Don't worry. It's the evening for it." I nodded at Tinkler in the kitchen, who waved.

"Hi, Helene."

"Hey, Jordon."

"No Erik?"

"No, sorry." She turned to me and spoke in a low voice. "I came by myself because I wanted to talk to you. Alone."

"Okay."

"Is there somewhere...?" she shrugged expressively.

Tinkler was in the kitchen. The living room was echoing with the mayhem of the wrecking crew in the back garden. That left the spare room, jam-packed with Nevada's stock of vintage clothing and my overflow vinyl. Or the bathroom, or bedroom. None of which seemed suitable.

So we stepped back out the front door and stood in the little sheltered area which consisted of our front gate and the raised flowerbeds in concrete planters on either side of it. I closed the door behind us and almost immediately there was a rattling of the cat flap as Fanny emerged to peer at us.

Helene and I sat down side by side on one of the planters and Fanny jumped up and rustled through the flowers behind us before settling down to keep an eye on me.

"There was something I wanted to say," said Helene. "I didn't tell you the other day because I was ashamed."

I waited.

She carefully studied her fingernails. They were varnished a glossy black, but trimmed quite short. Guitarist's nails. "Do you remember when I said Saxon Ghost might have another reason to get rid of me? Besides me not having slept with him?"

I nodded. I did remember. But all this sounded very different, and rather odd, now that I had met the man himself. In this new context it seemed utterly implausible that Saxon Ghost would be capable of killing anyone.

But then, you never can tell.

"You see," said Helene, "the thing is, I outed him."

"Saxon's gay?" The *Barbarella* home décor made more sense than ever.

But Helene was shaking her head. "No. He's illiterate."

"Illiterate?"

"Yeah. He can't read or write."

"Jesus Christ." How was such a thing even possible in our century?

"At least, he couldn't back then. He'd never learned. He'd left school like that. That's why Lenny looked after all the paperwork for the record label. It was Saxon's dark secret. He was ashamed of it and he didn't want anybody to know. Went to great lengths to make sure nobody found out. He'd developed all these strategies for making people think he could read."

"Christ."

"But I found out," said Helene. "And I told *everyone*. And he was furious."

Hardly surprising, I thought.

"And I don't think he's ever forgiven me."

I turned this new information over in my mind. Was it sufficient motivation for murder, let alone after four decades? I tried to imagine the scalding humiliation Saxon must have experienced when his secret was revealed, and concluded that, in principle, it certainly was.

On the other hand, having got to know him a little, it just didn't feel right. He seemed too content, too comfortable in his own skin.

Helene was saying, "I really don't know why he got quite so upset. I mean, being unable to read or write was deemed kind of cool back in the punk scene. I think he even got laid on the strength of it. Still, he never forgave me." She leaned back and her black leather jacket creaked and suddenly I remembered what it reminded me of.

Or, rather, who it reminded me of.

"We had a visitor the other night," I said. "Actually in the middle of the night."

Her red-rimmed eyes flickered at me with interest. "Who was that?"

"Monika Dunkley."

Helene stared at me blankly for a moment and then said, "Oh, *Monika*. What did she want?"

"She seemed very concerned about your safety."

"That's sweet. She's an odd girl, though. Don't you think so?"

I did think so, but something in her tone irritated me. I said, "You didn't mention her when you were talking about the band."

"Well, she wasn't part of the band."

"She certainly seems to think she was."

"Well, not really. Not properly." She laughed, and said, "At school we used to call her Limpet Lass. She was never really part of our circle, and she was never really welcome in it, but she used to always hang around with us. Clinging to us like a limpet clings to… whatever it is that limpets cling to." *Rocks*, I thought. *Docks. Piers. Submerged munitions.*

"So, when we formed the band we decided that if she was going to be clinging to us she might as well at least be useful. So we made her the roadie."

I thought this was rather cruel, though practical. As if picking up on this, Helene looked at me and said, "She was downright delighted."

"Delighted?"

"To be invited along for the ride. To be part of the Blue Tits experience. It gave her her moment. Her chance to achieve her little footnote in history. Which I very much doubt she would have got a shot at otherwise."

"And you've stayed in touch all these years?"

"Sorry?"

"Well, she obviously knows about you and Erik and your recent… troubles."

"Oh yes, well. She's been very helpful whenever we need stuff moved. I've had most of my musical gear moved over to Erik's, so it's handy for gigs at the pub, jam sessions and so on."

So Monika was still doing her menial duties as a roadie. Again, a little cruel. But there didn't seem much to gain from pointing this out.

"Anyway," she said, "I wanted to tell you about Saxon so you could put him at the top of your list, and maybe check him out."

"I've already gone to see him," I said.

Her eyes widened in surprise, the red make-up heightening the effect. "Really?"

"Yes."

"What did you think of him?"

I didn't feel any need to tell her that I'd just spent a portion of my afternoon digging out my spare Japanese inner sleeves to save his record collection. "He seems to have done very well for himself."

"Oh yes. Financially. He's done very well for himself financially. Made a lot of money out of us, while we didn't see much of it at all."

This was a common complaint among musicians, and generally a justified one. She peered at me. "Do you think he might be behind it?"

I shrugged. "I'm keeping an open mind. Meanwhile, I'll go on looking. For the LP." I didn't need to add, *And for your would-be killer.*

"Fair enough," said Helene. "Who's next?"

"Do you remember someone called Fanzine Frank?"

"Oh yes. Oh. Yes. He was all over us like a rash. Very creepy. Very into the Blue Tits. You know, he was absolutely our biggest fan." She made this sound like a pathological condition.

"Do you know his full name?"

She pondered. "Hmm. Frank... Frank something.

Something beginning with 'F'. Yes, definitely something beginning with 'F'." This wasn't much help, and to her credit Helene realised it. "He's still around, you know. Still putting out the fanzine. An old-fashioned paper fanzine, if you can believe it. The Internet age doesn't seem to have made any inroads with Frank."

"Do you have any copies?" I said. "Of the fanzine?"

"Oh, Christ no. I never hung on to any of those. But he's definitely still active. He's always pestering me for interviews."

"Do you have his number then, or his email address?"

"Nope, sorry. I don't have any of his contact details. And I make damned sure he doesn't have any of mine."

"Then how does he get in touch?" I said. "When he pesters you for an interview?"

"Through Monika, usually. Monika and Frank are as thick as thieves."

"Okay," I said. "Great. Can you give me her number?" It hadn't occurred to us to get it the other night when she broke into our garden.

"I'll text it to you."

Speaking of the garden, Nevada chose that moment to open the front door. Possibly in the interest of decency, she'd put her shirt back on and her safety goggles were hanging around her neck. "Helene!"

"Nevada!"

The women flung themselves together. "What are you doing out here?" said Nevada.

"Just filling me in on some details," I said.

"Well, come out to the back, Helene, and let *me* fill you in on some details." Accompanied by Tinkler we led our guest through the house and out into the garden, where we introduced Helene to Agatha, who had put her grave-robbing T-shirt back on. The evening had suddenly turned a mite chilly.

"It turns out Nevada and Helene went to the same school," Tinkler told her. "Isn't that incredible? I mean, who would ever have thought that Nevada went to school?"

Nevada, who had donned some heavy gloves, was busy picking up fragments of concrete rubble and putting them in a plastic sack. But now she paused to thump Tinkler on the arm with one of those heavily gloved fists, then returned to putting rubble in the sack.

Tinkler massaged his bruised arm. "Women like hitting me," he said. "Which is lucky, because I like being hit by women."

Helene was inspecting the shattered slab of concrete with approval, and with the encouragement of the other women, she picked up the sledgehammer and hefted it. Agatha gave her her goggles and Helene put these on and began to swing enthusiastically at the concrete with the hammer as Tinkler and I hastily retreated inside again.

7: TANIA'S TOWER

Saxon Ghost proved to be as good as his word. He set up a meeting for me with Tania Strack—Tongue Strap in her Blue Tit days—and he didn't waste any time about it.

To my amazement I found myself booked into her busy diary the very next day. I got a text in the morning giving me a whole hour's notice, with the ominous rider that if I couldn't make that meeting she wouldn't be able to see me for 'several weeks at the earliest'.

I was making coffee in the kitchen when the text arrived, and I was making coffee and cursing colourfully by the time I'd finished reading it. As it happened, however, an hour's notice wasn't impossible, because it turned out that Tania lived nearby—on Upper Richmond Road close to East Putney Tube station.

I drank my coffee, left a note for Nevada, who was still sleeping peacefully after a hard evening of concrete-smashing with the girls, and put out some biscuits for the cats. They were busy snaffling these up as I left the house and set out on a brisk but pleasant walk through the common, where the morning's tide of commuters had given way to assorted dog walkers. I took the path through the woods—the scenic route, past the water meadow—and caught the train from Barnes Station to Putney, a journey of only about three minutes. I found myself walking along Upper Richmond Road with almost a quarter of an hour to spare. Unfortunately all the charity shops were down the other end of Putney, heading towards the bridge. Here it was all estate agents flogging stratospherically priced properties, and bars selling coffee or booze.

I was pleased to see that the Brazilian Naval Commission was still present. I found its somewhat surreal presence in this London suburb, in the throes of transforming itself from dodgy to posh, rather reassuring.

As I approached the shadow of the looming railway bridge running into East Putney station, the nature of the neighbourhood began to change. The bars and restaurants fell away and the blocks of luxury flats began. Stratospherically priced indeed. Tania Strack lived in a new luxury development called Plaza Gardens, in the modestly named Grand Tower, a building of curved glass and white stone with a stack of triangular balconies jutting dramatically out from one of its narrower sides.

I was just about to enter this architectural fantasia when my phone rang. It was Nevada.

"Where the hell are you? I wake up and find a note—"

"I'm only just up the road in Putney."

"It doesn't matter where you are. Something could

happen anywhere." She was genuinely angry. "We agreed after yesterday that you wouldn't go it alone."

"I'm sorry," I said. I told her about the sudden summons to a meeting and gave her Tania Strack's address.

"I'll meet you there," she said. Her voice softened a little. "And then we can do the charity shops on Putney High Street."

I was able to orientate myself when I got out of the elevator on Tania's floor and I realised that she must be the proud possessor of one of those dramatic pie-wedge balconies. As I walked along the hushed, carpeted corridor towards her apartment the front door popped open and a woman stepped out.

She was poised, stylishly dressed, black, with feline eyes. She regarded me with a steady, assessing gaze and wasn't impressed. I stood aside to let her pass and she conferred a cloud of subtle perfume on me, murmuring something polite-sounding but indistinct as she went by, heading for the elevator. She didn't touch me, but I felt the force of her passing.

I suppose you'd call it charisma.

Tania Strack stood waiting for me in her open doorway.

"Who was that?" I said, indicating the disappearing figure.

"Cecelia Tyburn McAllister-Thames. She found some time in her busy schedule to drop by for a brief discussion of my political career, or rather the absence of it." She smiled at me with a cynical look in her eye. "She's a force of nature, wouldn't you say?"

"I wouldn't like to hazard a guess."

She chuckled, leading me into her flat. "Cecelia's an Oxford graduate, a political fixer, and now seated on the boards of a number of large companies. Not to mention in the House of Lords. But I knew her back when she was going to her first Sex Pistols gig and didn't have the nerve to shove the safety pin through her nose. Perhaps it's just as well. It might look a bit dodgy in her photo in Hansard."

I did my best to chuckle politely, too. We sat down, me on the sofa, her on the chair—just like with Saxon Ghost yesterday—but there the resemblance ended.

The sofa and chairs were upholstered in what looked like, and might even have been, real silk, in a blue and white fleur-de-lys pattern. The whole place was similarly tastefully and expensively furnished, but it somehow didn't feel like anyone lived here. It was all too clean, too orderly. Like a high-end hotel. I imagined that if I went into the bathroom the soap would be stylishly wrapped in paper.

The sliding windows, floor-to-ceiling of course, led out to the balcony and let in plenty of daylight, while also providing a spectacular view of dodgy downtown Putney.

The walls of the apartments were hung with paintings of Queen Elizabeth I, including a familiar one featuring her with those giant sleeves and a tiny white head. There was also a grand panorama with good old Gloriana in the foreground and a vast fleet of ships, like crude cut-outs on an equally unconvincing English Channel, presumably prefatory to kicking the shit out of the Spanish Armada.

There were a couple of hefty colour art books about the period resting on a coffee table and the whole place was decorated with a fixation on the Elizabethan theme, the only exception being a large framed poster depicting my host photographed from the waist up with her arms folded, looking stern but relatable against a white background with some giant red numbers looming behind her which were the frequency of a London radio station. *Talking Tough with Tania* announced some lettering at the bottom.

Apparently Ms Strack was a power in talk radio. I'd had no idea. But then, I only ever listened to music radio.

Tania Strack had gained weight since the Blue Tit days, but her sleekly tailored business suit did a remarkably good job of concealing this. She sat sideways to me in her chair, so that she was in three-quarter profile, not unlike her pose on the poster. Her hair was short and black, contoured closely to her head like a helmet. This, along with her sharp nose and round rimless spectacles that enlarged her eyes, gave her something of the appearance of an alert corvid.

"So, Saxon said you were interested in interviewing me."

"Well, in having a chat," I said. "It's not exactly an interview."

"Oh, I see," said Tania, and I felt our encounter go through a sudden and profound gear change. Nothing perceptibly altered in her appearance, but I sensed what little interest she had in our meeting draining rapidly away. Her eyes dropped for an instant to a small table beside her chair.

I saw her phone was lying on it. She was checking the time.

It seemed that mine was running out, and swiftly.

I needed to make some kind of connection with her right now. And somehow I knew just launching in with questions about her days as a punk rocker with the Blue Tits wasn't going to work.

Unfortunately she didn't have a record collection I could rescue...

I stared at all the Elizabethan paraphernalia, wracked my brains, and took the plunge. "Her court astrologer used to live up the road," I said.

Tania Strack's eyebrows went up, but nothing else about her face altered. "I beg your pardon?"

"Elizabeth's official astrologer was a necromancer called John Dee."

"I know who John Dee was."

"Well, he was a local boy," I said. "Used to live just up the road in Mortlake."

Her eyebrows came down now, knitting together sceptically.

"Are you sure?"

"Oh yes."

She picked up her phone and did a quick search.

"My god, you're right. Just up the road. His house survived for centuries. It was once a girls' school. Then some philistines demolished it and now there's a block of flats there." I wondered what had been demolished to create the very block of flats we were now sitting in, but I didn't spoil the vibe by bringing that up. "The new building is called John Dee House." Tania grinned. "Presumably to placate his spirit."

She was still staring at her phone with happy concentration as she scrolled down a website. "Still might be worth a visit, though. He was buried in the chancel of the church next door. A lot of that is gone, too, but the church tower survives. It very definitely might be worth a visit." She tore her gaze from the phone and looked up at me. Her face had come to life in some subtle way and she no longer looked like she was posing for her poster.

"Thank you for that," she said. "Saxon told me you were a useful chap to know, and he's always been a first rate spotter of talent."

The reason I knew about John Dee, homeboy and sorcerer made good, was that both Valerian and Black Dog had written songs about him. The 1960s music scene had been rife with occultism. Personally, I didn't believe any of that malarkey, Tinkler's ability to psychically sense Agatha's sports bra notwithstanding.

Tania made a show of switching off her phone and setting it aside. "Now, what can I do for you?"

I figured that straightforward honesty was the way to go. Or at least a minimum of lying.

"I'm trying to get hold of one of your records and, I know it's a long shot, but Saxon thought it was just possible you might still have a copy."

"One of my records?"

"One of the Blue Tits albums."

"Ah, I see. Which one?"

"The first one."

"You don't mean on CD, do you?"

"No," I said. "On vinyl. And I'm actually looking for a first pressing. You know, the one which was withdrawn from sale."

"Oh yes. That thing. Why would you want one of those?"

"Because it's now very rare and worth a lot of money. And I have a buyer lined up who's willing to pay through the nose for a copy."

When I said this I saw Tania loosen up perceptibly and completely. We had now established that it was money I was interested in, and that was a motive she could understand.

"No, I'm terribly sorry but I don't think I've seen one of those for years. I don't know why Saxon would even think I might have one."

"Like I said, he did say it was a long shot, but he thought you might have kept one stashed away as an investment. He said you were very shrewd like that."

She liked this. "Oh well, that's very kind of him. And he's right. I certainly might have hung onto one if I'd had the slightest inkling that it would ever be worth anything. But one just can't foresee how things are going to turn out, can one?"

Amen to that.

"I'm just sorry that you had a wasted journey." She did indeed sound sincerely sorry. But her mention of being an aspiring politician suggested that I shouldn't take any sincerity too seriously. "Is there anything else I can do for you?"

"Yes, possibly. Do you remember a guy called Fanzine Frank?"

"Frank Fewston. Yes, of course."

Fewston. A surname. I asked her to spell it, and she said, "Would you like his address or phone number?"

This was a windfall. Of course Monika the roadie allegedly knew Fanzine Frank, and Helene had promised to give me Monika's number, but I had the sense that anything that depended on Monika coming through was a distinctly dodgy prospect. Whereas this was definite and here and now.

"Yes please. Both please. You're still in touch with him, then?"

"Oh yes. He lives not far from me."

"He lives in Putney?" Better and better.

"No. Not far from my home. In Epsom." She looked around the sunlit apartment, which must have cost a cool half a million at least. "This is just my little pied-à-terre for when I'm in town." Well that explained the anonymous feel of the place. She didn't really live here. "It's very handy for Putney station," she said, "which runs straight into Waterloo. Excellent transit links, you know."

I said I knew and thanked her for Frank's details, which she was now busily texting me. "I really appreciate your help," I said. "And Saxon's."

"Saxon Ghost is a lovely man," she declared. She said the name with an utterly straight face. But again, that might have been the politician in her.

I decided to take a chance on something. "This is rather a delicate matter," I said.

She immediately leaned forward, all ears. "Yes? What is?"

I hesitated for a second, not faking my diffidence about this. "Someone told me that Saxon was illiterate."

She considered this. "That's such a cruel word. But it's true. He was. *Was*. Back in the days when I first knew him. But he's overcome that handicap now. Thereby showing, I think, great personal courage and determination. It is truly amazing what people can do, don't you think?" We were well and truly in party political broadcast territory here, but I said I agreed anyway. "In fact Saxon offered to help me out," said Tania. "He was going to be my czar for adult literacy. Which was going to be one of the major campaign issues I intended to focus on when I ran for office." Her mouth tightened.

"Of course, all that's off the table now," she said bitterly.

I emerged from the Grand Tower into the sunlight of Upper Richmond Road and turned right, heading back towards the High Street. I was a little surprised that I hadn't heard from Nevada yet. I'd expected her to be waiting outside the building for me. Indeed, I'd thought she might have crashed our little party. Not that it would have done any harm for her to arrive during my interview with Tania. When Nevada wants to turn on the charm, even hardened radio talk show hosts with thwarted political ambitions and an Elizabethan history obsession have been known to melt.

I was halfway to the junction with the high street when my phone rang. I was relieved to see it was Nevada.

"I just came out of Tania's building," I said.

"I know. I saw you."

"You saw me? You're here?" I lowered the phone and began to turn my head.

"Don't look around," said Nevada quickly.

I pressed the phone to my ear again. "What's going on?"

"I don't want to be seen. Someone is following you and I don't want them to know that I'm onto them."

"I'm being followed? Christ." I felt like I'd caught a shameful disease.

"Just keep walking. Look natural."

"I'll do my best," I said.

"I came here to meet you and I was just approaching that tower—"

"Tania's Tower."

"Yes, I was just approaching Tania's Tower when I saw you come out of it. And I saw this van that was parked— quite illegally I might add—pull away and follow you."

"What kind of van?"

"A white one."

Of course. You couldn't be much more anonymous in terms of vehicles in London than by driving a white van. They were everywhere. Which led naturally to my next question.

"Are you sure they're following me?" There were so many white vans, driving in so many random different directions I wasn't sure how we could be sure of anything.

"Well," said Nevada patiently. "They started their engine and pulled away when you came out, and they had to turn around almost completely to follow you, so they clearly hadn't been planning to set off in that direction. I think they were just waiting to see which way you went."

"But it could just be—"

"No, I don't think it could just be a coincidence," she said, deftly anticipating my argument. "They drove only a little way ahead of you and then stopped and waited for you to walk past before they drove ahead and stopped again."

"Jesus. Where are they now?"

"Just behind you."

"What should I do?"

"Take the next turning on your right and we'll see if we can flush them out."

8: WHITE VAN

The next turning on my right proved to be Oxford Road, SW15. I had hardly started to walk down it when a battered and somewhat grimy white van rattled past me and pulled up a short distance ahead.

"I'm with you now," said a voice behind me. I turned around to see Nevada, who fell into step at my side. We walked slowly towards the shabby white van together.

I said, "What do you want to do now?"

"This could go on all day, and I'm getting impatient," said Nevada. "Let's put a stop to it, shall we? Right—you take the driver's side, I'll take the passenger side. *Go.*" She broke into a run and I followed her. We peeled apart and reached the van just as its taillights flashed red and the engine rumbled shakily to life.

I realised why Nevada had taken the passenger side. It meant she was standing in the road beside the car and blocking their getaway. A much more dangerous position.

But from where I was standing I could see inside the van.

I could see the driver.

Monika Dunkley. She was wearing a plaid cap that concealed her mohawk, but it was her all right.

She wound down her window, frowning, and said with a note of accusation, "You two scared the shit out of me!"

We got Monika to leave the van in the Sainsbury's car park while we took her off for a chat.

We found a trendy little coffee shop—in this neighbourhood the real challenge would have been not finding one—and took a quiet table at the back.

"All right," I said. "Why were you following me?"

"I wanted to talk to you."

Nevada wasn't buying this. "So why didn't you just get out of the van and say that?"

"After the other night I wasn't sure you'd *want* to talk to me." Monika dropped her eyes and rubbed industriously at a stain on the table with her thumbnail. "Especially after I promised not to drive my van away and I did. You know, you didn't want me driving and I promised not to, because I was drunk and that."

"So because of that you were… ashamed?" said Nevada.

"Yeah, something like that, I suppose. A bit."

I said, "So today you were just planning to drive around, following me?"

"I wasn't really planning anything. I was trying to make up my mind. I thought if I could make bumping into you look like an accident—you know, 'Oh, what a coincidence, fancy meeting you here,' sort of thing—then it wouldn't be so bad. You know. Me turning up like that. Not like…"

"Not like you were stalking him."

"Yeah. Not like that."

"So you were just waiting outside Tania's place, were you?" I said. "Waiting for me to come out?"

"Yeah."

"How did you know where she lived?" said Nevada.

"Oh, I've stayed in touch with Tania. I've tried to stay in touch with all the girls, and I've managed pretty good. Except with Ophelia. She's dropped off the radar. No one's quite sure where Ophelia has got to."

All this was massively missing the point, I thought. I said, "But how did you know I'd be at Tania's in the first place?"

"How did I know you'd be there?"

"Yes."

"Well, you'd gone there to have a chat with her."

"Yes, but how did you know that?"

"Saxon told me," said Monika.

I almost said, *Saxon Ghost?* But there could hardly be two. "Saxon told you that I was going to see Tania?"

"Yes."

"And he told you exactly what time I was going to be there?"

"Well, Tania told him and then Saxon told me."

Nevada leaned a little closer towards Monika. This could have been friendly, or it could have been menacing. Take your pick. "And you just happened to call up Saxon Ghost and ask about us?"

"No. He called me."

"He called you?"

"Yeah."

"Just out of the blue he calls you up?"

"Pretty much. He does that from time to time. It was a, you know, booty call."

"A booty call?" said Nevada. For the first time since she'd spotted the white van she seemed wrong-footed. Not to mention disarmed.

"Yeah, we used to have a thing going. Back in the day. Back in the Blue Tits day. And we still hook up now and then."

This wasn't as unlikely as it initially sounded. I remembered Helene saying that Saxon hadn't managed to sleep with any of the girls in the band. But it seemed entirely possible that he might have scored with their roadie. If at first you don't succeed... In fact, thinking about it, Saxon and Monika were a fairly plausible couple. They were even a little alike physically.

I also remembered how he had instantly known who I was talking about when I mentioned her name. *That sounds like Monika*, he'd said, as if he knew her rather well.

I'd assumed all this was just fond memories, but it made a lot more sense if they were still in touch.

So to speak.

"And so, in the course of this 'booty call'," said Nevada, "you just got talking to Saxon Ghost about us?"

Monika bobbed her head. "I wanted to see you guys again, but I couldn't come by your house. Not after I disgraced myself the other night. I told him I'd like to, you know, sort of engineer an encounter, and he told me about this meeting you'd arranged with Tania and I asked if he could find out what time it was, and he did." She smiled at me. "So I could hook up with you." Then she glanced worriedly at Nevada and hastily added, "I don't mean hook up hook up."

"No, of course not," said Nevada diffidently. "One booty call at a time." But under the table her hand found mine and clasped it.

"So that's it." Monika shrugged. "I came along this morning so I could be there after your meeting with Tania. How did it go?"

My first instinct was to be cagey. But, thinking about it, there was no harm in telling her. And I wondered if she might be able to add some useful insights of her own. "It went pretty well," I said. "She was able to give me contact details for Frank Fewston."

"Fanzine Frank? Oh, I could have given you those. Why, do you want to go see him?"

"I thought I'd have a chat."

"You're barking up the wrong tree there."

"Really, you think so?"

"Yeah, Fanzine Frank would never try and kill Helene. He loves Helene. In fact, he loves all the girls. But especially Helene, I reckon. She's like his little favourite."

"Okay," said Nevada. "So if he isn't a likely suspect, who is?"

Monika shrugged truculently and stared at me. "I thought he was the detective. Isn't that what he's supposed to be finding out?"

Nevada shot me a look compounded of annoyance and despair.

"But that's part of being a detective," I said patiently. "Talking to someone who knows all the principals, all the people involved. Someone who might have insights into the situation. Someone like you."

Monika bought into this with gratifying speed. She immediately began nodding her head in vigorous agreement. "Yeah, that makes sense," she said. "That makes sense, all right. So, what would you like to know?"

"If Fanzine Frank doesn't want to kill Helene, who does?"

"Ah, hello. Tania for a start."

"Tania Strack wants to kill Helene?"

"I'm not saying that," said Monika, although she just had. "I'm just saying she has a *motive*."

"And what would that motive be?"

"Well, you know about Tania's big plans?"

I said, "Why don't you just assume we know nothing about Tania Strack. Except that she used to be in the Blue Tits and play the..." I realised that I'd forgotten what instrument Tania had played in the band.

"She was the lead vocalist," said Monika with comfortable condescension. I could see that it gave her a warm and gratifying feeling to be in a position to tell us things we didn't know. Which was fine with me. Those were exactly the kind of things I liked being told. "She was the singer in the band."

"That's right. I remember now," I said. "Helene said she couldn't get into the school choir. She wasn't good enough."

Monika giggled. It was a surprisingly girlish sound, coming from this rather hulking middle-aged woman. "She was rubbish. And *anyone* could get into the choir. Even I was in the choir." She fell silent for a moment, lost in thought. "That was back at Emily Kelso," she said.

"We know," said Nevada.

"The Emily Kelso Academy for Young Ladies."

"We know." I noticed that Nevada didn't volunteer the information that she too was an old girl of that famed institution. Clearly she didn't want to send this conversation off on a tangent.

But evidently it was off on one anyway. "You should really look into that place," said Monika.

"The school?" I said. "Why?"

"Because there were a lot of people there who were really pissed off at Helene. Because of her starting the band. She got up a lot of people's noses. Not to mention all the grief the school got when the newspapers found out that us Blue Tits were all from there." I noticed she'd upgraded herself to band member status again.

"We brought the place into disrepute. In fact, the headmistress got sacked because of it." She was nodding enthusiastically now. "I never thought about that before, but that's someone else who might have a grudge against Helene."

"The headmistress of Emily Kelso?" She'd have to be a ripe old age by now. Still, we shouldn't ageist about prospective murderers...

"Yeah, but not just her. There were loads of people at that school, both pupils and staff, who got really ticked off because of what she did. Because of what we did."

It was a long way from being ticked off to attempting murder, I thought, but Monika clearly had embraced this new notion. "You should really look into that place," she repeated.

"We will," said Nevada. "But you were going to tell us about Tania Strack."

"You asked me about people who might want to kill Helene," said Monika in an aggrieved voice. "Not just Tania. Or do you want me to just concentrate on Tania and not bother mentioning anyone else?" She gave us a look that would have done credit to a sulky child. *See if I care*, it said.

"No," I said wearily. "Please tell us about anyone who you think might be a likely candidate."

"Well, there's the Bride of Frankenstein for a start."

"Who?"

"Bill Bridenstine. That was just our nickname for him."

This was a relief. After the Saxon Ghost experience I'd been ready to believe anything.

"Who is Bill Bridenstine?" said Nevada. She looked at me. "The name rings a bell."

"TV chat show host, I think," I said.

"That's right." Monika was nodding vigorously again.

"And why might he want to kill Helene?" said Nevada.

"Because of what happened," said Monika.

Nevada and I glanced at each other. This obviously wasn't going to be easy. But I was willing to do what was necessary. "And what happened?" I said.

With the uttering of these magic words, Monika began to tell us the whole sordid story.

After Saxon Ghost had rerecorded and rereleased the Blue Tits' first album, the band suddenly found themselves with a hit on their hands. Saxon had then proceeded publicising them to the hilt. One of his coups had been getting them on *Bickering with Bridey*, an early-evening chat show on Thames Television that went out nationally. As the title suggested, the show's appeal—if that's what you could call it—consisted of the gladiatorial spectacle of the host Bill Bridenstine being obnoxious to his guests.

If those guests in turn got a little combative, so much the better.

But one bitterly cold grey autumn evening in 1977, when the members of the Blue Tits walked into his studio, Bridenstine got more than he'd bargained for.

"One thing you have to realise," said Monika, "is what television was like back then. There was no political correctness. There was no health and safety. And long lunches were the order of the day. Lengthy, lavish, expense-account lunches. So old Billy boy wanders in to get ready for the show, and he is well refreshed. Very well refreshed indeed." Monika looked at us. "Pissed," she said, in case we hadn't got it. "Out of his skull. He could still walk. And talk. And if you didn't get close enough to smell him, you might even think he was sober. But if you came within ten feet you could smell the whisky coming off him in clouds."

Not beer, then, I thought, remembering Monika in the garden the other night and her own adventuresome aroma.

"And if you got a bit closer, you could see his eyes— the lights were on but no one was home. You know what I mean? None of which meant he wasn't functioning. He was. This was his standard mode, apparently. This was how he did his show every week. He figured that he was such a pro, such an old hand, that he was good enough to do it pissed. But he hadn't met the Blue Tits." Monika giggled again.

"He had us down as just a bunch of brainless little sluts. And his plan was to slut-shame us, show us up for the morons we were, condemn our general moral depravity and, with a little luck, get us to flash a bit of tit. Then it would be job done, back to the bar for a quick one while groping his secretary before getting a taxi home."

Monika grinned a wolfish grin. "But it didn't work out like that. For one thing, any one of us had twice the brains he had. So together we had ten times the brains of Bill Bridenstine." I noticed that Monika was firmly part of the band now. "It might have been different if he'd bothered to read the notes his researcher had prepared for him. But that would have cut into his drinking time and the almighty Bridenstine decided he could just wing it. So he didn't know that we'd all gone to a private school. And his first salvo was about how we were a bunch of uneducated yobs. Which went badly awry when Ophelia started making insulting comments about him in Latin, with the correct declension of all nouns, pronouns and adjectives. And there were some very good adjectives."

Her smile was beatific now, as she savoured the treasured memory. "The audience started howling with laughter— this was all being transmitted live, you know, in front of a live audience—and suddenly they were on our side, and

Bridenstine *really* didn't like that. So he started trying to regain lost ground. Then he started getting nasty. But we just wiped the floor with him. Made him look an absolute tool. Such an absolute tool that his career never recovered."

"All right, so that explains why he might have a grudge against the Blue Tits in general," said Nevada. "But why Helene in particular?"

And why would he go to the lengths of trying to kill her, I wondered. None of this sounded plausible to me.

"Because she said the C-word," said Monika.

"What?"

"Helene dropped the C-bomb."

"You mean…"

"She called Bridenstine a cunt. Live. On national television. Can you believe that they didn't have some kind of transmission delay so they could censor things like that? But they didn't. And Helene said it. The worst word of all. Never mind 'fuck' or 'shit' or 'piss'. This was like the ultimate taboo. And millions of people heard her say it. The next day it was all over the newspapers. All over them. The Blue Tits *owned* the front pages." Monika's big, nostalgic smile grew bigger.

"Saxon was so pleased. You can't buy that kind of notoriety, he said. And notoriety sells records, he said. And boy did it ever. When I told you before that the album had been a hit, I meant it was an indie-label punk-rock first-album kind of hit. But now it went through the roof. It totally made our careers." Her smile changed to something much nastier. "And it totally destroyed Bill Bridenstine's.

No more expense-account lunches for darling Billy. He lost the show, lost his job. Went from being one of the top television personalities of the day to being a pariah. Last I heard he was working on local radio, reporting about sheep shagging in the Outer Hebrides or somewhere like that."

There was a genuine note of pride in Monika's voice. "And all because one little girl said one little word."

Okay, I thought. *Now, that might just be a motive for murder…*

Monika slapped her hands down on the table in an authoritative fashion, as if drawing a line under the previous discussion. "But anyway, I wanted to tell you about *Tania*." She gave her head an impatient little shake, as if to say, *I haven't got all day. You're wasting my valuable time with these constant detours of yours*. "Now, Tania Strack has definitely got form with Helene. And I'm not talking about something that happened forty-odd years ago. I'm talking about now."

"Okay," said Nevada. "Keep talking about now. Please."

Monika looked at me. "You said you didn't know what Tania has been up to since she left the band."

"That's right. Though I did see a poster in her flat. She's on the radio? Has her own show?" *And not about animal molestation in the Western Isles*, I thought.

"She does. And she's very popular with a certain segment of the population. The thing you have to understand about Tania is that she's got very right wing in her old age, and that plays really well in some quarters. So she has this show and she is doing very nicely with it. She has a highly successful career. And Tania also has a shitload of money, both from the radio gig and from her investments. She invested every penny she ever made from the Blue Tits. Not like some of us. Some of us pissed it up the wall. But Tania always had her head screwed on. She put her money into real estate. In London. In the 1970s. Can you imagine?"

I could see that Nevada was indeed imagining. Enviously. Well, this explained how Tania could afford a house in Epsom plus a Putney pied-à-terre.

Monika blinked and looked at us. "Where was I?" she said. "I was going somewhere with this."

"Motive for murder," said Nevada succinctly.

"That's right. But a successful career and a shit ton of money just aren't enough for our girl Tania. She also wants a career in politics. But she's not going to get one."

"Isn't she?" said Nevada. She was intrigued now, and so was I.

"No, because Helene won't let her. Helene really hates how reactionary Tania's become. She says it's like a betrayal of everything we stood for in our Blue Tit days. It's bad enough having Tania pump out her poison on the radio, but going into politics? Running for parliament? That's where Helene draws the line. She told Tania she won't let her do that."

"And how does she propose to stop her?" said Nevada.

"She proposes to stop her by publishing her memoirs. Helene has been threatening to publish her memoirs for yonks. But she said if Tania didn't back down she'd really do it this time. And Helene promised her these memoirs would be warts and all. She actually said *genital* warts and all. Ha! Good old Helene."

I said, "So did Tania back down?" This was beginning to shed light on some of the things she had said to me, and the bitter tone in which she'd said them.

"Oh yeah. You bet. Because Helene knows about all the skeletons in the cupboard. She knows where all the bodies are buried. She knows where all the skeletons are buried. She could really dish the dirt." Presumably on top of the buried skeletons. "Because Tania wasn't always a tight-arsed little Tory. She used to be quite the fun merchant. She got up to a great deal of mischief, and I mean serious mischief, when she was still one of the girls."

She nodded her head in agreement with herself. "Now, Tania's never pretended she wasn't a Blue Tit. In fact, she's found it quite useful for her image. Gives her a bit of street cred, you know. Former punk rocker. Adds a little spice to the biography. But there's such a thing as too much spice, and if Helene really dished the dirt on her, it wouldn't just torpedo Tania's hot little political dreams, it might well finish off her radio career, too."

Monika nodded decisively. "So, that's where things stand. If Tania wants to fulfil her true-blue dreams, it will be over Helene's dead body."

9: MAY FAIR

I used the number Tania had given me for Fanzine Frank and commenced what turned out to be a long game of telephone tag. As I was busy leaving messages for him and he was busy leaving messages for me, it became very clear that nothing was going to happen in a hurry.

So I discussed our options with Nevada and we decided that I should set up meetings with the other members of the Blue Tits. They were prime candidates to still own a copy of the suppressed first album.

And these former bandmates also might be able to shed light on who would have a sufficiently serious grudge against Helene to want to kill her.

"Plus of course they might want to kill Helene themselves," said Nevada. "The way that Tania does."

"The way Tania allegedly does."

"As alleged by Monika the roadie."

"When you put it like that," I said, "it sounds a lot less likely."

"True, but if what she said was right about Tania's political aspirations having been deliberately stymied by Helene…"

"Then that's genuinely a motive for murder," I said.

"Yes."

"But it won't do Tania any good if she kills Helene and then the dirt gets published anyway."

Nevada shook her head. "I get the feeling that this dirt hasn't been written down yet. I mean, Helene doesn't exactly give the impression of being a dedicated memoirist who's been sitting in a cork-lined study for long hours devotedly recording the minutiae of her earlier life."

"No. She certainly doesn't give that impression."

"I mean, we can check with Erik," said Nevada. "Or indeed with Helene herself, and find out for certain. But my impression is that, at the moment, all those juicy punk rock scandals still only exist in Helene's head."

"Which would explain the urgency of someone wanting to kill her—"

"Before she has a chance to write them down," said Nevada. "Exactly."

We looked at each other for a long moment as the penny slowly dropped. Perhaps drawn by the sudden silence, Fanny came trotting in and made a high-pitched plea for food. For once we ignored her.

"We have to get in touch with Helene," I said.

"Right now," said Nevada. She had already picked up her phone. "I'll call Helene. You try Erik."

I grabbed my own phone and dialled Erik's number. As

I did so, Nevada frowned and turned to me, shaking her head decisively. "Voicemail. Should I leave a message and tell her?"

We think someone, Tania being the top candidate, but, come to think of it, it could be anyone from the old days, is trying to kill you because of what you might reveal in your memoirs. So you have to write said memoirs right away and also arrange for them to be immediately published if you should die. And also widely publicise the fact that…

"Let's try and talk to her in person first," I said.

"Right." Nevada began speaking brightly into the phone. "Helene? This is Nevada. Agatha and I had an utterly lovely time smashing the crap out of that concrete slab with you the other night. But that's not what I'm ringing you about. I need to talk to you rather urgently. So do please call me back as soon as you get this message."

While Nevada was busy being charming to Helene's voicemail, I wasn't getting any voicemail at all on Erik's number. It just rang and rang and rang. Maybe he hadn't even set up voicemail, it being too much for his rock-star brain. But, wait a minute, hadn't I left messages for him before? I was sure I had. So perhaps Erik had changed his phone provider or his package, or something, and his voicemail had dropped off into oblivion. Because ensuring that it wouldn't drop off into oblivion had been too much for his rock-star brain.

This was incredibly frustrating and I was beginning to get angry, and Nevada was starting to look at me anxiously, because now the anger had turned to fear. Erik's lack of voicemail and the endlessly ringing phone had suddenly taken on a far more sinister connotation.

"Is something wrong?" said Nevada.

"There's no answer. No answer and no voicemail."

"Maybe—" said Nevada.

But at that instant, the phone was answered.

"Hello. Erik's phone," said a clipped and supercilious voice.

I was speechless for a second. "Tinkler? Is that you?"

"Oh, hi!"

"Why are you answering Erik's phone? And what's with the stupid voice?"

"I thought it might be somebody important calling."

"Well, tell Erik if somebody important is likely to call him he should get his fucking voicemail fixed."

"I know, I know," said Tinkler. "It's a complete bummer, isn't it? You see, what happened is that Erik's phone provider notified him that anyone with the Super Phone Plus package was going to be charged a penny every time they accessed their voicemail—"

"Tinkler…"

"So, in a towering fury, he cancelled the Super Phone Plus package and reverted to the Standard Phone Plus package, thinking that would include voicemail. I mean, you would think that it would include voicemail, wouldn't you? Being Plus and all. But—"

"Tinkler, is Erik there?"

"If he was here he would have answered his own phone, wouldn't he?" The superciliousness began to creep in again.

"Where is he?" I said.

"Out in the garden."

"Well, go and get him."

"I can't do that," said Tinkler. And his voice dropped to a low, conspiratorial tone. "He's gone out to the boulder. And when he goes out to the boulder, he likes to be left alone."

The boulder? Erik's drug stash. "Tinkler, are you guys stoned?"

"Not as stoned as we are going to be, my friend. Not remotely as stoned as we are going to be."

"Tinkler, listen to me, this is very important."

"Yeah, yeah, yeah."

"No, seriously, Tinkler. Tell Erik that Helene has to start writing her memoirs. Or at the very least put down all the most scandalous and salacious stuff." Nevada was nodding in fervent agreement as she listened to me. "Put it down on record," I said, "and make sure she names names. So that if she is, heaven forbid, killed…"

"Sorry," said Tinkler. "I nodded off for a moment. You said something about Scandinavian Sally Stuff and, what, a record of names?"

"Tinkler…" I said, through clenched teeth.

There was a gurgle of laughter on the other end of the line. "Just messing with you, bro," said Tinkler. "You are so easy to wind up."

"Tinkler, for Christ's sake…" At the edge of my vision I could see Nevada making throat-throttling motions with her hands.

"Okay, relax," said Tinkler. "You want me to tell Erik to tell Helene to make a summary of all the juiciest bits from the memoirs she's planning to write, all the reprehensible stuff that might piss other people off, and they might want to prevent her disclosing, and arrange so that it's put in the public domain if anything happens to her."

Nevada stopped making strangling gestures and stared at me. I imagine I made an arresting sight, with my jaw on the floor.

"Tinkler," I said, "that's exactly right."

"So you reckon that could be the motive behind the murder attempts?"

"Yes," I said. "We think it might be." Nevada was nodding enthusiastically again.

"Good call," said Tinkler. "Helene will have to make damned sure that everybody knows she's done that, though, or it won't be any protection for her."

"Yes."

"I'll suggest the enthusiastic and extensive application of social media. Finally it will prove useful for something."

"Yes."

"Anything else?"

"No."

"Can I go and get stoned with my friend now?"

"Only if you tell him to fix his voicemail."

"That comes under the heading of anything else. Learn to be orderly in your presentation of entreaties. *Ciao*." Tinkler chortled and hung up.

I looked at Nevada. "Tinkler is on the case."

"Is that a good thing?"

"In this one instance, apparently yes."

Richmond is an affluent suburb of London with a rather lovely bridge across the Thames that I'm very fond of, and not just because Piero Piccioni wrote a great song about it. There's also an excellent selection of charity shops there, especially just across said bridge, and a load of good pubs and cafés and restaurants.

Most importantly, it is just a quick bus or train ride from our place. This morning Nevada and I had caught the train. It was Saturday and we set off early, or at least early by Saturday morning standards, because it was the Richmond May Fair.

We paused at Paul to get some sandwiches, and at Oxfam so I could check out the records and Nevada could sneer at the clothes. Then we turned off the Quadrant and headed down Duke Street towards Richmond Green, which was where the May Fair was held every year.

They were still setting up, which was the point of getting here at this time. Early birds, worms, and so forth. Some of the stalls were devoted to selling food or new items or running raffles. These were just a waste of space as far as we were concerned. We wanted second-hand stuff— potential treasures.

As we walked towards the green I felt the buzz of excitement, and I knew Nevada felt it as well.

But we had something else on our agenda today, too.

"Have we got time for a quick look around before we go after him?" said Nevada.

"Of course we have. I don't know if he's even here yet."

Nevada nodded happily and peeled off to check out the possibility of designer clothes discoveries, while I made a beeline for the record stall on the far side of the green, run by Patrick the Cat Protector.

We called him that partly because I could never remember his last name, but mostly because his profits went to the charity Cats Protection. A worthier cause it was hard for us to imagine. Patrick was reliably here every year, but nonetheless every year I was relieved to see him, because he wasn't getting any younger. His stall consisted of a couple of folding tables covered with cardboard boxes full of LPs. Those were my kind of cardboard boxes. Plus more on the ground under the table.

Patrick also brought large sheets of plastic with him and waited beadily to drape them over his boxes at the first sign of rain. Most years he wasn't disappointed, but today it was fine and dry.

He saw me coming and waved. He was a small, smiling man with rather feverish eyes who had a habit of wearing button-up sweaters with a proper shirt and tie on underneath. I handed him the bag I'd brought for him, full of LP inner sleeves and outer covers which I'd removed from records I'd bought over the last year—I had my own very definite ideas about how a well-dressed piece of vinyl should be clad, and it was much more gratifying to recycle my castoffs via Patrick than to just bin them. Anyway, it was an impressively large bag and he accepted it gratefully. I then set about searching through the boxes.

Patrick the Cat Protector was strong on big bands and jazz vocalists, and there was nothing wrong with that. Almost immediately I found a British grey label mono Warner Bros. pressing of a Joanie Sommers album arranged by Neal Hefti. What's more, it had a deep groove, which was very unusual if not downright weird for a British pressing. I bought it immediately.

"No original Blue Notes, I'm afraid," said Patrick as he made change for me. No surprises there, then.

"Any punk rock?" I said.

"There's some U.K. Subs in that box."

"Nothing by the Blue Tits?"

"Not likely. Their stuff sells really quickly."

"No chance of a first pressing of the first album?"

Patrick sucked his lower lip meditatively. "I might have one back at the house."

This being his standard answer to all such enquiries. The thing was, he quite often did have a copy back at his house in Sudbury. Before I could take this thought any further, a shadow fell across the box of LPs I was looking through.

"My spies told me you'd be here."

I turned to see Saxon Ghost beaming at me. He was wearing oxblood Doc Martens, jeans that looked uncomfortably tight for a man of his girth and a biker's jacket of classic design except that it was fashioned from white leather. I'd never dreamt that such a thing could exist. In a well-ordered world, it probably couldn't.

We shook hands and I said, "By your spies, you mean Monika?"

"Yes, she said she rang you up and told you about Bridenstine being here."

So he knew about our plans to try and meet Bill Bridenstine today. "That's right," I said. "That was very helpful of her."

"Wasn't it just? And very handy that he's turned up here, what with you wanting a word with him and all." There was a somewhat needling quality to the way he said this and I sensed that our friend the Ghost wasn't happy about something. "Anyway," he said, "I knew you'd be here and I thought I'd pop along and say hello."

"Hello," said Nevada.

We turned to see her approaching us, carrying a very large paperback book. As Saxon inspected her, his odd little eyebrows crept up on his forehead.

I said, "This is Nevada, my other half." Saxon's eyebrows crept a little higher still and I sensed my status had just received a sudden upgrade.

"Hello, Nevada. I'd say something about unusual names, but I'm called Saxon Ghost, for Christ's sake."

We all laughed and Nevada said, "Well, fancy meeting you here."

"I come along every year." This made perfect sense, since he was a local. "Also, like I was just telling your bloke here, Monika said that you were going to be about, so I thought I'd pop along."

"Mr Ghost," said Nevada.

"Call me Saxon, love."

"All right, I will, but only after noting for the record that 'Mr Ghost' is the coolest name ever. Saxon, I wanted to say thank you for the very welcome injection of funds you provided for us."

Nevada had looked at our account the previous day and had given a little shriek. "We just got £500 from Saxon Ghost," she'd told me.

"What?"

"Apparently, according to the accompanying message, you saved his record collection."

"Well, I suppose you could say that."

"Well, he certainly said that."

Now Saxon Ghost was smiling at us and said, "My pleasure, love. Saxon Ghost always pays handsomely for services rendered." He looked at me. "You were right about those poly-lined sleeves. One of them had already started to stick to a record. The Kertész *Bruckner: Symphony Number Four*. Like you said, the bugger left marks all over the playing surface."

I said, "If the adhesion process has only just started you might be able to remove them by washing with a really good record-cleaning machine. And I mean a really good one. You're welcome to use my Moth, but—"

"I'm way ahead of you, son. I've got an ultrasonic cleaner all lined up. But in any event, the point is, you saved my record collection."

"You didn't have to pay us five hundred quid," I said.

Nevada seized my arm. "Don't try and talk the nice man

out of his generous gesture, honey. It's rude. And besides, I've already used the money to book a holiday."

Saxon laughed. "Going somewhere nice, love?"

"Wine tour of the Rhône."

"Lovely. You didn't know, then, mate?" The latter was directed at me, based on the fact that I was gaping at Nevada.

"No," I said.

"It's a surprise," said Nevada complacently.

I said, "What about…"

"I've already booked Agatha to look after the twins."

"You have kids?" said Saxon.

"We have *cats*," said Nevada. "Considerably less chance of Social Services being called in when you abandon them to go off on a wine tour of the Rhône."

"And did Agatha say yes to cat sitting?" I said.

"Oh yes. Thrilled at the prospect. But that's only because I didn't tell her where we're going. We'd better brace ourselves for some serious sulking when she finds out." She looked at Saxon. "Clean Head will be upset about missing out on the wine tour." She took my hand. "But I wanted it to be a romantic little number for just we two."

"Clean Head is Agatha?"

"Yes, sorry. Force of habit."

"Got a shaved bonce, has she?"

"She does at that. Looks rather good on her, too."

Saxon Ghost eyed me sardonically. "Did you name her that, then? After Eddie Cleanhead Vinson?"

Nevada was staring at him. "Yes, he did. How did you know?"

"Well, he's Mr Jazz, isn't he? Never mind me being Mr Ghost."

"And how did you know *that*?" I said.

"Had a look at your website." He smiled at me. I realised how easy it would be to underestimate this man. And also, possibly, how dangerous. He turned and looked around the green, which was now filling with people as the stall holders finished setting up. "Any sign of him yet?" he said, smiling.

"Who?" said Nevada.

"Bill Bridenstine. Monika told you he was going to be here, didn't she?"

"Ah, yes. Yes, she did."

Saxon Ghost turned and looked at us. The smile was gone. I sensed we were about to get to the nub of the matter. Something had pissed off Mr Ghost and now he was going to tell us about it. "But what I don't understand is why you want to talk to him. He won't have a copy of that Blue Tits record you're after. He's just about the last person in the world who's likely to have a copy."

This was certainly true, given the havoc the band had wreaked on Bridenstine's career. I decided it was time to come clean. "I'm not just looking for the record," I said.

"Yes, mate. I know, mate. So I understand. You're looking for some nutcase who's been trying to top Helene Hilditch."

"Monika told you that too, did she?" Good old Monika.

"Yes," said Saxon. "But why didn't *you* tell me that? I could help you try and find out who's doing it. I mean, it's fucking awful. Someone trying to kill Helene? Why didn't you tell me?"

I braced myself and started to speak. But Nevada beat me to it. "Because you were a prime suspect."

Saxon stared at us. "Me? Why?" He seemed genuinely perplexed. Not to mention hurt.

I braced myself again. "Because Helene revealed to the world that you couldn't read or write," I said.

He shrugged. "Well, that was true, mate. I couldn't."

"But it must have been incredibly hurtful," said Nevada. "To be... exposed like that."

Saxon smiled ruefully. "Oh yeah, I'll say. And I won't pretend I wasn't angry." His smile faded and he looked me right in the eye. "And I might even have said at the time, in the heat of the moment, said that I wanted to murder her, or something along those lines. But actually, I reckon she did me a favour. It hurt like hell at the time and it was total humiliation, but at the end of the day it was the best thing that ever happened to me. Made me get my finger out and finally learn to read."

He reached over and took the book Nevada was holding, then held it up in front of his face like a revivalist preacher ostentatiously presenting a Bible, and proceeded to read the cover blurb.

"'One of the best film biographies ever written.' And then there are those three dots that you call an ellipsis. And then, 'Joseph McBride has written the biography that John Ford deserves. There can be no higher compliment than that.'"

He handed the book back to Nevada and smiled at us.

"I don't suppose you'd consider reading the rest of it,

just like that?" said Nevada. "It would save me the bother."

Saxon chuckled. "That's the sort of thing Monika says. She loves me reading to her, she does."

"So you two are quite an item?" said Nevada.

The sunlight gleamed in highlights on Saxon's shaved skull as he shook his head decisively. "No, not really. She's too unstable for a full-time relationship."

Any enquiry by us about just what intriguing form Monika's instability might take was cut off by a sudden blast from the public address system.

"Welcome to the Richmond May Fair!" announced a smoothly booming voice, full of contrived cheer and bonhomie. "And what a lovely day it is for it, too. Ah, the month of May, the fairest month of all." The voice now took on a tone of unctuous profundity. "As the Bard would say, 'As full of spirit as the month of May'."

We were all looking at each other. "Is that him?" said Nevada.

Saxon Ghost nodded. "In the flesh. Billy Bridenstine. The Bride of Frankenstein himself."

"'Love, whose month is ever May'," continued the voice. "'Rough winds do shake the darling buds of May'."

Christ, I thought. *He's really hammering this Shakespeare theme into the ground.*

"And while you're savouring the darling buds of May be sure to try one of the delectable May Fair burgers from the Richmond Burger Bar tent and let the rough winds shake you some toothsome candy floss from the Surrey Sweet Society. Though please remember that children are only allowed to use the bouncy castle while under the supervision of at least one adult."

I had now isolated the exact source of this booming hucksterism: a distant platform where we could see a man standing proudly holding a microphone. I looked at Nevada. "I suppose we'd better go and introduce ourselves."

"And I better make myself scarce," said Saxon. "What with me being instrumental in the fact that Mr Bridenstine's career now consists of playing second fiddle to a bouncy castle." I have to say, he didn't sound contrite.

Indeed, he sounded positively gleeful.

10: BRIDE OF FRANKENSTEIN

Bill Bridenstine was tall, perhaps six foot six, and big and rangy with broad shoulders. The ruggedness of his physique was strangely at odds with the sort of prissy outfit he was wearing: moccasins with tassels, tight white trousers, and a lemon-yellow V-neck sweater with a powder-blue paisley cravat at his throat. Hanging outside the cravat was a gold cross on a thin gold chain. His face was ravaged, knobbly and a startling shade of red, except for the broken blue veins in his cheeks and nose. That nose was a remarkable thing, looking like the sort of misshapen potato that would never make it through the cosmetic quality control of a supermarket selection process. His hair was a dyed dead shade of black, like shoe polish, and worn in what would once have been called a duck's ass cut.

Looking at that nose and the fine mesh of blue veins, I couldn't help remembering what Monika had said about him being a heavy drinker. We'd approached him in full charm mode and asked if he would grant us an interview. He'd been enthusiastic right up to the point where I'd mentioned the Blue Tits.

Now he was shaking his head.

"Sorry, I'm just too busy."

"It won't take long," I said.

"I'm sorry, but I simply don't have the time."

"We could fit it in whenever."

"I just simply don't have the time."

"We can pay you," said Nevada.

"Pay me?" Bridenstine turned to the woman who seemed to be in charge of the public announcements with him. "Alanna, let me see the script schedule."

Alanna was tiny—I suppose the polite word would be petite but she was almost childlike. She had a deep tan and tawny hair worn in a long braid tied with red ribbons. She wore khaki shorts and a T-shirt with the stylised cartoon image of a fish on it. *More Christian iconography*, I thought. She was barefoot and her toenails were painted red to match the hair ribbon.

Bridenstine and Alanna went into a huddle over the script schedule—a rather grand name for a piece of paper with a scant few notes jotted on it. After much frowning and calculating the great man allowed that he might be able to sit down with us and answer a few questions.

Three minutes later we were seated in the cool quiet shadows of a pub in a side street near the Richmond Theatre.

"What would you like to drink?" said Nevada.

"Just a soda water, please."

"Are you sure?"

Bridenstine grimaced. "Oh, certainly. My drinking days are behind me. Far behind me. I haven't touched a drop for years."

I was intrigued to get his version of what had occurred on that autumn night at the television studios when the Blue Tits had shocked the nation and shattered his career. Monika's account would inevitably have been partial.

"Have you seen it?" he said.

"Sorry, no. Long before my time," I said. "Our time," I corrected myself, including Nevada, who was taking a backseat in our 'interview' while she carefully studied the pub's wine list. Apparently she had yet to find anything that met her exacting standards.

"Why don't you watch it on the Internet?" said Bridenstine sourly, and I cursed myself for not having thought of doing just that. I considered saying that I hadn't known it was available, but I decided that would just dig me deeper into the unprofessional interviewer hole.

Anyway, Bridenstine was already in full flood with his own less than fond recollections of the Blue Tits. "They turned up late and I knew they were going to be trouble. You can always tell. There was hardly time to get them through make-up, not that any amount of make-up would have improved the look of that lot. As soon as we went on the air, it was like feeding time at the monkey house. Now, as a television professional I pride myself on my ability to control a live studio situation, but this lot were uncontrollable. Categorically uncontrollable. Can I have a straw in that, sweetheart?"

This last was directed at the barmaid who had arrived with his soda water.

He got his straw and used it to stir the ice cubes around in his glass, staring into its fizzing depths as though searching for the secret of existence. Evidently he didn't find it.

"From that point on it became an exercise in damage limitation. I just wanted to get through to the end credits with the show's reputation intact. And, less importantly, my own reputation intact. To my abiding and utter shame, I failed in both those objectives, but I sincerely doubt anyone could have done any better. These were stupid little girls, hysterical little hellions. The experience of appearing on television had simply gone to their heads. They were completely inexperienced, total amateurs. The big mistake was letting them on the show in the first place, and in that regard I am not willing to take any blame." He paused and sucked gloomily at his soda water. "That was down to my brilliant researcher and my bold producer. It was they who deemed it such a dazzling idea to feature the Blue Tits."

He uttered the band's name with an odd kind of relish, shooting Nevada a furtive glance as he did so. Maybe he just got a thrill out of saying 'tits' in front of a young woman. Nevada, intent on scrutinising the list of New World whites, didn't even notice.

"Oh well," said Bridenstine, "both my researcher and my producer were out of a job the following day. As was I... as was I."

I said, "It happened that quickly?"

His hand crept up and touched the cross he was wearing, as if to remind himself that it was still there. "The papers came out the following morning. By the afternoon we were on the carpet being told how we'd let everyone down, ourselves included they said, the condescending turds, and by that evening we were gone. Gone. My producer was in tears, the gutless little runt. I waited until I knew everybody from the studio would be at the pub, at our local, and then I went in, too. The whole place went quiet. Just like in one of those Westerns when the stranger walks into the saloon. And then I stood drinks for everybody. Bought a round for the entire pub. And, you know what? They applauded me. Everybody applauded me." His voice was thickening with emotion now, and there was a gleam of tears in his eyes. I found myself feeling sorry for him.

"They all knew it could have been them, you see. It could so easily have been them, any one of them. What can you do if you're on a live broadcast and somebody steps outside the boundaries of decency? If they go beyond the pale? We all live by what you might call an unspoken code. A tacit agreement that everyone will respect the parameters. The parameters of civilised behaviour. And, by and large, people do. By and large. But what happens when you're confronted by savages? When you're sitting there under the studio lights with the cameras pointing at you, and you're lumbered with a pack of creatures who are hardly human?"

The tears were gone from his eyes now, replaced by a hard glint of anger. "What do you do? There's nothing you can do. You're at their mercy. Everyone knew that. It could have been them with their career down the toilet, if someone had come onto their show and said 'cunt'."

He uttered the word with a strange loving precision. I abruptly stopped feeling sorry for him as he shot another sly glance at Nevada. She looked up from the wine list and gave him her best *Mona Lisa* smile.

I was glad that he'd put paid to any sympathy I'd felt. It made the next bit easier. Time for the jackpot question.

"It must have made you very angry," I said. Bridenstine looked at me with keen attention as I spoke, as though he was back on his talk show and I was a guest cueing him for a memorable remark of his own, which he was now carefully formulating.

"Especially with the girl who did it," I said. "It was Helene Hilditch, wasn't it? After all, she was responsible for what happened. It was really only her, wasn't it? You must have been really angry with her in particular."

Rather than tensing up, as I had expected, Bridenstine now became oddly calm. He sighed and sank back in his chair and shook his head.

"I know it seems odd," he said, "but I am grateful it happened."

He was right, it seemed very odd. What was even odder was that he sounded like he meant it.

He leaned forward, his face lighting up, a strange, hesitant smile coming and going, flickering across his lips. "Because, you see, if it hadn't happened then I would never have known the light of the Lord. I would never have felt that healing light shining in me, fulfilling me, filling me up and nourishing me and lifting me up, carrying me to a new place. A new and better place. I now live in the light of the Lord, every moment of my life, washed in that warmth, renewed in it, bathed in it. I abide in his merciful light."

As he spoke, he reached for the cross that hung at his throat again and absent-mindedly stroked it. His voice, which previously had been smooth and impressive but rather oily in its wheedling insistence, as it had been earlier on the public address system, was now soft and melodious, and marked by an entirely new and quite persuasive sincerity. The eyes staring out of his ravaged face were those of a man transformed.

I shot a glance at Nevada. She was as transfixed by this metamorphosis as I was, even to the extent of putting the wine list aside.

"It's…" He cleared his throat. "It's a little difficult talking about this. Talking about those times."

"Of course. Thank you for making the time to tell us about it." *After we offered to pay you.*

"You see, it's such a rollercoaster of emotion. My downfall, and then my being uplifted again—"

He suddenly leaned forward and spoke to the girl drying glasses behind the bar. "Excuse me, dear, but do you by any chance have any Irish whiskeys?"

The girl smiled and nodded. "Oh yeah, you bet your boots. We've got Redbreast, Red Spot, Green Spot, Yellow Spot, Midleton, Connemara, Teeling, Gelston's and of course Bushmills and Jameson."

"Is the Gelston's the twelve-year-old?"

"Oh yes."

"Sherry cask finish?"

The girl made an exaggeratedly contrite face. "Nope. Rum cask. Sorry!"

"The Red Spot, is that twelve years old?"

"Fifteen."

"I'll have the Red Spot." He turned to Nevada and me. "You don't mind if I have a little drink? A wee drinkie?"

"No... I suppose... But didn't you say...?"

"And you won't mind picking up the bill? Ha-ha, bit cheeky of me to ask I know, but after all, you are interviewing me."

"No. That's fine."

Bridenstine swivelled on his stool and called after the barmaid. "Darling, make it a double, would you?"

The tumbler of whiskey came, and he smiled, nodded and accepted it, and then downed it in one. He sighed, and looked at the empty glass with a slightly perplexed expression as though trying to work out how this weird phenomenon had come about. Then his face brightened and he smiled and called to the barmaid. "Same again, please, sweetness."

The girl came back and took his tumbler. "Thirsty, eh?" she said. She refilled it and placed it in front of him. Bridenstine left it sitting there on the bar in front of him and studied it carefully for a long moment. If the answer to life's mystery hadn't been in the soda water, surely it must be in the amber depths of this expensive whiskey?

Which Nevada and I were paying for.

Or rather, that Erik would be paying for when we submitted today's expenses to him.

Bridenstine's hand shot out to seize the glass as though it had been about to escape. He held it to his misshapen nose and inhaled the aroma carefully, then drank it down in one long ecstatic swallow.

"Hello, sweetie, hello, dear," he called cheerily to the barmaid. "There seems to be something wrong with this glass. It keeps becoming empty." The girl came back, gave him a professional smile and refilled it with the third double.

I looked over at Nevada. She gave an imperceptible nod. I could guess what she was thinking. Maybe the whiskey would loosen his lips—it could hardly do anything else, with him drinking it at this rate.

And maybe we would learn something.

This time he took an immediate sip of his drink, but only a small one, then he set it aside and turned away from it, like he was playing hard to get. I was starting to be impressed by the variety of his drinking strategies.

"Helene Hilditch?" he said, as if I had only just uttered the name. "Helene. Hill. Ditch." He turned back to the bar and looked with elaborate surprise at his drink sitting there. Where had this come from? He picked it up and inspected it to make sure it was real, and then he threw it back with a natty snap of the neck. The glass was empty again. "Hello, flower," he called to the barmaid. "Coo-ee." She came back down the bar to us. "You will never guess what I'm going to say, darling," he said, eyes twinkling with good humour.

She smiled indulgently as she filled the glass again. This brought it to the equivalent of eight single whiskies. He took the newly filled glass and instead of drinking it, he held it to his chest as he swivelled on his bar stool to look at us. As he spoke he continued to hold it close to him, like it was something precious, in need of protection.

"Helene Hilditch," he said, "was a fiendish little bitch." I wondered for a moment if this was going to be a light-hearted poetry recital. But no such luck. "When she said it," he said, "I couldn't believe my ears. I could not believe it. I literally couldn't. I thought I was hallucinating. I mean, things like that just don't happen." His voice had taken on a note of wonder. "Can you imagine?" he said.

He glanced down at the glass he was holding to his chest. Maybe the bouquet of the whiskey had suddenly penetrated to his potato nose. He lifted the glass to eye level and studied the golden liquid inside. A weirdly exalted expression came on his face. "It was a pivotal moment. It was *the* pivotal moment in my life. You don't get many of those. And you don't usually know when they come, I mean as they're actually happening. But I knew. I knew all right."

He put the glass to his lips again and emptied it in a suave series of sips. Then he set it down on the bar, very carefully, and wiped his mouth with the sleeve of his lemon-yellow sweater. He looked at us. "I wasn't the cunt," he said, as if revealing a great and unexpected truth. "She was the cunt. She was the cunt cunt cunt."

He turned back to the bar. "Excuse me, darling."

I leaned over towards him and spoke in a low voice. "Perhaps you've had enough," I suggested.

He turned sharply and looked at me, and I instantly knew I'd said the wrong thing—though I didn't yet realise quite how wrong.

"Had enough? Had enough? I've had enough, have I? Who are you? Who are you to tell me I've had enough?"

The bar in this pub was constructed in the currently fashionable manner with a granite top in rectangular sections, which meant there were some very hard edges and unforgiving corners on it. Bridenstine now picked up his empty whiskey tumbler and, moving in a businesslike way, swiftly and neatly smashed it against one of the granite corners. He did this in such a manner that the base of the tumbler remained intact in his hand while all that remained of the rest was a viciously sharp curve of glass rising from it like the blade of a knife.

He's done this before, I thought, as he lunged at me and jammed the sharp edge against my throat, right under my chin, hard enough to just break the skin, pressed firmly against the big blood vessels that clustered there.

I tried to back away to relieve the pressure, but I already had my back against the bar. I felt my blood pulsing against the sharp tip of the glass. Bridenstine was leaning towards me, his ravaged features split by a rictus of a grin, breathing hot whiskey fumes into my face. "I've had enough, have I?" he said, in a tone of polite enquiry.

Nevada had instantly jumped to her feet and moved towards us, but she now stood frozen, doing nothing.

I appreciated her problem. There was nothing she could do without increasing the likelihood of this lunatic drunk cutting my throat open. Grabbing his elbow, for example, would be a particularly bad idea.

Behind the bar, the girl was staring at this tableau in dumbstruck horror. I locked eyes with Nevada. I couldn't believe it was going to end like this, on a sunny spring morning, thanks to an idiot drunk with an improvised weapon and a killing rage.

But if it did end here, I wanted to be looking at her as I went.

"Bill!"

The voice cut through the silence, terse and angry and standing for no nonsense, like someone reprimanding a misbehaving dog.

Bridenstine turned to face the person who had called out.

It was the woman from the public address system, the tiny barefoot woman. She was holding the piece of paper. What had they called it? The something script. No, the script something. The script schedule.

As soon as he saw her, he instantly pulled the glass away from my throat and hid it behind his back like a guilty child.

"Bill. What on earth are you doing?"

"Alanna, I'm sorry. Oh, I'm sorry, my love. I've let you down again, haven't I?"

He sank back down on his bar stool. The remains of the glass dropped from his hand and cracked on the floor.

Nevada was instantly upon me, her arms around me.

Standing between me and Bridenstine, shielding me with her body.

"Billy, Billy, Billy," said the woman softly. "What have you done?"

Bridenstine was staring blankly into space. He said nothing, but a pungent ammoniac smell suddenly rose sharply in the room and I saw with horror that there was a dark patch spreading at the crotch of his white trousers.

"Come on, let's get you out of here," said the woman softly. It was as if she were talking to a child, or an invalid. Bridenstine slid obediently off the barstool.

The woman turned to us. "I am so sorry. He's a lovely, lovely man but he has such a vicious temper. That's his cross to carry. And, I suppose, mine too."

She led him off, tiny beside him, like a child leading a bear.

As they disappeared out the door into the brilliant daylight, the barmaid came and stood near us, leaning across the bar to get nearer still.

"Jesus wept," she said.

I said, "We'll pay for that glass he broke."

My voice was impressively clear and steady but somehow sounded artificial, as though it were my first time using a phrase in a new language I'd recently learned.

"Like hell you will," she said. "It wasn't your fault. It was that fucking creamer's fault. I saw what happened. He's out of his fucking mind. He's off his loaf. He shouldn't be roaming the streets. He isn't safe. Here. Have a drink. On the house."

She grabbed three glasses and the nearest bottle of whiskey, and sploshed sloppy servings in all the glasses. Her hand was shaking so much that the neck of the bottle rang musically against the rim of the glasses.

While she poured the drinks Nevada came closer to me and put her hand against my chest. My heart was beating so hard that I could distinctly feel the outline of each of her fingertips against it.

11: THE MOST UN-PUNK THING

Perhaps not surprisingly, I decided to take it easy the following day. I slept in with both the cats huddled on the bed beside me, making use of different parts of my body for pillows, dozing and dreaming and faintly aware of Nevada bustling around in the kitchen.

I was finally woken by the sound of the coffee grinder. Or rather, by the cats' reaction to it—their identical outraged leaps from the bed in protest at this audio atrocity. I just smiled contentedly. My beloved was doing the prep work for my morning coffee. I put on a dressing gown and went through to the kitchen to finish the task.

As I made the coffee Nevada lightly toasted some Putney Sourdough and put out a selection of spreads and fruit—sliced bananas, strawberries and grapes—on the table. We ate breakfast together and then Nevada went out to the back garden to finish replanting the Japanese rose in its new flowerbed, the one created by the recent concrete-smashing antics.

I poured myself a second cup of coffee, switched on the monoblocks and settled down on the sofa in the sweet spot to catch up on my backlog of album listening. I still hadn't had a chance to properly explore the Liberty pressing of Grant Green's *Idle Moments* that I'd bought with our first flush of new funds.

Idle Moments was a perfect title for a lazy Sunday, come to think of it.

It was gorgeous. Who was that playing tenor saxophone? Joe Henderson.

Fanny came and joined me on the sofa while Turk went outside, clattering through the cat flap to supervise Nevada's gardening activities. I rubbed Fanny's head as we listened to Grant Green's delving, articulate solo on 'Django'. I was successfully losing myself in the rich rounded tones of the guitar, and determinedly not thinking about what had happened yesterday, or about Helene or her situation.

This strategy worked perfectly well until the phone rang.

It was Saxon Ghost. "Mate," he said. He packed an impressive range of emotion into that one word. Shock. Anger. Camaraderie.

"Uh, what?" I said.

"I heard. About what happened."

"What happened?"

"I heard about Bridenstine and what he did. What he tried to do. That scumbag. I wish I'd come along with you to the pub now. That vicious little scumbag. I should never have left you two alone with him. I'm kicking myself. I am so sorry, mate. I wish I'd been there. I would have shown him what happens to someone who goes after a friend of mine with a broken pint mug. He would have ended up with it in his face. With it up his arse."

"It wasn't a pint mug."

"So sorry, mate. So how are you doing? Are you all right?"

"I'm fine." Or I would be if I didn't have to listen to someone on the phone making me relive it all.

"He's the scum of the earth, that Bridenstine."

"He's just pitiful," I said. And I meant it.

"You're right there. He always was. He always was. Well, take care, mate."

We said our goodbyes and he hung up.

Nevada came in from the garden with a decorative smear of dirt on her forehead. "Who was that?"

"Mr Ghost."

"Oh, Saxon. You know, I really quite like him."

"He knew about Bill Bridenstine trying to cut my throat with a whiskey glass. Well, he got the glass wrong, but he knew about everything else."

"Oh, you poor thing," said Nevada. "Absolutely the last thing you want to talk about. But he meant well."

"But how did he know about it?" I said. "How the hell did he know what happened?"

"I suppose Monika must have told him."

"How did Monika know?"

"Helene must have told her," said Nevada.

"How did Helene know?"

"Erik must have told her." Nevada paused. "After I told him."

"Why did you tell Erik?"

Nevada smiled grimly. "Because if this job is going to be so dangerous, your day rate is going up."

"I've got a day rate now?" I said.

"And rather a generous one, as of yesterday."

Nevada went back out into the garden and Fanny emerged from under the armchair where she had retired in disgust at the interruption. I went to the Garrard to restart *Idle Moments*. I decided I might as well go back to the first track. Fanny appeared to approve and we relaxed on the sofa while the music filled the room as only a vintage Van Gelder-mastered Blue Note can. Everything sounded solid, immediate, real.

Though not quite as immediate and real as the ringing of the phone. Again.

It was Tinkler.

"How are you?"

"I'm okay. Did Erik tell you about it?"

"Of course he did. Are you sure you're all right?"

"It really wasn't such a big deal."

"Not from what I heard. Listen, my friend…"

"Yes?" I said.

Tinkler chuckled. "You weren't supposed to take it *literally* when I said the vintage vinyl business is cut-throat."

"I think that's a classic, Tinkler. Wait until I tell Nevada. Oh, how she'll laugh."

"I mean, god," he continued, oblivious, "you are so literal-minded."

After a bit more buffoonery and some threats about coming over to visit, he rang off.

I went back to the turntable. The stylus of the Ortofon drifted slowly down to meet the playing surface again and the slow spooky chords of the title track rose around me once more, filling the room. I settled down on the sofa with Fanny slumped against me, head on my thigh, and we let the music start to wash over us.

Then the doorbell rang.

I sighed and got up. Fanny gave a squeak of reprimand— where are you going *now*?—as I trotted to the front door and opened it.

Standing there were Erik and Helene in their Sunday best. She was wearing black jeans and a pink denim jacket. He was wearing black jeans and a bright red Hawaiian shirt open halfway to his navel to expose wiry grey chest hair and an assortment of necklaces. Both were shod in black cowboy boots, polished to a high gleam.

They were holding a bottle of pink champagne and a large heart-shaped box of expensive-looking chocolates. For one surreal, vertiginous moment I thought it was Valentine's Day. Then I remembered that I'd only very recently attended a memorable festivity to celebrate the merry month of May.

"Hey!" said Erik with a big friendly smile.

By contrast, Helene's face was creased with sadness and concern. "You poor guy," she murmured. Erik, realising that he'd got the vibe wrong, immediately rearranged his features into a suitably sombre configuration and dropped his voice a considerable number of decibels.

"Hey, man," he muttered in tones appropriate to, say, standardised funeral commiseration.

"Can we come in?" said Helene.

"Yes, of course. Please." I stood back and they walked past me into the house.

As soon as I closed the door Helene threw her arms around me. "I am so sorry." She gave me a powerful hug. Her body felt extraordinarily skinny and birdlike, all bones and wiry strength. As soon as she let go of me, Erik moved in for some hugging of his own. His aftershave made a striking contrast to Helene's perfume, though they were both clearly big-ticket items. His embrace was a ferocious bear hug.

"We're so sorry, dude," he said.

Then they both stood back to look at me.

I was acutely aware that I was unshaved, unwashed and undressed. But this didn't seem to bother my rock-and-roll visitors.

Hugs concluded, they just strode in and commenced to make themselves at home: Helene by going into the kitchen, setting the chocolates on the counter and then opening the fridge and rummaging inside to make room to stash the champagne; Erik by standing in the middle of the living room and waiting for someone to attend to his needs. I went to the turntable and lifted the tone arm up, cutting off poor Grant Green in his prime again.

The back door popped open and Nevada came in. Erik's face lit up. "Hey!" Then he remembered this was supposed to be a downbeat and serious occasion, so he forced himself to look appropriately gloomy once more.

"Erik," said Nevada happily, and kissed him on the

cheek. Which meant Erik had to struggle to stop himself grinning again.

Helene stepped in from the kitchen and the two women exchanged delighted cries and kisses. "We heard what happened," said Helene. "And we just wanted to stop by and…" She held up the box of chocolates, which resulted in more delighted cries, though not as many as the bottle of champagne when Helene cracked the fridge open to display it.

"Bollinger Rosé," said Nevada. "Very nice. We shall uncork this little item in just a moment. First come outside and see the fruits of our labours with that sledgehammer."

The two women went out to the garden; Erik and I looked at each other.

"So are you, ah, all right, bruv?"

I realised he was staring at my throat, looking for a mark. There was indeed a mark there. But it might just have been an insect bite—pink, puffy, unremarkable.

"Yeah," I said. "I'm fine."

"Of course you are, big bollocks. Of course you are. Nice one. Good." Erik nodded decisively, as if to conclude the matter. We were, after all, men, and no more need be said. He pounded me powerfully on the back a few times, presumably to supplement my injuries, and then sank contentedly into an armchair. He peered around the room and then, already bored with the lack of stimulation as only a retired rock-star can be, he hunkered forward to bring himself closer to Fanny, who was perched on the arm of the sofa. "Hey, pussycat." He extended his hand for her to sniff.

Fanny gave him a sneering yawn and promptly jumped down from the sofa and disappeared, obviously having concluded that Grant Green was off the playlist for now. Intelligent cat.

Erik was staring at my record collection.

"You got any more Mellencamp?"

"Certainly." I took *Idle Moments* off the turntable and restored it carefully to its protective sleeve. Then I went to the appropriate shelf and selected *The Lonesome Jubilee*, potentially John Mellencamp's masterpiece. Though of course there is also *Big Daddy*.

I held the album cover up to show Erik. "Okay. Nice one." He nodded to signify his grudging approval.

The women came back in from the garden. I didn't know what they'd been talking about, but Helene came immediately over to me and seized both my hands in hers. "You poor, poor guy. You are so brave."

"Uh, thank you. You know what, if it's okay, I'll go put some clothes on." I was still standing there in my dressing gown. It was a stylish dressing gown, chosen by Nevada. But, still…

"Of course. You go ahead." Helene released my hands. I turned and started towards the bedroom. I'd gone about three steps in that direction when I heard a piercing wolf whistle. I turned back to see Helene with two fingers between her lips. "Nice legs," she said roguishly.

"They're not bad, are they?" I heard Nevada drawl, with a smug note of ownership, as I hurried off.

* * *

When I returned from the bedroom looking slightly more respectable, I found that the gathering had taken on a businesslike atmosphere—despite, or perhaps because of, the glasses of pink champagne on the table. Nevada, Helene and Erik were all seated there and I joined them.

"So," said Helene. "The first thing we wanted to ask is if you think we should call the police now."

"The police?" I pondered for a moment. "Well, we've certainly got witnesses."

"Witnesses?"

"Well, there's Nevada. And the barmaid."

"Ah, no," Erik was shaking his head, looking a little embarrassed. "We don't mean about what happened to you yesterday."

"Although that was bad enough," added Helene hastily.

"Yeah, of course that was terrible, man, terrible…"

"What we meant," said Helene, "was should we call the police and tell them that Bridenstine has been trying to kill *me*."

Nevada and I exchanged a look. We'd already given this considerable thought, and discussion.

Helene caught the look. "You don't think it's Bill Bridenstine?"

"Well," I said, "he certainly has the murderous rage." I realised I was touching my throat as I said this. Luckily there wouldn't be any scarring from his whiskey-glass dagger. At least, not on the outside. "But we don't think he's sufficiently organised to have done the meticulous planning required in all those various attempts on you."

"Maybe he had some help," said Erik.

A thought flashed through my mind: a small, barefoot woman in a cartoon fish T-shirt. I shook my head, both to dismiss the image and to gently contradict Erik. "As much as I dislike the bastard, I just don't see it being him."

"Why not?" said Erik stubbornly. "He's the one with the big juicy motive."

Helene suddenly slammed her fist down on the table, causing all of us to jump, as well as some spillage from the champagne flutes, which no one had touched yet. "I am so sick of people having a go at me about that," she said. She was genuinely angry.

"No one's having a go, doll," said Erik quickly.

"No, not you. But everyone else. No one will let go of it. They won't let me forget what I did. Was it really so bad? Was it really so—so transgressive?"

"No, doll, of course not."

"If it wasn't for our uptight society, no one would have batted an eyelash. If it had been in Sweden or somewhere no one would have cared."

Actually, I seemed to recall that Sweden was quite a conservative, church-going culture, but I wasn't about to offer this refutation to Helene, who was in full swing. "Anyway," she said. "It wasn't even my fault. It was all Ophelia's fault."

This I had to pick her up on. "Really?" I said mildly. "How so?"

"Because of the way she started spouting Latin. Did you know about that?" Both Nevada and I were nodding obediently, but that didn't stop Helene giving a full recap of the situation: Bill Bridenstine antagonising them and insulting them on his talk show. "He just blithely assumed we were all stupid little slags from the slums. So Ophelia starts showing off her Latin. She was always such a little show-off. And as soon as she started doing that, my blood ran cold. There we were, on live television being watched by millions of people, we're supposed to be the cutting-edge new punk band and she's *speaking Latin*. Perfect Latin. Can you imagine? It was the most un-punk thing ever. We were about to completely lose it. We were about ten seconds away from the end of the Blue Tits. And I knew it was down to me. I had to do something to save the day. I had to restore our street cred."

She paused. And then she said, proudly, "So I did."

"You really did, babes," said Erik, rubbing her gently on the arm.

We all picked up our glasses and toasted the utterance of ground-breaking obscenities live on prime-time television. Helene was relaxed and happy again.

But we were no closer to identifying who was trying to kill her. And I said as much.

"You really don't think it's Bridenstine?" said Helene.

"Believe me, if I thought we could get him put away in prison forever I would be only too delighted. But whatever else is wrong with him, I don't think he's the one."

"All right, then. If it's not him then who is it?"

demanded Erik truculently. He'd obviously forgotten that I was supposed to be the object of sympathy today.

"Well, Tania Strack for a start."

"Oh, yes," said Helene, "I meant to thank you for your advice. Very sensible."

"Oh yeah, nice one," said Erik. I was suddenly back in his good books again. "Tinkler gave us your message and we got right on it."

"I put down all the dirt I could remember about the olden days." Helene sounded very pleased with herself. "All the really primo dirt. And we've announced on social media that if anything should happen to me we'll release it to the world. Bong Cha has been a great help."

"Bong's very big on social media," said Erik.

Nevada was looking pensive. "So, did you tell everyone that someone was actually trying to kill you?" *That could make our job a lot more difficult.*

"Oh no," said Erik. "That would be a real downer. The way we phrased it was that we know everyone is gagging to read Helene's memoirs, and so we've made sure that the highlights will go into the public domain if, heaven forbid, anything should ever happen to her."

That was smart.

"So," said Helene, "who are you looking at, if not Bill Bridenstine?"

"How about Fanzine Frank?" I said.

Helene seized on this immediately. "Of course. *Him.* And I was supposed to give you Monika's number, wasn't I? So you could reach him. Damn it. Here, let me—"

"Thanks, I've already got it." From Tania Strack in her Putney penthouse.

"You know what," said Helene, "I don't know why I didn't think of it before. I suppose I've known him so long that he's just blended into the background of my life. But he's a prime candidate. A total stalker type, and always monitoring my movements, supposedly because they'll be of interest to the readers of his... publication. Which is basically *Hello!* magazine for punk rock obsessives."

For someone who acted like she always threw it in the bin, she seemed to know rather a lot about this periodical.

But we all agreed Fanzine Frank was the next person to check out.

Erik and Helene soon made their excuses and left. But they helped us finish the champagne first.

12: PYTHONESQUE EUPHEMISM

It was one thing to decide that Fanzine Frank was the next person we should talk to—pinning him down and actually talking to him was quite another.

In fact, he proved so elusive that Nevada and I finally decided we should leave him for the time being, prime suspect though he was—not to mention being the purchaser of several boxes of the original LP—and instead interview the remaining members of the Blue Tits.

Ophelia Brydent (drums) and Dylis Lispector (bass).

When Monika the roadie had said Ophelia had dropped off the radar I hadn't taken this very seriously. But unfortunately, it proved to be an accurate analysis of the situation. No one—Erik, Monika, Helene, Saxon, Lenny— had any idea where she was, or how she could be reached. Even the stalker's best friend, the Internet, proved to be no help. I wondered, however, if Tania Strack might be able to provide us with a useful lead.

Monika had assured us that she wouldn't know where

Ophelia was, either. If Tania knew, Monika said that she would know that she knew.

I wasn't entirely convinced by this tortuous logic and I decided I would approach Tania as a last resort. "Why not a first resort?" said Nevada.

"Because I also want to ask her if she's trying to kill Helene because Helene killed her political career, and I haven't yet figured out a tactful way of doing that."

"Ah. I see your problem."

So we turned our attention to Dylis Lispector, formerly Dildo Inspector in her punkadelic heyday. She proved remarkably easy to track down, and to contact by email, but she was out of the country until next week. So, a dead end if only temporarily.

Which left one other line of enquiry.

Helene (and Nevada's) old school, the Emily Kelso Academy for Young Ladies.

Monika had been adamant that the place was a hotbed of people with reasons to hate Helene, so I felt we had to at least make some gesture towards checking it out, although I didn't hold out much hope for getting cooperation from an institution like this on what was a tenuous and frankly rather weird line of enquiry.

Nevertheless I found the phone number for the school, spoke to the head teacher's secretary and then, to my surprise, the head teacher herself, one Enrica Morado.

I sensed she was a busy woman so I quickly outlined my request. I was researching a documentary about the Blue Tits—that old lie—and I was eager to visit the Emily

Kelso Academy to speak to anyone who might remember the ageing punksters from their days as girls at the school.

"That would be me," said Ms Morado. "I remember them very well. I was a junior teacher here then."

"Really?" I said. "That's fantastic. If you could spare a little time, we'd love to meet you. I've already spoken to Helene Hilditch and Tania Strack—"

"Oh, Tania. She's *marvellous*. One of our most prestigious old girls. And very active on our board of governors, not to mention being the most breathtakingly generous of patrons."

I'd already felt I was making progress with Ms Morado, but I'd clearly hit the jackpot by mentioning Tania Strack. "I'm sure Tania would be happy to vouch for me," I said.

"Oh there's no need for that. We would be delighted to talk to you. I personally would be delighted to talk to you."

We arranged a date and time, I confirmed the route to the school, and it was as simple as that.

Agatha and her black cab had another paying job that day, and a lucrative one, so we decided to give her time off for good conduct and drive down in Tinkler's car. This meant we had to take Tinkler along, too, but he promised to be on his best behaviour. Which was just as well, because the words 'Tinkler' and 'girls' school' should never be in the same sentence.

Tinkler's car was a Volvo DAF which had for a long time been merely an old banger, but was now rapidly in danger of becoming a vintage automobile. It was a pity Agatha wasn't available, because she liked driving it.

The car was an odd shade of red and we called it Kind of Red, for historical reasons involving us all almost getting killed. I was designated to drive because Nevada liked to navigate and Tinkler liked to be driven around in his own car. "It makes me feel like a sultan," he said. "Now all I need is the harem."

"There's a spiderweb on your wing mirror, Tinkler."

"I'm amazed there's only one."

We drove along Abbey Avenue and then across Clarence Lane to Roehampton Lane. We headed down to the A3, past the large Asda, past Putney Vale Crematorium—that cheery landmark—and, more happily, past the big field which regularly hosted the big boot fair where Nevada and I had once gone hunting for a rare jazz record in the early days of our courtship.

Out of London into Surrey.

I knew we'd definitively left the city and reached the country when I had to slow down for a girl on a horse. The girl wore a yellow high-vis vest, the horse wore black socks on his back legs and red socks on the front. We drove past country pubs, along winding roads lined with greenery and shadowed by tall shady trees.

Our destination was Ashtead and we approached it along green tunnels of road, branches of trees not quite closing up to screen off the hot blue sky overhead. On either side of us were old brick walls covered with ivy. They soon gave way to more modern, very high red brick walls.

"Those are some serious walls," said Tinkler, peering out the window.

"To keep the inmates inside," said Nevada, who didn't seem particularly thrilled about revisiting her alma mater.

"It's really not far from the M25 here," I said. The M25 was the famed London Orbital Motorway. The only British motorway to have provided a cool name for a band.

"It was certainly handy for hitchhiking when we skived off," said Nevada.

We turned off the main road onto a narrow, winding approach lane.

"This is actually the back entrance," said Nevada. "No vile jokes, Tinkler."

"I'm shocked you would even suggest such a thing."

The lane led us to a narrow opening in the red brick wall flanked by rusty white gates and a small, matching rusty white gatehouse. The gatehouse was empty and the gates were propped open with bricks, weeds lapping up to obscure their lower edges.

"Not exactly high security," said Tinkler.

"There used to be a nasty little man in that gatehouse," said Nevada. "I guess economy measures have put paid to his position."

"But they've got a surveillance camera up there," I said. It was mounted on the roof of the empty gatehouse and carefully angled to cover the entire approach, either by road or on foot.

"So they have," said Nevada. "Smile and wave."

The school was effectively a gated community consisting

of scattered buildings set in their own rambling grounds. As we approached it we drove over a stone bridge across a dried-up overgrown brook choked with greenery. Beyond the bridge the road widened out again into a well-maintained two-lane blacktop with tall, broadly spreading trees on either side of us, and big expanses of neat lawns. White painted stones were distributed as a kind of punctuation along the grass at the side of the road.

We drove past giant hedges, richly green and perfectly spherical. "My god, look at those hedges," said Tinkler. "Big balls. I bet you girls had some amusing names for those."

"We did, actually," said Nevada.

Rather than one or two large buildings, the school seemed to be dispersed into small, cottage-like structures. Ms Morado's office was in a slightly grander version of one of these, approached by a footpath across a wide and luxuriant expanse of grass dotted with big trees, and the occasional green wooden bench. We parked the car some distance away in a circular gravelled area, also ringed with white stones, and set off along the footpath.

As we neared our destination Tinkler suddenly said, "I think I'll wait here," and plonked himself down on a bench in a shady spot under a large oak.

"Don't you think you should come with us, Tinkler?"

"What would I bring to the party? I wouldn't bring anything to the party. You kids have fun."

Nevada and I stood looking at him indecisively. "Tinkler…" she said.

"Strictly sixteen-plus fantasies," he said, and waved his hand at us. "Go. See the headmistress."

"Head teacher."

"Knock yourself out." He eased himself back on the bench in a luxuriant sprawl and took out his phone.

We left him there, albeit reluctantly, and went on to the cottage. There was a sign on the door inviting us to please enter, so we did, finding ourselves in a small reception area with a woman at a desk covered with miniature cacti in brightly painted pots. She looked up from her screen and told us that Ms Morado was expecting us. I noticed that, among the other screens behind the desert flora on her desk, there was one providing a high-resolution view of the approach to the gatehouse where we'd just driven in.

No wonder they were expecting us.

We walked through a further door and into a big comfortable room full of sunlight. There was a thick green carpet stretching out before us and the walls were lined with books.

Ms Morado was a slender woman in her sixties with a bulldog jaw and maroon hair with dark highlights—I suppose you'd call them lowlights. She was wearing a purple business suit, black sweater and a string of white pearls with a purple gem at the centre. Her earrings were matching purple gems.

She rose from her desk, smiling as we came in, and then suddenly froze, staring.

"Nevada—what are you doing here?"

Nevada nodded at me. "I'm his partner in crime. And everything else."

"Well, what a surprise, what a lovely surprise. Nevada... Warren, isn't it?" It took her a moment to conjure up the surname from the depths of her memory, but I could see how happy it made her when she did. "Please, do come in and sit down. Both of you."

She led us to a sofa and a set of armchairs. We established ourselves on the sofa, but instead of taking one of the armchairs in the time-honoured way, Ms Morado perched on the corner of her desk nearest to us. She was silent for a moment, as if gathering her thoughts, and she kept staring at Nevada. The unannounced presence of my honeypie had clearly thrown her.

"Well... thank you for coming all this way to see us."

"Thank you for seeing *us*," I said.

"Ah, not at all. Only too pleased. Delighted, in fact. As I told you, Tania Strack is a truly marvellous patron of the school." She was already smiling, but at the mention of Tania her smile widened to the point that it began to look painful. Maybe it was, because it faded, leaving Ms Morado looking businesslike and perhaps a little wary.

"So, how may I help you?"

"You said you were at the school when the Blue Tits were here."

She pursed her lips and her eyes flickered upwards and to one side, just for an instant. "Oh yes, yes. You must forgive me if I have a tiny bit of cognitive dissonance any time that name is mentioned—I mean, in that context."

"As the name of the band, you mean?"

"Yes, well exactly. Because you see—" she peered at us as though a thought had just struck her "—I may be telling you things that Nevada has already told you, so I apologise if that's the case, but you see Blue Tits is also the name of one of our school houses here at Emily Kelso. So whenever I hear the name, that's where my mind immediately goes at first."

I smiled what I hoped was my most ingratiating smile and said, "Yes, of course. And I did know about the house name." I glanced at Nevada, sat at my side, looking benignly inscrutable and gazing out the window with apparent fascination. "But it was Helene who told me."

"Oh, yes, I see. Helene. Helene Hilditch, Tania Strack, Ophelia Brydent, Dylis Lispector." She pronounced each name with a little triumphant flourish as if she was reading them off some kind of internalised roll call, then smiled at me as if expecting congratulations. It was a pretty impressive feat of memory, assuming she hadn't mugged up on the subject just before we arrived. I supposed remembering the names of students from decades earlier was the kind of accomplishment that a teacher might pride herself on.

"And Monika Dunkley, of course," I added. At the edge of my vision I thought I saw a ghost of a smile on Nevada's lips for a split second before her poker face resumed.

Ms Morado's fleeting expression of puzzlement was all I could have wished for. "Monika? But she wasn't... Oh yes, that's right, she was the *road manager* for the band, wasn't she?" I thought road manager was rather a grandiose designation, but then so was band for that matter, given the general level of musicianship involved. But I just smiled and nodded.

"That's right. Although she seems to feel she's a fully fledged member of the Blue Tits."

"Fully fledged! Oh, very good," said Ms Morado, smiling a big generous smile, and I felt a warm flush of pleasure at the praise. For a moment it was foolishly like being back at school and basking in the approval of your teacher—but without the immediate sequel of worrying that your classmates would beat the hell out of you later for sucking up.

Ms Morado kept the big smile on her face and rotated her gaze to Nevada. "You see, fully fledged is an expression which pertains to birds."

"When they get their feathers and are mature enough to fly," said Nevada, speaking for the first time since we'd sat down.

"Of course, you knew that. How silly of me. And how condescending. You must forgive me."

"Nothing to forgive," said Nevada.

A casual listener would have just heard two women exchanging polite small talk. But I wasn't a casual listener, and I was now keenly aware of the bristling hostility underlying this gracious chat.

"But you see, it was just so apt," said Ms Morado. "That's why it was such a perfect turn of phrase. Because of course Tania and Helene and Ophelia and Dylis did spread their wings and fly away from the nest."

"And Monika," said Nevada.

"Yes," conceded Ms Morado. "And Monika, too. They all left the school like birds taking flight. Flapping their wings and sailing into the world, the big wide world, for the first time."

"Hardly the first time."

"As did you, Nevada. As did you," said Ms Morado, ignoring Nevada's remark. She was smiling again but her eyes were cold as bottle glass. "But at least Tania and the others completed their studies and fulfilled their academic obligations and obtained their qualifications."

"Yeah, and they really put those to good use, didn't they?" said Nevada, and she smiled back at the woman. They seemed to be in a competition to see who could show the most teeth. It was like a display of ritualised hostility between carnivores.

I didn't fully understand the source of this hostility, which I could feel swelling steadily in the room, but that hardly mattered. What mattered was that I didn't think we had time for it, no matter how veiled and mannerly the skirmishing might be.

Eyes on the ball, please, folks.

I said, "You were going to tell us about your memories of the girls, Ms Morado. Your personal observations would be really valuable for my research." I'd gone from *our* to *my* to keep Nevada out of the equation for now. At least until I understood why Ms Morado seemed to have it in for her.

Nevada and Ms Morado were still staring at each other, for all the world as if they were vying to see who would blink first. But now Ms Morado turned to me and said, "Of course. What specifically would you like to know? Their academic achievements, perhaps?"

Hell, no.

"Actually, I'm more interested in the period just after they left the school."

"After they left?" Ms Morado was doing her best puzzled look. "But, by definition, that was the point at which I no longer had any contact with them." She said this as if I'd presented her with an interesting anomaly, too polite to imply that I was merely an idiot. "I'm afraid I can't help you there. They were gone, and I was still here at the school." Now the idiot interpretation was definitely in play. So much for my bonus marks for fully fledged.

I said, "Yes, but because you were here you were in the perfect position to observe the reaction of the others to what they got up to."

"The others? Do you mean the staff or the pupils?"

"Both. I would be very interested to know how the staff and pupils reacted when these girls formed their group and achieved infamy."

"Ah, infamy. Exactly. Well put." I was back in teacher's good books.

"I understand that some people were quite upset," I said. This at least had been Monika's assessment. Upset enough to potentially want to kill Helene all these years later, according to her.

Ms Morado seemed lost in thought for a moment. Her hands floated up and carefully touched the purple gems in her earlobes as if attempting some fine adjustment of them. "I wouldn't say *upset*. Of course there was a certain amount of envy on the part of the girls. And shock among the more straitlaced members of staff. But our headmistress at the time, Mrs Strickland, very sensibly decided to embrace the opportunity."

"How so?"

"Well, you see Marsha Strickland was a very young and open-minded woman. Highly progressive. She was a breath of fresh air. As you can well imagine, the Emily Kelso Academy had emerged from the 1950s and 1960s as rather a moribund institution, and it was badly in need of a breath of fresh air. At least the board of governors were sensible enough to realise this, to know that times had changed, and that they needed to change with them. So they hired Marsha."

I noticed that we'd gone from Mrs Strickland to Marsha with remarkable speed.

Perhaps Ms Morado realised this too, because she said, "Marsha was a friend of mine. Or rather, she became one. I like to think that she became one. I very much admired her. She was the person responsible for hiring me, as part of her policy of introducing fresh blood to the school." She turned to Nevada, "I know it's hard to imagine that the decrepit hulk you see before you could ever come under the category of fresh blood."

I didn't want to get sidetracked into another terribly refined catfight, so I cut in. "You said she embraced the opportunity?"

Ms Morado looked away from Nevada and smiled at me. "Yes, yes. You see, as a progressive, modern headmistress she thought it was actually rather wonderful that some of our girls had left and formed a punk band, and a very successful one to boot. She thought it was, or at least could be, a cause for celebration. She even suggested the possibility of getting them back to the school to give a talk to the younger girls." Her smile faded and the enthusiasm in her eyes died. "But unfortunately things went horribly wrong."

"How so?"

"As you might well imagine, there was initially considerable resistance to Marsha's position on this. The older and more hidebound members of staff and the board of governors were hideously offended by the whole notion. They felt the good name of the school was being besmirched, dragged through the mud, etcetera, etcetera. But Marsha argued that there was no way we could possibly conceal the fact that the band consisted entirely of girls from Emily Kelso, even their road manager, so we might as well capitalise on it. Use it as an opportunity to show how modern and—to use a current word—*inclusive* we were. She also said that we were bound to be the subject of publicity anyway, so we might as well turn that to our advantage. If you can't beat them, join them. That sort of thing. Do you see what I'm saying?"

"Yes."

"So she got photographs of the four girls from our files—I'm afraid Monika wasn't included—and had them enlarged and framed, then hung the pictures in the vestibule of the assembly hall in the same place where we celebrate notable feats of sporting prowess and academic achievement, with trophies and cups and certificates and so on. And she had one of their records framed and hung it up with the photos."

Suddenly I was on full alert. "One of their records?"

"Yes, one of their long-playing records."

Nevada and I looked at each other. I dug out my phone and hastily called up an image of the Blue Tits' first album. The original version. I held my phone out and Ms Morado bent down and squinted at it.

"Yes," she said. "That's the one."

Nevada and I exchanged another glance. I resisted the urge to immediately ask what had happened to the framed record. We had to work out how to handle this. And I sensed that Nevada was thinking—furiously and swiftly—along similar lines.

In any case, Ms Morado had swept inexorably on with her narrative.

"Marsha also had herself photographed in the act of hanging the record on the wall, with a view to releasing this image to the newspapers. A publicity shot, if you will. She was planning an entire campaign around the girls and their band, to show that here at Emily Kelso we were not old-fashioned or stuffy or superannuated. But already the old-fashioned, stuffy and superannuated forces were massing against her. It all came down to a crucial meeting with the board of governors, which took place one evening in the autumn of 1977."

I had a sudden unsettling premonition of where this was heading.

"It happened to be the same evening when the girls in the band were making their first appearance on television."

Uh-oh.

"A programme that was very popular at the time called *Bickering with Bridey.*"

Oh shit.

"So Marsha was in this meeting, a meeting to determine the future of the school—and indeed her own future—and while this meeting was taking place, that programme was going out on the air. As it happened, I was watching it as it went out. I needed something to distract me because I was very nervous, on behalf of Marsha. I was, as the saying goes, having kittens. Because I knew how important the meeting was for her. Her entire future was at stake."

I looked over at Nevada. Like me, she was riveted by this narrative and the inevitable disaster in the offing.

"At first it seemed like a good omen, the fact that the girls were getting such wonderful publicity just at the exact moment that Marsha was passionately defending them in front of these... dinosaurs."

Ms Morado had lowered her gaze. She seemed to be studying the carpet with great care. "And initially it was all going so well. The programme, I mean. The host Bridenstine was this dreadful boor and he very clearly had it in for our girls, but they were holding their own. Indeed, more than holding their own. There was this magnificent moment when Ophelia demonstrated that she hadn't been asleep in Latin after all. But then Helene..."

I saw her mouth tighten with distaste as she pronounced Helene's name. But that was replaced immediately with perplexity as she paused and tried to work out how to describe what happened next. "You see, Helene called the host... she said... she insulted..."

"Oh really?" said Nevada, suddenly all bright-eyed innocence. "What exactly did she do?"

"She said—"

"What *did* she say?"

"Ah... well..." We watched Ms Morado trying to tiptoe delicately around what Helene had called Bridenstine. It was as though she was picking her way across a minefield.

Finally she said, rather startlingly, "Are you familiar with *Monty Python*?"

"Yes," said Nevada and I in unison.

Ms Morado wilted with relief. "Well, then you have no doubt seen the travel agent sketch. And, to put it in *Monty Python* terms, Helene effectively called this chap a 'silly bunt'."

Oh, nice save, I thought.

"Except Helene didn't use any such Pythonesque euphemism," added Ms Morado coldly. She sighed. "And the enormous tragedy is that at this point Marsha had *succeeded*. She had in fact managed to convince the board of governors to adopt her policy. We were going to celebrate the girls and their achievements, publicise them rather than try to disavow them. It was going to be a thrilling new chapter in the history of the school. When she emerged from the meeting Marsha was *radiant*." A flicker of a smile crossed Ms Morado's face at the memory, but only for a second.

"But then she had to be told. Someone had to tell her what had happened on the television while she was shut up

in that meeting. And I am afraid that that someone was me."
She looked up from the carpet and gazed at us bleakly. "I
wish it hadn't been me. I wish I'd been more of a coward,
and I'd funked it and left it to someone else. But I was the
one who told her. And I had to watch the radiance fade
from her face. Forever, as it happened. At that exact instant
it was all over."

I remembered what Bridenstine had said about pivotal
moments in life, and how you usually didn't know when
they came along. But here was another one, triggered by
Helene and her willingness to utter one little word.

Then I realised that thinking about Bridenstine and that
day in the pub had caused me to unconsciously put my hand
to my throat. I forced myself to take it away. I saw Nevada
looking at me and I suspected her thoughts were running on
similar lines.

"All over," repeated Ms Morado. "In that instant. All
over for poor Marsha. She wasn't just forced to abandon
her programme of modernisation and liberalisation, she
was forced to resign from her post. She had forfeited her
job. She had been one of the youngest headmistresses in
the country—and certainly the most progressive. She'd had
such high hopes, such dreams and ambitions. And now,
at a stroke, that was all over. It veritably destroyed her. It
entirely crushed her. And, more than that..." Ms Morado
fell silent for a long moment.

Finally she said, "I suppose Marsha Strickland was
what today we would call bipolar. She was capable of long
spells of boundless energy and enthusiasm, intense, almost

microscopic attention to detail, radiating immense charm and personal magnetism all the while. But when she was knocked off her perch she could easily be precipitated into a period of the most utter, dark despair. And that was what happened then. Just when she needed her energy and optimism the most, when she needed to be knocking on doors and making telephone calls and sending out her CV, putting her best foot forward and looking for a new post. We tried to help her—her husband Ray and I. We did everything we could. But it has to be said that the outlook was bleak, even if she had applied herself diligently to hunting for another job. Her career had been permanently damaged."

Again, the parallel with Bridenstine.

Ms Morado shrugged. "But we'll never know."

"Why not?" I said, though I had an unhappy premonition that I knew exactly why.

"Because Marsha took her own life. She went to bed one night, turned on all the gas rings in the kitchen and went to sleep forever."

13: ARCHIVE COMPLEX

Nevada and I looked at each other. In bed while the gas from the kitchen was doing its lethal work: exactly like one of the attempts on Helene's life.

"Ray came home and found her that way," said Ms Morado in a matter-of-fact voice. "He smashed all the windows to get rid of the gas. He must have known it was too late, but he smashed them all anyway. I don't blame him. I'm sure I would have done the same thing. Smashed all the windows in the world, in fact." Ms Morado fell silent again.

"I'm sorry," said Nevada quietly.

Ms Morado looked at her in surprise. "It's not your fault, dear."

"I'm sorry it happened."

"That's kind of you."

Both women fell silent now. I waited for what I thought was a decent interval and then I said, "What happened to Ray?"

Ms Morado frowned at me. "What do you mean? He

was devastated of course. Broke down at the funeral, broke down utterly. It was quite terrible."

"But he didn't..." I searched for an appropriate euphemism. "He didn't also take his own life?"

Ms Morado shook her head emphatically. "Oh no. He of all people understood only too well the devastation and damage that suicide causes. No one knew that better than he did. It is, in a way, the ultimate act of selfishness. Almost one of narcissism; certainly one of solipsism. No, Ray never would have done anything like that."

"So what happened to him," I said, "after that?"

Ms Morado shrugged again. It was somehow a strange-looking gesture on her bony shoulders, much too informal for this very formal woman. "I don't really know. I don't think anyone really knows. He just dropped out of sight. The rumour was that he went off to India. I can't honestly say if he did, or if he ever came back. Certainly he never got in touch with me again."

"I see." Now I had to ask the other question that was burning to be answered. "You know that record?"

"Record?"

"The LP by the Blue Tits, the one which was framed."

"Ah, yes." I thought Ms Morado might have been offended or annoyed by this sudden change of subject, moving from the tragic to the trivial, as she was bound to see it. But instead she seemed profoundly relieved and grateful to be moving on to a more banal topic.

"You were very definite about it being the same one I showed you on my phone."

"Yes."

"You're absolutely certain that it was the same one, with the same cover?"

"Yes." Ms Morado rose from the corner of the desk where she had been perched and went and sat down behind it. I wondered if this was a way of hinting that it was time to terminate our interview.

But instead she took one of the small framed photographs on her desk and turned it around to face us. It was a colour photo in an ornate antique silver frame. It showed a tall, slender woman with fluffy blonde hair wearing a dark flowered dress that came down to her ankles.

The woman was smiling and holding up a framed album, ready to hang it on the wall. The glass on the framed record reflected a bright white smear of flashbulb glare in one corner, but nonetheless, under the glass there was clearly a copy of the first pressing of the first Blue Tits LP.

"That's fantastic," I said, and I meant it. Here was firm evidence, depicting the album in the flesh. Or in the vinyl, as it were.

"Thank you." Ms Morado turned the photo around and regarded it fondly. "She looks so happy there, doesn't she?"

Both because I didn't want to get back onto the painful topic of Marsha Strickland's tragic demise, and because I'd have to raise the subject sooner or later, I said, "And do you have any idea where that record is now?"

Ms Morado looked up from the picture. I thought she was puzzled by the question, but apparently she was just thinking hard, because she said, "Yes, I'm sure I do. It would be in the school archives."

I sensed Nevada going very still at my side, deliberately not looking at me or doing anything else to give the game away. I began to feel that low, slow excitement that appeared whenever there was the possibility of a really outstanding find.

"Would it be possible to look at it?" I said.

"I don't see why not." Ms Morado was all brisk business now. "In fact I can take you over to the archive complex myself if you like."

"That would be very kind of you."

"Perhaps you wouldn't mind waiting for me outside?"

"Of course," I said.

"Thank you. I just have a few calls to make. I won't be long, and it's a lovely day. There are some benches…"

"I know," I said. "We left a friend sitting on one of them." Suddenly I realised that Tinkler had been left entirely to his own devices for quite a while. Some might say for far too long. But how much trouble could he get into, sitting on a bench?

Well, I didn't have time to concern myself with that now. I had bigger fish to fry.

As Nevada and I got to our feet I said, "Oh, and I was wondering one other thing."

Ms Morado had opened a desk drawer and taken out a small purple notebook, which I surmised contained phone numbers because she was holding it in one hand while she held her phone in the other. She looked up at me with polite attention. "Yes?"

It was the bonanza question and I tried to keep my voice as casual as possible. "I was wondering if you'd consider parting with the record?"

"Parting with it?"

"Yes. Selling it to me, actually. You see, I need a copy for this project and I've been actively looking for one, but it's proved rather hard to find. So having this one turn up is a real stroke of luck." Every word of this was true, though I'd skilfully avoided saying things like *priceless collector's item*.

Ms Morado began to shake the little book she was holding, as if in a gesture of scolding reprimand. "We couldn't sell it to you," she said firmly.

"Oh," I said. "What a pity." I didn't try to conceal my disappointment, and maybe this was actually a smart move.

Because then her face brightened and she said, "But you could make a donation to the school fund."

We emerged from Ms Morado's cottage into warmth, sunlight and the smell of freshly cut grass. Nevada took my arm.

"Nice move," she said. "I can't believe you not only discovered that she had a copy of the record, but got her to agree to dig it out for you and what's more, *sell it to us*." She began to hum a happy little tune, visions of bonuses from Erik Make Loud no doubt dancing through her head.

I said, "I think we may have to make a substantial contribution to that school fund, though."

Nevada stopped humming. "Why—do you think she's

in there googling it, even as we speak? Checking the price on Disc Goggles?"

"Discogs," I said automatically. "No, I don't think there's a huge chance of that, given that she's a woman who still keeps phone numbers handwritten in a little purple book."

"Yes, that was a rather nice retro touch, wasn't it?"

"But I still think we ought to pay her a decent sum."

Nevada considered this. "To prevent blowback when and if she does discover that the record is worth a small fortune?"

"Exactly."

Nevada shrugged. "Oh well. What the hell. Erik is the one who's going to be paying for it, ultimately."

"Exactly, again."

"Still, it sticks in my craw to have to give the old bag anything. I don't suppose we could just return under the cover of darkness and simply *steal* it."

"That wouldn't be my preferred course of action."

Nevada chuckled. "Pity. I know plenty of ways into this place. And I begrudge giving that woman the sweat off my brow. I wonder if the brow is connected to the craw? The brow bone connected to the craw bone…"

"There certainly seems to be bad blood between the two of you."

"That? Oh, that. That was just because I left the school under something of a cloud. Under a giant fucking slab of roiling cumulonimbus in fact, if you want to know."

"Actually," I said, "I wouldn't mind knowing. You never talk about your schooldays."

Nevada shrugged. "There's nothing to say." Then, perhaps because it was a usefully distracting segue, or in fact because of what she had just seen, she suddenly said, "Shit. Tinkler."

I turned and looked over at where we'd left him.

Tinkler was still slouched on the bench under the large oak tree. The only thing that had changed about the picture was that he was now surrounded by a circle of teenage girls in school uniform sitting at his feet and listening to him with rapt expressions as he expounded on some point, with numerous elaborate hand gestures.

The girls—in compliance with his avowed policy, they did indeed all appear to be sixteen-plus—looked up at our approach and began to rise from the ground, brushing bits of grass off their skirts. The group had pretty much broken up and moved away as we drew near. The few remaining girls looked at us with wide-eyed interest. One of them came up to me.

"Your friend's *sick*," she said happily.

"Don't we know it."

Tinkler beamed at us. "Welcome back, chums. Bye, girls!" He waved to the last departing stragglers and they waved back. Tinkler returned his attention to us. "You do realise," he said, "that 'sick' is a term of high praise by today's youth, meaning really, really cool?"

"Surely that particular usage has fallen by the wayside," said Nevada. "And the term has reverted to its original meaning?"

"Let's just agree to disagree."

"Tinkler, what on earth were you talking to those girls about?"

"Oh, they saw us getting out of the car and they wanted to know who we were. In particular they wanted to know who *you* were." He indicated Nevada. "I told them you were an old girl, a former member of this fine institution, indeed a former member of Blue Tits house. And when they asked what you'd been up to since leaving I said you'd been gainfully employed throwing bricks into the faces of neo-Nazis."

"Just the one," said Nevada modestly. "And it was a breeze block, actually."

"Then I told them about your vintage clothes scam—sorry, business—and that got them really quite excited. So I gave them your web address. I think you've made some sales already."

Nevada was looking at her phone. "Christ, he's right."

"Oh, and one other thing." He looked at me with his big, innocent eyes. "When they asked how we were all connected I sort of hinted, well actually came right out and said, that Nevada and I are, ahem, life partners."

"You did what?"

"Which is, you know, a polite way of saying that we're making jiggy on a regular basis. The old horizontal mambo. I must say that when I told them *that* they looked at me with a new respect that I found rather gratifying. I think I'm going to have to try shamelessly lying a lot more in the future."

"How did you explain away my presence?" I said.

"I said you were her gay best friend who helps her choose clothes. Perfectly plausible."

"Great. Thanks."

"Always happy to help."

Nevada now proceeded to kiss me in such a way as to undermine all aspects of Tinkler's story, if anyone was watching. "Honestly, Tinkler," she said, when we came up for air. "We're going to have to get you laid."

"Yes please."

"Or, more likely, buy you a life-size doll."

"Almost as good as that, I might be seeing Opal again."

"Wait. What? I thought Opal moved to America."

"She's back in the UK, at least for a while." Tinkler grinned. "And we're back in touch. And I'm inexorably weaving my web of charm around her. My *lurv* charm."

Opal was a young woman of keen intelligence, despite her having dated Tinkler, and considerable beauty, ditto, and ruthless ambition. It was the latter attribute that had led to her dumping Tinkler last time, moving to the States to pursue it.

"Well, just don't get your heart broken again," said Nevada.

"So long as I get my ashes hauled, who cares?"

"Ashes hauled?"

"You've obviously never listened to the blues, young lady. Ashes hauled means leg over. End away. Wick dipped. Oil changed..."

This fascinating tour of the riches of the English language was cut short by the appearance of Ms Morado. "I'm sorry about that," she said as she joined us. "I didn't mean to keep you waiting so long."

"No problem at all."

Tinkler rose from the bench and we all started walking, following Ms Morado. I said, "This is Jordon Tinkler. I suppose you'd call him a friend."

"Oh, ignore him," said Tinkler. "He's just still smarting about the gay remark."

Ms Morado gave a polite, uncomprehending laugh and increased her pace somewhat.

We walked along winding footpaths through the lawns and gardens of the school, past a variety of small buildings, mostly in the cottage style. Several of these had circular stained-glass windows beside the front doors with quite beautiful images of birds carefully wrought on them, rather in the style of the British painter William Nicholson.

These were clearly the famed school houses with their ornithological names. We saw an owl and an eagle. And then one that was more infamous than famed, with a particularly adorable little blue and yellow bird on its window.

As we walked past it I looked at Nevada and she nodded and took my hand. "That's it," she said. "The den of iniquity."

"You don't want to go and look inside? For old times' sake?"

"God no." She mimed an elaborate shudder and squeezed my hand hard.

A moment later Ms Morado said, "Ah, here we are."

We had arrived at three long, low rectangular buildings set around an open area of flowerbeds like three sides of a square. Unlike the cottages we'd seen up to now these were modern-looking—grey, undecorated functional boxes made mostly of concrete.

"I'm afraid 'archive complex' is rather a grand name for these," said Ms Morado apologetically. "They were once stables and then garages and now… they are as you see them." She seemed genuinely worried that we might be disappointed. She said, "Indeed, 'archive' is rather a grand name for what they contain. This has become essentially a dumping ground for all the clobber that no one wants any longer, but which no one can quite bring themselves to throw away. I'm sure you're familiar with the principle, on a smaller domestic scale. Like an attic or a garage or a cupboard under the stairs."

Far from putting me off, this just sharpened my interest. She'd just named three places that would be prime hunting grounds for old records—though attics tended to get a bit too hot for my liking, as a location for decent LP storage. Vinyl warps.

"Now, let me see," said Ms Morado, chewing at her lower lip. She hesitated between the building on our right and the one on our left. The one directly in front of us seemed to be out of the running. Suddenly and decisively she turned to the left, took out a large, clattering ring of keys and unlocked the door of the building.

We stepped with her into cool, dust-smelling gloom. For a moment Ms Morado fumbled for a light switch in the darkness. Then there was a click followed by a buzzing sound as long fluorescent tubes came alive on the ceiling, throwing a white glare so harsh and sharp that we shielded our eyes.

We were in a long, narrow, windowless storeroom lined with grey and green metal shelving covered with cardboard boxes. The boxes all had numbers on them, either written on with black marker pen or on small typewritten squares of yellowing paper affixed with equally yellowing tape. Some had a few words on them in addition to the numbers.

There were a lot of shelves, and a great many boxes, but Ms Morado moved among them decisively and with every sign of confidence, occasionally slashing irritably at a cobweb with her hand. Did no one dust in this place? "It should be... No... I'm sure it is... Ah, yes. Here."

She stopped in front of a large brown cardboard carton that had once contained boxes of a popular breakfast cereal. The shelf it rested on was at eye level and I moved quickly forward to help her reach it down. At the same moment, as if the two of us were a single, synchronised mechanism, Tinkler moved quickly backwards to avoid any possibility of being enlisted to assist.

Ms Morado and I wrestled the box to the floor, with Nevada helping. It was surprisingly heavy and I allowed myself a brief fantasy that it was full of nothing but records, all of them rare and valuable and in mint condition. Dust rose as we set it down, tingling spicily in my nostrils.

We stood for a moment, looking at the box at our feet, with faded and rather ghostly images of green cartoon roosters crowing happily upon it.

"When Marsha got the sack," said Ms Morado softly, "she walked out. Walked out and left everything behind in her office. All of her personal effects. It was dreadful to find everything abandoned like that, but we couldn't just leave it there. So we boxed it up to hold it for her to collect. But Marsha never came... and then she was gone. We waited for her husband to collect it. But Ray never did, either. So it ended up in here, collecting dust."

We all looked down at the box with sober respect, as if it might contain Marsha Strickland's ashes rather than just, potentially, a really rare record.

The box was sealed with tape. Ms Morado abruptly bent down and used one of her keys as an improvised blade, slicing it open with a shrill shrieking sound. She folded back the flaps of the box and bent down to delve inside.

"Here," she said, and my heart gave a lurch.

She began to pass us framed photographs. They were colour portraits, head and shoulder shots, carefully posed, of teenage girls in school uniform. I had no trouble immediately identifying Helene and Tania. They all looked heartbreakingly young and innocent, although Helene already had an incipiently punkish hairdo, which promised things to come.

Then came a frame larger than the rest, and square. Just right for displaying your favourite long-playing record. Ms Morado took it out and held it up to look at it, so that the back of the frame was towards us, a blank black panel.

"That's odd," she said.

She turned the frame over to show us. The other side was a blank white panel.

My heart sank.

She prised the two sections of the frame apart, removing the glass at the front from the backing. "It isn't even fastened together," she said, frowning. The backing of the frame contained a square of white mounting board. I took it from her and carefully removed the board to make sure there was nothing behind it. There wasn't. Just the back of the frame.

So that was that.

"Someone must have taken it," said Ms Morado. "Why would anyone do that?"

I bent down and looked at the box again. There was a square of paper fixed to the front with the words *Effects: M. Strickland* typed on it and some numbers. The paper was stuck to the box with tape that was beginning to peel away, brittle and so yellow that it was almost brown.

I folded down the lid of the box again and looked at the strip of tape which had sealed it, and which Ms Morado had so neatly sliced open with her key.

It wasn't yellow at all.

Ms Morado locked up the building and we said our goodbyes in an atmosphere of general gloom and defeat. She set off back towards her office without looking back and we turned and headed for our car.

After a minute or two of glum silence, Tinkler said, "This visit hasn't been a complete waste of time, though. My sexual street cred has been immeasurably enhanced."

"And we've found another candidate for Helene's would-be killer," said Nevada.

"Who's that?"

"The husband of the late Marsha Strickland," I said.

"The lady whose box we just violated?" said Tinkler. "Any filthy sexual insinuations in that sentence are purely accidental, or possibly just a spinal reflex."

"Yes."

"So why would her husband want to kill Helene?"

"Because she was another victim of the Howlin' Hellbitch's famous television broadcast. Didn't you get that from what Ms Morado said in there?"

"No," said Tinkler. "I was just waiting for her to shut the fuck up and look in the box for the record. Bummer that someone beat us to it, eh?"

"Yes," said Nevada tightly.

"And not that long ago judging by how recently that box was resealed," I said. The tape hadn't had time to discolour with age.

Tinkler nodded as if he'd spotted this, too. Perhaps he had. "I wonder who it could have been?"

"Oh, this place is full of thieves," said Nevada, staring around balefully at the beautifully maintained grounds and charming little buildings of her old school.

"But it would have to have been someone who knew the value of the record," I said.

"That could be anyone with access to the Internet," said Tinkler. "Did the box woman really die because of what Helene said on the TV show?"

"Pretty much, yeah. It finished off her career just like it did Bill Bridenstine's, and she couldn't handle that."

Tinkler shook his head and made *tutting* sounds. "Amazing what a four-letter word can do. It makes you think," he mused happily. "Talk about girl power."

We fell silent as we reached the parking area.

When we'd arrived earlier we had been the only car on the circle of gravel, but now there was another one there. It was a blue and white Nissan Figaro. I'd heard Clean Head remark that these dashing little vehicles were more like handbags than cars. Stylish handbags, though. I wondered idly who drove this one.

I was about to find out, because as we approached Kind of Red a figure stepped out from under the shade of a nearby cluster of trees.

"Nevada!"

We turned to look, and saw a handsome middle-aged woman with short cropped grey hair. She had striking blue eyes that looked oddly familiar. Her expression was stern in a take-no-prisoners kind of way. She wore a pair of faded blue jeans that fit her perfectly, grubby ivory ballet slippers, and a baggy oatmeal-coloured sweater, which she somehow made look effortlessly chic.

"Enrica told me you were here," she said to Nevada, who was standing frozen, staring at her in astonishment.

But Nevada rapidly regained her composure. "Oh great," she said. "My teachers are still ratting me out after all these years."

"That's what we pay them for."

"You're not paying them anymore. In fact, I seem to remember there was a lot of trouble getting you to pay them at the time."

"Oh, you know what I mean," said the woman. "Don't be difficult. And don't dig up the past. You always deliberately misunderstand things and twist them around. And you always dig up the past. In fact, one might say that's your specialty. Your two specialties."

"Yes, one might say that," said Nevada.

She sighed, and turned and looked at me with a wry smile.

"I don't believe you've met my mother."

14: WINE CELLAR

Having originally entered the school grounds through the narrow back gate, we now left through the rather grandiose front gate, driving in a truncated convoy consisting of Mrs Warren's Nissan Figaro in the lead and us in Tinkler's car behind. There were tall white stone pillars on either side of the main gate with sculpted eagles on them, and as we drove out I saw that the eagle on the left pillar was missing his head, which rather reduced the grandiosity. I thought I glimpsed it lying in the grass, looking pissed off with his undignified position, but then we were out of the school compound and heading for the main road with the Emily Kelso Academy rapidly disappearing behind us.

"I can't believe you have a mother," said Tinkler from the backseat.

Nevada shifted around to look at him. "Why not?"

"You just don't seem the type."

"Very funny," said Nevada. "Anyway, mother is perhaps too strong a word for what she is."

"Well, you can be as snippy as you like," said Tinkler. "But she's invited us to lunch, so she's already in my good books."

"You haven't tasted her cooking yet."

I was only following this bickering badinage with a very small portion of my attention. I was mostly concentrating on keeping up with Nevada's mother in the Nissan. She obviously knew this area better than I did and was driving fast, with no apparent concern about my ability to stay on her tail. I didn't want to lose her, so I soon found myself speeding along country roads a lot faster than I was comfortable with. But I managed to keep the nippy little blue and white car in sight, just about.

We passed a sign that said *Beware racehorses. Please drive slowly.*

Fat chance of that, I thought, praying that a blood-stained equine collision wasn't imminent.

A little later we passed another sign, a small brown and white one which simply announced *Borough of Epsom & Ewell.*

With surprising swiftness the country roads became urban, and all at once we were driving through a large town. "Oh, look," said Tinkler. "They've got Nando's here. So we haven't completely left civilisation behind."

"They've even got a Majestic Wine warehouse," said Nevada, who was checking our location on her phone. "But it's still not enough to redeem the place."

We drove past a pub called The Rifleman. We weren't moving at high speed anymore. However, the traffic grew heavier—which gave me a new and exciting reason to be worried about losing sight of Nevada's mother. But the little Nissan was slowing considerably now, and I had the feeling that our journey was nearing its end.

"I can't believe she's moved to Epsom," said Nevada. "It's so not her kind of town."

Up ahead, Mrs Warren's signal lights went on and we followed her as she took a right turn off the A24 onto Church Road. Then another right turn into a street where the Nissan pulled over.

"Perhaps I spoke too soon," said Nevada.

The street in front of us was strikingly different from everything we'd seen up until now. It was like we'd taken one of those storybook turns which lead into an enchanted realm.

On either side of us were neat terraces of small elegant houses, all uniformly flat-fronted, with no gaps between them. They were divided at intervals by black drainpipes and each one had two windows and a brightly coloured front door. Most of the houses themselves were painted white, but a few were in pastel shades—pale blue, lilac and pink. The effect was very beguiling and attractive, as if a picturesque Mediterranean street had been somehow uprooted and dropped down in the middle of urban Surrey.

The warmth of the day and the brilliant sunlight added considerably to the resemblance.

Mrs Warren got out of the Nissan and walked up to her house, which turned out to be the pink one. With hanging baskets of purple flowers outside, it was a well-kept, pretty place. We joined her as she stood by the dark blue front door, waiting for us rather impatiently.

In the window beside the door a black cat stared out at our small group and then quickly disappeared. "That's the spirit," said Nevada's mother. At the time I thought it was a rather enigmatic and sarcastic remark, expressing ironic approval for something we'd done, or perhaps to the cat for fleeing. But later I would learn that she was actually saying, "That's the Spirit." With a capital 'S'. Because it turned out to be the name of the cat.

Mrs Warren unlocked the door and we stepped into shaded, fragrant coolness. It was a small house and as soon as we were inside we could see down the hallway to a room at the back with large French windows through which the sunny garden was visible. "Come in," she said, "and see if you can find somewhere to sit in the sitting room. Or the dining room. It's the same room."

Nevada was gazing up the staircase towards the shadowy upper floor of the house. "Can I go up and have a nose around?" she said.

"No. You can stay down here with everyone else."

"Do you have any of my stuff here?" said Nevada.

"The stuff you so thoughtfully left behind when you took off?" said her mother. "Most of that's in storage in a unit over in Cheam. The Cheam Storage Centre. It's just a divine place. So delightful. Like a multi-storey car park, but without the romance."

"Well, thank you for not just throwing it out," said Nevada.

"You never know when something might come in handy," said her mother. She walked through to the dining room and we followed. There was a round wooden table in here, a dresser and four wooden chairs and two comfortable-looking white armchairs with cushions with a butterfly pattern on them.

The place was friendly and full of light, decorated in a kind of Normandy farmhouse style. Beyond the French windows was a surprisingly large garden, dense with flowers and greenery. Almost hidden by the plants were half a dozen small wooden structures with pitched roofs that looked like miniature houses. A bit too big to be dolls' houses—maybe garden gnomes' houses. I saw the black cat disappearing into the shrubbery, continuing its strategic retreat from this inundation of visitors, perhaps aiming to take up residence in one of those miniature houses with the gnomes.

I also noticed the cat flap through which it had escaped, set into the bottom of one of the glass panes of the French windows. Somebody had done a decent job of cutting the glass to fit it.

"Go on, sit down," said Mrs Warren, and we did. She paused and took a good look at us, as if assigning us points for which chairs we'd chosen, then went out through a door on the right-hand side of the room.

Nevada immediately hopped out of her chair, went to the door, opened it and peered after her mother. She shut it silently and returned to her chair. "Wine cellar," she said, sounding rather grudgingly impressed.

"Wine cellar?" said Tinkler.

"All right, it's not actually a cellar. It's not underground. But it's still a room devoted to wine. We had one in our old house and we always called it the wine cellar."

"How do you devote a room to wine?"

Nevada sighed. "You put up lots of shelves and you put lots of bottles of wine on them, on their sides—unless they have screw caps instead of corks, of course, in which case you use a different and more widely spaced set of shelves where you can stand them upright."

"Good to know. You wouldn't want those screw-cap bottles on their sides."

"No, you wouldn't. Because then the wine would be reacting with whatever lines the screw caps. Usually plastic. And there's a wine refrigerating unit in there."

Tinkler sniggered. "A wine refrigerating unit? You mean a fridge with wine in it?"

"No, I mean a Fisher and Paykel dedicated freestanding wine storage unit with two different temperature zones and an ultraviolet tempered glass door. It costs a couple of grand."

The door opened again and Mrs Warren, who had evidently been listening on the other side of it, said, "It also has a low vibration compressor, whatever that is, to guarantee that the wine remains undisturbed."

"Well, we wouldn't want the wine to be *disturbed*," said Tinkler.

Mrs Warren turned to study him. She was holding a bottle of wine in one hand, grasping it by the neck with her arm loosely at her side. It was exactly the way I'd often seen Nevada hold a wine bottle. Indeed it reminded me keenly of the way she'd held one the other night when she'd been preparing to defend our household against an intruder in the garden.

All of which suggested, at least to me, that Tinkler would be well advised not to get too mouthy.

"We do also have a *fridge* in there," said Mrs Warren, her gaze fixed on Tinkler. "Which is where this came from." She held up the bottle. "I'll go and open it now, because it's one of the ones without a screw cap." This last remark was directed at Nevada as Mrs Warren walked back out of the room and down the hallway we'd come in by.

"It's still a C-list wine," said Nevada, as soon as she was out of earshot.

"I'm impressed," I said. "You hardly even had a chance to glance at the label."

Nevada smiled at me. "I imagine you could judge the quality of an LP by its label from across the room." I smiled back at her.

"Ah," said Tinkler in a treacly voice. "Trainspotting lovebirds."

Mrs Warren came back in, holding the wine bottle in one hand and a professional-looking corkscrew in the other. She sat down at the table, unfolded a small knife blade from the handle of the corkscrew and, with a few swift decisive movements, sliced off the foil that concealed the cork—which Nevada had taught me to call the capsule—snapped the knife blade away again, inserted the corkscrew decisively into the cork, cinched and twisted it a few times and then pulled out the cork with a satisfying pop.

She set the bottle down on a small white saucer in the centre of the table, which was evidently stationed there for exactly that purpose, and set the cork down, upright, beside it, like a miniature sentinel to guard the wine.

"We'll let that breathe for a little while," she announced. "I'll get the glasses." She went out again.

"I bet we don't get the Riedels," said Nevada.

A moment later her mother came back carrying four wine glasses, hanging down from her hands with the stems between her fingers. Again I recognised that gesture very well indeed. As she set them down on the table Nevada turned to me with a look of triumph and silently mouthed the word 'Ikea'.

Her mother glanced sharply over her shoulder, as if sensing that some communication was going on behind her back. And, perhaps also, that it wasn't entirely complimentary. She looked steadily at Nevada. "Do you hear from your father much?" she said suddenly.

Nevada shrugged. "Not much. The occasional email. Christmas and birthdays."

"That's disgraceful."

"It's about the same I get from you."

"Is he still living with his teenage prostitute in Thailand?"

"She's not quite a teenager, Mum. And to be a prostitute you have to charge for it. And it's Goa now, not Thailand."

"You always stuck up for him," said Nevada's mother. "*Always*." She smiled a thin-lipped smile at me. "It is so reassuring to know that there are some fixed points in this crazy, ever-changing world—don't you think?"

I didn't know quite what to say.

Nevada stepped into the breach smoothly. "So you haven't got any of my stuff here?"

Mrs Warren shook her head. "You know very well that isn't what I said."

"You said it was in a storage unit in Cheam."

"I said most of it was. But your bow and arrows, for instance, are still here."

"My sixty-six inch Nano Max?" said Nevada. "And my Eastons?"

"I suppose so." Her mother turned and smiled at me. "Most girls have pictures of singers hanging on their bedroom wall. Not my little darling. She had a lethal weapon."

Nevada yawned casually then studied her fingernails with equally elaborate casualness. "I'm sure if I had had pictures of singers hanging on my bedroom wall they would only have antagonised you."

"I am sure they would," said Mrs Warren. "Not least because you would have chosen them solely for that express purpose."

"Damn right," said Nevada happily.

"You really were the most troublesome child," said her mother, in a tone of considered truculence.

Tinkler shot me an alarmed look, which I had no difficulty reading. It seemed like total domestic warfare was about to break out before our very eyes, and all he wanted was a free lunch.

"Excuse me, Mrs Warren," I said in my most polite voice.

She turned and regarded me coldly. "Yes?"

"It's very kind of you, the wine. But I'm going to have to drive so I was wondering if perhaps I could have some coffee instead?"

She sighed and got up and left the room without a word. Perhaps to make coffee, or perhaps to find a suitable weapon to dispatch a bothersome guest.

Tinkler wilted with relief. "Good move," he said. "Just in the nick of time, too. Normally I wouldn't mind a catfight. But this mother and daughter thing..." He paused thoughtfully. "Hang on, though, come to think of it, Mrs Warren is definitely in the MILF category."

"Tinkler," said Nevada, in a dangerous voice. "There is a line. And you have just crossed it."

Tinkler gave her a put-upon look. "What's the problem? I'm just designating her porn category. Now yours—yours would be—"

"Tinkler." Nevada's voice had now ratcheted up the danger factor considerably.

Hastily, continuing in my role of subject-changing peacekeeper, I said, "Speaking of cats..."

The black cat had returned from the garden and pushed his head through the cat flap, looking at us warily. He had yellow eyes and was very pretty, though of course not as pretty as our own felines.

"Well, come on in, silly cat," said Nevada. "Don't just stand there half inside and half outside."

The cat didn't move, continuing its wary appraisal of us newcomers. Then Mrs Warren came back in and he shot into the room, between her feet, and down the hall.

"Silly cat," she said, her voice suddenly and eerily echoing her daughter's. She was holding a white mug of what must have been instant coffee, considering the speed with which she'd produced it. Just the one, I noticed. Presumably on the principle that if anyone else had wanted coffee they should have asked for it at the time, and if they hadn't, bad luck.

Still, at least the diversion had served its purpose of averting hand-to-hand combat between two generations of the Warren women.

Or maybe not. Because as she sat down at the table, setting the mug of coffee on it in my general direction, but just tantalisingly out of reach, Nevada's mother started right in again where she'd left off.

"Nevada has been trouble to me ever since she was born," she said in a dry, pragmatic voice. "Since before that, in fact. From the moment she was conceived. I knew the exact moment she was conceived, you know."

"Oh, Mum, for Christ's sake, please…"

"I just *knew*," declared Mrs Warren. And she was so definite about it that I absolutely believed her.

"How did you know?" I said.

"Because my nipples started tingling."

At the mention of nipples, Tinkler made a small involuntary sound. Nevada's mother immediately swivelled her most baleful gaze on him. "Who are you, again," she said, "exactly?"

"Jordon Tingler… I mean Tingler… I mean Tingler… I mean *Tingler… I mean Tinkler!*"

Tinkler was now red-faced and gasping. A first.

Nevada's mother seemed in no way offended, however. In fact, she appeared quietly pleased with the chaos she'd wrought in poor Tinkler's brain. She nodded, a small mysterious *Mona Lisa* smile on her lips. This, too, was unsettlingly familiar.

Then she turned to me.

Oh good, I thought. *It's my turn.*

"You're the boyfriend?" she said.

"Please, Mum," said Nevada.

"Yes," I said. "I do have that privilege."

Mrs Warren was silent for a moment, peering at me with unnerving concentration. Finally she said, "You're not her usual type."

Tinkler got in there instantly. "What is her usual type, Mrs Warren?"

She considered for a split second, then said, "An embittered alcoholic ex-special forces officer traumatised by combat who's drinking himself to death."

It was such a perfectly delivered little zinger, and so unexpected coming from this dour woman, that both Tinkler and I gaped with astonishment and then burst into laughter.

We laughed and laughed.

And laughed.

Until finally it dawned on us that Nevada and her mother were not only not laughing, but were exchanging a complex look. It was unreadable, but it signified nothing good.

We were both thinking it, but Tinkler was the first to say it.

"Oh, shit."

15: MRS WARREN'S PROFESSION

Outside in the garden Nevada and I were alone, except for the black cat, who had elected to join us and eavesdrop on our very personal conversation. Tinkler and Nevada's mother remained politely inside, talking about god knows what.

Possibly porn categories.

We watched the black cat prowling among the beds of flowering herbs and listened to the hum of the bees. Since we'd stepped outside I'd realised that most of the plants were herbs of various kinds and that the little wooden 'houses' I'd seen were actually beehives.

Nevada took my hand. "I'm sorry I never told you about it," she said.

"That's all right. I knew there was something you didn't want to talk about." There had always been a portion of Nevada's past that had been a no-go area. Of course, I'd wondered about it. Not many young ladies of her age and background had such an extensive acquaintance with the use of weapons, for instance.

Nevada took a deep breath, as if she were about to jump off a high diving board. "His name was Willard Dunne," she said. "He was the archery instructor at Emily Kelso. Archery and languages were the two things I was any good at. Mum was right—he was ex-special forces, and he was a mess. Drinking too much was the least of it. I mean, why else would he have ended up teaching at a girls' school? I was far and away the best pupil he ever had, so he spent a lot of extra time with me. He was determined that he wouldn't get involved with any of the students but…"

But once he saw those big blue eyes he was lost, I thought.

"I fell for him and he fell for me. We started seeing each other. We were careful, but you can't keep a secret like that in a place like that. It all came out. They were going to fire him and discipline me. So we ran off together. We headed for the Continent. There was the problem of earning a living, but that proved a surprisingly easy problem to solve. Because Will had a very particular skill set. He just didn't have the ability to market it. Which is where I came in."

That made perfect sense. Nevada had a very good head for business.

"People are always looking for private security. We did particularly well in the south of France. There's a lot of money there, they wanted bodyguards and they were willing to pay top dollar. I had the language skills and I spruced Will up, got him dressed in good clothes so he looked the part and could fit in with the entourage of any oligarch on the Riviera. And I got him to train me—weapons, self-defence and tactics—so that we could both get jobs. We did very well for a time. But then Will started throwing our money away in the casinos. I put a stop to that. He didn't like a woman telling him what to do and he began to resent me. But it was the drink that was the real problem. He couldn't stop. He could do his job, he was a functioning alcoholic. But he *was* an alcoholic. The cracks were beginning to show."

Nevada fell silent for a moment. I wondered if she wanted me to say something, but instead it seemed a very private moment. Finally she said, "I told him he had to stop drinking and he wouldn't. I told him it was either me or the booze. And he chose the booze. He loved the drink more than he loved me."

Her voice was steady and calm. "That was the bottom line. He wasn't going to stop. So I left him. A couple of years later I heard he was gone. He'd drunk himself to death." She paused. "We were together for quite a long time and a lot of it was very good indeed. And it might have worked, if not for the drinking."

She looked at me, eyes suddenly luminous with the threat of tears.

"I'm sorry," she said. "Does it hurt to hear me say these things?"

"Perhaps it's a character flaw," I said, "but I just can't feel threatened by a guy called Willard."

She blinked a few times and then her shoulders started heaving with silent laughter. She came closer and hugged me. "It all worked out for the best," she said. "If it hadn't happened, I never would have met you. And the kittens would be growing up without a mum." She took a step back from me.

"Speaking of mothers…"

"Time we went back inside?"

"Yes," said Nevada. "I know she's a complete nightmare. I'm so sorry to have dragged you here. And Tinkler."

"I don't mind," I said. "As for Tinkler, he deserves everything he gets."

We walked back in through the French windows. Mrs Warren and Tinkler were sitting at the table, talking with every appearance of cordiality. The wine was still untouched, but two more mugs, presumably of coffee, had appeared. Nevada's mum was really pushing the boat out.

As we came in she was saying, "So I put a Flow Hive in the super. The super sits on top of the queen excluder." Tinkler was nodding as if he could conceivably be taking this in. "The Flow Hive is made of plastic and the traditional beekeepers are up in arms about it, but you have to move with the times." She turned and looked at us. "Did the bees bother you?"

"Not at all."

"That's good. They sometimes attack strangers."

Thanks for telling us that now, I thought.

"Apparently some of the little devils have cross-combed," said Tinkler.

Mrs Warren nodded grimly. "I didn't get around to putting in the other frame in time," she said.

Tinkler shook his head and made *tutting* sounds. "Rookie error."

Instead of throwing her coffee in his face, Mrs Warren said, "I know, I know," and shook her head. She even sounded a little contrite.

"So, how long have you had the bees?" said Nevada.

"Let me think… It was the same time the Spirit moved in. So, about three years ago now."

"The Spirit is the cat?" I said.

"That's right," said Mrs Warren. "I called him that because he turned up when I got the hives. As if he was part of the deal. Just turned up from nowhere, moved in and made himself at home."

"Ah," said Nevada. *"El Espíritu de la Colmena."* She looked at me. *"The Spirit of the Beehive."*

"I remember," I said. Nevada had a passion for the cinema, particularly foreign films—preferably pretentious and impenetrable specimens, but this one had actually been rather good. This revelation about nomenclature was a relief, because I'd thought there might have been some kind of alarmingly religious connotation involved. And you don't want that in a cat's name.

Mrs Warren was nodding. "Directed by Víctor Erice. Have you seen his other film, *El Sur*?" Apparently this was a shared family passion.

"Yes," said Nevada, not actually adding the words, *Of course, I'm not a philistine*, but abundantly implying them. "And I've also seen *El Sol del Membrillo*." She translated for me again. *"The Quince Tree Sun."*

"The Quince Tree Sun?" said Tinkler. "Christ, I've just got to see that. Remind me to stream it when I get home. Is there any nudity?"

Both the women ignored him. They were exchanging a steady gaze. I was wondering if they were about to bond over a shared love of Spanish films.

But the moment passed, like the sun being obscured by a cloud. Mrs Warren looked away and said, "How did you enjoy your reunion with Ms Morado?"

"It was sheer delight," said Nevada.

"What do you think of her in her new role as head teacher?"

"I mostly think she's hell-bent on living up to her name," said Nevada.

Reacting to our blank looks, her mother said, "Morado is Spanish for 'purple'."

"Oh, and she was dressed all in purple," said Tinkler.

"God you're quick, Tinkler," said Nevada.

"Did she hold forth about the beloved Marsha?" said her mother.

"The old headmistress? Yes, she seems pretty cut up about what happened to her."

"That's putting it mildly," said Mrs Warren. "She never got over it. She was in love with her, you know."

"Ms Morado?" I said. "With Marsha Strickland?"

"Oh yes. She virtually keeps a shrine to her in her flat. She never got over her death."

Nevada and I exchanged a quick look. This visit with her mother might not be a complete write-off after all—we'd just discovered a new suspect with a strong motive for wanting Helene dead.

"Well," said Mrs Warren, "I'd better get lunch started, so you can be off soon. I imagine you're eager to be getting back to London."

She rose from the table, gathering up the mugs. "I'm afraid this may take a little while. Just about every plate, glass and piece of cutlery I own is waiting to be washed up, so I'll have to do all that before I can even begin to prepare any food."

"We'll help you wash up," I said. "In fact we'll do it for you."

"My friend here often says crazy things," said Tinkler. "Which is fine just so long as it's clear that he doesn't speak for me."

"No, of course we'll help, Mum," said Nevada.

This offer of assistance didn't give rise to the grateful moans of pleasure one might have hoped for. Mrs Warren just said, "All right, but you're going to have to boil a kettle. Several kettles. That's why everything is waiting to be washed up. The boiler has broken down and there is no hot water."

With this grim pronouncement she turned and marched out of the room and we followed her. Or, rather, Nevada and I followed her while Tinkler remained where he was, to maintain the maximum distance between himself and any possibility of domestic chores.

The kitchen was small, bright and decorated in keeping with the rustic French theme. It was clean and neat, except for the impressive pile of unwashed cutlery, plates and glasses in the sink. Mrs Warren caught me looking at it and said, "The boiler has decided to quit. Just out of warranty, of course. It's going to cost me at least five hundred quid, not to mention being punished with cold baths until they deign to send an overpaid troglodyte to attend to it."

I looked at the boiler, which was mounted on the wall in the corner by the window, from which the cat had peered out at us earlier. I recognised this contraption. The same or a very similar one was mounted on the wall of our own kitchen. I went over to take a close look at it. The small display screen, where an error code normally would appear, just showed a string of numbers.

Hmm…

I turned to Mrs Warren, who was watching me with a kind of sardonic impatience. Nevada merely looked puzzled. "Do you have a screwdriver?" I said. "I need one with a Phillips head."

"No Phillips head," drawled Mrs Warren. "Tragically." She looked at me to see what I was going to do next.

"But you do have one?"

"Oh yes. A house is not a home without a screwdriver." She took one out of a drawer and handed it to me with sarcastic ceremony. "There you go. May the two of you be very happy together."

At this point, Tinkler wandered in, apparently drawn by the tenor of our conversation and the promise of an embarrassing scene. Certainly Nevada was staring at me, wondering what the hell I was up to.

I looked at the screwdriver. Luckily I recognised this, too. It was a flat head, but it was a DeWalt. I firmly gripped the blade, gave it a sharp tug, pulled it out of the screwdriver handle, reversed it, and stuck it back in again. *Voila*. All at once it was a Phillips.

Nevada's mother, Nevada and Tinkler were staring at

me now as if I'd performed a magic trick, which in a way I suppose I had. You could use one of those screwdrivers for years and not realise it was reversible. And, for a moment at least, Mrs Warren seemed to have exhausted her repertoire of snarky commentary.

Under the boiler was what looked like the largest collection of back issues of *Sight & Sound* in private hands. Nevada and I moved these, and even Tinkler got involved, to the extent of picking up one of the magazines and leafing through it, presumably in search of smut.

I now had access to the underside of the boiler. I used the screwdriver to loosen the Phillips screw beneath the unit and removed the face plate and passed it to Nevada, who set it on the floor. Her mother and Tinkler were standing side by side watching us with growing incredulity.

The interior of the boiler was now exposed. It looked like a car engine with a nest of pipes and wires behind it. Among these was the small black plastic object that I remembered was called the flow unit, or the flow sensor or something.

I reversed the screwdriver and used the rubber handle of it to give the thing a couple of firm whacks. Mrs Warren started to say something but then thought better of it. "Run the tap," I said. "Please."

Neither Tinkler nor Mrs Warren showed any inclination to move, so Nevada went to the sink and turned the water on. "The hot tap?"

"Yes please."

As Nevada turned the tap to hot, the boiler immediately rumbled to life, and I saw the welcome sight of the little flame icon spring up on the display screen. I picked up the face plate from the floor with the help of Tinkler, of all people, hung it back on the boiler and tightened the screw again. Then I started restacking the film magazines.

Nevada's mother had replaced Nevada at the sink. She was running the tap and staring at the steaming water. "You got it working," she said. Then she stared at me. I recognised the look. It was the same one my cats had given me when I had first switched on the underfloor heating after I'd installed it, converting the icy crypt of our home into a residence where a cat could sprawl sleepily on the warm floor anywhere her little paws took her.

"There's a thing in there called an impellor," I said. "It's like a propeller, but in reverse. The flow of water drives it. And when it's activated, it causes the boiler to heat up. But a piece of crud had blocked it, shutting down the system. So I shook it loose."

"A piece of crud?" said Mrs Warren. "Is that the technical term?" But there was a distinctly softer note to her sarcasm now.

"Pretty much, yes."

She switched off the tap, regarded it with suspicion for a moment, then turned it back on. The boiler sprang to life once more and the hot water flowed. She turned it off again, gave me an unreadable look, then left the room without a word. Nevada came over and kissed me. "Good work," she said.

"Yeah, good work," said Tinkler. "No kisses from me, though."

"We'd better get on with that washing up," I said, looking at the pile of dirty plates which had not magically shrunk since I'd last inspected it.

Nevada and I moved to the sink while Tinkler skedaddled.

I had just begun to wash the first item, Nevada at my side holding a tea towel and poised to dry it, when Mrs Warren came back in. "What are you doing?"

"We said we'd wash up—"

"Leave it. You go and sit in the sitting room with the Tingler. Nevada, would you go out in the garden and pick some mint please?" Mrs Warren had taken an apron off a hook on the back of the kitchen door and was putting it on. It depicted a giant fluffy black and yellow bumblebee. She shooed us from the sink and starting washing the dishes. "I'll do these." She shot a glance at the boiler, as if not quite trusting it not to quit again any second. "It's practically a pleasure now the damned thing is working again."

"You can cancel the overpaid troglodyte," said Nevada, as we left the kitchen.

"Yes, dear, so I can," said Mrs Warren with a note of satisfaction in her voice.

Back in the sitting room, Tinkler was ensconced in the most comfortable armchair, perusing the copy of *Sight & Sound* he'd liberated.

"Look at that," said Nevada softly.

"Not a pretty sight, I agree, but at least he can read."

"No, *that*," said Nevada. She pointed at the table. The wine bottle that had been there earlier, 'breathing', was now gone, and it had been replaced by another one, also opened.

I looked at Nevada. "Have we now been upgraded to the B-list wine?"

She went over to the table and picked it up and studied the label carefully. Finally she said, "The A-list, actually." She set it down again. "It's still Chablis. The woman is like your friend Lenny, obsessed with bloody Chablis. But now at least it's a really fucking good Chablis." She smiled at me. "I'd better go out and get that mint."

"Do you want a hand?"

"No, you stay here and bask in your victory. I'll see if I can make friends with that spooky little feline." She opened the French window, letting in a warm, perfumed breeze, and stepped out, heading for the black cat who was sitting on a tree stump, watching the beehives with apparent fascination.

As soon as she was gone, Tinkler lowered his magazine and gave me a droll look. "Bask in your victory," he said.

"That's what the lady said."

He set the magazine aside. "I thought your trick transforming the sonic screwdriver was quite impressive. But to be honest, from that point on I was sure you were going to fall flat on your face."

"Oh ye of little faith."

"But then I remembered that incident, many, many years ago, back in the period I like to think of as BNE— Before the Nevada Era—when your boiler broke down and that engineer who repaired it very kindly showed you how to fix it yourself if that particular fault ever recurred."

"You remember that, do you?"

Tinkler nodded. "That being the only conceivable boiler fault you could ever repair, even if someone had a gun to your head. Even if someone had a gun to your cat's head."

"Every word you say is true. Which is unusual."

Now Tinkler shook his own head. He shook it a lot. He shook it like a man stunned anew by the wonders of the world and the mysterious workings of the universe. "You are a lucky bastard," he said. "A lucky, lucky, lucky bastard."

I looked out the open French windows at Nevada, bending over to stroke the black cat, who deigned to accept her attention. Perhaps sensing my gaze, Nevada looked up and smiled at me. I smiled back.

"Don't I know it," I said.

Mrs Warren got through the washing up swiftly, and apparently cheerfully. Indeed, at one point we heard singing from the kitchen. Quite touchingly flat and tuneless singing—another attribute shared by mother and daughter. Then lunch was assembled in record time and served up on the table, which until now had been chiefly devoted to supporting a bottle of wine which needed to breathe.

The food was pre-prepared, all evidently from Marks & Spencer, and mostly from their deli section. It was very tasty and only a fool and a snob would have complained about it not being freshly hand-made, and I was arguably only one of those things. I thought it was terrific, and the wine was even better, judging by the small sip or two I allowed myself. When Nevada and Tinkler speedily demolished the bottle, with a little help from Mrs Warren, she immediately went back into the 'cellar' and got another one.

When she went back into the kitchen for something Nevada checked the bottle. "It's exactly the same one," she said. "The good stuff. She hasn't even gone for an inferior vintage."

Her mother returned from the kitchen and frowned at the glass of wine that I'd been nursing since the beginning of the meal. "You're not drinking your wine."

I shrugged. "I'm rationing it. I have to drive."

"Don't be ridiculous," she said. "There's no question of you going back tonight. You can sleep here." She indicated me and Nevada. "You two in the spare room upstairs. As for Mr Tingler, he can use a futon I've got, on the floor in here. If he has no objection."

"On the contrary," said Tinkler. "Far from having any objection, Mr Tingler is tingling with excitement at the prospect of a futon."

I looked at Nevada and she gave me an imperceptible nod. All afternoon I'd been braced for the longish drive back, but now I felt myself relax completely. I took a big sip of the wine as her mother watched with approval. It was very good.

"Thank you, Mrs Warren," I said. "That's very kind of you to let us stay."

"You're only entitled to stay if you drop that Mrs Warren nonsense. My name is Persephone. You can call me that. Or Penny. Or Pen. But absolutely never *Percy*."

"Right," said Tinkler. "Percy it is."

The second bottle of wine was duly emptied and another one fetched. For the first time in weeks I felt like the weight of the Helene situation had been lifted from my shoulders. I could stop worrying about who was trying to kill her, and how to stop them.

At least for a while.

The conversation moved on to Mrs Warren—sorry, Penny—and her bees.

"Do you get honey from them?" said Nevada.

"Of course I do. And with six hives I get quite a lot of it."

"How much is quite a lot?"

"Maybe five hundred jars a year."

"Christ. What do you do with it all?"

"Sell it, of course. And, though I say it myself, I'm doing rather well out of the stuff." It didn't surprise me that this woman had turned beekeeping into a successful business. Like mother like daughter.

Nevada was immediately intrigued. "How much do you charge for it?"

Penny picked up the wine bottle and efficiently topped up all our glasses. "Depends. From ten pounds for a standard jar up to just over a hundred pounds per jar for the special artisanal stuff."

"*A hundred pounds for a jar of honey?*"

"Yes. Just over."

"People actually pay that?"

"Yes."

"What makes the special artisanal stuff so special?" said Tinkler.

"Well, principally the drugs."

"Drugs?"

"Yes. I call it Hashish Honey, but that's mostly for the alliteration. You know, brand identity. It's actually infused with cannabis."

There might have been a shocked silence at this point if Tinkler hadn't immediately said, "How do you infuse honey with cannabis?" He sounded like his interest was more than academic.

"Much the same way you make cannabis butter," said Penny. "Do you want me to give you the recipe?"

"To hell with that," said Tinkler. "Just sell me a jar."

"How much of this stuff do you sell?" said Nevada.

"Oh, enough to get by."

"Do you grow the weed here? I didn't see any in the garden."

"No, of course not. That would be reckless given the state of prohibition which still obtains in this rather backwards nation."

"Yeah," said Tinkler. "Prohibition. Backwards. Obtains. Right on." He'd had a few drinks.

"I have a friend who grows it hydroponically in her attic," said Penny.

When lunch was finished—it went on so long, it was more like supper—we took our glasses of wine outside, along with our dessert. This consisted of Greek yoghurt with honey—not the doped stuff, much to Tinkler's disappointment, and my relief.

Penny pointed out the various kinds of flowering herbs

she'd planted for the delectation of the bees, as well as for their sheer beauty. The most impressive of these was the painted sage, which had four different-coloured flowers on the same plant: purple, pink, white and yellow. Rather reminiscent of the colours of the houses in the street outside.

She also showed us the wasp trap she'd made—apparently wasps had a nasty habit of attacking the bees. The trap was fashioned from a big plastic bottle of Coke cut in half with the funnel-like top section inverted into the bottom half that was still full of the sticky brown beverage. "Wasps love the stuff. Bees won't drink it. They have a more refined palate."

We also admired the cat. "The Spirit sits on the tree trunk all day watching the hive. He loves to watch the bees."

I was enjoying watching the bees myself, proverbially busy as they flew to and from their hives. I was more than a trifle drunk and simply glorying in not having to worry for the time being about anyone trying to kill anyone. It felt like I was on holiday. Penny was explaining the different kinds of bees she had—the name 'Buckfast' was the one which stuck in my mind—when my phone rang.

It was Fanzine Frank at last. He was eager to set a time for us to meet.

So much for my holiday.

16: BLACK LIGHT

The guest room was at the top of the stairs, immediately adjacent to what Penny—and Nevada—called the library. There were quite a few books in there, it was true. But there were even more films, on DVD and Blu-ray, neatly lined up in alphabetical order by surname of director, on floor-to-ceiling shelves.

As a man who did much the same thing with his LPs, I wasn't about to call anybody obsessive or anything disrespectful like that.

The bed in the guest room was a big double, but it was soft. Much too soft. Nevada and I sank into the mattress and it sagged at the centre, rolling us into a heap in the middle. Despite this, thanks to the excitements of the day, family reunions and boiler repair—plus the wine, of course—we were soon drifting off.

We were on the verge of sleep when the shadowy gap in the doorway, left open for ventilation, was filled with a more inky portion of shadow and Spirit the cat came in

and gave a single, loud peremptory yowl that shocked us both back to full consciousness. The Spirit observed our discomfiture with satisfaction and then withdrew, mission apparently accomplished.

"Okay, I'm wide awake now," said Nevada.

"Me too."

We lay in silence a while and then Nevada said, "What are you thinking?"

I was thinking about the little woman I'd come to regard as Bill Bridenstine's keeper—like a child leading a bear, as they were indelibly fixed in my memory. What was her name? Something Irish, beginning with 'A'.

I told Nevada this.

"Alanna," she said. "Why on earth are you thinking about her?"

"Well, do you remember when Erik and Helene came around after the…" I felt the words drying up in my throat with the remembered pressure of that lethal shard of glass.

"The incident in the pub?" said Nevada gently. "Yes. Rather a nice bottle of bubbly they brought with them. The very least they should have done for you, some might say."

"Okay, so when they came over they were very keen on the idea that Bridenstine was the one who was trying to kill Helene. But I told them they were wrong."

Nevada rolled over so she could lean on her elbow and look at me. Or at least, she did as good a job of this as the preposterously soft mattress would allow. "So? You were right. To tell them they were wrong. You said that Bridenstine was too much of a pitiful drunken mess to

organise anything as meticulously planned as the attempts on Helene. I mean, can you see him painstakingly building that booby-trapped guitar amp? Soldering iron in one hand and circuit diagram in the other, while receiving Irish whiskey intravenously, presumably."

"No," I said. "I can't see that, though the intravenous drip is a nice touch. But he could have paid somebody else to build it for him."

Nevada shook her head, a dark shape hanging above me in the dimness of the bedroom. Outside somewhere a dog howled briefly and mournfully and then was silent, commemorating some transient canine agony. "I don't even see him being organised enough to do *that*," she said. "And what about sneaking into her flat to turn on the gas, driving the hit-and-run car, getting hold of the cocaine and spiking it? All of those things require skill or subtlety. Finesse, careful planning. He is capable of none of those things. All he's capable of is insane rage and pissing his pants."

"Sure," I said. "But, again, he could have paid someone else to do all of those things. Maybe after all these years he's stumbled on his perfect partner in crime and he's out for revenge."

As Nevada shook her head, her hair brushed across my face, all the more ticklish for being invisible. "I think not. Because paying your perfect partner in crime requires money. And he struck me as someone so strapped for cash that, as our friend Mr Ghost put it, he was willing to play second fiddle to a bouncy castle. Ready, willing and able to do that. And you saw the way that he jumped at the chance

to earn a few quid when we offered to pay to interview him. He almost bit our hands off."

"I also saw the way that she looked at him."

"Who? The Christian midget?"

"Yes," I said. "Don't you think she loves him?"

Nevada sighed. Her breath flowed softly across my face. "I think she bloody adores him. The capacity for women to throw themselves away on creeps and pricks and fools is a tragedy beyond explanation."

I said, "When Erik and Helene came over, Erik kept saying that even if it wasn't Bridenstine doing it in person, someone could be helping him. And I kept thinking of Alanna. And I kept refusing to believe it could be her."

"Well, I reckon you're right."

"I told myself that she was a devout Christian..."

"And a midget," said Nevada.

"And a midget. And she seemed nice. And she seemed genuinely ashamed of Bridenstine's behaviour."

"Oh, she was. She was."

"So it seemed hugely implausible that she'd be involved in helping Bridenstine commit murder for revenge."

"Right on every point," said Nevada. "So, what's the problem?"

"The problem is, I was lying to myself. I was trying really hard to make a case for Bridenstine not being involved. I wanted to rule him out. I would have twisted the facts any way necessary to make them fit that conclusion."

"You didn't have to twist them much."

"But my mind was closed. And the reason it was closed

is because I don't want to go near Bridenstine again. Or near anyone associated with him." I looked at Nevada, a darker outline in the dark room. "Because I'm scared."

"Of course you are. That's only natural after what happened."

"It may be only natural, but it doesn't help."

She was silent for a moment, and then she said, "Right. Okay. So we'll put him back on the suspect list."

"At the top," I said.

"Well, relatively near the top," said Nevada. "After we've spoken to Fanzine Frank, we'll arrange to go and see the Christian midget and suss her out. And you don't need to be scared. Of anything. Because I've got your back." She moved closer to me. "I've also got your front."

She eased on top of me and opened her legs to encircle me. "One thing about this bed being so fucking soft," she said, "is that at least it won't make any noise."

She kissed me.

When we went downstairs the next morning we found the cat peacefully asleep on top of Tinkler, who was comfortably cocooned in a quilt on the famous futon on the floor of the sitting room.

"Did he keep you awake, the little bugger?" said Nevada as the cat fled at our approach.

"*Au contraire*, he's been a delightful little sleep aid. A warm and furry hot water bottle. And now you've chased him off, curse you."

Penny set out breakfast for us—Poilâne toast, unsalted butter and more honey—while I got on my phone and worked out where Fanzine Frank's house was in relation to where we were. It wasn't far; and it didn't make any sense to go back into London and drive out to Surrey again, so we decided to go and visit him before we went home.

Tinkler needed to get back to work, but he was happy to let us keep the car for the day providing we dropped him at a railway station where he could get a fast train back to London.

Penny came out to see us off. The cat called the Spirit watched inscrutably from the kitchen window as we unlocked Kind of Red and climbed inside. Penny kissed us goodbye and gave Nevada a carefully gift-wrapped package.

Tinkler leaned out of the back window. "Bye, Percy."

"Bye, Tingler."

I started the car, looked in the rear-view mirror to see her waving goodbye, and pulled away.

As much as I disliked being drawn back into the whole Helene situation, it felt good to be in motion again. I turned onto East Street, and headed in the direction of Tolworth. I noticed signs pointing the other way, towards Cheam, where Nevada's teenage belongings were becalmed in a storage unit.

Except for her bow and arrows, which were now in the back seat.

Also in the back seat was Tinkler, busily gloating over a rather beautifully wrapped package of his own. "Did you get given a jar of honey, too, Tinkler?" said Nevada.

"Well, not exactly."

"What do you mean, not exactly?"

"I got given a jar of the famed Hashish Honey."

"Jesus wept. I think my mother's taken a shine to you, Tinkler."

"Why wouldn't she?" he said.

"It's hard to know where to begin answering that question."

We dropped Tinkler at Chessington North station, from where it was a straight shot and a fast service into Clapham Junction. He hopped out of the car and waved to us cheerily, with his jar of hash honey clasped firmly in one hand.

"He'll probably have eaten it by the time he gets home," said Nevada.

"He isn't going home. He's going to work."

"Well, that's fine because, as we know, he does his best work when stoned."

We almost didn't make it to Fanzine Frank's house. We were just turning into his road when a rusty—and rust-coloured—old Range Rover came gunning out, in the wrong lane, straight towards us.

I said, "Fuck," and Nevada said, "Shit," as I urgently wrenched the steering wheel to the left. We almost ended up on the pavement, but we missed the Range Rover, which disappeared without even slowing down, presumably in a hurry to cause another accident somewhere else.

I adjusted our road position and we drove the last fifty metres or so without any further threats to life or limb.

Fanzine Frank Fewston lived in a surprisingly large Georgian semi-detached house in a cul-de-sac. There was a paved parking area made of grey bricks set into the ground, and some narrow flowerbeds tucked directly in front of the house. Here some tulips and other random flowers were competing with a jostling cluster of weeds.

After the bee-friendly glories of Penny's garden, these looked distinctly shabby.

We parked and locked Kind of Red, then went up to the front door. When I pressed the brass button, instead of the expected traditional door chimes there was a blast of savage electric guitar chords. Nevada and I looked at each other. Okay, now it was beginning to look like we were in business.

To our right was a bay window lined with milky opaque net curtains. These twitched as the guitar chords faded and vanished, perhaps into the Rock Hall of Fame. "Don't look now," said Nevada out of the corner of her mouth, "but we're being watched."

"Got it," I said.

There was a pause of sufficient length for us to begin to wonder whether this would be one of those embarrassing situations where someone pretended not to be at home, after having inadvertently given away their presence. It certainly hadn't been a breeze, or indeed a cat, moving those curtains.

But, finally, we heard footsteps from within, approaching rather quickly.

In fact, running towards us.

Nevada and I exchanged a perplexed look. And then we both stood to the side, so that if the door burst open and revealed, say, an Olympic sprinter outward bound at full speed, we wouldn't be in the way.

The door did burst open, but what it revealed was a potbellied middle-aged man with impressive—that's a polite word—tobacco-coloured facial hair. It was hard to categorise this exactly because it consisted of a fairly dramatic moustache, a small beard, and mutton chop sideburns all growing together in an incestuous mass. The mutton chops rose like dried brown foam on either side of his face, framing a pair of expensive Ray-Ban aviator sunglasses with an odd pink tint. These were perched a little too far forward on his nose, almost but not quite revealing the eyes behind them.

Which was a shame, because those eyes might have given a clue as to whether this person was high, or perhaps how high he was. There was certainly a slightly odd smell about him. It was familiar, and although I couldn't quite identify it, it definitely chimed in with the theme of him being potentially off his head.

Above the sunglasses he would have had a mass of long, ratty brown hair, except he was going seriously bald, so the mass was reduced to a fringe hanging lankly over his ears.

He was wearing a yellow sweatshirt which was far too tight for his portly girth. On it, in red, was printed the words NEVER TRUST AN ATOM. THEY MAKE UP EVERYTHING. And a picture of a smiling cartoon atom.

Beneath the sweatshirt, the lower part of his body was clad in a pair of shorts which had once been known as hot pants but were now called booty shorts. They were made of something like satin in a metallic royal blue shade and had printing on the elasticated waist band which read, mendaciously, BETTER BODIES.

Below the shorts, his legs were skinny to the point of being sticklike, and strangely hairless. Perhaps the growth of all that facial stuff had exhausted his follicles. On his feet was a pair of vintage American-style sneakers in a particularly unpleasant shade of orange with no laces in them.

This apparition now removed his sunglasses and was looking at us a little wildly, though, oddly, without any particular surprise, bafflement, or lack of recognition. He seemed to be expecting us, to know who we were, but nonetheless to still be looking at us a little wildly.

To test this theory, I said, "We spoke on the phone yesterday—"

"Yeah, yeah, yeah." His abundant facial hair wagged with urgency as he worked his jaws, uttering the words with such volume and emphasis that I was worried for a moment that we might be in for a string of a cappella Beatles hits.

Which would have been very un-punk.

But then he said, "Come on, come on, come *in*." He urgently gestured for us to come inside. As we did so, after an instant of understandable hesitation, he announced, "I've got to get back before it dries." Then he turned and ran, at top speed, away from us into the depths of the house. As he did so, I noticed that on the back of his head what remained of his hair was fastened in a man bun. Yet another fashion statement.

As he ran he yelled, with a remarkable whining note in his voice, "Mindy! The guests are here."

He could then be heard mumbling, more to himself than the world at large, "I *told* you. I told you." There was an irritatingly martyred note to this which meant that, when it was cut off by a door slamming, we didn't feel we were particularly being deprived of anything of value.

"Hello," said a new voice.

It was such a quiet voice that it took a moment to work out where it was coming from. We looked up the stairs and saw a woman standing on the first landing, or rather on the section of staircase immediately above it, and peering over the banister at us.

As soon as we made eye contact, she smiled and promptly started down the steps in our direction, moving so quickly that she was almost skipping down the stairs. Rapid locomotion seemed to be a hallmark of the denizens of this house.

The woman must have been in at least her fifties but she was oddly youthful-looking, with a remarkably open, unlined face. She was somewhat chubby, though nothing on the order of Frank—assuming that the individual in the atom sweatshirt had been Fanzine Frank—and was dressed in shorts made from cut-off jeans, flip flops and a kind of denim smock with brass buttons at the neck and a large pocket over her left breast.

Her skin was pale, and in terms of the general impression she made it was difficult to say whether she was mousy or buxom. Her hair was a pale brown shade hovering somewhere between chestnut and grey, and she wore it in a mannish cut.

Her smile, however, was appealingly bashful and tentatively welcoming. It was also, thankfully, sane.

"I'm sorry to keep you waiting," she said, as she came down the stairs, flip flops flapping. "Frank is right, I was supposed to answer the door when you got here, but when you did get here I suddenly panicked." She chuckled. It was an engaging little sound, self-deprecating and inviting you to savour the general silliness of existence. "I decided I had to rush upstairs and get changed."

Nevada flashed me a quick look, which I understood to mean, *Christ, if this is what she looks like after getting changed, what was she wearing before?*

The woman was now at the foot of the stairs and we stood back to give her room to join us in the hallway. She smiled again, brushed past us and closed the front door, which the apparition had left open and which we'd been loath to close in case we needed a quick escape.

When the door closed we were abruptly in darkness, but not for long. The woman flipped a switch and a light came on.

An ultraviolet light.

Suddenly what had looked like featureless yellow walls in the hallway and on the staircase were revealed to be covered with glowing pictures. These had been done in UV marker pen, or something similar. They were ghostly shades of lavender, blue and red and depicted musicians—punk musicians, of course—in the throes of performance.

Guitar heroes thrashing their instruments, drummers pretending they could drum, singers throttling their microphone stands.

They were somewhat crude, but energetic and vivid and altogether kind of impressive.

Our hostess, now reduced to a disembodied set of Cheshire Cat teeth glowing at us in the darkness, said, "Uh-oh. Wrong switch." There was another click, and normal electric light came on. The walls were featureless yellow again and the smile was reattached to the woman. "Sorry about that," she said. "Would you like a cup of tea?"

17: STOPPED CLOCK

Nevada said, "A cup of tea would be lovely."

"Then let's get you one. Or two, rather," the woman laughed. It was a polite, meaningless social laugh, but nonetheless rather engaging. We fell in behind her as she strode along, flip flops slapping softly on the pink carpet.

"You're Mindy?" I said.

She glanced back over her shoulder and smiled at me. Her teeth, even by normal light, were in very good shape. I don't know why that should have surprised me, but it did.

"Right first time. Mindy Fewston. How did you know? Was it Frank bellowing my name?"

"Afraid so," said Nevada. "For some reason he fled when he saw us. Opened the door and then fled. We're trying hard not to be offended."

"Yes, sorry about that. Please don't be. Offended, that is."

We were now walking through what I supposed you'd call a living room. It was a very large space and looked to me like it had originally been two rooms, which at some point had been turned into one by some ruthless removal of walls. Like most living rooms it had a sofa and armchairs, in this case actually two sofas, but there the resemblance ended.

Because this place was so crammed with wall shelves and freestanding display units that there was hardly room to move, let alone live. The display units were glass cubicles fitted with shelves and LED lights to illuminate what was on those shelves.

The spaces on the wall between shelving units were hung with framed posters, crammed uncomfortably close together. The posters were all for punk gigs, and as far as I could see all featured the Blue Tits. Some of the posters were crudely hand-lettered specimens, others were boringly typographic. But a few were striking examples of photography and design.

What's more, there were records. Not just LPs and 45s, but also CDs and cassettes. Exclusively by the Blue Tits, of course. As we followed Mindy through the room I did my best to scan all these while on the move without actually getting whiplash. I couldn't see the original pressing of the first album anywhere among them.

The recordings on show only made up a very small portion of the stuff in here. On the shelves was a daunting assortment of other items. These included stacks of books, magazines and newspapers, not to mention black leather dog collars bristling with chrome studs and spikes; black leather jackets similarly decorated; denim jackets covered with cloth patches featuring lettering or cartoons; a vast assortment of gleaming safety pins exhibited on black velvet as though they were precious items in a jeweller's window; a huge number of enamelled or tin badges, ditto; several electric guitars and bass guitars, in various states of disrepair but nonetheless displayed as if they were holy relics; baseball caps and T-shirts; boots and shoes; stockings—all black, all fishnet, all torn; some skirts in leather, spandex and latex; and a black bin liner which had been modified to form a kind of garment, and was displayed on a mannequin to prove it.

There were also some very crudely fashioned inflatable sex dolls, which caused me to remember Nevada's unkind comment to Tinkler, and some bondage masks. I wasn't sure if these were part of the punk paraphernalia or were signs of another area of interest. Which in this context would have seemed positively healthy.

In its single-minded devotion to such a narrow range of music it reminded me irresistibly of a small house in Los Angeles I had once visited which had been a virtual shrine to the great forgotten jazz singer Rita Mae Pollini. I was going to make the comparison to Nevada, but I caught myself just in time, realising that it hadn't been Nevada I was with when I'd visited that place.

So I kept quiet, contenting myself with the devout hope that we wouldn't stumble over a dead body here.

Mind you, if there was one it wouldn't be easy to spot it.

"Welcome to the inner sanctum," said Mindy, glancing back over her shoulder and flashing us a smile as she led us single file through this chamber. "Try not to profane the holy of holies by bumping into anything."

Not thus profaning the holy of holies wasn't easy, as we weaved our way through the room on a circuitous route as if trying to throw hounds off our trail. But eventually we made it to the doorway in the far wall. On one side of this stood a female mannequin of slightly alarming anatomical accuracy wearing combat boots and leather trousers but otherwise naked, if that was the word, from the waist up except for a bandolier of ammunition slanting from one shoulder and looping around the bare torso. The mannequin's head had been replaced by a surprisingly realistic-looking watermelon with a big slice out of it, a red gash in the green, like a savage smile. Up close this colourful fruit turned out to be made of wood.

Stationed on the other side was one of the inflatable sex dolls with a plastic apple stuffed in her gaping mouth.

I went through the door with a very tiny but very real sense that these gatekeepers were vetting me. For what, I don't know, because we then emerged into a kitchen—a wonderfully sane, boring and normal kitchen, all gadgets and stainless steel. Perhaps my relief showed on my face because Mindy said, "I don't let Frank put any of his gear in here. He keeps moaning that the collection needs somewhere to expand to. Expand! I think of it as one of those 1950s science fiction B-movies where the rampant protoplasm just keeps on growing and growing and growing."

"Like *The Blob*," said Nevada. I could see she was forcing herself not to utter the date of the film's release and the name of the director.

Mindy gave a delighted little squeal. "Exactly like *The Blob*. But it's not getting its slimy pseudopods into my kitchen. That's where I draw the line. Here and in my shed. That's where the lines are drawn." She nodded towards the window that looked out on the garden.

"You have a shed?" said Nevada. "Is it big?" I sensed some garden-envy coming on.

"It's a decent size, thank goodness. It's so nice to have somewhere that's me. I like to potter around in the garden and hang out in my shed. It's my personal space. There isn't much personal space in there." She pointed back towards the sitting room full of paraphernalia. "So it's nice to have a place of my own. Though just at the minute it isn't my own. Frank is using it." She smiled contentedly. "I'll kick him out soon, though."

"So, Frank is out in the shed?" I wondered if he was deliberately hiding from us.

"Yes. Very rude of him when he knew you were coming to visit."

"He said something about something drying. Is he painting?"

Mindy shook her head. "Not paint. Glue."

Glue. That was the smell I'd detected on him.

"What is he gluing?" said Nevada.

"Action figures? No, that's not the correct term. Action figures have moveable limbs and can be posed, as no doubt Frank would quickly remind me if he was here. But what he's gluing are little figures made of plastic—forgive me, *resin.* They come in kits and they're made in very limited editions in Japan. They're very expensive and Frank buys them, very avidly, as soon as they're released. Then it's off to the shed to glue them together. Oh, what joy. He does indeed paint them, but that's a tribulation for another day." She chuckled.

Nevada said, "And these little figures are of…"

"Members of the Blue Tits, of course. The Blue Tits are proverbially big in Japan. Still. Forty years on. But wait a minute, I'm supposed to be making you tea."

Normally I would have kept my mouth shut and allowed myself to be served tea, but this was an extremely well-equipped kitchen and among its many gleaming appliances was a rather beautiful red and silver Astoria espresso machine crouching on the counter as though impatient to leap into action. So I nodded at this lovely device and said, "I couldn't help noticing…"

Mindy's face immediately fell. "I am *so* sorry. The coffee machine is out of action. What bad luck." Arguing against this being a lie just to thwart me was the fact that she sounded genuinely grief-stricken and also that I now noticed the machine was unplugged and pulled away slightly from the wall. Damn.

"It's broken?" I said. It didn't look broken. Maybe if we just plugged it back in…

"Not *broken*," said Mindy pedantically. "Out of action. I'm modifying it."

"Oh, okay," I said. "Tea is fine, then."

And Nevada whispered in my ear, "You hero."

Mindy began to open cupboards and assemble tea-making essentials. "I'm sure Frank will be finished gluing his figurines soon. Then he'll remember his manners and come in for a chat." She paused in the act of opening an airtight stainless-steel cylinder with *Tea* printed on it. "And if he doesn't, we'll go and turf him out." She grinned happily at the thought.

She made the tea quickly and efficiently and we were soon drinking it. I suppose it was all right if you like that sort of thing. Mindy glanced up at the silent electric clock over the sink and said, "Right. That's long enough. It's time Frank emerged from his den and was sociable. Do you mind bringing your tea out to the garden?"

Far from minding, I was thrilled at the possibility of pouring it discreetly away among the vegetation. So we trooped after Mindy through the back door and out into the sunshine.

It was a big garden with high walls and big trees—on closer inspection, apple and pear trees—rising higher than the walls and providing shade in the garden. There had evidently once been well-defined lawns and flowerbeds, but these didn't appear to have been tended in recent decades and had been allowed to revert to the wild. This wasn't necessarily a bad thing, and the whole place was emphatically alive, teeming with bees, wasps, butterflies, moths and crickets. But any chance of it providing an idyllic environment was somewhat nullified by the Christmas decorations.

These consisted of brightly painted silhouettes, apparently cut from fibreboard using a jigsaw with more enthusiasm than skill to create mostly life-sized versions of Santa, Rudolph the Red-Nosed Reindeer, the three wise men—respectively riding a unicorn, a camel and a kangaroo—and a generic snowman.

This macabre procession stood among the long green grass and wild roses looking more than a little surreal. I noticed that Santa was depicted wearing sunglasses and with a safety pin through his nose, while Rudolph had a mohawk. *Thank heavens for that*, I thought. Or the whole thing might not have been in keeping with the punk rock theme.

The figures were all lavishly garlanded with strings of Christmas lights, now thankfully dormant.

Mindy caught us gaping at this gallimaufry. "Yes," she said. "I'm afraid that lot's been up since Christmas. And not last Christmas, either. I keep nagging Frank to take it down but he always says there are more urgent things to do. Like gluing figurines."

Behind the Christmas cavalcade, deep in the shadowed recesses of the garden, stood the shed we'd heard so much about. Windowless and made of unpainted pine, it was indeed large. On the wall of the shed was a big electrical switch with a painted arrow pointing towards it and the words *TIME FOR FUN!* in big red and green lettering. Christmas colours.

Snaking from the switch was a black cable that disappeared down into the grass and rose again to fasten itself to a grey plastic junction box connected to the strings of lights. The junction box was attached to the hindquarters of the wise man riding a camel. The one with the greatest claim to historical accuracy.

I guessed that when the time-for-fun switch was thrown, the whole mess would light up in a questionably festive fashion.

"The neighbours are getting mightily pissed off," said Mindy, with a certain amount of relish. "I mean, looking out your window and seeing this every day of your life... But Frank can't be persuaded to make it a priority."

Of course, Mindy could have dealt with this Christmas tat herself. But I sensed one of those domestic conflicts that gradually hardened into a stalemate that could last for decades. Poor neighbours.

"Still," said Nevada brightly. "Come December, you're all set."

"Right," said Mindy. "Once a year it's absolutely brilliant. Like the axiomatic stopped clock that's right twice a day. Come on, let's go get Frank." But as she began to wade through the long grass there was the distant sound of electric guitar chords.

The front door.

"Sorry," said Mindy. "I won't be a minute." She trotted back into the house and left us becalmed there in the overgrown garden. I took advantage of her absence to pour my tea out on a thirsty-looking plant. Nevada shook her head.

"Shame about that coffee machine," she said. "Do you think we should intrude on Frank in his shed?"

We looked at the silent wooden building at the shadowy far end of the garden, where glue was apparently being applied to expensive Japanese plastic in the shape of four young women.

We looked at each other.

"Probably best to wait for Mindy," I said.

"Probably best," agreed Nevada.

We only had to listen to the busy insect life for a moment or two before there was the sound of women's voices from inside the house. The back door of the house opened and Mindy came out followed by a fleshy, formidable-looking woman in a smart grey business suit.

Tania Strack.

"Well, I'll let you lot get acquainted," said Mindy. She started back for the house, calling over her shoulder, "Earl Grey, isn't it?"

"Yes, well remembered," said Tania Strack. "Milk, no sugar."

Mindy disappeared indoors and Tania turned to us with an expectant look. I made the introductions and she and Nevada began to chat with guarded cordiality, while I tried to assess the situation.

It was true that I'd wanted to go back to Tania and talk to her again, but I was utterly wrong-footed by her suddenly appearing like this. What's more, I could tell by the glances she was giving me and a trace of tension in her voice that something was up.

As soon as I saw a gap in the conversation I said, "This is quite a coincidence."

Tania looked squarely at me and said, "It isn't a coincidence at all. I told Frank to get in touch with me when you came to visit, so I could come and see you."

For a second I wondered how she knew that I was coming here, then I remembered that it was Tania who had given me Frank's details in the first place, in her Putney penthouse that day. "Okay," I said.

"I want to talk to you."

Nevada shot me a swift look; this didn't sound good.

"Okay," I said again.

"Is it true that you think I'm trying to kill Helene?"

That shut me up good and proper. When I finally thought of something to say, it was, "Who told you that?"

"Monika."

Good old Monika. Everybody's favourite roadie. I was caught somewhere between astonishment and fury. After all, it had been Monika who had been so adamant that Tania was a leading candidate for Helene's would-be killer. I resisted the temptation to point this out.

Instead I said, "Did she also tell you about what's been happening to Helene?"

Tania dismissed this with a curt wave of her hand. "She touched upon it. But to return to my question, do you think I'm trying to kill Helene Hilditch?"

"No," I said. Nevada gave me a surprised look and Tania glared at me with suspicion.

"No?" she said.

"No, I don't particularly think you're trying to kill her. You're merely one in a rich and varied field which includes you, Dylis Lispector, Ophelia Brydent, Saxon Ghost, Bill Bridenstine, Bill Bridenstine's Christian midget girlfriend, Lenny Nettleford, Enrica Morado, devoted friend of Marsha Strickland, the late Marsha Strickland's grieving husband," I nodded at the shed, "Fanzine Frank Fewston,"

I nodded at the house, "Mindy Fewston, the charmingly garrulous Monika herself and a person or persons unknown. Plus, quite possibly any domestic animals owned by any of the above. Except for goldfish. I think we can safely rule out goldfish."

There was silence except for the noise of industrious insects at work in the sunny garden.

"Oh," said Tania.

"I like 'charmingly garrulous'," said Nevada.

"So do I, actually," said Tania. Then, "But you *do* suspect me?"

"Yes," said Nevada. "And not least because Monika was very adamant that we should include you on the list."

Tania looked at me. "Is that true?"

I nodded. "So much so that I'm rather surprised she told you what we were up to."

Tania shook her head. "Oh, she'd been drinking. Monika will say anything when she's been drinking." She paused and seemed to be thinking something through very carefully. "Why would I want to kill Helene?"

"Because she scuppered your political ambitions."

"I see. And how is she supposed to have done that?"

"By threatening to dish the dirt on your colourful behaviour back in the good old Blue Tits days."

Tania nodded sagely. "I see. But assuming that such facts exist and that the whole thing isn't just a tapestry of lies, wouldn't it be remarkably stupid of me to kill Helene and to have the whole thing come out anyway, after she's dead?"

I felt a little thrill. It seemed word had got round in just the way we wanted it to. Full marks to Bong Cha and her ability to work social media.

"Because in that case," said Tania, "any such putative scandalous material would be in the public domain, which is the last place I would want it. And at the same time I would have been involved in a murder that could conceivably, no matter how careful I'd been to cover my tracks, be traced back to me. Wouldn't that be a remarkably stupid thing to do?"

"Yes, it would," said Nevada. "But the fact remains that someone has made a number of spirited and determined attempts to kill Helene."

Tania sighed, lowered her chin and began firmly shaking her head. "Helene has to be the centre of attention. It would be just like her to inflate some tiny accidental incident into a conspiracy. Or indeed, to invent such a conspiracy out of the whole cloth. It would be very much the sort of thing she'd do."

"I don't think there's any chance that's happening here," I said.

She glared at me pugnaciously. "Why not?"

So we told her the story of all the attempts on Helene's life. In detail. It was quite impressive to see her face gradually change. "Christ," she said, finally. "Someone really is trying to kill her."

"Yes."

"But it's not me."

"I know," I said.

She peered at me. "What do you mean, you know? How do you know?"

"Because if you had been trying to kill her you would have stopped as soon as you heard about the dead man's handle."

"The dead man's… Oh, you mean the fact that she's arranged to have her memoirs released if she dies."

"That's right. If you had been the one trying to murder her, you would have stopped at that moment. And, having stopped, there would be no point in you coming here and confronting us about it."

Tania digested this. "I might be deliberately doing so to remove suspicion from myself," she suggested.

"But why even open the question?" said Nevada. "Let sleeping cats lie."

"Sleeping cats?"

"I'm not a dog person."

Tania laughed and shook her head. "All right. So the threat to Helene is real, but I'm not behind it. Where does that leave us?"

"Tania!"

We turned to see that while we'd been talking Fanzine Frank had emerged silently—it was tempting to say stealthily—from his shed and had approached us unnoticed, his skinny white legs smoothly parting the long grass.

18: FANZINE FRANK

"Tania!" cried Fanzine Frank. "I thought I heard your voice." He scurried over to join us.

"I've just been gluing your head on!" he said, then lunged for Tania and kissed her. She did a remarkably convincing job of hiding any distaste she might have felt for that bearded visage grinding against hers. I was beginning to think that Tania really was a loss to politics.

Frank turned to look at us with a happy smile on his face, as if this was our first meeting. I suppose, in a way, it was, so we went through the formality of introductions and he pumped our hands, holding on to Nevada's just a shade too long. If she found his grip as sweaty as I did, it must have been a minor ordeal. But she smiled bravely.

"Now," said Frank, "you were saying on the phone that you're doing some kind of documentary about the girls, the Blue Tits?"

Knowing this was a lie Tania gave me a droll look, but thankfully said nothing. "I'm researching," I said.

"For a potential documentary."

"Well, you've come to the right place," said Frank. "It's hard to imagine what other place you could go, but there's certainly none better than right here."

"I certainly got that impression from your sitting room."

"Yes, not much room to sit, is there? My lady wife is always on at me to slim down the collection. But... you know..."

I did in fact know, but how did he know that I knew? Maybe there was a sign whereby a collector could always spot another collector. Like a scarlet letter, but only visible under the right conditions, like those ultraviolet murals in our host's hallway. Only in this case it could only be seen by a fellow nut.

This seemed like an opportunity to cut to the chase, so I said, "I see you've got their records in there, too."

"Oh, yes, all of them. Multiple copies in multiple formats."

All of them. I felt a bracing small jolt of excitement. How best to approach the next, delicate question?

"I didn't have a chance to have a proper look," I said.

"Well, you must, you must have a proper look."

"Thanks. Because I didn't spot a copy of the first album. I mean the very first one. The first pressing of the first album."

"Oh, the suppressed pressing?" said Frank. "The suppressed pressing..." I wondered if he was about to launch into a tongue twister, perhaps along the lines of being impressed but it was depressing. However, instead he fell profoundly silent.

"Saxon Ghost mentioned that he'd sold you some

copies," I said, to encourage him. I'd decided that I should put this fact into play before he denied ever seeing one, or made a similar assertion. Because that could be just plain embarrassing.

"Did he? Saxon did?"

"Yes, he actually said he sold you several boxes of them."

Frank rather unexpectedly broke into laughter at this disclosure. At the edge of my vision I saw the women tense up a little, in case this signalled that he had finally snapped. But it didn't seem that he had, because he shook his head ruefully as he continued to laugh, and said, "I did, I did. Several boxes. Seven, I think it was."

"Now," I said cautiously, "I know that this record has become very valuable."

"Oh, it has. Yes, that's right, it has."

"Because it's so scarce."

Although, I thought, *it probably doesn't seem quite so scarce to you when you've got seven boxes full of it. Which might enable me to drive the price down a bit.*

I didn't really have to do so, given that it was Erik who was paying, but professional pride meant I had to at least try.

"Oh yes," Frank was bobbing his head eagerly. "Very scarce indeed."

"As it happens, I'm looking for a copy."

"Looking for one?" said Frank.

"Looking to buy one. On behalf of an interested party. We're absolutely willing to pay a fair price."

Frank scratched his beard and pondered. "Well, I suppose we could always do with a bit of extra cash."

"Everyone can," said Nevada brightly, doing her best to help my sales pitch. She looked crestfallen when Frank shrugged.

"But I've already sold those LPs."

"Not all of them," I said. He looked at me in surprise.

I was as sure about this as I had ever been about anything. "You would have saved one for yourself."

He nodded and smiled a sad smile. "I planned to, you know. I was going to save one for myself. In fact, at first, I was going to save a whole box for myself. Then just twenty copies—there were thirty per box. Then twelve. Then ten. But the money I could get for them kept going up and up."

I could see Nevada following this argument, and finding it all too convincing.

"Finally it came down to just one copy," said Frank.

"And you would never have sold that one," I said. I was certain I had the measure of the man.

He shrugged again. The sad smile grew a little less sad. "You're right. I didn't."

I silently sighed with relief. It had been like pulling teeth, but finally he'd admitted he had a copy. Now the question was, how could I convince him to part with it?

"I didn't sell it," said Frank. "I *gave* it to someone."

At the instant he dropped this bombshell, as if she'd been planning her entrance for maximum impact, Mindy came out of the house with a mug in her hand. "Oh, Mindy," said Frank, his face suddenly brightening. It was as if he was surprised to see her, but was glad she'd turned up.

Mindy gave the mug to Tania, who thanked her. Steam was rising from it, which was a little startling. Given the length of time Mindy had been gone it seemed more likely that it would have had a layer of ice on it.

"I'm so sorry it took so long," she said. "I went in and I made the tea and then I opened a new bottle of milk and did that thing where you go to pour it and nothing comes out because it's turned into a solid mass. Yuck. So I ran out to the shop and got some more. And then I had to make the tea again. I'm sorry it took so long."

"You shouldn't have gone to all that trouble," said Tania, blowing on the tea.

"It was no problem."

"I could have had it without milk."

"Now you tell me," said Mindy, rolling her eyes and laughing. Frank joined in, although I could tell his heart wasn't in it. Maybe Mindy could, too, because she said, "What's up, love?"

"You know the Tits' first album?" I found this abbreviation of the band's name immediately distasteful and I quickly glanced over at Tania, but of course she was far too cool a customer to give anything away.

"Yes, dear."

"No, I mean the first first one. The rare one."

"Oh, that one," said Mindy, in such a way that I was far from convinced that she did actually know it, as opposed to saying whatever was easiest at the moment to just shut him up. I could sympathise.

"Well, this gentleman wants to buy a copy."

"Well, then sell him one."

"But I don't have any," said Frank with a return of the richly whining note which he had used to such effect earlier. I imagined he used it a lot. "I got rid of the last one. I'm sure."

"You've been sure about things before, and it's turned out you were wrong. Go and have a look."

I could see this didn't go over well with Frank. In fact I saw him beginning to get stubborn and dig in his heels like a moody child. But Mindy adroitly averted this by saying, "Go on, I'll come in with you and help you look."

She took Frank's hand and his sullen look was replaced by a rather endearing smile. Or at least it would have been endearing if it hadn't been buried in a nest of matted hair. Mindy led him by the hand back towards the house. "Sorry about this," she called to us. "We won't be long. You can sit in those chairs."

Both these statements struck me as obvious falsehoods. Given the nature of Frank and his collection, the idea of getting anything done promptly was downright laughable. And as for the chairs we'd been invited to sit in, they simply didn't exist.

Or at least, that's what I thought at first. Then I realised there actually was a stack of garden chairs, made of green plastic, half obscured by a vast, unruly rose bush and doing a remarkably effective job of blending in with it.

I wrestled three chairs off the stack—four actually, but the top one was covered with a geological layer of bird droppings, so I put that to one side. I set the chairs in a convivial little grouping and we all sat down. Tania was still working on her hard-won mug of tea but Nevada had finished hers and my own was no doubt by now nourishing the root system of some lucky flora.

"At least he seems eager to sell you the record," said Nevada in a confidential tone, leaning over towards me. "If he can find it."

"Yes," I said. "Frank seems fond of money." There had certainly been a note of happy nostalgia in his voice when he'd talked about how the price had just kept going up and up. "Which is a relief because I thought it was only Japanese resin figures."

"Well, they certainly need plenty of cash to fund this place. I don't mean just the house and that state-of-the art kitchen."

"But also all of Frank's toys." Frank struck me as a man who would never deny himself a toy.

"Oh, they're not hurting for money," said Tania quietly. We looked at her. She was watching us over the rim of her mug as she sipped. "Frank is a lot brighter than he looks."

"Without wishing to be offensive," I said, "that leaves a lot of scope for being brighter."

Tania snorted into her tea. "He's actually got a first class honours degree from Imperial College. In electrical engineering or electronic engineering or something. He's had highly paid jobs ever since he left uni and now he's retired on a whacking great final salary pension scheme. On top of which he still does consultancy work and gets paid top dollar for it."

I wondered if he wore the hot pants when he did his consultancy work.

"A first class honours degree?" said Nevada with a hint of wonder in her voice.

"Mindy's got a double first," said Tania. "They met at uni."

There was a pause now, but not an awkward one since we'd got most of the awkwardness, and indeed the unequivocal hostility, out of the way earlier. Nevada broke the silence by saying, "Is that a Reiss suit?"

Tania seemed pleased by this question. "Yes, it is. Well spotted."

"It's stunning. Classic but stylish."

"Thank you."

"You should take a look at Ted Baker. And The Fold, London."

Tania stared at her for a moment and then, without saying anything, set aside her mug and dug out her phone. Normally I would have taken this as the height of bad manners, but with Tania Strack I was beginning to regard it as a good sign. "Ted Baker I know, but that other was The... what, London?"

"Fold." Nevada looked at me and winked. Because Tania was now riveted to her screen, evidently liking what she saw. She studied the phone for what felt like an awfully long time. Finally she lowered it, saying, "Very nice. I'll have a proper look later." I wondered how long a proper look would entail. "Thank you for the tip."

"I mostly deal in vintage clothing," said Nevada, "but I can also help with contemporary pieces." She gave Tania her business card.

"Thank you," said Tania, putting it away carefully. "I may give you a buzz."

"I hope you do."

These preliminaries concluded, Tania evidently felt she could now ask us personal questions. "You guys have been together a long time?"

"Yes, mm-hm, quite a while."

She favoured me with a rather beady gaze. "So, are you actually searching for this record you're harassing Frank about, or was that a load of hokum, just a cover story for you trying to find Helene's assailant?"

"I'm actually searching for the record."

"That's good, because if it was the other, god knows how many laws you'd be breaking."

Probably none, I thought. But I said, "I was also telling the truth when I said we have a firm buyer."

"That's not all you're interested in, though, is it?"

"No, true. We're hoping in the course of searching for the record to flush out the would-be killer. It gives us a perfect cover story for getting close to the suspects, or who might be able to point us towards suspects."

"People like me and Frank," said Tania.

"Well, you're no longer in the first category but you're still definitely in the second."

Tania didn't take the hint implied by this. Instead she said, "What happens if you do flush out the killer?"

I said, "We'll go to the police," while at exactly the same moment Nevada said, "We'll cross that bridge when we come to it."

Tania laughed. "And you actually think Frank might be the culprit?"

"I don't know," I said. "I have an open mind. But I'll tell you one thing: I don't believe his story."

Tania folded her arms and looked at me sternly, as though I was giving evidence to a select committee, and I was sounding dodgy. "Which story is that?"

"About having sold the last copy of that extremely rare record."

Nevada corrected me. "Having given it away."

"Yes," I said. "That was even less plausible, wasn't it?"

"Why?" said Tania. But this sounded less like a cross-examination and more like she was really interested. So I told her.

"Because he's an anorak, a fanatic, a collector."

"Does it take one to know one?" said Tania with a note of sweet malice. Nevada shot her an annoyed look, but it didn't bother me.

"Perhaps it does. But either way, I'm not wrong. He's not the sort of person to surrender the last copy of a valuable collector's item, especially when it's pretty much the crowning glory of that entire obsessive assemblage in there."

"I'm afraid you're wrong about that," said Tania. "His crowning glory and most prized possession would never be an LP."

How wrong you are, I thought. But I said politely, "What would it be then?"

"Oh, a used pair of knickers, I should think. Underpants would be where it's at. And the more stained and filthy, the better." She laughed at the shocked expressions on our faces. It was a pity Tinkler wasn't here, because he would have been delighted with the turn the discussion had taken. "Providing it was one of *our* pairs of knickers."

"One of the Blue Tits'?"

"Oh, yes." Tania leaned back in her chair, the green plastic bending dangerously with her weight. "You see, I agree with most of what you said. Obviously you are right in your analysis of Frank as a compulsive and fanatical collector. He is exactly the sort of person who has to have it all, who has to collect the set. So you were entirely correct when you said he would never part with such a cherished and sought-after trophy. Never," she repeated, smiling broadly, "except in one very particular set of circumstances." She fell silent, savouring the drama of the situation.

I decided to allow her her little moment. But before I could reply, Nevada said, "Okay, we'll bite. What set of circumstances?"

"If one of the girls asked him for it. If one of *us* asked him for it."

Nevada and I looked at each other. I hadn't considered this. But now Tania had said it, it had the ring of truth. One obsession trumping another.

Tania was nodding vigorously, as if agreeing with herself. "If one of us so much as batted our eyelashes, we could get him to do anything we wanted. That's the way it always was. And for better or worse, the way it still is. We've always taken advantage of him shamelessly. Some of us more than others. Did you see all those guitars in there? And the electric basses?"

"Yes. It's an impressive selection."

"Every time we wanted a new instrument we just sold the old one to Frank for his museum. For more than we'd originally paid for it, even if we'd completely trashed it. It was rather cruel."

"You think?" I said.

She spread her hands in a helpless gesture. "What were we supposed to do? I suppose you could call it abuse of power, because we certainly had power over him. But we hadn't asked for him to become fixated on us. What exactly is the etiquette in a situation like that? And, if we exploited him, he certainly exploited us, too. He was definitely getting full value for his money, in terms of the creepy sexual thrills."

"I don't suppose," said Nevada, "that any of you actually ever…" she made a gesture in the air with her hand that was somehow both meaningless and entirely meaningful.

"Sleep with him?" said Tania. "Certainly not."

"None of you?"

"None of us." Tania paused and added, "Well, not in reality, that is."

Nevada and I looked at each other, the possible implications of this statement whirling through our minds. Then Nevada turned to Tania. "What exactly do you mean?" she said. "We're utterly agog and we absolutely have to know."

Tania laughed. "What I mean is that he would get Mindy to dress up like us and he slept with *her*."

"Dress up like you?"

"Well, dress up and do her hair and make-up and all the rest of it."

"Like all of you?"

"Well, not at once," said Tania. "One at a time. The various members of the band. In rotation. In their marital bed."

Nevada thought about this for a moment, and then said, "*Eeeeeeyuch.*"

"I think you speak for us all," I said. Though for me this revelation wasn't in itself so shocking as the discovery that the man with all that facial hair had a sex life.

Tania laughed. "To each his own, I say."

"And what does Mindy think about all this?" said Nevada.

"Why don't you ask her when she comes back?"

"Ask her?"

"Oh, sure," said Tania. "They're entirely open about their sex life and happy to discuss it."

"Christ," said Nevada. "Just when I thought it couldn't possibly get any worse."

"So, now perhaps it seems a little less reprehensible, the way that all of us always used to take advantage of him so shamelessly?"

I wasn't sure that it did. But then something seemed to occur to Tania. "Helene in particular, though," she said. "Helene really rode roughshod over Frank." She looked at us suddenly, struck by another thought. "How do you know Helene, anyway?"

"We're old friends of her new boyfriend," said Nevada.

"What's-his-name, the guitarist from Valerian?"

"That's right, Erik Make Loud."

"Ridiculous name," said Tania.

"What exactly is a tongue strap, again?" said Nevada.

"All right, all right, I'll give you that. Ridiculous names do rather go with the territory, I suppose. So, anyway, how long have you known Helene?"

"Not long at all," I said.

"All right then. So, here is what you need to know. Setting aside my quite justified personal animus and trying to look at things objectively, she is a genuinely dreadful person. I want you to know that." She seemed eager for us to believe this. I sensed many old grudges at work here, and some new ones, too.

"Why do you say that?" said Nevada.

"Because Helene rides roughshod over everyone in her life. It should be no surprise to anyone that someone wants to kill her. In fact, the really surprising thing is that it isn't the other way around."

"What do you mean?"

"That she isn't the murderer instead of the murder victim. Helene is quite capable of killing someone. She is altogether a nasty piece of work and, I might add, quite dangerous."

Tania leaned over to one side with considerable effort, the plastic chair bending with her, and carefully set her mug on the ground. Then, as if this signalled a sudden change of tone, she said, "Admittedly she was a lot of fun when we were in the band. We were great friends back then."

The door of the house opened and Mindy stepped out. "You got the chairs sorted. Good." She went to the rosebush, where the two remaining chairs were standing, one covered in bird shit. Not surprisingly it was the other one she dragged over to join our little group.

"How's the search going?" I said. I had begun to feel the tension of waiting, like a tight knot in my stomach. I tried to keep it from showing in my voice.

Mindy shook her head. "It doesn't look good, I'm afraid. Usually Frank is like the squirrel who's forgotten where he buried his nuts, but in this case it seems he's right. It looks like the last copy really is gone. Frank is just tidying up now. He pulled the place apart looking for it. We had a really good root around, but it just isn't there."

I didn't say anything. I didn't know what to say. It's never much fun to be thwarted—not that this was anything new. As a record hunter I'd had countless prizes slip from my grasp. On the other hand, I'd also stumbled on many unexpected treasures. I tried to dwell on these now instead of brooding, or going into the house to give a good kicking to Frank, whom I thoroughly blamed for this whole debacle. After all, he'd had seven boxes of the damned thing.

Perhaps to relieve the uncomfortable silence, Tania piped up cheerily, "I've been telling our friends about the costume parade."

"The costume parade?" said Nevada. "Oh, you mean…"

"Oh, that," said Mindy, with a good-natured sigh.

Nevada lowered her voice and leaned in closer to Mindy. "Do you actually…?"

"Dress up? In bed? For Frank? Oh yes."

"But isn't it a bit…"

"Oh, I don't mind. Why should I mind?"

"But I mean, it's a bit weird," said Nevada.

"Why is it weird?" said Mindy. She sounded genuinely puzzled.

"Well, for a start, here we are sitting with Tania, and presumably you dress up like Tania…"

"Yup, I do that," said Mindy.

"In my punk rock heyday," said Tania. "Right?"

"Yeah, of course."

"Not in my grey wool blend checked blazer and trousers."

"No, I'm afraid that just wouldn't do it," said Mindy. She and Tania shared a little laugh at the preposterousness of this suggestion and then Mindy turned to Nevada, who was following the proceedings with fascination.

"I dress up like all of the Blue Tits," said Mindy. "But not just them. I also do policewomen, nuns, nurses, cowgirls…"

"Hence the term 'costume parade'," added Tania unnecessarily.

"And it really doesn't bother you?" said Nevada.

Mindy chuckled. "Why should it bother me?" she said. "It's good fun. And even if it wasn't fun, I'd still do it. I mean, I just want Frank to be happy. I know it sounds drippy, and inane and stupid, but I'd like *everyone* to be happy. What the hell? The world wouldn't be such a mess if people were just happy."

Amen to that, I thought.

Frank emerged from the house clutching a can of energy drink. He loped over to join us, realised there wasn't a chair for him, detoured to the rosebush and collected the last remaining one. Its long history as an avian toilet didn't seem to deter him. He dragged it over, plonked it down beside Mindy's and promptly sat down on it, slurping at his drink.

"So, no record?" I said.

"Doesn't look like it," said Frank, avoiding my gaze. "Doesn't look like it at all, I'm afraid."

"You really did get rid of the last copy."

"So it would seem."

"And you gave it away?" I said.

"That's right."

"Who did you give it to?"

"Well," said Frank, meditatively sucking the spillage of the energy drink out of his beard, "you see, one of the girls really wanted a copy."

"One of the girls?" I said. Tania was giving me a look of triumph. "One of the girls in the band?"

"That's right," said Frank, taking a long swig of his drink.

"Who?" I said. "Which one?"

"Ophelia."

Mindy had been following this exchange with a concerned look on her face. Now she turned to me. "Do you think you might be able to buy it from her?"

"I might think that," I said. "But Ophelia has disappeared. Nobody knows where she is."

"I do," said Tania.

19: MUTANT CATS

The revelation about Ophelia had made the whole trip worthwhile. Nevertheless, plunging down the rabbit hole that was the world of Fanzine Frank Fewston had left Nevada and I decidedly rather drained.

So, feeling we owed ourselves a treat, we had lunch at a café called the Chalk Hills Bakery in Reigate, as recommended by Nevada's mum, and then went on a charity shop binge in Ashtead and Banstead.

"I can never remember," said Nevada, "is it a binge or a spree?"

"It's a spree until you find you can't stop doing it, and then it becomes a binge."

"Binge it is."

There was disappointingly little in the way of interesting vinyl in these towns, but Nevada managed to fill three large carrier bags, stuffing them with what she'd taken to calling schmata. This officially meant cheap, old or unfashionable rags, but when Nevada used the expression, it meant anything but. She was very pleased with her finds, and hummed a happy tuneless little tune all the way on our drive back, sitting beside me in Kind of Red.

I felt a pleasant sense of homecoming as we turned off Roehampton Lane onto Clarence Lane and drove past the high-rise towers of the Alton Estate, modernist slabs poised on their dainty little stilt-like legs. Then we were on Abbey Avenue, and then home again.

Somewhat to our surprise, there was no flurrying rush of felines to greet us as we approached the front door. Usually the sound of us opening the gate, or rattling our keys, would have occasioned an eruption of whiskery welcome through the cat flap.

We looked at each other. "I hope everything's all right," said Nevada.

"I'm sure Agatha would have let us know if anything…" I started to say.

Then a voice called, "Through here."

We walked into the living room to find our cat-sitter not sitting, but lying flat on her back on the sofa, with Turk curled on her feet and Fanny lying on her chest. Agatha's head was propped comfortably on a couple of cushions and she was reading a Black Lizard paperback of *Pick-Up* by Charles Willeford.

She lowered the book onto Fanny's back—Fanny didn't seem to mind—and said, "Apologies for not getting up, but obviously I can't move until the cats do."

"Obviously," said Nevada.

"Heaven knows what would have happened if you

guys hadn't turned up."

"We probably would have found a skeleton on the sofa, bones picked clean by a mysterious force of nature. For which read 'hungry cats'."

Agatha rubbed Fanny behind the ear and said, "You wouldn't pick your Aunty Agatha's bones clean, would you, Fanny? Would you, Turk? No you wouldn't." Fanny purred an unconvincing demurral. Turk opted for a diplomatic but noncommittal silence.

"Do you think you can drink a glass of wine while lying flat on your back like that?"

"I'm certainly willing to try."

"Okay," said Nevada. "Wine coming up."

"It's a tough life," said Agatha from her prone position.

I sat on the armchair next to the sofa. "Thank you for looking after the little wrongdoers."

"Any time."

"But we thought you were only staying until this morning."

"That was the plan. But then I had a job fall through and finished up earlier than expected, so I thought I'd come back here and make sure these two hadn't starved to death since breakfast. And then I decided to lurk in wait until you came back and hit you up for a free meal."

"Sounds like a plan," I said.

"That's what I thought."

Nevada came back from the kitchen with three glasses of white wine. "This is the Marcel Deiss Alsace I was telling you about." She handed one glass to me and one to Agatha. "It is fucking dynamite, if you will pardon the unladylike expression."

"Ain't no ladies here," said Agatha, and proceeded to try and sip the wine while remaining horizontal and otherwise motionless, so as not to disturb her valuable cargo of cats. This was difficult to achieve without pouring a biodynamic blend of Gewurztraminer, Pinot Gris, Riesling and Pinot Blanc into her left ear, but she was a resourceful woman and she managed it.

"Our home invader here thinks she can score a free meal," I said.

"Well, you better get cooking then," said Nevada.

"Oh, let him drink his wine first," said Agatha.

Nevada smiled at me. "I suppose we have to allow him that."

Agatha set her glass on the floor and turned her head so she could look at me. Fanny shifted on her chest, not approving of even this small movement. "So, have you found that record yet?"

"Sort of."

"And what does that mean?"

"We've been told about someone who definitely has a copy."

"Definitely definitely or maybe definitely?"

"About as definitely as you can get with these jokers," I said. "The nice thing is that the person who owns it is also the person we were looking for."

"Oh, Ophelia something," said Agatha.

"That's right."

"I thought she was supposed to have vanished off the face of the earth."

"Basically she had," I said.

"She's deliberately dropped out of sight," said Nevada. "She doesn't want anyone to know what happened to her or where she is."

"Why?"

"Well, she's had rather a rough time of it," said Nevada.

This was an understatement. Tania had given us the selected highlights of Ophelia Brydent's life since her golden days as Feel Up Rodent. "We were all pretty wild," she'd said. "But Ophelia never knew where to draw the line. I doubt she even knew there was a line. We all boozed." Then she'd given us her most frank and candid look. "We all dabbled in drugs. But Ophelia didn't just dabble. She got seriously into the stuff. Heroin, specifically. And that was that."

Apparently heroin addiction had swallowed years of Ophelia's life. Decades. She had lost everything—home, friends, family, all her money, her health—and spiralled inexorably downwards.

"But when she hit bottom she began to come up again," Tania had told us. "She's been slowly climbing out of the hole she dug for herself and I've been doing everything I can to help." So she had been subsidising Ophelia in her period of recovery and had found a place for her to stay.

"She sounds like a good friend," said Agatha, lying on our sofa covered with cats. "Remind me, which one is Tania again?"

"The Tory in the tower," said Nevada helpfully.

"Oh right, got you. Sorry, I'm having trouble keeping track of the Tits. Normally there's only two of them."

Somehow Agatha abbreviating the name of the band didn't bother me the way it had when Fanzine Frank had done it.

"She told us something else about Ophelia, though," I said.

Agatha looked at me with alert interest, moving her head only fractionally so as not to dislodge the indolent Fanny. "What?"

"Oh, god, yes," said Nevada.

"What?" repeated Clean Head.

I said, "She told us who got Ophelia on heroin in the first place."

"Who?"

"Guess."

Agatha paused and considered for a moment and then said, "Helene."

"Right first time."

"Jesus. So it wouldn't be surprising if…"

"If Ophelia was nursing a grudge against Helene," said Nevada.

"And she wanted to get even," I said.

Agatha started to nod and then thought better of it under Fanny's stern gaze. "In other words, a motive for wanting to kill Helene."

"Right again."

"Jesus, is there anyone who *doesn't* have a motive to kill this woman?"

"Not that we've found yet," I said.

"But, on a positive note," said Nevada, "we haven't finished looking."

"One other thing," I said. "Helene and Erik were almost killed by someone who spiked their coke with Fentanyl."

"And who would know better where to score Fentanyl..." said Agatha.

"Than a regular drug user like Ophelia. Right."

There was a moment of silence and then Agatha said, "So, Tania's the woman with the phone-in programme, right?"

"Right-wing radio rabble-rouser," said Nevada. "Correct. I quite like her, though. I might sell her some clothes."

"You'd sell clothes to your worst enemy," said Agatha. "If they coughed up enough money."

"That's true."

"So when do you go to see Ophelia, reformed junkie and potential murderer, to try and get the record?"

"We're waiting for Tania to get in touch with her and find out if she's willing to speak to us," said Nevada.

"So it could still all fall through?"

"That's right," I said. "Think positive."

Both the women laughed, and the vibrations of mirth through Agatha's body proved too much for the cats, who both leapt off her. "Oh, they're off," she said. "Just as well. I was going to need the loo at some point. And would you mind if I took a bath?"

"Be our guest. Or rather, continue to be our guest."

"Thanks. I'm feeling a bit grubby. It got pretty hot in the cab today."

"I thought you had air conditioning."

"I had it off most of the time. Trying to save the planet."

"In that case you deserve a clean towel. There's one in the hamper in the spare room."

"Thanks."

She went out. Nevada and I sipped our wine. Nevada was watching me closely. "So, what do you think? Of the wine, I mean."

I considered carefully. "A fantastic collection of flavours."

"Yes?"

"It started out like candied pear and now it's headed in the general direction of violets and honey."

"Yes!" She came over and kissed me. "I couldn't have put it better myself."

Agatha must have overheard our tasting notes because she came padding back in, wearing nothing but a fluffy white towel tucked tightly under her arms. "I forgot my wine," she said.

"Well, we can't have that."

I moved to pick up her glass from the floor for her, but she performed a graceful swoop, sinking on her knees to retrieve it, and then rising again. It was an impressive move, entirely achieved without disturbing her towel. I'd forgotten about all the yoga Agatha did.

She sampled a little more of the wine.

"So, what do you think?" said Nevada eagerly.

"I could express my approval, but it wouldn't be very ladylike."

"Fucking dynamite, isn't it?"

"Yes indeed."

The women stood there chatting and sipping their wine, one with her towel in grave danger of falling from her lithe, naked frame, and just then the doorbell rang.

"Now, who could that possibly be?" I said.

I opened the door. Sure enough, it was Tinkler.

"I thought I'd drop by and pick up the car," he said. "Is this a good time?"

"Only if your definition of good encompasses Clean Head taking off all her clothes."

"Ha! Nice try. Like that's going to happen agai— Oh my sweet lord."

"Hello, Tinkler," said Agatha. She finished her wine, set the glass on the table and then sashayed away down the hall. Tinkler stared after her, eyes straining to reach into the x-ray spectrum far enough to penetrate a single layer of fluffy towel.

As she disappeared behind the bathroom door Tinkler made a small moaning sound and then turned back to stare imploringly at me and Nevada. "Why isn't my house full of gorgeous women, some of them naked?"

Nevada shook her head and made *tutting* noises. "You can't have a beautiful cat-sitter unless you have some beautiful cats."

Tinkler subsided into a chair. "I wouldn't mind getting some cats. The only thing that puts me off is this business of having to continually feed them. Now, if they were capable of feeding *me*, that would be a different matter. And surely with genome editing, that's just around the corner?"

"You don't get enough exercise as it is," said Nevada. "If you had mutant cat slaves to wait on you it would finish you off."

"Typical lack of vision."

"How about some wine?" said Nevada. "We've polished off the top bottle but you're just in time to join us for second best."

"Story of my life," said Tinkler.

Nevada poured the wine. "Now why don't you go in the kitchen and see if you can be of assistance to the chef?"

"How likely is that?"

"Well, at least it will take your mind off the splashing noises from the bathroom and the thoughts of water droplets gleaming on Agatha's taut, nubile bod." There were indeed some splashing noises coming from the bathroom.

Tinkler got up and said, "You take joy in causing me anguish, don't you?"

"It's low on my list of joys, but it's there."

In the kitchen I began to get ingredients out of the fridge—a lemon, some green beans, some chestnut mushrooms, a wedge of Parmesan—while I brought Tinkler up to speed on the developments of the day.

"I like the sound of that costume parade," he said. "Is this Mindy a looker?"

"Not up to your high standards," I said.

"Speaking of which, you'll never guess who's now constantly getting in touch with me. I'll give you a clue. It's Opal. I think she's missed me. I think she's obsessed with me. I may well have a stalker. It will be my first. Anyway, I am beginning to believe it's entirely possible that she will be mine, mine, mine once more."

"That must be why you're not showing any interest in other women."

We paused and listened to the boiler on the wall—a boiler I would always regard fondly now—responding to Agatha's demands for more hot bathwater.

"Oh well," said Tinkler. "I'm still a player. I have to keep multiple honeys on the string. And speaking of honeys, did you notice how Persephone gave me the good stuff while you and what's-her-name only got the standard stuff despite what's-her-name being her daughter?"

I got the bag of basil leaves out of the bowl by the window where we keep it, basil not liking refrigeration. "To me that's a feature not a bug. You can keep the drugged stuff."

"*Au contraire*, my friend. I shall *share* the drugged stuff. In fact I've got it with me. In fact we can all have some tonight."

I sighed, "Do we have to?" I selected a generous number of small plum tomatoes which we kept in a bowl by the basil for the same reason, and also because they seemed like good friends and natural partners.

"You may be opposed to the use of recreational drugs, old buddy, but I suspect the gals will leap at the chance. What on earth might you be about to do with all those tasty-looking ingredients?"

I picked up the conical chrome grater, the lemon squeezer and the large ceramic mixing bowl and moved them to the food prep area—the corner of the counter where the cats were theoretically forbidden to roam, which simply meant they waited until we went out before shamelessly gambolling there.

"Grate the lemon zest…" I said, beginning to do just that.

"I love that word. So zesty."

"Squeeze out the juice. Add an equal or greater amount of olive oil." I got the extra virgin Sicilian out of the cupboard. Perhaps it was a romantic illusion but I thought it had a citrus hint, which went well with the lemon juice. I glugged it into the bowl, the deep green oil curling attractively with the pale yellow juice. "Grate in the Parmesan, add torn basil, steamed fine green beans, sliced mushrooms, add half the zest, add spaghetti cooked al dente, toss together with more Parmesan, lemon zest and sliced plum tomatoes and serve."

"You make it sound so simple. Although I'm sure it would prove not only difficult but potentially dangerous for anyone but a trained professional like yourself to prepare."

Tinkler knew very well I wasn't a trained professional. "It really is simple," I said. "You should try making it."

"What, and deprive that food delivery app with the cute little cartoon kangaroo of its chance to exploit its employees? Forgive me, independent contractors."

I refilled Tinkler's wine glass, not just to shut him up, and got on with making supper. "So you now have to wait for word from Tania," he said. "About whether the mysterious Ophelia is going to grant you an interview."

"How do you know that?"

"Nevada told her mum and her mum told me."

"Why were you talking to Nevada's mum, Tinkler?"

"Checking if she did a bulk discount on the honey for large orders. The *special* honey." He wagged his eyebrows.

"Well, as it happens that's right. We're going to have to wait for Tania to get back to us. But while we're waiting there are other people we need to look into."

"Like who?"

I hesitated for a moment, because I didn't even like to say the name. "Bill Bridenstine for a start."

"Christ, you are a glutton for punishment, aren't you?"

"It's not him we want to talk to."

"I hope not. I doubt your jugular vein could stand the strain."

"But he has this girlfriend—"

"Shit, why is it that everyone has a girlfriend except me? Even psychopathic alcoholic losers of ex-television personalities."

"When your rant is over," I said, "I was going to say that we're considering the possibility that she could be behind the attempts to kill Helene. So perhaps you can stop feeling envious now."

"Oh, I don't know," said Tinkler. "I'd happily date a psychopathic killer if she had compensating features. Is she a looker?"

"She's a Christian midget."

"I still haven't entirely lost interest. But how are you going to go about determining if she's the culprit?"

"I don't know yet. I don't even know her full name or where to find her."

"Ah, the true professional at work. You never disappoint."

"But while we're finding out those things, there is one other lead to chase up. The fourth and final Blue Tit."

"Oh yeah. Dildo Something. Dildo Inspector?"

"That's right," I said. "Dylis Lispector. It turns out she lives just this side of Hammersmith Bridge."

"Well, Jesus, she could hardly be closer. Why haven't you spoken to her already?"

"Because I got in touch and it turns out she's in New Zealand."

"Oh. I see your problem. That is, indeed, outside the London travel zone."

"But she just got back today," I said.

"Excellent," said Tinkler. "So the game is afoot." He rubbed his hands. "Now, what's for dessert? It had better go with hashish honey or I'm going to give you a really shitty review on TripAdvisor."

20: JET LAG

Dylis Lispector lived in one of the side streets off Castelnau just before the bridge. Nevada and I could have caught the bus there, but we opted to walk because that meant Nevada could ravage all the charity shops in Barnes en route and also feed her Marcel Deiss addiction by picking up another bottle or two at Lea and Sandeman.

"The only problem with this plan," said Nevada, "is that unless I'm phenomenally unlucky I'm going to end up carrying a load of purchases with me. Is it unprofessional of us to turn up at Dylis's place dragging a load of shopping? Even if it transpires that she is a depraved killer, one wants to make a good first impression."

"Bring along a posh and stylish bag to put everything in," I suggested.

"Posh, stylish and capacious," said Nevada. "Excellent idea."

It might have been an excellent idea, but it involved an extra fifteen minutes waiting while she went through her bag collection looking for something suitable. But finally we set off. It was another dazzling spring day and, once we'd crossed the main road and left the traffic behind, it was positively idyllic. And we were able to get over both the level crossings on Vine Road without having to wait for any trains to pass—a near miraculous occurrence.

"You see," said Nevada. "We've made up for all that time lost in bag selection. So you can stop fretting now."

This was true. As it happened we were able to trawl our favourite shops in a leisurely fashion—though we were lucky it was too early in the week for Olympic Studios Records to be open, otherwise that would have put a serious dent in our schedule.

We ended up at the Red Lion with time to spare and set off walking north on Castelnau. With Hammersmith Bridge closed, a massive volume of vehicles had been forced to find other ways to cross the river, and it was blissfully peaceful. Soon enough the bridge itself was in sight, looking far too well built and Victorian to really be in need of any serious repair. Perhaps it was all merely a massive and very cheeky traffic-calming measure. The temptation to stroll onto the bridge and just stand there watching the big khaki river go by was considerable.

"We'll walk across it and go into Hammersmith afterwards," said Nevada.

This sounded like a fine idea.

It was a pity it was never going to happen.

* * *

The nearer you got to the Thames, the more elite the properties in this neighbourhood became, peaking in Riverview Gardens, the street where Dylis lived. It was lined with big handsome buildings made of red brick with thin layers of white brick, like a cinnamon cake with vanilla filling. Moving down the road, modern buildings gave way to older Edwardian ones, all built in keeping with the same design scheme—all big, and all no doubt attached to a multi-million price tag.

"Jesus," said Nevada. "How did a punk rock— What did she play?"

"Bass."

"How did a punk rock bass player end up with a house here?"

It was a very good question. "I guess she's like Tania. She was born at the right time and she invested wisely."

"Very wisely."

Dylis's building was one of the older ones, with a double front door and elegant wrought-iron balconies. It was the sort of place where you check your reflection in the window before ringing the bell.

Nevada caught me doing this. "You look fine," she said and gave me a kiss. "Best foot forward." I pushed the button with Dylis's name beside it. For a long moment nothing happened, then there was a buzzing noise and the door clicked open. We entered a sunlit entry space with a floor made of a mosaic of small red and white tiles. We didn't have long to admire it because a door opened to our left and a rather croaky voice called, "Come in."

We hastened to where a woman stood waiting. She was deeply tanned with silver hair tied back in a ponytail. She wore a long, rather Arabic-looking blue and white striped dressing gown over leopard skin-print leggings and a T-shirt the colour of milky tea that was cropped to show a band of tanned, flat midriff. Her feet were bare. Her body looked very toned and fit. Her face looked haggard and exhausted.

"Please," she croaked, waving her hand for us to follow her. We went through a white door set with panels of glass in art nouveau shapes. While we'd been standing outside the house I hadn't been able to tell how many flats this building was divided into, or what size they were. The answers were: four, and large. Very large. It appeared that Dylis inhabited this entire floor of the building except for the small entrance hall.

We were in a sunlit sitting room with very high ceilings and gleaming wooden floors, big and comfortable-looking dove-grey chairs and sofas, piles of books and magazines and a bright yellow bicycle leaning against the wall just inside the door. On the far side of the room was a baby grand piano, shiny and black, looking gleaming and pampered. Hanging on the wall above it, an electric bass guitar.

This being displayed in a position of such prominence suggested that Dylis was very proud of her musical past. The fact that it was hanging on the wall, high and out of reach, suggested that she had no plans to pick it up again any time soon.

She moved across the room slowly, intermittently hanging onto furniture like an unsteady drunk, and sat down on the piano stool facing us.

"Sorry about the voice," she croaked, "and for taking a while to buzz you in."

"No, it's fine. We—"

"And for looking such a mess."

"You look—"

"And for still being in my pyjamas."

"No, don't worry—"

"Where's my juice?"

This last was clearly a rhetorical question, so we remained tactfully silent while Dylis looked around the room with a puzzled expression, searching for her juice. Then she turned back to us. "Sorry," she said. "I just got back from New Zealand yesterday and I haven't quite landed yet, if you know what I mean."

"It's a long flight," I said.

"Have you been?" There was a sudden spark of interest in her voice.

"No, but I can imagine."

"You can't imagine," said Dylis firmly. "You *can't* imagine. I fly over there twice a year, god help me. I mean, it's lovely. It's paradise on earth, and I love it. But it is the other end of the planet. Quite literally the other end. Of the planet. And I am flying there… twice a year…"

"Do you go on business?" said Nevada.

"On *family* business." She laughed a croaky little laugh at her own joke. "So it's actually pleasure. My son moved there first and when we went to visit him my daughter was so impressed with his lifestyle that she had to move there, too. But they've always been like that. Competitive. There was no way Stephanie was going to let him have a nicer house in a nicer country than she did. So basically it now means I have to—well, I don't have to, but I *want* to—fly there twice a year. Once for each of them."

She coughed croakily into her fist and then thumped her chest. "They live at opposite ends of the island, of course, as far from each other as possible. So that's two months out of my year. There's no point going over there for less than a month at a time. It's the other end of the planet."

"Do you ever get to Central Otago?" said Nevada.

"No. Have you been there?"

"No, but I understand it's a fabulously good wine-making region."

"I understand that too," said Dylis. "But it's on the southern island. My brood are on the northern island. In Lower Hutt, which is near Wellington. And Kaitaia, which isn't near anywhere." Then she glanced around the room in annoyance, as if we'd been deliberately distracting her from more serious matters. "Where's my pomegranate juice?"

Nevada and I looked at each other helplessly. If only we could help the poor woman in her quest to find her juice.

After a moment's profound deliberation Dylis said, "Maybe the kitchen…" Having achieved this feat of reasoning, she rose from the piano stool and started out of the room, down a short hallway presumably heading kitchen-wards. We hesitated for a moment and then followed. Which is just as well, because she croaked an impatient, "Come on through."

The kitchen was as big as the sitting room and looked out onto some well-maintained gardens at the back of the building. A big window was open just wide enough to let a cool flow of breeze in. Beyond the lawns and flowerbeds, I realised with a foolish shock, was the vast green drift of the Thames itself. Riverview Gardens actually provided a view of the river from its gardens.

But in my defence, in a world where names like Sunny Meadows invariably betoken a gloomy cul-de-sac, my surprise may not have been entirely foolish.

Nevada and I stood for a moment, just staring out the window at the view. It was well worth the four or five million pounds it must now command. It was like an Impressionist canvas. Seurat, maybe.

As she moved restlessly across the kitchen, presumably in search of juice, Dylis stumbled and grabbed onto the counter to steady herself. We moved forward to help her but she waved us back. "It's all right. I'm not drunk. I just spent twenty-three hours on a plane, and I haven't got my land legs back yet."

She demonstrated this by standing in the middle of the kitchen and weaving woozily around as if her feet were glued to the floor while the rest of her body was slowly swaying. It was a bit like a hula hoop competition. "It's like being on a surfboard on a gentle swell. But you're standing on solid ground. It takes about a day and a half to normalise." She collapsed on a high stool beside the counter and stared around her. "Where's my pomegranate juice?"

"I'm afraid we don't know," said Nevada politely.

"Of course you don't know. You're here to talk to me about the Blue Tits, right?"

It was a relief that she was tracking at least to this degree. "That's right," I said. "I'm sorry if we've called at a bad time."

"No, it's fine. It's not a bad time. I told you to come around, didn't I?"

This seemed like a genuine question rather than another rhetorical one, so I said, "Yes, when we emailed you."

"That's right. You emailed me. Sorry, I'm a bit slow on the uptake. I've just flown through god knows how many time zones. I'm not clear about small matters like dates and times and which way is up."

"Would you like us to come back later?"

"No, no." She shook her head, her grey ponytail sweeping back and forth like its namesake. "Let's…" I had a strong impression that she was about to say, *Let's get it over with*. But she politely corrected herself and instead said, "Let's talk now."

Nevada looked at me to take the lead. "Okay," I said. "So we've been interviewing all the members of the Blue Tits…"

"Have you spoken to Helene?"

"Yes."

"How is she?"

"She's fine."

"She nearly got killed, you know," said Dylis.

Nevada and I looked at each other. "Yes, we heard something about that."

"In fact, I understand she nearly got killed, what was it? Four times? That's pushing it a bit, don't you think?" Dylis reached down, grabbed her stool and twisted it around, screeching on the kitchen floor tiles, so she was facing us more squarely. Suddenly, despite the jet lag, her eyes seemed very clear and the mind behind them very sharp.

"Don't you think?" she repeated. Her voice was harsh now, and it wasn't anything to do with the croak in it.

"Yes, it's a bit excessive," said Nevada.

All at once the mood in the room had changed. Sunlight was still pouring in, and the heat of the day hadn't diminished, but suddenly it felt distinctly chilly. The spring breeze flowing in through the window had a frigid bite to it.

Dylis Lispector held out her right hand towards us, balled into a tight fist. She extended her first finger, as if she was pointing at Nevada. "She was nearly run over." She extended her second finger. "Then the gas was left on in her flat." A third finger. "Then someone tried to give her a lethal Fentanyl overdose." A fourth finger. "And then she was almost fried by an electrical short in her guitar."

"That's right," I said.

"You know all about that, then?"

"Yes," I said. "But I'm surprised that you do."

"Why?" Dylis suddenly swivelled round on her stool so that she was facing away from us towards the counter. In front of her was a toaster, a blender and a chunky, highly polished wooden block with an impressive array of kitchen knives displayed in it. She continued speaking with her back to us.

"She's an old friend and bandmate. Why would it be surprising that I know what's going on in her life?"

She abruptly reached forward and pulled one of the knives out of the wooden block then set it down on the counter beside her. Then she swivelled around to face us again, leaning back so her elbows were planted casually on the surface of the counter.

This also had the incidental and interesting effect of putting her hand very close to the knife.

She looked at us, her eyes tired but alert. And cynical. And wary. "My question," she said, "is how on earth *you* know all about that?"

"Helene told us," said Nevada. She was keeping her eyes fixed on that knife, and on the hand which was so close to it.

"Helene and Erik," I said.

"Who's Erik?"

"Her boyfriend."

"Oh, the guitarist."

"That's right. He's very concerned about her."

"Is that right?" said Dylis. "Where does Erik live, again? It's in Wimbledon, isn't it?"

"No," I said. "He lives right here in Barnes."

"By the river," said Nevada. "By the Bull's Head."

"Oh yes, that's right," said Dylis. "Funny that I forgot that."

She turned around again, picked up the knife from the counter and slipped it back into the wooden block. Out of the corner of my eye I saw Nevada relax.

Still with her back to us, Dylis said, "Everyone must know that. Where he lives. I mean, it must be easy to find that out. All a person has to do to find that out is look on the Internet, right?"

"Actually," I said, "Erik and I are old friends." As soon as I said it, I wished I hadn't, because it sounded false even in my own ears. The thing was, I had indeed known Erik for years. But for most of that time we certainly hadn't been friends, and I wasn't even sure that I would call us that now.

Maybe because she caught that false note, or for other compelling reasons of her own, Dylis Lispector reached for the block again and drew out another knife, a much larger and much sharper one.

She twisted around to face us and set the knife down, elbows casually back on the counter again. Her hand wasn't just close to the knife this time, her fingers were actually touching its handle.

At my side Nevada was very still indeed. "What's with the knives?" she said. Her voice was casual and relaxed.

Dylis shrugged. The movement didn't cause her fingers to leave the knife. "Avocado for breakfast. Got to slice the avocado. Need a decent knife for avocado slicing."

"I thought you were having pomegranate juice," said Nevada. She made it sound cordial, conversational.

Dylis seemed to forget about the knife for a moment. "Where is my frigging pomegranate juice?" she said.

"In the fridge, presumably."

"Of course it's not in the frigging fridge. I leave it out overnight."

"To warm up?"

"To oxidise the phytochemicals so that they have a more beneficial effect when clearing the body of free radicals."

I knew bullshit when I heard it, and I was very close to saying as much. But then there was the small matter that our hostess had her hand on a fucking huge, sharp knife. So I stayed silent and let Nevada do the talking.

"It would be a really friendly gesture if you put that back in the block where it came from."

"Would it?" said Dylis, not moving.

"Have we said something…?"

"You've said a lot of things," she said.

Now the mood in the room underwent a profound change. I don't believe in anything resembling the paranormal—Tinkler's nude-Agatha radar notwithstanding—but I really did feel something at this moment. When I discussed it later with Nevada, she said she'd felt it too.

There was genuinely a sense of something in the room.

Maybe when an event like this is about to happen there's a preliminary tremor, like those subsonic signatures of an approaching earthquake that animals can sense.

We didn't know what was going to happen, but we knew that it was coming.

And that it was going to be bad.

And we were both working like hell to avert it.

"Would it be best if we just get up and leave?" said Nevada.

"Don't get up and do anything," said Dylis. "Don't move from where you are, please." At least we were still at the please and thank you stage.

"Do you have some kind of doubt that we're who we say we are?" said Nevada.

Dylis kept her hand on the knife. "No. Because you haven't said who you are."

"It was all in the email. I've got a copy on my phone."

"Don't touch your phone."

I moved my hand slowly away from the vicinity of my pocket. Nevada nodded imperceptibly that she agreed this was the right thing to do. She was dividing her attention carefully between me and Dylis.

"You want us to confirm who we are?" said Nevada.

"That would be nice."

"Why don't you call Helene?"

"Because I don't have my phone here with me," said Dylis with heavy sarcasm.

"Let one of us get it for you."

"Stay where you are."

"Call her on one of our phones," I said. "We both have our phones here."

Dylis thought about this. She looked at Nevada. "All right. You put your phone down on the end of the counter and slide it towards me." Nevada unlocked her phone and then did exactly as she was told.

Dylis picked up the phone with one hand. She was now actively holding the knife in the other one. She peered at the phone. "You've got a lot of pictures of cats."

"Tell me about it. You just press the contacts icon…"

"I know how to work a phone," said Dylis tetchily.

"Well, anyway, her number's programmed in."

Dylis lowered the phone. "How do I know it's her number?"

I said, "Call it. If she answers, it's her number."

Dylis lowered the phone further. Our objective seemed to be steadily receding. "But what if it's not her?"

"What," I said, "you mean because we have a voice actor on standby ready to impersonate her?"

She gave me a venomous look and punched the number. We waited for a long time in a tense silence, then Dylis put Nevada's phone to her ear as the call connected.

We waited another long time, presumably while it rang. And rang.

Then she lowered the phone and looked at it.

"No answer."

"Well, try Monika's number then. Monika Dunkley."

She hesitated for a moment and then said, "Okay." Maybe she was just enjoying using Nevada's phone. She scrolled through our contacts and punched another number. This time there was an answer at the other end, and promptly, too.

"Monika? Hello. No, no. It's not. It's Dylis. Yes. That's sort of why I've rung. What? Oh, yes. Yes. Just got back. Really? Well, that is a coincidence. But before we get on to that—oh no. Don't be silly. I'm not prejudging what you want to talk to me about. I have no idea what you want to talk to me about. And I am certainly not judging *you*."

Even though we were only getting half of it, this was definitely beginning to sound like a conversation with our friend the roadie.

"But, before we get on to that, whatever 'that' might be, can we briefly discuss what I rang you up about. Thank you. Thanks. Yes. I am. I am using her phone. That's why I rung. These people say that they know you. What? You're right. You are right. Good point. I hadn't thought of that. Okay…"

Dylis peered closely at us through her jet-lagged eyes and proceeded to describe us over the phone to Monika.

And none too flatteringly. She listened and then she covered the phone and said to us, "She says she can't be sure."

"She can't be sure?"

"That it's really you."

"Oh, for Christ's sake, give me the phone. Shove it over to me."

Dylis shook her head. "Use your own phone."

I didn't point out that in recent memory I had been strictly instructed not to touch my phone. Instead I took it out and dialled Monika. "Tell her to hang up or it will go to voicemail."

"He says to hang up or it will go to voicemail. Yes. Speak in a minute." She lowered Nevada's phone and watched me.

My call connected. "Hello?" said a familiar voice.

"Monika."

"Hi! How's it going?"

"Not too well at the moment."

"Why not?"

I stared across the room at our hostess with the knife. "Let's not get into all the details just at the minute, but suffice to say it would be really helpful if you could simply tell Dylis that we are who we say we are."

"You know, I don't know…"

"What do you mean you don't know?"

"How can I be sure?"

"Look, Monika, you do realise that you're speaking to me and I'm sitting here in the kitchen with Dylis." *And a sharp fucking knife*, I didn't add. "You are actually speaking to me. You do acknowledge that this is really me?"

"Yes…"

"And by extension that it is Nevada sitting beside me."

"Yes."

"So you can vouch for us. You can tell Dylis that this is really us, the people you know."

"Yes… but…"

"But what?"

"I just wouldn't feel comfortable taking that responsibility."

"What?" I said, unable to believe my ears.

"I mean, what if—"

"What if what?"

"I don't know," said Monika. "That's what I'm saying."

There was then a long stubborn silence. In my imagination I could see Monika's pouty face all too clearly. Pudgy and grim and determined.

Nevada and Dylis were both looking at me. I could feel sweat flowing freely down my ribcage.

"Are you still there?" I said finally.

"Yes."

"But you're not going to vouch for us?"

"Oh, I didn't say that."

"So you'll call Dylis back? Right now?"

"Yes."

"And you'll say that we're really who we say we are?"

"Of course," said Monika. "I'll say it's you."

"Great, thank you."

Her voice softened apologetically. "But I just can't tell her to trust you."

"What?"

"I just can't take that responsibility."

"Why not?"

"Because it wouldn't be appropriate," she said primly.

"Thanks a bunch."

"Sorry," said Monika. "Can you pass me back to Dylis? I need to speak to her."

"No, I can't pass you back. Call her back on Nevada's fucking phone."

"Oh yes, right. Sorry." She hung up and, a moment later, Nevada's phone rang in Dylis's hand.

She answered it and listened impatiently to what was apparently a monologue from Monika. It went on quite a while and Dylis's impatience only grew. Finally she said, "Yeah, let me think about it." And hung up. She switched off the phone and set it on the counter and looked at us. "Sorry if I used up your minutes."

"What was that all about?" said Nevada.

"Oh, she wanted to borrow some money. And not for the first time. Poor Monika never really got her shit together."

This seemed to sound a more convivial note. In any case, it was something we could all certainly agree on. So it made sense that Nevada said, "Do you think you can put the knife away now?"

This suggestion appeared to enrage the woman. "Do what? Why would I do that? Why in God's name should I trust you? You worm your way in here to try and tell me that you're looking for Helene's killer…" Monika must have told her this, because we hadn't.

"Actually," I said, "we wormed our way in here to try and tell you that we're looking for a record."

"A record?"

"The very first pressing of the very first Blue Tits album."

"The first one? The original one?"

"Yes."

"The one with all the guitar solos?"

"Yes."

"Those were pretty good solos."

"So I understand."

"That record changes hands for a lot of money these days."

I said, "We would be very happy to provide a lot of money so a copy could change hands today."

"I'm sorry?"

"If you happen to have a copy," said Nevada.

"We would be delighted to buy it from you," I finished.

"For a fair price," said Nevada.

Dylis was giving us a very seriously assessing look. I was beginning to think she might have the record, never mind the one supposedly in Ophelia's possession. It would hardly beggar belief that two members of the same band had retained a copy of their first ever professional recording.

"You would have to pay a lot of money for that record," said Dylis. "Assuming I did have a copy. A great deal of money."

Because you need it living in a place like this, I didn't say.

"After all, it may be the only copy in existence."

"Actually, we know of at least one other," I said.

She looked at me sceptically. "Really? Where?"

"Ophelia Brydent has a copy."

"Oh, does she really? Well, good luck with that. Jolly good luck, because Ophelia has vanished from human ken.

Nobody knows where she is." She smiled at us, pleased by the decisive way she had trussed us up with her logic.

"Tania does."

"She doesn't," said Dylis with confidence.

"Well, she claims she does. And she sounds pretty sure of herself."

"I don't believe you," said Dylis. And then, before we could suggest it, she picked up Nevada's phone again, and began scrolling down the screen. "Christ," she said in a chagrined voice, "is there anybody's number you haven't got in here?"

She tapped Tania's number and put the phone to her ear.

It seemed to be answered very swiftly. "Hi! What? No. It's me. Dylis. Yes. Yes. Well, it's a long story. I'll get to all that in a minute. What I want is to verify who these people are and if they are to be trusted." She looked up at us again. "I'll describe them," she said.

I wasn't inclined to sit through another one of her caustic verbal portraits of us, so I said, "Let me talk to her."

Dylis shook her head emphatically, as she was listening to something Tania was saying. "Okay," she said, "*you* describe them." She listened some more and then began saying, "Yes, yup, yup, that sounds about right. No, that's great. Thank you. Oh, wait—there is just one more thing. Apparently you know where Ophelia is… Well, how do you think? Okay. Okay. I'll tell them."

She looked up at us. "She said you weren't supposed to tell anyone that she knows where Ophelia is."

"Tell her we got freaked out because you're brandishing a huge fucking knife in our direction."

She laughed merrily and said into the phone, "Did you hear that? He said they're freaked out because I'm brandishing a huge fucking knife at them. Yes. Oh, the, ah…" She looked at the knife in her hand. "The Global G2 Chef. Oh yes, they're great, aren't they? Do you use the ceramic sharpener? I know. Me too, it's outrageous. It's almost cheaper to buy a new one. I suppose that's what they want you to do. Yes. That would be great. Can't wait. Ciao."

She hung up and turned to Nevada. "She said I should do a fashion consultation with you."

"That was nice of her," said Nevada.

But Dylis was staring down at her leopard-print leggings. "I must say I found it rather offensive. And a little hurtful." This wasn't great news, because the last thing I wanted was this woman upset.

But she just set the knife aside, as simple as that. She moved away from the counter, towards the refrigerator, saying, "You know, we should put our heads together and try and work out who's trying to kill Helene." She grasped the refrigerator door for stability and turned to look at us. "I'm so sorry for thinking it was you."

"That's okay," I said. "I was beginning to think it was you."

She looked genuinely confounded. "Me? Why me?"

"The Global G2 Chef," said Nevada, nodding at the knife on the counter.

"That and your dates," I said. "If you've just been in New Zealand for a month, that means you were still here in London for the relevant period when someone was trying to dispatch Helene. And while you've been away, things have been suspiciously quiet."

She gaped at me and then started laughing. "You think I'm a potential killer? Look at yourselves!"

Nevada and I looked at each other. I thought we looked pretty good.

"For a start," said Dylis, "what's in that massive, sinister frigging bag? A full murder and torture kit?"

Nevada involuntarily clutched her snazzy shoulder bag, as though it were a child who was being insulted. I could see that she was rather hurt by this comment about a fashion accessory it had taken her a full quarter of an hour to choose this morning. Then, without warning, she slung the bag off her shoulder and onto the counter. She did this so abruptly that both Dylis and I jumped a little.

"All right," said Nevada tightly, unzipping the bag. "You want to see what's in here?"

"No, really, it's fine," said Dylis feebly, and quite ineffectually, since Nevada's blood was now up. She proceeded to unpack her bag with great sarcasm, if such a thing is possible, itemising the various high fashion finds she'd bought on our tour of the shops this morning.

Dylis gaped at the designer clothes piling up on her counter. "My god, you got those all today?"

"Yes," said Nevada tightly.

"In a charity shop?"

"In fairness, in a series of charity shops."

"How much did you pay?"

Nevada told her.

"Jesus wept," said Dylis. "I'm going to have to start going to those shops." Confirming, yet again, that nobody likes a bargain better than a rich person.

The sincerity of Dylis's envy seemed to have mollified Nevada. She concluded by taking out the two bottles of Marcel Deiss wine to show her—we'd gone for the Rotenberg as well as the Alsace.

"That looks good," said Dylis, perhaps by way of an olive branch. But the sight of the wine apparently reminded her of something. "What could I possibly have done with my pomegranate juice?"

Nevada shrugged a *that's-your-problem* shrug and began to repack her bag.

"I always leave it in the sitting room," said Dylis, "so I can drink it in there first thing in the morning, watching the sun come up." She paused for a moment, nibbling on her lower lip, and then a big smile spread across her face. "Oh, I remember now. It's in the bedroom. I left it there last night so I could drink it in bed, in case I was too tired to get up."

She hopped down happily from her stool and trotted out of the room.

I looked at Nevada. "At least that's one mystery solved."

"Praise be."

Dylis came back in, beaming, and holding up a glass with both hands as if it were a sporting trophy. Or perhaps a votive offering. It was a large glass full of a somewhat unappetising brownish red liquid that looked like slightly-off tomato juice. "You see," she said, as if we'd staunchly and consistently denied that such a thing could exist.

Admittedly, I had begun to doubt that it did.

Dylis sat down on her stool again and set the juice on the counter. She grabbed the belt of her dressing gown, knotted it tightly around herself and gave a big sigh.

That was the moment when we should have done something, if only we'd known.

But we didn't, and she picked up the glass and sipped.

Almost immediately a change came over her face. She set the glass down shakily, reached both her hands up to her mouth and tried to say something.

All that came out was a tight, strangled sound as though her throat was closing. Her face had gone milk white and her eyes were staring blindly in front of her.

She stood up and took one step towards us.

Then she collapsed to the floor, falling hard, like trash casually tossed from a giant hand.

21: VANILLA VODKA

"She was poisoned?" said Bong Cha.

"It looks like it," I said.

Bong Cha was a short, solid-looking woman with a face superbly designed for scowling. She invariably wore sweater and blazer combos that looked like downmarket knockoffs of Tania Strack's business suits. Bong was theoretically Erik Make Loud's live-in housekeeper, but over the years they had become more like flat mates. Or perhaps a mildly bickering married couple. Either way, there had been an inevitable decline in the scope and frequency of her domestic chores.

She had, however, deigned to personally open the door to myself and Nevada today. No doubt because she wanted to be the first to hear the news. "So what happened?" she said eagerly.

"If you don't mind, I'd like to tell everybody at the same time. It will save me repeating myself over and over again."

"Oh well, if it will save your precious *time*," she snarled. Then she put on her nicest smile and said, "Hello, Nevada."

"Hello, Bong."

The women exchanged cheek kisses and then Bong Cha glowered at me again. "Everybody is upstairs waiting in the audio-visual room. So you will be able to tell us all at the same time. You know the way, go on up."

"Thanks."

"Don't say anything until I've come up to join you," said Bong Cha as she disappeared in the direction of the kitchen. "Or you might have to *repeat yourself.*"

The audio-visual room was a big room at the rear of the house, facing away from the river. It was much as I remembered it, pretentious name and all, except that the television, once the largest I'd ever seen, had begun to look somewhat shrunken and antiquated—time for an upgrade, surely?—and the blackout blinds had been opened to let in the evening sunlight.

Tinkler was sitting on the sofa, Erik and Helene in the reclining armchairs on either side of it. They weren't reclining at the moment; they were sitting bolt upright. And they all sprang to their feet as Nevada and I came in.

Helene ran to Nevada and hugged her. Tinkler and Erik converged on me.

"Are you guys all right?" said Helene.

"Luckily we don't drink pomegranate juice," I said.

"Christ, who does?" said Tinkler.

"Dylis Lispector."

"Not even her anymore, by the sound of it," said Tinkler.

Helene gave a little sob. "Is she dead?"

I shook my head. "No."

"Thank god."

"But she is reportedly in a critical condition, in a coma."

"Bummer," said Tinkler.

There was silence for a moment and then Erik said, "What happened?"

"Wait, wait," yelled a voice from the doorway. Bong Cha came barging in, pushing an unnecessarily elaborate-looking office chair with a wheeled base. Stacked rather precariously on the seat of the chair were white ceramic trays of canapés, matching plates, black paper napkins—very rock and roll—some chunky glass tumblers and a bottle in a silver chiller sleeve. "Wait for me. Otherwise he might have to say something twice."

She shot me a vindictive look, but I went and helped her with the trays anyway, setting them on the driftwood coffee table in front of the sofa, first moving aside a six-disc Blu-ray set of the Ken Burns documentaries about World War Two. Tinkler's hand shot out and snagged a canapé immediately, not waiting for the plates or napkins which were distributed a moment later.

Drinks were poured—the bottle was vodka, of course, but it turned out to be Stolichnaya Vanilla, which was a startling break with tradition. Blueberry vodka had generally been Erik's house tipple. Maybe this was Helene's influence. And then everybody sat down, Bong Cha in the chair she'd just wheeled in, Nevada and Tinkler and I on the sofa.

We described our visit to Dylis. Helene gave a little gasp when she heard about the knife. Tinkler just said, "I've always said you two look like dodgy characters. It's surprising you don't get knives pulled on you more often."

"And she was constantly banging on about this juice she was looking for," said Nevada. "She'd set the glass down somewhere and couldn't remember where she'd put it."

"But she did remember," said Erik.

"Unfortunately, yes."

"And they're sure the stuff was in the juice?" said Bong Cha.

"As soon as she drank it, she went down like a felled tree."

Nevada had instantly started performing first aid—though she'd wisely avoided mouth-to-mouth resuscitation. It was obvious to us that the drink was responsible, and Dylis's mouth would have been contaminated with it.

Meanwhile, I had called for an ambulance.

"The ambulance came from the accident and emergency department at Charing Cross Hospital, which was good news, because it could hardly have been much closer. The bad news was that Hammersmith Bridge was closed, so they had to come via Putney. Which was like going around three sides of a square instead of coming straight down to us."

"That fucking bridge being closed is a fucking nightmare," moaned Erik.

"It's not a nightmare for everyone," said Bong Cha. "I know people who live up by the bridge who are turning backflips with joy."

"All I know is, every time we head north over the river we have to go across Putney or Chiswick," said Erik stubbornly. We seemed to be getting off topic here.

I said, "All the while we were waiting, Nevada was

performing CPR. She showed me what to do so I could relieve her, then she would take over again, and then I would relieve her again, and so on."

"Jesus," said Helene. "You poor things."

"Poor Dylis," I said. "We broke a number of her ribs."

Erik winced. Nevada said, "It's almost inevitable if you're doing it properly and doing it for a long time."

"That's right," said Bong Cha firmly.

"Anyway," I said, "the ambulance finally got there and they took over, and then they had to drive around three sides of the square to go back."

"Poor Dylis," said Helene.

"So she's now in a coma in Charing Cross Hospital."

"I was once in a coma there," said Tinkler nostalgically. This was actually true.

"Let's hope she comes out of it too," said Nevada.

"Do they know what it was?" said Erik. "What it was in the pomegranate juice that caused her to have that reaction?"

"Luckily they've got almost a whole glass of the stuff to analyse. She only took a sip…"

"Just a sip? Jesus."

"But apparently it will take weeks to identify the toxin."

"Toxin," said Helene softly, and shuddered.

"Are they sure it wasn't just that the pomegranate juice was off?" said Erik.

"They're sure."

"So, someone…"

"Yes," I said. "Someone deliberately put something in the juice so she would drink it and this would happen. Actually, not so this would happen, but rather so that she would drink it when she was alone and no one was around to help."

"No one to break her ribs performing CPR," said Tinkler.

"Exactly. If we hadn't been with her, that would have been it."

"But why would anyone want to try and kill Dylis?" said Helene.

"Why would anyone want to try and kill *you*?" said Erik staunchly.

"Actually, I've got a theory about exactly that," I said.

They all turned to look at me, Tinkler draining his glass as he did so. "A theory? Great. Is there any more of this vodka?"

As he got his refill, I began to set it out before them. "It's proving difficult to kill Helene," I said.

"Damn right." There was a note of pride in Erik's voice. "And the fuckers are going to find out that it will continue to prove difficult."

"Good," I said. "Okay. But what if it was so difficult that they gave up?"

"Gave up?" said Erik incredulously. "They never gave up. They made four attempts."

"But they've stopped now. For the time being at least."

"That's because we're onto them. And because our guard is up."

"Exactly," I said. "So it's become too difficult for them. So what if they changed their tactics and decided to kill Dylis instead?"

The room went silent. They were all staring at me except Nevada. We'd discussed this earlier.

"That doesn't make any sense," said Bong Cha. "Kill Dylis *instead*?"

I said, "It does make sense if they didn't necessarily want to kill Helene."

Erik nearly popped a blood vessel. "What do you mean didn't necessarily want to kill her? Do you think we were lying to you about what happened? Do you think we were mistaken?"

"Easy, doll, easy," said Helene. Fortunately Erik heeded her and began to calm down. Otherwise we might have been called upon to do some more cardiopulmonary resuscitation, and I was still aching from last time.

I spoke slowly and carefully. "I meant what if they didn't necessarily want to specifically kill Helene, *at that time*. Not specifically her. So they could give up on her for the time being and come back for her later. Because, what I'm saying is, they don't want to *just* kill Helene."

Everyone was listening to me with full attention now.

"It all falls into place," I said. "It makes perfect sense if they want to kill them all."

"Them all?" said Erik.

"All the Blue Tits?" said Helene.

"Yes," I said. "I think someone wants to kill all the members of your band."

324

22: LEECH LANE

Erik's reaction startled me, though I suppose it shouldn't have. He rejected my theory out of hand. Talking about it later, after we'd returned home, Nevada and I realised that one of the problems with it, for Erik, was that it deprived Helene and her plight of a certain, dare I say it, romantic aspect.

When she was the only damsel in distress, the one woman facing death, that made her special.

And no doubt she genuinely was special to Erik.

But as soon as she became part of a sequence, figures moving past the gun in a shooting gallery, she lost that uniqueness. She was reduced in importance. And Erik couldn't have that.

In a way, none of this mattered, because Erik and Helene, like Erik said, had their guard up now and were exercising great caution. This was perfect, and it mustn't change, so their attitude towards me didn't matter. They were safe for the time being. That's what mattered.

Interestingly, Helene for her part listened to my thesis

thoughtfully and kept her counsel, quietly reserving judgement.

Erik wasn't quiet, and he didn't reserve judgement. He thought I was crazy.

Tania didn't.

I phoned her up and told her what I believed was happening. She got it right away. "So, what you're saying is that I need to be on my guard, too."

"That's right. And what's more, it's imperative that someone warns Ophelia."

There was silence on the line. Then she said, "I can do that."

"Okay, but do it right away."

"I will."

"I still want to see her myself, though. And talk to her." And buy the record from her for Erik—whatever thoughts he might have about my hypothesis, it hadn't altered our deal, although I didn't think this was a suitable time to bring up the subject of rare vinyl.

"Glad to hear you have at least some sensitivity," said Tinkler when I told him about it later. "So has she agreed to tell you where Ophelia is?"

"She's agreed to discuss it."

"Okay. That doesn't sound good."

"She's asked us to come down to her house in Surrey and talk to her about the situation."

"I suppose you want to drive my car down there," said Tinkler. "Well, sorry, my friend. You can't expect me to just drop everything and take more time off work to come with you."

"Actually," I said, "I want Clean Head to drive your car down there. She's agreed to help us."

"You know, come to think of it, I've still got plenty of annual leave to take before the end of the year. And if you don't use it, you lose it."

"Funny, I thought you might say that," I said.

"This is terrific," said Tinkler. "The whole gang is getting together and going on a mission. Admittedly, it's to Surrey, but you can't have everything. Hey, maybe we can visit Persephone again?"

"Maybe we can," said Nevada, coming in from the spare room with a rucksack. "But we've got a lot to do."

"You know, we never did have that hashish honey," said Tinkler. "Why don't we eat it in the car on the way down?"

"Tinkler…"

Tinkler nodded at me. "We can get old killjoy here to drive, if that's what you're worried about. He won't want to partake anyway."

"I'm not sure I'm going to partake, either," said Nevada. She set the rucksack down on the floor with a thump that suggested its contents were heavy.

"What?" said Tinkler. "You can't do that. That would be no fun. I count on you as my partner in pharmaceutical mayhem. Don't turn into a killjoy."

"I think I'd better keep a clear head," said Nevada.

"Oh, come on. Why?"

"Because we're in a situation where there may be more than joy getting killed." Nevada went back into the spare room.

Tinkler shrugged. "Well, more for me. And for Agatha. And who knows, she might find my honey strangely arousing."

"Yes, it certainly would be strange if she found that," I said. "Anyway, I thought you had set your sights on Opal."

"That reminds me, I must sext her."

"Don't do it while you're here," said Nevada.

"Of course not. I do have some sense of decorum. So anyway, what's the objective when we go and see Tania?" said Tinkler. Without waiting for an answer, he went on. "Get her to take you to Ophelia, get the record and then get the hell back to London? That makes sense. Then we can eat the honey on the drive back. Perfect. We'll *fly* home."

I shook my head. "It won't be just a quick in-and-out."

"Pity, I like a bit of quick in-and-out. What else are you planning to do?"

"There's also the matter of Tania's safety."

"What? Who cares about that? Leave it to the police."

"The police aren't about to provide around-the-clock protection for a threat they don't believe exists. In fact, in these straitened times, they couldn't provide around-the-clock protection for a threat they do believe exists."

"So, tell Tania to take a long holiday in a magical land somewhere far, far away."

"We did, as it so happens. We did exactly that. It would have been the perfect solution. But she says she has to stay here. Too many important business commitments and so on."

"Well then, if the police can't help and she's such an important businesswoman she'd better hire her own round-the-clock protection. She certainly has enough money."

"That's what I told her," I said. "In fact I recommended someone."

"Who do you know who could do something like that?" said Tinkler.

Nevada came back in from the spare room, carrying her bow and arrow.

Tinkler looked at her, then at the heavy rucksack on the floor and then at me again. "You've got to be kidding," he said.

"No," said Nevada. "This could be the start of a lucrative sideline."

We were driving through the countryside again, only this time Agatha was at the wheel, so we were driving considerably more quickly. We passed low, ancient-looking stone walls and big barn-like buildings behind dense hedges. In the distance we could see white chalk cliffs exposed high on a green hill.

"Christ," said Tinkler. "That reminds me of Dover. It gives me the heebie-jeebies."

"You went to school there, right?" said Agatha.

"Yes, and I have nothing resembling fond memories of the place."

"Except for the turntable," I said.

"Oh yes, that's right. I did steal a very nice turntable," said Tinkler proudly.

"That's actually a former quarry up there, that chalk," said Nevada. "It leads to Box Hill, hence the name 'Chalk Hills Bakery'. Which is actually a café where we had a lovely lunch." She leaned forward so she was almost whispering in

Tinkler's ear—he was in the front passenger seat so he could be as close to Agatha as possible. "We waited until you went back to London," she said, "and then we had a lovely lunch."

"Typical."

We drove along a narrow, shaded, winding lane with the trees arched in a canopy overhead. Deep shadow alternated with sunlight as we passed signs that read *Pebble Hill*.

"Is Bam-Bam Hill nearby?" said Tinkler. Then, "*Flintstones* gag."

"We got it," I said.

"We're heading for a place called Headley," said Nevada.

"Oh, look, another picturesque place name," said Tinkler. "Leech Lane. That's probably still the cutting-edge medical treatment for the yokels around here. Leeches."

"Leeches actually are a cutting-edge therapy," said Nevada, "for reconnecting severed blood vessels."

"Don't try and make the yokels sound less dim-witted," said Tinkler. "And no more talk of severed blood vessels, please."

The tunnel of trees was so dark now that an approaching car had its headlights on. Then abruptly we weren't driving among trees, but through a strikingly ugly concrete box.

"What the hell was that?" said Agatha as we flashed through it.

"One of the supports for the motorway bridge," said Nevada, who had made a careful study of the whole area. "The M25 encircles this place. Turn left here."

Agatha smoothly executed the turn and suddenly we were on a gravel drive that curled around a circular patch of grass with a huge, thick tree in the centre of it, covered with ivy. She found a patch of shade and braked neatly to a stop.

We got out of the car. To our left was the house, an enormous red brick structure. To our right was a collection of outbuildings with blue and black plastic wheelie bins against their walls. Beyond the outbuildings was a dark cluster of trees. There were apple trees on either side of the drive, covered in pink blossom. Immediately in front of us was a section of lawn completely carpeted with bright yellow daffodils.

It was a warm and sunny day, the air smelled sweet and it would have been utterly idyllic and peaceful, but for the continual drone of traffic from the motorway in the distance.

Walking towards us across the yellow carpet of daffodils was Tania Strack. In deference to the country setting, instead of her usual business outfit she was wearing a tweed suit. Tania had already met me and Nevada, of course, but introductions were in order for Agatha and Tinkler. Everybody shook hands.

Whether it was the smooth political operator in her or not, I have to say that Tania seemed genuinely pleased to see us. Which was quite a feat when Tinkler was part of the equation.

"My god," said Nevada, looking at the red brick building towering over us. "What a house. Talk us through it, please."

Tania grinned. Nevada had clearly chosen the right subject. The only thing better would have been a question about Elizabethan history. "Where do I start? Well, it was built in the nineteenth century by a banking family. It has fourteen bedrooms."

"Fourteen," murmured Nevada. Perhaps she was thinking about how many caches of vintage clothes and spare cats such a place could accommodate. I was thinking along similar lines, though for clothes read vinyl.

"It's divided into three sections, the west and east wings and the central portion. From the air it's an H-shape. The banking family consisted of three brothers and their wives and children. Each brother had his own wing and, apparently, each family stuck to their own part of the house and was strongly discouraged from setting foot in any of the others."

"Why not just have separate houses?" said Tinkler. "They had enough money." Considering its source, this was a surprisingly sensible question.

"The brothers had grown up crammed together in a ghetto in Frankfurt," said Tania. "As much as they might have grown to dislike each other, they were accustomed to living in close proximity."

We crossed the lawn to an open door in the nearest wall of the house and Tania took us on a lightning tour, just of the ground floor of the west wing, but that was plenty. Immediately as we came in the door there were white bricks on the floor and a large number of wellington boots—I wasn't overly surprised to see that they were all green—flanking the entrance. An adjacent room had a sink and floor-to-ceiling dark wood cupboards in two sections. "Those were the gun cupboards," said Tania.

"Gun cupboards?"

"You know, for the shooting parties."

There were dark wood floors and dark wood beams criss-crossing the whitewashed ceilings. The house could have been gloomy but everywhere doors and windows were open to the warm, sunny garden. The sitting room had big fireplaces, but nothing compared to the library, which had a fireplace you could have parked a car in. The main hallway had a blue and white tiled floor and a dark wood staircase zigzagging upwards. Visible through a window was the gravelled courtyard in front of the central section of the house.

Deeper in the heart of the house, away from the open doors and windows, it had begun to seem like a labyrinth of dark, shadowy corridors.

Tania led us back towards daylight. We came into the kitchen—where I noticed the big cooking range was not an Aga but something called a Rangemaster Elan, a major break with tradition—and out the back door into the garden again.

"But you didn't come down here to see my house," she said, looking at me.

"True."

"You want to talk to Ophelia."

"That's right."

"All right," said Tania, as if she'd come to a decision. "Follow me."

23: CASHMERE RUSTLERS

"That used to be the croquet lawn," said Tania, as she led us away from the house. There was still no sign of Ophelia, but at least we were still getting our informative guided tour.

"Are all these grounds around the house yours?" said Nevada.

Tania nodded. "Yes. It's about a twenty-acre plot."

"My god, what an extraordinarily beautiful place."

"Well, it was before they built the M25 next to it," said our hostess bitterly. But she wasn't wrong. Here we were, deep in the countryside with all the flowers, fresh air and sunlight you could wish for, and yet there was no escape from the distant, constant roar of the motorway, like the perpetual sound of the engines of a jet airliner on a long flight.

"That paddock used to be a tennis court," said Tania, pointing to an empty grassed area with a fence made of wooden rails. As soon as she said this, it was obvious from the neat rectangular shape of it. Beside it was a sunken gravelled space with a wooden picnic table. "And there's the barbecue area."

We had reached the outbuildings. "Here are the stables," announced Tania as we walked past one, peering in through the open doors at the wooden stalls and the stacks of hay. The smell brought back childhood memories of hamster cages, though on a more massive scale.

"No horses?" said Agatha with a hint of disappointment in her voice.

"I don't own any," said Tania. "Horse owning is second only to boat owning as a money drain. However, friends do stable their noble beasts with me. It so happens there is one in residence at the moment."

There were two sets of stables and a paddock adjoining each of them. It was in the furthest of these that we saw a large, lazy-looking brown horse. He was chewing away at hay that was stuffed in a giant red string bag hung over the paddock fence.

He also happened to be wearing what looked like a mask.

"Hey," said Tinkler. "A gimp mask. Kinky horse."

"It's to keep the flies off him, you oaf," said Agatha.

Tania stopped beside the paddock and gazed at the horse. "This is Charlie. He's pretty much a permanent guest here." She leaned over the fence and stroked the horse's big face just below the anti-fly mask. "He's been having a bad time lately, haven't you, boy?"

Charlie nodded that big head, either in agreement or to shake her hand off. "Why has he been having a bad time?" said Agatha.

Tania sighed and turned away from the horse, resuming our stroll. "We have some goats on the grounds, too. One day one of the goats got into Charlie's paddock. We raced over, thinking there might be trouble, but quite the contrary. Charlie and the goat—whose name was Archibald—were getting along famously. They became the best of friends. Every morning Archibald would trot over to the stables and wait for Charlie to be brought out to the paddock, like a kid calling around at his best mate's house. And they'd spend the day together, every day."

Tinkler inserted his head between mine and Nevada's. "I reckon they were having interspecies sex," he whispered. "That's what it was all about. I told you that horse was kinky."

"Then one day Archibald disappeared, and ever since then Charlie has been inconsolable." We all looked back at the horse in his paddock. Munching on his hay, he didn't look inconsolable. He looked well fed and complacent. But then, I'm no expert on horse moods.

We walked away from the outbuildings, leaving the well-tended lawns behind as we strode through long grass towards a belt of trees. The sun was now high and the shade of the trees was welcome. Sticky green strands of weeds tugged at our ankles as we waded through the overgrown foliage. We came to a stamped-down barbed-wire fence rising up from the weeds in mashed curves. We stepped over it carefully.

"You can walk across the bridleways to the church and the pub without ever setting foot on a road," said Tania. The sound of crickets seething in the grass had grown louder than the distant traffic on the motorway and the sour, pleasant smell of growing things was all around us.

We were looking out across a big oval field with a rail fence at its circumference. "That's a training track," said Tania. "For racehorses."

In the middle of the oval space stood a green metal structure. "Is that a feeding station for the horses?" said Nevada.

"It's a release gate," said Tania. "To train them for races."

At the top of the oval, to our left, was a Tudor cottage. At the bottom, to our right, a blue tractor stood in the shadow of some trees. Directly in front of us, on the other side of the field, was a run-down-looking barn, and near it a big blunt silver bullet shape. It had a long green horizontal stripe along the side with windows in it and a short vertical stripe, which I realised was a door.

It was a caravan.

Surrounding the caravan were animals which, at this distance, could just be identified as goats.

Tania stopped at the fence and leaned on it, gazing across the field. We seemed to have come to some kind of definitive halt. So I said, "Are we meeting Ophelia here?"

"No, I've arranged for you to have a chat with her at her place."

"Where's her place?"

Tania pointed to the silver caravan.

As we approached the caravan, the goats withdrew, casting suspicious glances back at us. It was just Nevada and me—we'd left the others on the far side of the field—but that still seemed to be plenty enough to spook these critters. Now that we were closer, I could see that there were green hubcaps on the tyres with the word *Bluebird* embossed on them.

There was also a porthole window in the green door of the caravan. The other windows had fringed green awnings over them and in the largest window, in the centre of the vehicle, I suddenly noticed that a woman was looking out at us.

She was sitting smoking a cigarette and regarding us without surprise. As soon as she realised that she'd been spotted she stood up and walked out of sight for a second before her face reappeared in the round window of the door.

She opened it and looked out at us.

She was wearing a black T-shirt and faded pink dungarees with narrow blue stripes on them. They were grass-stained and had been patched at the knees. Her feet were in sandals. Her thin, bare arms had elaborate tattoos in inky black swirls forming sleeves between her wrists and elbows. On her head she wore a shapeless olive-green woollen hat of the kind that always made me think of the French Revolution. A strand of grey hair had escaped from the hat and she tucked it back in as she looked at us.

"Ophelia?" I said.

"I suppose you'd better come in," she said without enthusiasm, and retreated back into the caravan, leaving the door open. There was a tree stump that served as a doorstep so we stepped on this and up into the caravan.

I felt it shift ever so slightly with our weight as we entered.

We were now in a narrow gangway that ran most of the length of the vehicle. It had a green and white chequered linoleum floor. On the left there were kitchen cabinets, on the right a sink and cooker, and a small seating alcove in green leatherette with a fold-down table. Ophelia had resumed her seat here by the window.

"May we come in?"

"I said you could." She picked up her cigarette from an ashtray on the table. It was hand rolled and it had gone out, so she ignited it again with her lighter. Nevada and I came further in and, after a moment's hesitation, we sat down in some chairs fashioned of chrome with green leatherette cushions. There was space in the alcove with Ophelia and we could have sat there with her, but that seemed too cosy by far.

She puffed on her rollie for a moment, studying us, and then said, "So you've come here for three reasons." She exhaled smoke in our direction. "Number one, you want to know if I've been trying to kill Helene. I haven't."

Okay, so that's that, I thought. What more evidence does one need?

"Number two, you want to buy a copy of our first album, the original one, from me. Okay."

"What?" said Nevada and I simultaneously.

"I said okay. I've got a copy and you can buy it from me." She pinched out her cigarette and laid it carefully in the ashtray, presumably to finish later. Waste not, want not. She half rose from her seat. "I can get it for you now."

"Okay," said Nevada and I, simultaneously again.

But instead of getting up, Ophelia sat down again. "I suppose we should talk price first." She didn't sound enthusiastic about it. This wasn't a bad idea, although I would have liked to see the LP—or at least been fully convinced of its existence—before we started haggling.

"All right," I said.

Ophelia lit her rollie again and resumed smoking it for a moment or two of intense concentration. And then she named a sum that was so outrageous that I burst out laughing. She didn't like this, and I don't blame her.

Nevada, who had been looking at Ophelia with horror because of the price, was now instead looking at me with horror because of my breach of etiquette.

But I really hadn't been able to stop myself.

"What's so funny?" said Ophelia.

"So, here's the thing," I said. "There are no copies of this record for sale anywhere online at the moment." I knew this because of course I was constantly checking, and had been ever since I'd accepted Erik's assignment.

"That sounds about right," said Ophelia.

"But they do turn up from time to time. And I'm sure one will turn up in the next couple of months." This was a generally sound assumption, although maybe I was being a bit optimistic about how long we'd have to wait.

Ophelia shrugged, shoulders rising on either side of her frayed dungaree straps. "So what?"

"So, when copies do turn up, the price is only a tenth, sometimes less—a twentieth—of the amount of money you're asking for."

Ophelia looked at her cigarette, which had gone out again, and irritably mashed it to fragments in the ashtray. That was one she wouldn't be smoking later. "Look," she said. "Have you seen how Helene lives? Have you seen where she lives?"

"I haven't actually seen Helene's flat," I said carefully. "But she's more or less living with Erik Make Loud now. And it's true he certainly does have a nice house in a nice part of town."

"And what about Dylis? Have you seen her place?"

"True again," I said.

"That has to be the most fantastic flat I've ever seen in London," added Nevada.

"Too bad you can't enjoy the view when you're in a coma," I said.

Ophelia gave me a bug-eyed stare, and I thought I'd gone too far. But then she started coughing, covering her mouth and looking so embarrassed that I couldn't help feeling sorry for her.

"Sorry," she said as the coughing fit subsided. "I shouldn't have mentioned Dylis. Poor Dylis. I forgot for a second what had happened to her. But the point I'm making is—look at where they live. And look at where Tania lives. And now…" She gestured around her. "Look where I'm living. Okay, let's be clear about this, I am in no way, shape or form slagging off Tania. Without Tania, I wouldn't even have this. I'm just saying that they've got theirs and it's time I got mine. Just a tiny slice of something for myself."

She looked around the caravan. "Tania lets me live here. And she's let me start raising my goats. You saw them, right?"

"Yes, they're very lovely," said Nevada, lying fluently.

"They're cashmere goats," said Ophelia. "They are lovely. They take a lot of grooming, but they're lovely.

When I can get them established and they're producing a decent quantity of fleece I can set up in partnership with a local spinner, or even learn to do the spinning myself, and I can begin to earn a living."

She delved into the big central pocket in the chest of her dungarees and drew out a tobacco tin. "A living. At last. That's all I ask. But it's going to take money to get established. I need to buy this land I'm using from Tania. It's all very well for her to let me live here for free, but I want to pay my own way."

She had popped open her tobacco tin and begun to delve inside, but now she looked up at us fiercely. "I want to pay my own way," she repeated.

"Fair enough," I said. I didn't add, *You still aren't going to get a fraction of what you're asking for that record.*

"And it's not just the land. I need everything else to get started with the goats. Including, god help me, the goats themselves. The ones you see out there are about half of what I had." She turned and peered out the window, looking anxiously for her goats.

"What happened to the others?" said Nevada.

"Someone stole them."

Cashmere rustlers, I thought. "Including Archibald?" I said.

She seemed to wilt. Her whole formidable façade vanished and her manner suddenly softened. "Yes, including Archibald. He was such a lovely little chap. And poor Charlie is heartbroken."

It took me a second to remember that Charlie was the horse.

342

"Are you sure they were stolen?" said Nevada.

"Yes."

"Who'd do something like that?"

"Oh, I know exactly who did it. Fucking Fancher."

"Who's fucking Fancher?" I said.

"Farmer. Fucking fascist farmer. Lives less than a mile from here. He got wind of my plans to raise goats for cashmere and did the maths and realised it could be quite lucrative. So he decided to take a crack at it himself." She picked up her tobacco tin again and extracted a pack of rolling papers from it. "He purchased some suitable goats and he brought them back to his farm in a trailer, then..." She paused as she expertly sifted a pinch of tobacco into a cigarette paper. "Then he got drunk and forgot about them. It was a particularly hot weekend and he just forgot about them and left them in the trailer."

"Jesus."

Ophelia rolled the cigarette, licked it and lit it. "And by the time he remembered, they were all dead."

"Jesus Christ."

"So he decided he would save money on replacing them by stealing some of mine instead."

"But can't you do something?" said Nevada. I could see she was scandalised about the nightmare deaths of those poor goats. And, to tell the truth, so was I. "I mean, if you know who stole them..."

"I don't have any proof," said Ophelia. She took the cigarette out of her mouth, picked a strand of tobacco off her lip and put it in the ashtray.

"But if he's got your goats…" Nevada paused, realising she'd almost said something comical.

"Including Archibald," I said quickly.

"Including Archibald," added Nevada, shooting me a grateful look.

"I would have to get access to his property," said Ophelia. "And then I'd somehow have to prove the goats were mine in the first place. Believe me, I've thought about it, and I've discussed it with Tania, but there's really nothing she can do. I mean, what is she going to say to him? She has to live here, and I suppose I do, too. She doesn't want to confront him and make an enemy of a neighbour. I mean, she probably *would* if I kicked up a big stink about it, but she's done too much for me already."

She took a drag on her cigarette and studied us. She now seemed more sad than formidable. "Anyway, now you know why I need that money."

"Okay," I said. "But it still doesn't alter the fact that Erik won't pay that much for the record. Even if he wanted to, he couldn't afford to." Rich retired rock star he might be, but Mr Make Loud couldn't afford to throw away tens of thousands of pounds.

Except on drugs, of course.

"Look," said Ophelia, her voice low and imploring. "Just ask him, all right?"

"Okay," I said. "Sure. No harm in that." No harm except him possibly bursting a major blood vessel when he heard.

"Okay, thank you," said Ophelia. "Now, about that third reason." I didn't know for a moment what she was talking about, then I remembered that she had announced that she knew we'd come here for three reasons.

She took a long drag on her cigarette and then exhaled. Since it was a rollie it wasn't as obnoxious as tobacco smoke usually was, but nevertheless it was annoying and inconsiderate. Maybe something in my demeanour conveyed this to her, because she leaned over and opened the window. Then she turned to me and said, "It seems you've managed to convince Tania that her life is in danger."

"We believe it really is. And so is yours." The open window brought in the far-off sound of the motorway, and a current of fresh air, along with the faint smell of goat.

Ophelia gave us a crooked smile. "So now you're charging Tania to provide protection for us?" She shook her head. "I don't like to see my friends being taken advantage of."

"What makes you think we're taking advantage of her?"

She gestured with her cigarette in the direction of Tania's estate. "Staying down here in a cosy bedroom at the big house. It's like a country hotel jaunt for you two, isn't it? And what could you possibly do to protect us, anyway?"

"A lot," said Nevada. "And we won't be staying in a bedroom at the big house."

Ophelia gave us her crooked smile again. "Really? You mean you won't even be on the premises?"

"We'll be very much on the premises. But we'll be sleeping in a tent."

"A tent?"

Nevada nodded. "Perhaps you can help us choose a spot where we can be tucked away out of sight but keep an eye on Tania's house."

Ophelia was staring at her. "All right," she said.

"In fact," said Nevada, "perhaps if you wouldn't mind we could have a look for a suitable spot now? I'd like to get the tent set up."

"All right." Ophelia stubbed out her cigarette and got up.

As the two women went off and explored the perimeter of the oval field together I waited outside the caravan and got on the phone to Erik. I started by telling him that we'd met with Ophelia and that she claimed to have the record, but to brace himself because the price she was asking was completely insane.

"How much?"

He fell gloomily silent when I told him. After a moment or two, to relieve the silence, and the gloom, I went on to explain what she wanted the money for, and I told him about her feelings regarding where she was in her life versus the other Blue Tits. Feelings which I felt were entirely justified, but it wasn't my job to tell Erik that.

It was my job to try and get hold of the record.

Nevertheless, I made sure he understood her situation.

This led to more silence, but somehow it wasn't so gloomy this time. "I have an idea," he said.

By the time the two women came back, Nevada seemed to have won Ophelia over completely. They were chatting away cheerfully, although the subject was far from cheerful. Ophelia was saying, "But what if you do happen to find someone? An intruder? A potential murderer?"

"We apprehend them."

"But how?"

"Well, there's a range of options," said Nevada. I knew that amongst these was the hand Taser she'd bought the day before with Tania's money. I say 'Taser' but it was actually a 20 million volt, 4.5 milliamp Runt rechargeable stun gun complete with built-in flashlight and the special wrist strap disable pin. It also came in a vibrant range of colours.

Nevada had chosen shocking pink, no pun intended, both because it went with the punk theme and because we got a substantial discount for that model.

We'd purchased it from a place called the Spook Store from a man with some very odd stubble, along with an assortment of other interesting items.

All of which were also paid for by Tania.

But at the moment my thoughts were elsewhere. "I spoke to Erik," I said.

"Oh," said Nevada.

"Oh yeah, right," said Ophelia. I could tell she was dreading his response. She was in the odd position of knowing she was asking an impossible price for the record, but also feeling she had no other choice. "What did he say?"

"He had a very interesting suggestion," I said.

Nevada was watching me with a half-smile on her face. "And what was that?"

"To use his own words, think of Live Aid, but with goats."

24: RELEASE GATE

Nevada spent the better part of an hour attending to her new duties as a 'security consultant' for Tania, and then we went back to the house to collect Agatha, Tinkler and Tania herself.

We sat waiting in the kitchen while Tania went to dig out a laptop we could use—we wanted something with a bigger screen than a phone. As soon as she was out of sight Agatha said, "Did you guys know she was married?"

"Tania?" said Nevada. "We just assumed she was divorced like everybody else her age."

"No, she's currently married. And he's here."

"What, here in the house? Now?"

"That's right," said Tinkler. "We haven't seen him because he's this shameful demented lunatic and they keep him locked away."

"We haven't seen him because this house is the size of Blenheim Palace," said Agatha.

"Still," I said. "It's a bit strange that he hasn't come to say hello."

"According to Tania, he sends his apologies but he's tied up in meetings."

"Meetings here in the house?" I said. I hadn't seen any cars or any other sign of anyone else besides ourselves and Tania. Even this husband seemed a bit of a will o' the wisp.

"Online meetings, on his computer," said Agatha.

"Duh," said Tinkler.

"Has anybody actually seen this guy?" I said.

Agatha shook her head. "No."

"No, but my money is still on shameful demented lunatic, probably with disfiguring scars," said Tinkler. "Let's, for the sake of the argument, call him the Phantom."

Agatha sighed and clouted him on the shoulder. It was a gentle and exasperated sort of blow. Almost affectionate. "His name is Derren Ghir. And he's apparently fairly well off."

"For which read filthy rich," said Nevada.

"He's one of those strange eccentric reclusive Howard Hughes types," said Tinkler. "You know, untold millions in the bank and mason jars full of urine."

"Shut up, Tinkler. Tania told me that they met when she was travelling through India. In fact, specifically, they met one night outside the Taj Mahal, in the moonlight, and he swept her off her feet. How romantic is that?"

"It sets a fairly high bar," I said.

"Anyway, never mind about the Phantom of the Taj Mahal," said Tinkler. "What is this insane scheme cooked up by my friend Erik?"

Agatha seemed pretty intrigued too. "Did you say he wants to hold a benefit gig to raise funds for Ophelia?"

"That's right," I said. "And I think she deserves funds. Anything to narrow the gap."

"What gap?" said Tinkler.

"Between Tania in this mansion," said Nevada, "and Ophelia living in an old caravan in the woods."

"With goats," said Agatha.

Nevada nodded. "It has to be said they are very nice goats. What's more they're going to be a money-spinner as an endlessly renewable source of cashmere jumpers."

"And cheese, too," said Tania, coming back in with a laptop under her arm. "Shall we go and try some?"

Ten minutes later we were all sitting inside Ophelia's caravan. I would have sworn there wouldn't be enough room for this many people, but it was surprisingly comfortable. Tania, Nevada and I sat close to Ophelia in the alcove, with Tania's laptop shut on the table in front of us.

More importantly, also on the table were bread, goat's cheese, olives and a bottle of wine. Sitting on barstools at the counter further down the gangway, Tinkler and Agatha also had plates of bread and cheese and olives and their own bottle of wine.

Ophelia had provided the food, and the wine had come courtesy of Nevada. We'd unloaded it from Kind of Red on our walk from the house—we'd come down with an assortment of bottles in accord with Nevada's precept to never travel anywhere without a supply of good wine.

It was a red, the Matetic Pinot Noir.

Ophelia loved the wine and Tania was guardedly impressed, all of which made Nevada a happy bunny.

"It's Chilean. They also do an excellent Syrah and some interesting whites."

We ate and we drank, and from time to time goats peered inquisitively in at us through the open door as if they wanted to join the party. Ophelia seemed relaxed and happy, enjoying the company and the attention. She was hardly recognisable as the woman we'd first met, chain-smoking rollies and regarding us with suspicion.

When I judged the moment was right, I said, "Okay, shall we do it?"

Ophelia immediately tensed up, but Tania nodded and opened the laptop. "I'll make the call," she said.

A few seconds later, the faces of Helene and Erik appeared on the screen. After the usual teething problems of sound and vision—I sensed the unseen presence of Bong Cha at the other end, walking the rock-and-roll couple through how to operate this suspicious new-fangled technology—communication was finally established. Tania angled the screen to face Ophelia. Ophelia lit a rollie.

Some rather tense pleasantries ensued and then Erik got down to business. He mentioned live streaming, YouTube, crowdfunding and Kickstarter, all in the manner of a man who had been recently briefed by his housekeeper about such things.

Ophelia nervously sucked on her cigarette. "So what you're suggesting is that we get the band back together," she said.

"Just for this one gig," said Helene.

"Which will make it really special," said Erik. "People

love these band reunions. And they'll pay through the nose if they know it's a one-off."

Ophelia's hair was escaping from her woolly hat again. She irritably shoved it back out of sight. "Just one problem. Our bassist is in a coma."

"Of course we've thought about that," said Helene. "But we don't think it's disrespectful or anything. We'll make an announcement and say our thoughts and prayers are with Dylis."

"And although it sounds horrible," said Tania, "having her in the hospital might actually sharpen people's interest."

"You mean because none of us are getting any younger," said Ophelia. "So they'd better catch us before another one drops off the tree?"

"Something like that."

"And you're up for it?" Ophelia gave Tania a steady, assessing look.

Tania smiled back, a slightly crooked smile. "Maybe it will generate a whole new following for me. Or at least consolidate the old one."

Ophelia nodded thoughtfully. "Okay. But that still doesn't solve the problem of who's going to play bass."

On the screen Helene smiled. "I know someone who might step into the breach."

"Who? Oh…"

Erik smiled modestly. "People say I play bass like a girl anyway."

A smile twitched on Ophelia's lips. "Okay, I'll think about it."

"Thank you! That's great!" said Erik.

"I just said I'll think about it."

"Of course, of course," said Helene.

"But if we *were* to go ahead with this…" said Ophelia. "How exactly do we make any money from it?"

"You let us worry about that," said Erik. Which translated as, *We'll get Bong Cha to explain that to us.*

Goodbyes were said, all very civil, then the laptop was shut and Nevada refilled everybody's wine glass. Now that they'd finished eating, Tinkler and Agatha had moved in close to the table.

Ophelia was deep in thought. "We're going to have to film this gig," she said.

"We might be able to help you with that," I said.

Nevada was busy opening another bottle of wine with her Swiss Army knife, but now she looked up and added, "That's right. We know a cameraman. Camerawoman actually. And a sound woman."

"You mean Sydney the giantess?" said Agatha. "And Foxy Foxcroft?"

"Exactly."

"Oh my lord," said Tinkler. "Women are drawn to me as if by some strange magnetic force." By which he meant he'd failed to sleep with Foxy Foxcroft once and was now being given the opportunity to fail again.

"But they work for Stinky Stanmer," said Agatha. "If we enlist them, Stinky is bound to find out what we're doing."

"And…?"

It took a moment for the penny to drop. "My god," said

Agatha. "You're right. For once we *want* Stinky to know what we're up to—because we need the publicity. It's brilliant."

Ophelia had been listening to this with keen interest.

"You know Stinky Stanmer?" she said.

"I'm afraid so."

"And you think you can get him to come down here to cover our gig?"

"Once he gets wind of it, the problem would be to try and keep him away."

A big smile blossomed on Ophelia's face. "This might actually work," she murmured. "Stinky Stanmer…"

"Just one thing," said Tinkler. "You may want to put chastity belts on your goats, to make sure Stinky doesn't try to shag them."

To her credit, Ophelia didn't even blink. She said, "Even the male ones?"

"Especially the male ones."

Night was falling and the moon was up, bright and white and as big as a house, as we made our way back from Ophelia's caravan. We walked past the big oval field, towards Tania's mansion. Tania indicated that she wanted to talk to me, so I hung back with her as Nevada, Tinkler and Agatha forged ahead.

"I thought that went pretty well," I said.

Tania's head bobbed, her eyes invisible in the spring night. "Yes, I agree. But that isn't what I wanted to talk to you about. I've been in touch with the hospital."

Sensing that something significant was afoot, Nevada dropped back and joined us.

"News about Dylis," I told her.

"That's right," said Tania. "And it's not good."

"Oh shit."

"No," said Tania hastily. "She's still alive. And her condition hasn't deteriorated. On the contrary she's beginning to improve."

"Then what's the bad news?"

"Someone tried to kill her."

"Tried—again, you mean?"

"Yes, in the intensive care unit of the hospital."

"What happened?"

"Someone injected a substance into the bag feeding her saline drip. It would have worked, too, but a nurse spotted that something was wrong. She changed the bag and saved Dylis's life."

"Thank god for that. She deserves a medal."

"I agree, but instead she's being blamed for what is being described as a mix-up in administering drugs. The nurse is incredibly pissed off. She's the one who spotted the error and she's gone from being a hero to being the scapegoat. She's livid. Not least because there was video footage which clearly shows an intruder by Dylis's bed."

"An intruder?"

"In hospital garb. They must have been aware of the cameras because the intruder took great pains not to let their face be seen at any time. It wasn't even possible to tell if it was a man or woman."

"Wasn't?" I said. Her use of the past tense seemed unsettling.

"Yes. The footage from the security camera mysteriously vanished. When they went back to look at it again, it was wiped. Like I say, this intruder was aware of the camera. They had apparently thought out carefully how to neutralise it as part of their campaign."

There was silence except for the distant murmur of Tinkler and Agatha in conversation and the swishing of our shoes through the long grass. The cold bright light of the moon fell across the fields around us.

"So we're up against the sort of person who can do shit like that," said Nevada.

"Someone very dangerous," said Tania.

"We've got to leave this to the police," I said.

"The police don't believe a word of it. They don't think there ever was an intruder at the hospital. They think there was an incompetent nurse who is now covering her arse. And the nurse isn't having any of it. She's kicking up a stink, so there's going to be some kind of enquiry. One day. Much good it will do us."

When we reached the house we said goodbye to Tinkler and Agatha, who were driving back to London. As they pulled away, I said, "Those two are getting on surprisingly well."

"Clean Head's keeping a close eye on him now that Opal's back on the scene."

"Is she jealous?" I said.

"Our girl Agatha doesn't do jealousy. She's keeping him under observation because we have a wager."

"We?"

"She and I. Though we'd be happy to cut you in on it."

"A wager? Let me guess…"

"That's right," said Nevada. "On whether Tinkler will, what is the phrase he used? Get his ashes hauled." She looked at me. "Do you want in on the bet?"

"What are the odds on ash-hauling actually happening?"

"Astronomically against."

25: TECHNICOLOR YAWN

It turns out that goats eat grass pellets. Not tin cans as Tinkler had helpfully suggested earlier.

Tinkler had rejoined us at Tania's the following day. "We thought we'd got rid of you," said Nevada when he turned up, beaming.

"I got a lift here. You know how I love getting a lift."

"Yes, for a man who owns a car you seem remarkably reluctant to drive it."

"Speaking of driving cars, I asked Clean Head if she wanted to come too, but she had some far-fetched story about having to work."

"Having to work and, much more importantly, look after our cats," said Nevada.

"Like that isn't work," said Tinkler.

The three of us were crossing the field towards Ophelia's caravan. The late morning sun was just starting to burn off the dew in the long grass, which was still wet enough to feel cool through our shoes. It was going to be another hot day, and the early coolness was welcome.

We were making slow progress because Nevada and I were lugging large and rather heavy plastic sacks. Tinkler, characteristically, was carrying nothing. The sacks contained grass pellets—something I hadn't known existed before today. They'd arrived in a delivery this morning and Tania had suggested we might take them over for Ophelia.

"They'll help you make friends with the goats," she said.

She wasn't wrong. As we approached the silver caravan the goats, who had always previously retreated whenever we arrived, instead came drifting tentatively towards us.

"Watch out, they're closing in," said Tinkler.

"Do you think they can smell this stuff?" said Nevada, setting her bag on the ground with an emphatic thud.

"Or they recognise it," I said, thudding my own one down beside it.

"Do goats have good eyes?"

"They have *weird* eyes," said Tinkler. "Unless you're the Lord Satan, in which case they have perfectly normal eyes."

It was true that the goats' eyes were extraordinary, with eerie black horizontal rectangular slits that served as pupils. We could see several examples now among the group peering warily as they drew close to us. Us and the bags of food.

"And that's not all," said Tinkler. "That one's got a comb-over. A bad comb-over. A bad goat comb-over."

This was also true, one of the boldest of our new friends having strands of longer hair on his back, curling across as if they'd been combed to conceal a bald patch. He and his companions also had rather cute pink noses with grey spots. Another one of the group, now advancing on us with growing boldness, had the traditional wispy billy goat beard.

"There's more of them coming through the trees," said Tinkler. "It's like a zombie movie. Shouldn't we secure a line of retreat?"

For all the goatish activity outside, there was no sign of life within Ophelia's caravan. The curtains in the windows were firmly closed. But we were preoccupied with the goats, who definitely were exhibiting signs of life and had gathered around us in a semi-circle. "I think they want feeding," said Nevada.

"I think you're right." The plastic sack I'd hauled over from the house had a thin line of perforations along the top. I used this to split it open and Nevada did the same with hers. We reached inside the bags and drew out handfuls of the grass pellets. They were small and neat, dry brownish green and rather sweet-smelling.

Tinkler was peering over my shoulder. "That stuff reminds me of cannabis buds," he said.

"Everything reminds you of cannabis buds," said Nevada.

Nevada and I extended our hands, full of these pellets, towards the waiting goats. They immediately began to jostle forward.

"Careful," said Tinkler. "If you get your hand bitten off you will not only have lost a valuable appendage, you will also always have to tell the humiliating story of how you lost it to a *goat*."

Comb-over Goat was the boldest, and the first to begin to feed. He put his warm chin on my hand and his tongue darted out repeatedly with machine gun rapidity, sweeping up the grass pellets and leaving me with a damp palm. I stuck my hands back in the bag and this time came out with two handfuls. Even so, there was jostling competition amongst the eager crowd and it wasn't easy ensuring that everyone got a fair share.

It was fun, though, and soon even Tinkler was joining in the feeding.

"What are those things on their throats?" he said.

Some of the goats did indeed have odd attachments growing from their necks which looked like the dangly things you get on those woolly Peruvian hats.

"They're neck bollocks," said Tinkler, always eager to put a prurient interpretation on anything. Though they did kind of look like that.

"They're called toggles," said a voice behind us.

We turned to see Ophelia standing there in her dungarees, barefoot, smoking a rollie. We had been so preoccupied with feeding the masses that we hadn't noticed her emerge from her caravan. "They're scent glands," she said. "They use them for putting markings on trees."

"Just like we men use our bollocks," volunteered Tinkler.

Having finally stuffed themselves sufficiently, the goats began to wander off again to whatever pressing business goats have in a field in Surrey. "Thank you for bringing the food over," said Ophelia.

"We also came to collect you," said Nevada.

"Collect me?"

"Tania says it's time to get started. We'll walk with you to the house. To provide moral support."

"Or in my case, immoral support," said Tinkler.

Ophelia shook her head. "That's very sweet of you, but I've changed my mind."

"Oh no," said Nevada, genuinely aghast.

Ophelia sucked intently on her cigarette and continued shaking her head. "I'm sorry, but I just don't think I can do it."

"You really ought to come over," said Nevada. "Perhaps just for a few minutes?"

"No, I…"

"You have to see the drum kit Tania got for you," I said.

Ophelia dropped her cigarette to the grass and ground it out with her bare foot, staring down as if this action required her complete and dedicated attention. "She did what?" she asked quietly.

"She's bought you this fantastic drum kit."

Ophelia gradually raised her head and looked at us. Her eyes had filled with tears. "She's been so good to me," she said in a harsh, choked whisper.

"You don't want to let her down now, do you?" said Nevada gently.

Ophelia shook her head and wiped her eyes.

We waited while she went back into the caravan to change, which involved her putting on a leather jacket and a ratty old pair of sneakers. Then we all walked together back towards the big house.

"Have those goats ever taken anybody's hand off?" said Tinkler.

* * *

The rehearsal was scheduled to take place in the drawing room of Tania's mansion. "For a drawing room it's very short of drawing materials," said Tinkler.

"The term is short for withdrawing room," said Nevada. "Back in the Neanderthal times, by which I mean the eighteenth and nineteenth centuries, after a meal the men would withdraw to a room like this to smoke and drink booze and abandon the women."

"What a great tradition," said Tinkler. "Such a shame it's fallen into disuse."

Booze was in evidence, though, in the shape of a number of bottles of excellent wine, both red and white, that Nevada had chosen. These were sitting on a sideboard against the wall to our left. Most of the other furniture, old maroon leather chairs and sofas of varying degrees of antique ugliness, had been moved here to join it. The billiard table had been pushed to the opposite wall—fortunately facilitated by wheels on its fat little legs. This wall also featured a large fireplace and a number of ugly oil paintings of grim-looking men.

By contrast, the wall directly in front of us was bright and sunny, with a row of tall windows that faced out towards the garden and the woods. There was a built-in bench seat running under the length of the windows, upholstered in maroon leather, of course.

Moving the furniture had left the bulk of the room essentially empty. The vast dusty pink carpet which had covered the floor had been rolled back to reveal an expanse of dark wood. In the middle of this there now stood guitar amps—although as yet no guitars—a microphone stand, and a gleaming black and silver Saturn V MH 'Exotic Rock' three-piece drum kit.

Nevada, Tinkler and I walked further into the room, our voices and footsteps echoing in the uncarpeted space. Ophelia followed shyly and hesitantly, like one of her goats venturing into a strange and potentially dangerous place.

She wandered over to the drum kit and gingerly took her seat behind it. Then she leaned forward and ran her fingernails across the drum skins on the low tom-tom, creating an eerie sound.

As if she'd been waiting in hiding to spring out at this exact moment, Tania now came in to join us. Rather than her usual business suit or country lady attire she was wearing jeans, a black turtleneck sweater and, surprisingly, Doc Marten shoes, polished to a high shine.

She smiled at Ophelia sitting behind the drums. "You look good there," she said.

"You shouldn't have bought this," said Ophelia, reaching out to caress a cymbal. "It must have cost a fortune."

"You can pay me back from the proceeds," said Tania, still smiling.

"The proceeds…" said Ophelia.

"The gig is going to be a big success."

"A big success," repeated Ophelia. She didn't sound convinced. A moment later she looked up sharply as if she'd heard something she didn't like, but the big empty room was silent. "Where's Helene?" she said.

"Out in her car."

"Out in her car?"

"Well, in her boyfriend's car," said Tania. "She's been sitting there since she arrived."

It was Helene who was responsible for Tinkler being here. He had cadged a lift down with her, in Erik's car. Erik himself, however, was nowhere to be seen, having remained in London.

"What is she doing sitting out there in her boyfriend's car?" asked Ophelia. Legitimately, I thought.

"She said she had to make some calls," said Tania disdainfully. "But I think she's just listening to music on her phone. Because she's scared to come in."

"Scared?" repeated Ophelia, her voice heavy with contempt. She seemed to have forgotten her own earlier fear. "Well, if she doesn't have the balls to get out of the car we're not going to get anywhere."

"We'll go and get her," said Nevada, in her brightest eager-to-assist mode. Tinkler and I followed her through the maze of dark hallways of the big house to the front door, which opened onto blazing sunshine and a gleaming blue Jaguar XF saloon parked in the driveway. Sure enough, Helene was sitting behind the steering wheel peering at her phone.

"Nice car," I said to Tinkler. "No wonder you wanted a ride in it."

"My heart belongs to Kind of Red. I am forever true to that automobile."

"Your heart isn't forever true enough to drive it, though."

"It's complicated," said Tinkler.

Nevada touched my arm. "Let me go and talk to her."

"Okay," I said, rather relieved to be let off the hook. She walked over to the car, waving at Helene, who looked up from her phone at Nevada's approach. That, at least, was a good sign, I thought.

Whatever Nevada said to Helene, it got her out of the car. She kissed Nevada and then came over and kissed me. Having spent an hour in the car with Tinkler driving down from London she didn't seem to want to kiss him again. Who would?

Interestingly, given the purpose of her visit today, Helene was dressed less like a rock chick than at any time since I'd met her. She was wearing a white T-shirt and peach-coloured trousers with the ankle cuffs turned up, over pink socks and white plimsolls. A black blazer had its cuffs turned up too, revealing a navy-blue silk lining. A pair of red sunglasses nestled in her blonde hair.

She'd obviously chosen this ensemble with care, though what message she was trying to send was anybody's guess. The only unambiguous signal came from the guitar slung over her shoulder.

"No Erik?" I said.

"He thought it was best if I had a chance to get reacquainted with the girls on my own."

"That was thoughtful of him," said Nevada.

I smelled reprehensible cowardice rather than commendable sensitivity, but I didn't mention that. Instead I said, "Who's going to play bass for your rehearsal?"

Before Helene could reply there was the sound of an approaching engine followed by crunching gravel as a vehicle pulled into the driveway. It was a very familiar-looking shabby white van. Through the windscreen Monika the roadie was staring at us fixedly, as though baffled by our very existence.

Helene smiled. "There's your answer."

"Monika?"

"It's been a lifelong ambition of hers to be a proper member of the band. Well, this is her moment in the sun."

"Can she even play the bass?" I said.

"After a fashion. Which means almost as well as Dylis."

We all fell silent at this point, thinking about Dylis lying in a coma in her hospital bed with someone still trying to kill her.

Meanwhile Monika emerged from the van. She was dressed in the same leather jacket, jeans and tartan shirt as when she'd first invaded our garden in the wee small hours. Gripped in a precarious fashion under her left arm she had two blue and white cardboard cartons, each containing, they declared, twenty-four bottles of Corona Extra Mexican beer. In her right hand she clutched a transparent plastic bag containing a number of odd-looking, small yellow and black bottles. She must have seen me staring at it because as she walked past she brandished the bag in my face and yelled, "Party time!"

Judging by the smell coming off her, she had already made a considerable dent in the beers she was carrying. I winced to think that she had been driving in that condition.

Monika apparently felt her cheery announcement was sufficient greeting, since she now hurried into the house without another word.

Helene looked at us, a droll eyebrow raised, and said, "Party time."

Then she went and looked in Monika's van and took something off the front seat. A bass guitar. She held it up to show it to us. "This might be useful," she said.

She carried it with her as we went into the house. Two-Guitar Helene.

By the time we got to the drawing room Monika had already launched into her heartfelt reunion with her long lost bandmate. Indeed she was still gripping the bemused Ophelia in a bear hug beside the drum kit as we trooped in.

The cartons of beer were on the sideboard now. Monika had contemptuously shoved aside our wine bottles to make room for them, pushing the carefully curated selection of reds and whites back and almost out of sight. She evidently didn't think wine was sufficiently punk rock.

I could see Nevada was rather piqued at this.

The plastic bag had been thrown right across the room to land on the billiard table where several of the small yellow bottles had rolled out onto the green felt. I went over to inspect them. I eventually deciphered the rather hard to read logo as *Pig Sweat*. This was accompanied by a cartoon of a muscular and evidently gay pig in black leathers looking very pleased with himself and the words *Content: 15ml*. What the hell? Pig sweat?

I was just recalling the fascinating fact, learned on Halig Island, that pigs don't actually sweat, because they don't have sweat glands, when Tania came hurrying into the room and stopped dead.

Monika and Ophelia were still standing locked in their rather one-sided embrace, swaying slightly. Ophelia looked like she wanted to be rescued.

Helene turned to her. "Hello, Tan," she said. "How's it going?"

"Couldn't be better," said Tania in a tense, clipped voice. Then, to Monika, "I see you've brought the beer."

"That's not all," said Monika, releasing the relieved Ophelia and trotting over to the billiard table. She lifted the plastic bag, spilling a few more bottles out onto the green felt. "Drugs too!"

The room fell into an icy silence as Ophelia's expression changed gradually from relief to anger. "You do understand that I'm a recovering heroin addict?"

Monika nodded eagerly. "That's why I brought amyl nitrite."

She tried to hop up onto the billiard table to sit on it, fell off, tried again, then once more, and finally managed it, sitting there swinging her legs and smiling blissfully. She was clearly so drunk as to be impervious to Ophelia's rage, so Ophelia scanned the room for another target.

She didn't have to look far.

"Well, if it isn't Helene," she said.

"Hi, Oaf." Helene was busy at the amps, plugging in her guitar and Monika's bass.

"The very person who was responsible."

Helene didn't look up. "Responsible for what?"

"For me having something to recover from."

"What?"

"For getting me on that shit in the first place."

Now Helene spun around and glared at Ophelia. "Oh, Christ," she said. "Why don't you take ownership of your actions for just once in your miserable little life?"

Ophelia turned away from her, to Tania. She spoke in a tightly controlled voice, vibrating with strained politeness. "I am so sorry, Tania. I know you've gone to a lot of trouble and expense. But this just isn't going to work."

"I agree," snapped Helene. She began unplugging her guitar again.

"Wait a minute," said Tania.

"No," said Ophelia. "This was all a big mistake." She started for the door.

"You're right there," said Helene, also starting for the door, clasping her guitar.

"Wait," said Tania.

"No," said Helene. But she did wait, because both she and Ophelia had arrived at the door at the same time, and apparently neither of them wanted to be the first to go through it, so they had stopped and were standing there glaring at each other.

"I have a suggestion," said Monika, from her perch on the edge of the billiard table. Actually, she shouted it, with such force that everyone turned to look at her.

"I have a suggestion," repeated Monika at a more normal volume. Then she nodded wisely and opened her mouth, presumably to offer her suggestion.

But instead she shuddered abruptly and, rather than words coming out, there was an abrupt and noisome torrent of yellowish liquid dotted, by way of striking contrast, with tiny green spheres—my best guess, undigested peas.

This noisome regurgitated mass splashed onto the floor to form a yellow and green puddle that seemed such a cunningly engineered restatement of the colour scheme of the amyl nitrite bottles on the billiard table that I wondered for a crazed second if Monika had considerately contrived an art installation for us.

"I have a suggestion," repeated Monika again, in a thoughtful voice, studying the widening puddle of puke on the dark wooden floor. But we didn't get to hear what it was, because she toppled forward off the billiard table and fell into said puddle.

Helene was staring at this spectacle, white-faced and aghast. "Someone is poisoning our bass players," she whispered.

"She poisoned herself, honey," said Ophelia.

Then the two of them went over together to lift Monika out of her vomit.

I went into the kitchen to put the food on hold. I had been designated to do the catering for the Blue Tits' big reunion rehearsal, but after Monika's exhibition I surmised that no one would have much appetite for a while.

For the occasion I'd made my Jim Harrison tomato sauce. This was the one I regularly cooked to go with pasta, but it also served superbly as a pizza topping, and I'd figured pizzas would be a good casual kind of finger food for today. I hadn't made my own pizza bases this time, not least because I was wary of Tania's farmhouse oven, which

I was still coming to terms with. Instead I'd bought some good M&S pitta bread. When—and if—people wanted to eat I would spoon the sauce onto the pittas and add an assortment of toppings, including, of course, goat's cheese.

I was sneaking a small snack under the guise of checking the sauce when Tania and Tinkler came in. "Poor Monika," said Tania. "She's like an overexcited child at a birthday party." She sighed as she opened the cupboard under the sink. "Thank god I rolled up the carpet," she added.

"Good point," said Tinkler, joining me at the stove, clearly also in search of a snack. I cut him half a pitta bread and was putting some sauce on it as Tania took a bright blue plastic bucket and bright yellow rubber gloves out of the cupboard.

"In any case, we'll soon get it cleaned up," she said, and hurried off.

"I can't believe she doesn't have some domestic slaves—I mean help," said Tinkler. It was characteristic that he had fled the drawing room not at the first sign of vomit but the first sign of manual labour to clean it up.

"Apparently her husband doesn't like strangers under his roof."

"Really?" said Tinkler. "The Phantom of the Taj Mahal won't allow strangers in the house?"

"Well, I guess he allows some. I mean, we're here, aren't we?"

"Good point. I'm still not sure I believe in the existence of the Phantom, though."

"His name is Derren," I said. "And he's out there now." I pointed out of the kitchen window, where Derren could be seen on the driveway, talking to a man who'd apparently just driven up in a Mercedes-Benz.

"Wow, is that really him? He must have escaped from the attic."

Derren was a somewhat colourless man with thin mousy hair and a toothbrush moustache who wandered around the house in the strange combination of shorts and a buttoned-up sweater. Oh, and sandals with socks. This was the ensemble he was wearing now.

The man he was talking to was tall, thin and dressed in a green waxed cotton jacket despite the heat. From where I was standing, I wasn't able to see his face.

Up to now Derren had struck me as reserved and humourless, but he and the other man seemed thick as thieves, chatting animatedly. I had no way of hearing what they were saying but they were now sharing a hearty laugh. I was just beginning to wonder in earnest who the hell this guy was when Tania and Nevada came in.

"We need another pair of rubber gloves," said Tania.

"For Helene," said Nevada.

"She and Ophelia are cleaning up the mess," said Tania. "And looking after Monika, too."

"The two of them are working together," said Nevada, giving me a significant look.

"It's wonderful," said Tania, opening the cupboard under the sink again. She sounded happy—and relaxed, for the first time today. "They do seem to be getting along."

"That's right," said Tinkler. "Monika's Technicolor yawn broke the ice, so to speak. They're rallying around her."

As Tania stood up, triumphantly holding a second pair of yellow rubber gloves, I said, "Who's that?" and nodded to the window.

She and Nevada came over just in time to see the visitor get into the Mercedes and drive away.

"Oh, that's just Fancher," said Tania.

"The farmer?" I said.

"That's right."

"The one who let his goats die?" said Nevada, with an edge to her voice. "And then stole Ophelia's?"

"I'm afraid that's just rumour and speculation," said Tania, slipping smoothly into politician mode. "Excuse me." She went out with the rubber gloves. Tinkler, surprisingly, followed her. I guess he was reassured that the clean-up was well in hand and there was no danger of him being enlisted to help.

This left Nevada and me alone in the kitchen. So she got out one of the bottles of the good wine and set about opening it while I cut up some pittas and began assembling mini pizzas. After all, we had a responsibility to do a quality control check before serving them to the guests, didn't we?

We were thus gainfully occupied when Derren came in from the garden, sandals slapping on the tiled floor. He looked cheerful. His conversation with Farmer Fancher had left him more animated than I'd seen him up until now.

"Something smells good," he said.

"That guy you were talking to, he was your neighbour the farmer?" I asked, trying to sound casual.

"That's right."

"What was he doing here?" said Nevada. I realised that since she had been hired to look after security on the premises she could ask blunt questions like this.

Derren grinned toothily. "He said he'd been having a lot of trouble with foxes lately and asked if we'd seen any, perhaps around the stables. I said no foxes—unless you counted this morning's influx of foxy women. We had a good laugh about that."

Just then, as if in riposte to the foxy women comment, there was a blast of noise from the direction of the drawing room. It seemed to shake the foundations of the house and we all looked up in shock before realising that this was the Blue Tits in full cry.

"Ah, sounds like the girls have got started," said Derren. He promptly pirouetted 180 degrees and strode back out into the garden. The music was causing the copper-bottomed cookware hanging on the kitchen wall to resonate eerily.

"Should we go and listen?" said Nevada.

"Not if we value our hearing."

"I suppose it's rather a personal moment for them and we shouldn't intrude."

"Exactly."

Judging by the booming bassline either Monika was back in action or someone else had stepped into the breach. I listened carefully, trying to isolate the bass. It wasn't Carol Kaye, but it carried the beat, more or less. And then the vocals began, a banshee scream that modulated into aggressive chanting, all impressively different from Tania as slick political operator.

Tinkler came hurrying into the kitchen again, as if blown by the force of the music. "The band is back together," he announced.

"So we hear," said Nevada.

"And that's Monika playing with them?" I asked.

"Yes. She's had some amyl nitrite and she's feeling much better."

The rehearsal continued all afternoon and into the evening. By the time the reconstituted Blue Tits packed it in, sweaty and happy, the light had faded and the fragrant summer night had begun in earnest.

We ate supper outside on the picnic table. Nevada's wine selections were sufficiently praised and she was finally mollified, her ruffled fur smoothed again, to use a cat metaphor. It was a good occasion, everyone friendly and cheerful, though no one wanted to sit directly opposite Monika and be in the line of fire, so to speak, in case there was another episode of gastric distress.

When the meal was over, Tinkler left, getting an Uber and then a late train back to London. He could easily have spent the night at Tania's, but since Opal was back on the scene he'd been obsessed with the frankly ludicrous possibility that she might turn up on his doorstep—or, rather, in his bed—and he wanted to be around in case of that unlikely eventuality.

Helene, who'd had far too much to drink to consider driving, did spend the night. Her unhesitating agreement when Tania suggested this was a further cheering indication that old enmities had been resolved, or at least suspended, as was Ophelia's decision to stay in the big house too.

She apparently did this occasionally, and there were certainly enough bedrooms. "I don't think the goats will miss me if I get back early tomorrow," she said. And then, looking at me and Nevada, "And you did give them a good feed today."

Even Monika was dissuaded from driving home blind drunk, and agreed to sleep over in the mansion.

Finally we said our goodnights and Nevada and I strolled through the moonlight to our tent, which we had set up in a concealed glade at the eastern end of the oval field, not far from Ophelia's caravan and those well-fed goats.

We zipped ourselves into the tent, climbed into our double sleeping bag and lay there, sealed away in our dark little womb. We talked for a while, and then we lay listening to the traffic on the M25. It was like the sound of the ocean in the distance, soft, recurring, never ending.

Then we slept.

I was jolted awake three hours later with a sense that something was wrong. Nevada was hunched forward in the darkness of the tent, her face turned to look at me, illuminated by the light of her tablet screen. "We've got an intruder."

Nevada had set up motion detectors and motion-activated cameras at strategic points in a loose perimeter around

Tania's house and Ophelia's caravan. It was one of these that had been triggered and had woken her.

Of course a wandering goat could activate a motion detector. Which was where the cameras came in.

This wasn't a goat.

It was a figure who'd approached from the far side of the field and was now standing by the release gate. The moon had gone in, which was presumably a factor in their choosing to approach now. Without the aid of moonlight, the intruder was just a shadow lost in shadows.

Until Nevada took out the night-vision goggles that we'd bought some years ago, about the time she'd thrown a breezeblock in the face of a neo-Nazi.

We took turns looking through them at the person by the release gate.

The intruder was small, wearing a hooded camouflaged jacket, combat trousers and sneakers. Something about the way they moved suggested a woman. They were now in motion again, traversing the field at an angle towards the copse of trees where Ophelia's caravan was situated.

Nevada handed me the Taser device. Its shocking pink carapace was just a colourless paleness in the night. "You know what to do?"

I nodded. I did. I had spent several hours under her supervision learning how to operate the damned thing.

Nevada grinned, her teeth a pale crescent in the night. She picked up her bow and arrows and whispered, "Let's intercept."

We were closer to Ophelia's caravan than the intruder, so we got there first, moving quietly from the cover of one cluster of trees to another until we reached Nevada's chosen position and stayed still.

The intruder's approach was going to bring them right past us.

"Get ready," murmured Nevada. She moved a small distance away and settled into shadow.

I was hidden by the trunk of one tree, Nevada by another, and the intruder was going to pass between us. As the figure got nearer I could see they were carrying something, but I couldn't make out what it was.

The field was heavy with dew and their boots were cutting through the grass with a wet whispering sound.

My breathing sounded so loud that I was sure it would give me away. I opened my mouth wide to make it quieter. Then I thought I could hear my heart, which was beating hard at the back of my throat.

The figure was now directly between me and Nevada.

Nevada rose up out of the shadow and said, "Stay where you are please. Or you risk getting an arrow through you."

Far from staying where they were, the figure turned and ran.

Right towards me.

I stood up, blocking their way, holding out the Taser and switching on its built-in flashlight.

The beam landed with a preposterous perfection of aim right on the face of the intruder.

It was a frightened face, terrified even.

But very familiar.

"Opal," I said.

Immediately Opal stopped moving. Nevada surged up behind her, bow and arrow held ready for action, but she was already beginning to lower them.

"Oh, it's you," said Opal, shading her eyes with her hands as she peered at me. "Would you mind not shining that at me?" I switched off the flashlight. Then she turned and looked at Nevada. "And you."

"And it's you," said Nevada with disgust.

"Jordon said you guys were still together, but I didn't believe him. You're so clearly incompatible." For a woman who had been in terror of her life a few seconds earlier, Opal had developed a relaxed and snotty attitude with impressive speed.

Nevada eased over by my side. "Can I please use the Taser on her?" she whispered in my ear. "Just a little?"

26: GOAT AID

"She'd never heard of Live Aid," said Tinkler. "I had to explain that it was this huge global charity fundraising concert event. Opal had never heard of it. Can you believe that?"

"Yes," said Nevada. "That's about what one would expect from a bimbo like her. What we can't believe is that you told your vile little ex-girlfriend—"

"I thought she was a bimbo," said Tinkler. "Or are they overlapping categories?"

"We still can't believe you told her what was going on with the Blue Tits."

"I didn't think there would be any harm in it."

Tinkler should have known better than that. The bimbo and vile ex-girlfriend, or Opal Gadon as she was more formally known, had enjoyed considerable success several years ago with a documentary based on the fascinating and tragic tale of her great-grandmother.

Ever since then she'd been looking for another true story which would have similarly wide appeal. When Tinkler had recently, in the course of a trying-to-get-laid phone call, inadvisably told her all about the situation between Ophelia and Helene, a light bulb must have gone on over Opal's, admittedly attractive, head.

A one-time punk rock star who became a penniless junkie and who was now struggling to rebuild her life, burying the hatchet with the ex-friend who had got her hooked in the first place, who also happened to be another one-time punk rock star. The two of them using the medium of music to work out their differences.

It was a classic tale of redemption.

Plus goats.

Opal was nothing if not ruthless, ambitious and unprincipled, and had come down here to sniff out the details. The objects she had been carrying the night we intercepted her turned out to be some small and robust spy cameras—Nevada suspected that they'd been purchased at the Spook Store; "I'm going to have a word with the owner," she'd said—which Opal had planned to conceal in the vicinity of Ophelia's caravan.

For 'research' purposes.

"You really outdid yourself this time, Tinkler," Nevada said.

"But I had no idea she was going to try and infiltrate the goat farm. I mean, who would? And I didn't tell her *everything*, did I? I didn't tell her that you were providing security on the premises."

"Luckily for you. You're going to have to watch that big mouth of yours."

Sensing that he was as good as off the hook, Tinkler smiled and said, "Well, all's well that ends well, right? I mean, here we are," he gestured expansively at Tania's house and grounds, which were seething with activity. "The big day. The day of the big concert. And it's going to be big. Did I mention that? Opal's going to help with filming and publicising it."

"She'd better steer clear of me," said Nevada.

Sensing that he might not be as off the hook as he'd imagined, and that a change of subject might be a good idea, Tinkler hastily said, "Look what I've got…"

"Don't try and change the subject."

But Tinkler was happily unzipping his jacket to reveal the T-shirt underneath. It was black, with the white cartoon face of a goat emblazoned on it. The goat's eyes were twin pink whirlpool spirals suggesting madness, but the big fat joint the goat was smoking indicated that instead it might just be really, really stoned. The emphatic white lettering above the goat's head read, in a comic font, GOAT AID.

"Great, isn't it?" said Tinkler. "I commissioned the design online and ordered a bunch of them in all sizes. Amazing what you can do now, eh? It's not true that the Internet is just for pornography." He beamed at us. "I gave Clean Head one and she loves it. The T-shirt, I mean."

"Where's ours?" demanded Nevada. It was actually a pretty cool shirt.

"They're available for sale at Ophelia's caravan. We've set up a pop-up gift shop. For one day only!"

Most of this was lost on Nevada, who had fastened on just one fact. "For sale?" she said, her voice dangerously soft.

"That's right. Tell Opal you get the friends and family discount."

"Opal?" Nevada's voice wasn't getting any less dangerous.

"Yeah, she volunteered to staff the gift shop."

"What she's volunteered to do," I said, "is to nose around Ophelia's caravan and see if she can dig up any useful dirt for her documentary."

"Shit. Do you think so?" Tinkler looked genuinely crestfallen.

"Absolutely," said Nevada grimly.

Tinkler shook his head. "Why are beautiful women so treacherous?"

"Beautiful is an exaggeration in her case," said Nevada. "And I still can't believe you're going to charge us for those T-shirts."

"It's all for a good cause," said Tinkler sanctimoniously.

"Did you charge Agatha?"

"That's different, I'm sexually obsessed with her. I wish she could have come along today." He looked around as if expecting her to appear. But Agatha was back in London, unable to attend due to work commitments.

We were sitting on the benches beside the picnic table where we'd dined the other night, in the barbecue area next to Tania's stables. It was a good position because we could see whenever anybody arrived and parked in the driveway. They also had to walk past us on the way to the big oval field where the gig was taking place.

The latest vehicle to arrive was a metallic green Mini, from which Sydney the camerawoman now emerged. This was in itself an impressive feat because she was very tall and the car was very small. When she saw us she waved and came over. Any hard feelings about what had happened on Halig Island, when she'd put us under surveillance, and we'd done our best to thwart her, were apparently long forgotten.

She sat down at the picnic table after shaking hands with us—Tinkler actually got a kiss, which cheered him up. "I've got all the kit in the car," she said. "I'll get it out in a minute."

"No hurry. The band is still setting up and Stinky hasn't even arrived yet."

"Why am I not surprised?" said Sydney. Apparently there was no love lost between her and her erstwhile employer. "Well, I think I'll make a start anyway."

As she left, Tinkler said, "Hey look. They let the madman out of the attic again."

"A little louder, Tinkler. I don't think he quite heard you."

Derren had been impressively energised by the preparations for the gig. He'd even abandoned his usual shorts and sweaters and had been racing around all morning in green rubber boots and a yellow high-vis vest. At the moment he was racing into the kitchen before emerging a moment later clutching a cup of coffee and loping up the driveway.

Tania then appeared from the kitchen with a tray covered with more mugs of coffee and some plates of biscuits. She was looking pretty energised herself. She came over to join us, setting the coffee out on the picnic table. I forced myself not to immediately snatch up a mug. It was good stuff, properly made. Tania sat down with us.

"Derren seems to be enjoying himself," said Nevada.

"He's having a field day. He's vetting all the approaching vehicles, working out whether they're part of what he calls the 'production team' or merely punters. He worked out we could charge the punters parking on top of the ticket fee. He hasn't had so much fun in years."

Regarding the ticket fee, we had decided to allow a small and select live audience for the concert besides streaming it to subscribers. Tania had grown quite excited at this prospect and suggested selling special deluxe VIP tickets 'for up to a hundred pounds per head'. We had to break it to her gently that, these days, even standard concert tickets sold for a hundred pounds a head. And often considerably more.

So now there were a selection of VIP packages available for Goat Aid, ranging from five hundred to fifteen hundred pounds, with the biggest ticket items providing admission to the after-party—in Ophelia's caravan—and including the opportunity to share wine and goat's cheese with the stars.

Guess who chose the wine.

Tania rose from the bench. "Well, I'd better get ready for my close-up, Mr DeMille."

"Thank you for the coffee. And the biscuits."

"My pleasure. Give the extras to anyone who turns up."

We said we would, though I'd mentally earmarked a second cup of coffee for myself. Tania went back into the house. As soon as she was gone, Tinkler looked at me and Nevada and said, "Thank you, guys."

Nevada was instantly suspicious. "What for?"

"For not completely taking my head off for the Opal thing. Loose lips sink ships and all that."

"You just got lucky," said Nevada. "We're saving our energy this morning for dealing with someone else."

"Who?"

"Your mate Erik."

"Why, what's happening with Erik?" said Tinkler. But then he looked over at the driveway where a silver Nissan Leaf was pulling up silently. "Alicia," he cried. Alicia Foxcroft, better known as Foxy, was another acquaintance of ours from Halig Island. She was a petite red-headed sound technician who'd somewhat led Tinkler up the garden path. But apparently all was forgiven in connection with this, judging by the way Tinkler hurried over to the car and kissed her as she was getting out.

"Romance is in the air," said Nevada cynically. And then, "Watch out. Here comes trouble."

Trouble was Erik Make Loud, ambling towards us, all amiable lanky rock star. With no idea what was about to befall him. We waved and he waved back. "I'll let you start off," said Nevada, speaking quietly and rapidly as he approached. "You can be the bad cop. Then I'll come in as the good cop." She paused.

"What is it?" I said.

"Nothing. Well, actually, I find the idea of you as a bad cop quite stimulating." She kissed me quickly. "But we'll return to that later."

"Right. And if the bad cop/good cop routine doesn't look like it's working," I said, "we'll wheel out our secret weapon."

Nevada nodded and took out her phone. "Right."

Erik had reached us now and gave us a big grin as he settled onto the bench. He was looking forward to the gig. The poor guy. "That coffee smells good."

"It's excellent. Help yourself."

"And biscuits. Hey. Chocolate ones."

As Erik availed himself of the free refreshments I steeled myself and said, "I'm glad you came by. We wanted to talk to you."

"Nice one. Talk about what?"

"About the line-up at the gig."

"The line-up? Do you mean the set list?" Erik smiled condescendingly at me as he crunched a biscuit. "The set list is the songs we play. The line-up is the people who're playing."

"Yep," I said. "I'm afraid it's the line-up."

Erik froze in mid biscuit-crunch. His highly developed musician's sensibilities—or, if you prefer, paranoia—allowed him to instantly leap to the correct conclusion.

"You don't want me to play?"

"That's what we wanted to talk to you about."

"You don't want me to play. This is completely out of fucking order. This whole fucking shebang is my idea. And I've been *rehearsing*. I brought down my solid state bass amp *especially*. Does Helene know about this?"

Nevada stepped in. It was clearly time for the good cop. "You see we discussed it and everybody agreed—"

"I didn't agree. I didn't agree to anything." He paused and stared at us as a new realisation dawned on him. "Wait a minute. Wait just a fucking minute. If I'm not playing bass, who is?"

"Ah, well…"

"Dylis is still in a coma, right?"

"She's out of her coma actually, but she's still in hospital, in intensive care."

"Then who is it?"

Nevada and I looked at each other. Since I was the bad cop, I decided I'd better answer. "Monika," I said.

"Monika?" For a moment Erik was genuinely puzzled. He couldn't place the name in this context. Then, with a growing look of horror, he said, "You don't mean Monika the roadie?"

"Yes. Yes, we do."

Horror turned to laughter. "Please tell me you're joking."

"Sorry." I shook my head. "No."

Erik stopped laughing. "But she was just standing in for me during the rehearsals, down here with the girls."

I shrugged. "I guess the girls liked playing with her."

"Playing with her? She can't even *play* bass."

"That's sort of the point," I said.

He stared at us silently. Then he said, "You've got to be kidding."

"No."

"So it's the fucking famous punk DIY ethic, is it?"

"Yes, that's exactly what it is. At least it's partly that."

"Oh, I see, it's partly that, is it? Well what else is it, *partly*?" Erik was getting more angry rather than less and I was relieved to see Nevada quickly sending a text on her phone.

"It's also partly that they owe it to Monika," I said.

"Who does?" said Erik. "I don't owe it to her."

"No, but the rest of the band does. They owe her the chance to be a real part of the Blue Tits for once." This feeling had begun to grow when she'd bonded successfully with the others during rehearsals. After puking everywhere.

"It's what she's wanted all her life," said Nevada.

"Well, isn't that lovely," said Erik. "That's the main thing, isn't it? I mean, if that's what she's wanted all her little life…"

"And she knows the songs," I said.

"I know the songs, mate. I have been rehearsing the songs."

I could see this argument bogging down and becoming trench warfare, so I was relieved that our secret weapon turned up at this moment, beaming, bald and still looking very much like a Buddha who'd hired a personal trainer. Strange to say, the tracksuit and trainers contributed to this impression.

"Have you met Saxon Ghost?" said Nevada in her best hostess mode.

"Yeah. Earlier. Hello, Saxon. But to get back to *our* discussion, you can't pull this sort of shit. People will be expecting me to play. We publicised this event telling people I'd be playing."

Saxon smiled and settled comfortably onto the bench opposite Erik. He had been fully briefed. "You will play, mate," he said. "There's going to be a jam session afterwards and you're not only going to play on that, you're going to be the guest of honour."

"Jam session," muttered Erik in disgust. But I could see that the words 'guest of honour' had hit home.

"And we'll want you to play on the record."

"The record?"

Saxon leaned closer to Erik. "Yeah, mate. The response to this gig has been so strong it would be crazy not to release an album on the back of it. And you'll be the cornerstone of that. Not just for your blinding guitar playing, but because of all your experience in the studio."

Erik shrugged sulkily. "What do you need me for? You've produced plenty of records yourself."

"Yeah, but I was never that into the nuts and bolts of production, was I? I was never that into perfecting the sound. We need somebody with the skills to do that."

Erik didn't seem to be listening. Instead he was muttering, "Fucking Monika, fucking Monika, fucking Monika." But, on the whole, I took this as a good sign.

Saxon, sensing that he was weakening, leaned closer still, elbows on the picnic table, his head now conspiratorially near to Erik's. "Plus, during those long, difficult recording sessions we're going to need an experienced professional to help us do all that blow."

Erik stopped muttering and his face lit up. "Oh yeah?"

Saxon nodded and smiled. "Oh yeah."

Erik sat for a moment, silent and surprised, like a child promised an unexpected treat. It was beginning to look like Saxon had made a friend for life.

But then Erik remembered that he was supposed to be angry. "All right," he snarled. "I'll do it. Or perhaps I should say I *won't* do it. I'll let fucking Monika do it."

He turned to me and pointed an angry finger in my direction. "But she's not using my fucking amp."

"Uh, all right."

Erik got up and stalked off. It was a good exit, rather spoiled when he doubled back to grab a handful of chocolate biscuits. When he was eventually gone, Saxon swivelled around on the bench and looked at us. "That went okay, right?"

"Better than we expected."

"Oh, by the way," said Saxon. "I looked into that matter you asked me to. The whereabouts of the old Bride of Frankenstein."

"And the Christian midget?" said Nevada.

Saxon chuckled. "That's right, Alanna Fairmont. I found a friend of a friend of a friend who knows them, or at least knows where they live. Some dump in West Drayton. I can send you the address."

"Thank you," said Nevada. I didn't say anything. I had experienced an uncomfortable feeling in my throat at the mention of Bill Bridenstine. He was literally a pain in the neck to me.

"Not that it will do you much good," said Saxon Ghost.

"Why not?" I said.

"Because they've both dropped out of sight." He saw our faces and added, "Don't jump to any conclusions about that. Reading between the lines, I think the bugger has gone somewhere to dry out—gone into rehab as you kids would say."

"And the Christian midget has gone with him?" said Nevada.

"So it seems. She's very devoted to him. Fuck knows why."

Nevada shrugged. "Well, that's that for the time being." She looked at me. "At least we know he's out of circulation, safely shut away in a therapeutic institution somewhere."

Unless it's the Abbey, I thought, which we can see from our back window. The notion gave me a sudden sick feeling in the pit of my stomach. I forced myself to be rational. Bridenstine wouldn't have had the money to afford the Abbey.

"Okay," said Saxon, rising from the bench, "I better get back to it. Lots of egos to be soothed before the gig begins." He bustled off, looking like a man who was happy to be back in action at something he did well.

"Oh Christ," said Nevada.

"What?" I said.

"Don't look now, but..."

Derren the passionate traffic controller had evidently allowed another vehicle the privilege of access to his driveway. Which was a little surprising because it was a mud-spattered and disreputable-looking Land Rover. For a moment I thought that Farmer Fancher might have changed his Mercedes-Benz for something more characteristic and that we were about to properly meet the goat rustler.

Sorry, alleged goat rustler.

But it was much worse than that. Much, much worse.

27: APPLE BLOSSOM

As the Land Rover followed the curve of the drive, searching for somewhere to park, the figure sitting in the passenger seat became visible.

Stinky Stanmer.

The Land Rover came to a jerky halt and before it was entirely stationary, the door popped open and Stinky leapt out. Apparently he had seen us and he headed straight for us.

"Oh shit, is he really coming over to talk to us?"

"He never misses an opportunity," I said.

Stinky smiled as he approached. At least, I think it was supposed to be a smile. He was wearing a black leather jacket—perhaps it was his attempt at the punk thing—black Beatle boots and white chinos. It would turn out later that the last item of clothing was a bad mistake.

"At least the beard's gone," said Nevada. The beard had made Stinky look like a surfer dude trying to be a rabbi. Or perhaps vice versa.

Now he was upon us.

"We were just saying that at least the beard's gone," said Nevada.

Stinky chuckled richly as if he was in on the joke and then, despite the fact that we'd made a point of not making room for him, sat down with us on the bench, with his legs wide apart in what someone had no doubt told him was an alpha male power stance. He smiled briefly at Nevada, and then turned to me and said, "Never let a woman drive when she's upset, mate."

The driver's side door of the Land Rover had finally opened and sure enough a woman—a young woman—got out. She was smartly dressed in corduroy jodhpurs and a tweed jacket, both cut to flatter her trim figure. Even at this distance she looked very young and strikingly pretty. And very upset.

Stinky was saying, "I can't begin to tell you. Never, never, never. Let one drive. When she's upset." He slapped me on the shoulder; it seemed he had perfected this gesture since we'd last met. Perhaps Erik had been training him. "So, how's it going?"

"Pretty good," I said.

"Been having fun, then?"

"Yes," said Nevada, despite, or more likely because of the fact that he wasn't addressing her. "Particularly when you stole our idea for a festival on Halig Island."

"Drowning Man, you mean?"

"Yes, that's what we mean."

"That was a great festival. That was a great idea. That was a great idea for a great festival."

"And it was our idea," said Nevada.

"Well, can anyone really own an idea?" said Stinky airily, and he turned to look at the young woman in jodhpurs whose circumspect approach had nevertheless brought her right up to the picnic table. At close quarters she looked about seventeen, very posh, and it was clear that she had been crying. "This is the famous Vinyl Detective," said Stinky. He made air quotes around the word famous. "And his girlfriend Arizona."

"Nice to meet you," said the young woman, smiling and putting on a brave face. "I'm Araminta." Of course Stinky hadn't thought to complete the introductions by including her. "Very nice to meet you," she repeated, "but if you don't mind..." She turned urgently towards Stinky, lowering her voice. "Could we just talk for a moment, please?"

"You did plenty of talking in the car." Stinky yawned. "You did enough. You did plenty enough."

"Stinky, please..."

Stinky shot her an angry look and she immediately wilted. She dropped her eyes and said, "Mr Stanmer, please..."

I looked at Nevada. She looked as angry as I felt. Having to put up with Stinky was bad enough. Having to watch the humiliation of this pitiable girl was too much. Stinky was now digging in his pockets, apparently looking for something, which involved taking out all the contents and spilling them onto the table. Among the objects thus revealed were a phone, its black screen spider-webbed with white cracks, a sachet of lemon-scented wet wipes, some vape cartridges in assorted exotic fruit flavours and a pack of condoms, ditto.

At the sight of the condoms Araminta literally went pale. This phenomenon must have caused us to stare at her because Stinky looked up at her, too. Then he turned back to me and winked. He picked up the condoms and put them back in his pocket.

"Because you never know when you might be called upon to make love to a beautiful woman, mate," he said.

I waited for him to punch me on the shoulder, so I could punch him in the face. But, perhaps realising this, he didn't.

Araminta looked like somebody had hit her with a club. I guessed the condoms were a sign, or a confirmation, that Stinky was sleeping with someone else besides her. She leaned over towards Nevada, gave a sickly smile and said, "Excuse me, is there a loo anywhere?"

"In the house," said Nevada. "I'll show you. My name is Nevada, by the way. *Not Arizona*."

She got up and led the girl off, shooting a look back at Stinky that should have curled his hair. Stinky had finally found his vape pen, evidently the object of his extensive pocket search. "You're not going to use that here," I said. I didn't make it a question.

"No, mate, no." He hastily put it back in his pocket. Then he quickly looked around as if to make sure the coast was clear, leaned towards me and said, without any preliminaries, "Hampshire and Foat. Have you heard them?"

"I've heard *Galaxies Like Grains of Sand*," I said.

"What did you think of it?"

"It's terrific."

"Yeah." Stinky nodded decisively. "It's terrific, isn't it? Terrific."

"It's got sort of a Morricone meets Eno thing going on," I said.

Stinky nodded some more as he took out his phone. He pushed a button on its cracked screen and spoke into what was clearly a voice recording app. "Hampshire and Foat. Terrific. Got sort of a Morricone meets Eno thing going on."

"Stinky, you do realise I am sitting right here?"

"Yeah, ha-ha, mate. I do realise that." He slapped me on the shoulder, put his phone away and rose to his feet. "Now, do you know where I can buy one of those T-shirts of the stoned goat?"

I considered saying I had no idea, but the money would go to a good cause. So I pointed and said, "Over there. On the far side of the field you'll see a silver caravan. That's where the pop-up gift shop is."

"Silver caravan. Gift shop. Right. Laters." He made a half-hearted attempt at a wave and walked off, almost bumping into Erik Make Loud, who was approaching fast, clearly in an evil temper, carrying an amp. He shot me a poisonous look as he walked past. At first I thought he was heading for his own car, but in fact he was on his way to Monika's battered white van.

I realised that his fury at Monika was what you might call nuanced. He probably wouldn't speak to her for weeks as a result of her replacing him on bass guitar, but he still expected her to haul his amp back to London for him.

The van was parked just off the driveway, nosed up to one of the apple trees, its windscreen pressed into the mass of pink blossom on the lowest branches.

Erik wrenched the rear door open with great violence and then set his amp inside very gently. He spent a moment adjusting it and fussing over it, making sure it was safe and secure, and then slammed the door of the van shut, again with great violence.

He looked at me as he went past, to make sure I'd registered his tantrum—sorry, his displeasure—then he headed back towards the oval field, where the concert would soon begin.

Nevada came out of the house with Araminta, both of them carrying glasses of white wine. I could see that Nevada was doing her best, but the girl's shoulders were still slumped. She looked beaten and defeated, and as soon as she saw that Stinky was gone, a look of alarm flashed on her face.

"Stinky—Mr Stanmer— Where did he...?"

I gave her the same directions I'd given Stinky and she rushed off after him.

"She's a glutton for punishment," said Nevada. She gave me one of the two glasses she was carrying and then reached over for the glass Araminta had abandoned and drew it close to us, too. We sipped our wine and watched a yellow Volvo estate car pull up. It was old but it was in very good condition. In the driver's seat was Fanzine Frank Fewston, which I found surprising. The notion that he could do something as complicated as drive a car had never occurred to me.

Sitting beside him was not his wife Mindy, but rather Monika.

"How the hell did she end up with him?" I said. "Her van's parked right here."

"Exactly what I was thinking."

We smiled and waved as they got out of the Volvo. I was appalled to see that they were both wearing Tinkler's goat T-shirts. "Has everyone got one of those except us?" said Nevada.

Frank and Monika had paused to delve in the back of the car, and now Monika was carrying a bass guitar that looked oddly familiar and Frank was chivalrously carrying the amp for it.

They came over and joined us, setting the amp and guitar on the picnic table. After the initial flurry of greetings I asked Monika about the guitar, which I had now recognised. "That looks like Dylis's bass."

"That's because it *is* Dylis's bass. I got it from her flat." There was a note of pride in her voice.

"You've got a key?"

"No, I went in through the garden window. Anybody can get in there. I've been warning Dylis about that for years." She looked at the bass fondly, and then she patted the amp like a faithful pet. "And this I'm borrowing from Frank."

"We took it out of the collection," said Frank with more than a hint of pride.

We weren't paying a lot of attention to Frank, or the amp. Nevada was looking at me. All this business about easy access through the window explained how someone could have got into Dylis's Riverview Gardens flat while she slept in order to poison her juice. Which reminded me forcefully of something else.

"It's good to see you, Frank."

"It's good to see you, too. Isn't this a great idea?" He stared around. "And so great of Tania to let us do it on her property." I noticed the 'us'.

"I wanted to ask you something, Frank," I said.

"Sure, yes, of course. I think you'll find I know as much about the Blue Tits as any other resource you'll chance upon." I could tell from his pious tone that he was being modest. He actually reckoned that he knew more than any other resource. And indeed, I was willing to believe this.

"As a matter of fact, it is the Blue Tits I want to talk about," I said.

"Of course it is." Frank looked a little bewildered at the suggestion there could be anything else worth discussing.

I glanced at Nevada, who gave me the silent go-ahead, and then at Monika, who was looking slightly alarmed. "So, have you heard about what's been happening to Helene? How she nearly got killed four times?"

Frank tried not to look in Monika's direction and failed. "Yeah, I had heard about that. It's horrible, horrible. Horrible."

"Yes, it is horrible."

"And then Dylis drinking that toxic juice. What an awful coincidence."

"We don't think it's a coincidence, Frank."

"Don't you?" He stared at me. "Why don't you think that?"

"Because we're convinced that someone wants to kill not just Dylis and Helene, but Tania and Ophelia as well. In fact, all the members of the Blue Tits."

"Including me," said Monika quickly. She sounded a little pissed off at not being included in the band, and maybe with justification, because she might be right. For all we knew, the killer or killers might well be after her, too. I kicked myself for not realising this, and I could see Nevada was thinking along similar lines. She gave me a chagrined look.

Frank was shaking his head, the fringe of hair around his bald spot swaying as he did so, like some kind of exotic percussion instrument. I half expected it to make a catchy Latin sound. "That doesn't make any sense. Why would anyone want to do that?"

"You're talking about motive, Frank," I said. "Let's set that aside for a moment." Not least because there were more potential motives for killing Helene alone than you could shake a stick at. "Instead, let's talk about means."

"Means?"

"Yes," said Nevada, neatly picking up the ball from me. "We want to talk to you about how someone is managing to make these murder attempts."

"You wanted to talk to me?" He sounded aghast. "You don't think I'm doing it, do you?"

Well, yes, Frank, you are high on our list, I thought. But let's not go into that right now. "Of course not," I said soothingly. "But we do think you could have inadvertently helped the killer. The would-be killer."

"Helped them?" He was staring at me, appalled. I wondered if he could be this good an actor. I was beginning to be swiftly convinced of his innocence. "How?"

"You see," said Nevada, "whoever is doing this knows a lot about the girls in the band. About their habits and movements."

"Like where and when Helene goes jogging," I said. "And the pub where she and Erik have a regular jam session, and when that is. And Dylis's daily juice regime."

"You see what we're getting at," said Nevada.

"You mean I know all those things?" said Frank. "Because I've researched them in interviews with the gals?"

"It's not just that you know them," I said. "You also publish them."

"In the fanzine," said Frank. He was unable to stop a smile spreading among his facial hair at this mention of his baby. "Like when I publish one of my 'Day in the Life' features?"

"Yes, exactly like that."

"You think someone is using that information to go after the gals?"

"That's exactly what we think."

Frank pondered this, sucking on the ends of his moustache. "But I haven't published everything."

"What do you mean?"

He glanced at Monika again. "Didn't someone tamper with Erik Make Loud's drugs?"

"That's right."

"Well, okay, so I never wrote anything about his drugs in my fanzine."

Nevada and I had discussed this. Now she said, "We think that someone got enough information from the fanzine to allow them to take it from there."

"Take it from there?"

"Yes." In fact Nevada had called the fanzine a 'stalker's starter kit'. "They could learn enough about the girls and their routines to begin to follow them around and put them under surveillance. And then finding out about Erik's drugs would be straightforward enough." Because the idiot kept them in the garden.

"So what we want, Frank," I said, "is your mailing list."

"Oh."

"You sell your fanzine by mail order, correct?"

"Yes. Almost exclusively."

"So you have the names and addresses of your customers."

"I guess so." This was where Frank's Internet aversion was going to come in really handy. If he just ran a website and published his content online there would have been no way we could trace any of the users. "But I don't think I can share that with you." He peered at us out of his hairy face.

"Don't you? Why don't you think that?"

"Ah, data protection, privacy issues…"

"Frank," I said gently. "We're talking about saving the lives of the gals."

He mulled this over for a moment, and then gave way to logic. Or what you might call common sense. "Okay," he said reluctantly. "I guess it's okay. I've already shared it with Tania anyway."

Nevada was as surprised as I was. "Really? Why did you do that?"

Frank waved his hands around, taking in Tania's house, this whole place, this whole day. "So she had a database of hardcore fans to approach."

Smart move, Tania. No wonder ticket sales had been so strong. "How many names are on that list?" I said. "Roughly?"

"About seven hundred."

Jesus. I glanced at Nevada. This wasn't going to be easy.

Monika was staring at her wristwatch and frowning. "Shit. We've gotta go, Frank," she said. Frank nodded and got up. They picked up the bass and amp from the table. "See you guys later."

We watched them depart, an odd couple if ever there was one. Nevada and I looked at each other. "What now?" I said.

"Monika's right," she said. "The concert will be starting soon."

"You think we should put in an appearance?"

"Albeit briefly."

So we made our way to the oval field. We'd been blessed with a long spell of dry weather, which was just as well, because otherwise all the foot traffic would have churned the place into muddy ruin.

The stage had been set up in front of the release gates and a large roped-off section of the field had been established in front of the stage, demarcating the official audience area. It had been necessary to extend this several times due to the expanding size of the crowd, which had now grown so large that we couldn't have got close to the stage if we wanted to. The fact that we didn't particularly want to might have seemed anti-social, or disloyal, or something, but the fact was, this wasn't going to be my kind of music, and additionally it was going to be played at the sort of volume which would have made tinnitus a thrilling possibility.

Indeed, we already had our earplugs in, but just the soundcheck was enough to drive us back. We retreated speedily, in the general direction of Ophelia's caravan. Ophelia herself could be seen on the stage, seated behind her gleaming new drum kit and getting ready to beat the hell out of it. Her smile was so huge I could see it from this distance.

I looked towards her caravan where a group of goats were staring in horror at the source of the seismic noise. "I think now would be a good time to go and get our T-shirts," I said.

"Good idea. And also, with a bit of luck, catch the loathsome Opal in the act of going through Ophelia's knicker drawer."

"That too."

The goats fled as we drew near, perhaps because we didn't come bearing food, or perhaps because they had correctly concluded that we were partly responsible for the thundering din that had destroyed the peaceful silence they normally enjoyed. Well, peaceful silence plus motorway noise.

The exterior of Ophelia's caravan was plastered with posters for the gig in Day-Glo punk colours, yellow and pink, which went oddly well with the green stripe. The door of the caravan was wide open, so we hopped on the tree stump and stepped inside. Every available surface had been piled with copies of the posters, stacks of glossy souvenir programmes and piles of neatly folded T-shirts. Several of the T-shirts were on hangers attached to the caravan's ceiling, to display them in all their glory.

The stoned goats stared down at us balefully. To paraphrase Henry Ford, the shirts were available in any colour you wanted, so long as that colour was black with swirling pink eyes.

Sitting in the alcove with a cashbox and a credit card reader, the person entrusted with selling all this merchandise was not, as we'd been promised, Opal, but rather Araminta, Stinky's heartbroken driver.

"Hey," I said. "What happened to Opal?"

Araminta looked like she was going to start crying again. "She went off with Stinky."

"Went off with Stinky?" said Nevada. "Why?"

"Well, they started talking and seemed to rather hit it off..."

"Hit it off?" said Nevada tightly. "Christ."

"And now they've gone off together to..."

"Oh, we can guess what they've gone off to do together."

"No." Araminta was desperately shaking her head. "It's nothing like that. I'm sure."

Nevada gazed at her sadly and said nothing, but it was clear she didn't agree. "Really," said Araminta. "It's nothing like that. Stinky said they were just going off to find somewhere to take cocaine."

"Oh, well," I said, "that's all right then." Any irony I intended was quite lost on Araminta, who shot me a grateful look.

We bought our T-shirts, making damned sure we got the friends and family discount, and left young Araminta to pine over Stinky until his return. As we walked back towards the field we had a panoramic view of the stage with its rapt audience, as well as, in the distance, Tania's fourteen-bedroom house and the vehicles parked outside it.

The concert was just beginning in earnest. I saw the tiny figure of Tania herself appear on stage, now clad in a black leather jumpsuit, and seize the microphone stand. An enormous cheer rose up to greet her from the crowd while behind her Helene and Monika began to play—blasting out thrashing chords, enormously amplified, causing a flock of crows to burst from the nearby trees where they'd been roosting and swirl away.

At the same moment the music started there was an enormous thudding sound, like the biggest bass drum in the world. Followed almost instantly by a crashing and tinkling that might have emanated from a matching set of cymbals.

This wasn't coming from the stage, though.

It was coming from the direction of the house, where we saw Monika's van bouncing on its tyres and shuddering like a dying animal as grey smoke poured out of its shattered windscreen and a vast cloud of pink apple blossom rose above it.

28: HELLO, MY LOVELY

A few people in the audience turned around, aware that something had happened, but most of them were completely focused on the stage, where the Blue Tits were playing their hearts out and blasting forth their greatest hits.

Meanwhile, Nevada and I were running for all we were worth towards Monika's van. As we neared it we saw a woman step—or rather, stagger—out from where she'd been concealed on the far side of the vehicle.

It was Opal.

And it was a measure of how shaken she was that she ran without hesitation straight towards us, only too happy to see us.

"What happened?" I said.

"The van. It just—it just blew up."

"We know," said Nevada. "We saw."

"And Stinky... Stinky and I... we were about to get into it..." Opal's voice, admirably steady up to now, abruptly acquired a serious quiver.

She turned and stared at the van. There was still smoke pouring up out of its smashed windscreen—although now we were closer I realised it was more dust than smoke. The apple tree in front of it had been stripped of its blossom and the bark of its trunk looked strangely lacerated.

"You were going to *get into it*?" said Nevada.

"We were just about to open the door at the back. We were looking for somewhere…" she halted.

"To do your coke," I said.

Opal nodded gratefully, realising this was no time to be coquettish about such matters.

"Stinky was just reaching for the door…"

"Jesus, is he—?"

"No, he's all right. I mean, he's sort of all right. He was reaching for the door of the van and then it exploded. I mean, the van. I mean, there was an explosion inside it." She stared at us. "Like a bomb going off."

Nevada nodded. "Yes. Like a bomb going off."

I started moving towards the van and she called out sharply, "Don't, love. There might be a secondary device." I looked at her and then I looked at the van. Christ… A secondary device?

"Where's Stinky?" I said.

Opal nodded towards the cluster of apple trees on the far side of the van. "He's behind those trees. He won't come out." She lowered her voice. "He shat himself."

"I beg your pardon?" said Nevada. I couldn't tell if she genuinely hadn't heard, or if she just wanted to hear it again.

"He shit his pants," said Opal. "Now he doesn't want to come out and he doesn't want anyone to come near him."

I moved past the smouldering van, giving it a wide berth. I couldn't see anyone among the trees on the other side, but I called out anyway.

"Stinky?"

There was a pause, and then a small voice said, "Yeah."

"Are you all right?"

"Yeah." And then, in an even smaller voice, "I had to take my trousers off."

"Okay, well you just stay there."

I turned to Nevada and Opal, who had now joined me. Nevada was trying hard not to smile, but she couldn't stop herself. She leaned over and whispered in my ear, "Stinky really is stinky now."

Poor Stinky. It was a very human thing that could easily have happened to any of us.

But it *was* rather funny.

"What on earth," called a loud, aggrieved and very firm voice. Approaching along the driveway from the direction of the front gate was Tania's husband Derren in his yellow high-vis vest and green wellies. He was moving quickly and he looked riled.

"What on earth is all this?" he demanded. "What was that I heard?"

"Everyone's all right," I said. "No one was hurt." I paused, trying to work out how to say this without it coming out sounding like a joke. "Though one of our party needs a new pair of trousers."

Derren didn't seem to be listening, let alone laughing. I can't say that I blamed him. "That wasn't music," he said with a kind of fierce decisiveness. "That wasn't the girls. That was some kind of explosion."

"Yes," said Nevada. "In the van."

"In the…" He turned and glared at Monika's van for a long moment, as if it was personally responsible for this situation. And then he hurried over towards the vehicle, perhaps to give it a good talking to.

"Don't get too close," said Nevada.

Derren paused and looked back at her.

"You think there might be a secondary?"

"There might be."

"Timed to catch rescuers or medical personnel." Derren nodded briskly. "Nasty things." He reluctantly backed away from the van and went over to inspect the trees nearby. They had marks on their trunks as though an animal had been scratching them. A very big animal. He looked at the marks and then looked at me.

"Shrapnel?" I said.

He nodded and took out a penknife, then dug it into the bark, extracting something. He examined it with satisfaction. "Ball bearings," he declared.

He threw it at me and I surprised myself by catching it one-handed—a tiny metal globe about the size of a marble. It was still surprisingly shiny and, though it might have been my imagination, it felt warm.

"Ball bearings," repeated Derren. "Very nasty. Very effective." He returned to the van and walked around it, inspecting it thoughtfully.

He was gradually drifting closer and Nevada said, "Don't you think…"

But just then Derren lunged forward and wrenched the back door of the van open—I was amazed that it still worked—and then he was peering inside. Nevada and Opal and I all backed hastily away. A smell came out of the van that reminded me of an overheated metal saucepan left on the stove after it had boiled dry.

Derren made a barking sound of satisfaction. "Nothing in here that could be another device. Come and have a look." We approached slowly, with trepidation, and looked in over his shoulder. "What a mess," he said.

The interior was blackened and scorched, the walls dimpled and pockmarked with the savage impact of the ball bearings. The seats at the front had been shredded, revealing the pale foam inside as if someone had taken a giant cheese grater to them. Fresh clean air was coming in through the jagged hole where the windscreen had been and I could hear birds in the trees pluckily starting to sing again.

"That thing, whatever it was, is what contained the device," said Derren. He indicated the splayed fragments of what had once been Erik's bass amp. I turned and looked at Nevada. "It was triggered to go off at the exact moment the concert began," I said.

She nodded. "If it had been in place as planned, it would have wiped out everyone on stage."

"Oh my god," said Opal. We all stood there looking at each other. The only one who seemed unmoved by this near-miracle of an escape—which had almost involved the death of his own wife—was Derren. He had wandered around to the front of the van and was now inspecting the apple tree that had taken most of the blast.

He turned to us and shrugged philosophically. "Oh well, the blossom would all have been off that one in a couple of days anyway."

He turned and walked back towards the house. "I'll get you those trousers."

The strangest thing was that, far from spoiling the day, the demolition of Monika's van largely went unnoticed. In fact the concert was a massive success, though Nevada and Opal and I didn't see any of it. We sat at the picnic table drinking wine and keeping a close eye on the wreckage of the van, in case it might have some further surprises to spring on us.

We'd raised the issue of calling the police and Derren had said to leave it to him.

Stinky, clutching the trousers borrowed from Derren and wrapped from the waist down in a borrowed towel, had scurried from his concealing trees into the house and disappeared, not to be seen again. Presumably he was busy in one of its many bathrooms.

Derren had fetched a shovel from somewhere, gone in among those trees and located Stinky's despoiled white chinos where he had abandoned them. Then, in his efficient, pragmatic way, he'd buried them on the spot, like a soldier fallen on the battlefield.

The afternoon had gradually turned to evening and we'd finished several bottles of wine, with the occasional assistance of Derren, when Stinky's lovelorn driver Araminta turned up. There was still no sign of Stinky himself. Araminta explained that Fanzine Frank had relieved her in the caravan and he would handle the anticipated post-gig rush for merchandise.

From where we sat, the music from the distant stage was an agreeable murmur, obscuring the ever-present underlying drone of the motorway. Erik was playing now, in the jam session section of the concert, which explained why Frank had been willing to surrender his place in the crowd in front of the stage.

Araminta was halfway through her glass of wine—it was the same wine, though a different bottle, as the one she'd abandoned earlier, so she hadn't missed anything—when she lowered it and said, "My god, what happened to that van?"

We let Opal tell her and as soon as she heard what had happened to Stinky she slammed down her glass on the table, said, "Why didn't you tell me before?" and dashed into the house.

Opal shook her head. "What does she see in Stinky?"

"I don't know," said Nevada. "What did you see in him?"

"The chance to pick his brains for my documentary."

"You could have saved yourself the trouble. Stinky doesn't have any brains to pick."

In the oval field the concert ended with a final convulsion of guitar soloing and a final crash of drums, and then the applause rose like the crackling of a big fire. It subsided slowly and people began to disperse, with high-vis Derren making sure they exited by way of the road on the far side of the field, only allowing the privileged few back this way, towards the house.

The first of these was Erik Make Loud, stripped to the waist, hair soaked with sweat, grinning. Performing had transformed him. He came marching towards us, exultant, his bass guitar slung backwards over his shoulder like the rifle of a returning warrior.

He waved to us, a god on Olympus acknowledging mortals far below.

Then he caught sight of the van.

His grin vanished and he dashed over to peer into the dark maw of the blasted vehicle. The sun was going down fast but evidently there was still enough light to see inside, because he turned back to us and howled, "What the fuck happened to my amp?" He started towards the picnic table, his face like thunder.

Also hastening towards our table, and as if to provide an interesting contrast, was a jubilant Tinkler. "Goat shirt sales are buoyant," he called, seizing a glass of wine in passing. "What's more, we've made our target on ticket sales alone today."

"Our target? You mean they got enough money for Ophelia's goat farm?" I said.

"And more. Considerably more." He sipped his wine as he hurried into the house, presumably in search of the loo.

I turned to Erik, who was now standing beside the picnic table with the oddest expression on his face.

"Looks like you will get your LP after all," I told him.

"Yeah."

"And your idea of a benefit gig worked beautifully."

"Yeah."

"So," I said, "I can't really take any credit for securing that record for you." Nevada looked at me in alarm. Was I sabotaging our chance of getting a bonus? But it was true: the LP had been obtained thanks to Erik's quick thinking and hard work. I was willing to take a finder's fee, but that was about it.

But we needn't have worried.

Because, for all his recent amp-mourning histrionics, Erik was no fool. In the time it had taken to walk to the table he had put it all together in his head. What would have happened if he'd gone on stage with that amp. He was staring at me.

"It was a bomb, wasn't it?" he said.

"Yes. Detonated just as the concert started."

Erik looked quickly around. "Does that mean by somebody here?"

I shrugged. "It could be. Or it could be anybody watching on the Internet."

"We figure it was remotely detonated by phone," said Nevada. "So they could have done it from virtually anywhere."

Erik set his guitar on the table, pulled his T-shirt out of the back of his jeans, where it was hanging, and put it on. Then he leaned over and pounded me on the back. "You saved my life," he said. "You saved all our lives. I didn't want to back down about playing the bass, but you insisted."

I opened my mouth to say that I'd had no idea that's what I'd been doing, and anyway, it had been Saxon who'd really talked him into stepping down. But at a look from Nevada I fell silent and let him give me the credit.

I guess in a way I had saved all their lives.

While Erik expounded on this theme, Tinkler returned from the house. He reached our table, suddenly stared and said, "Holy fuckaroo. What happened to that van?"

"Only just noticed that, have we?" said Erik. He chuckled affectionately and slapped Tinkler on the back. As we brought Tinkler up to speed, Fanzine Frank came wandering over to join us, having been booted out of the caravan to make room for the after-party.

After the after-party—goat's cheese and wine with the stars in the cramped space of Ophelia's home—the VIP ticket holders were politely ushered away by Derren towards their cars, parked in a distant field.

He returned soon, taking off his yellow vest and gratefully accepting a glass of wine.

A little while later the Blue Tits all came back as a single unit, arms linked, drunk and happy, with Monika among them, for once absolutely as an equal. I was quite moved by the sight, and by her obvious joy. But then she noticed the van.

"My van!"

She ran to it, gaped at it for a moment and then sank sobbing to her knees.

While the other Blue Tits were variously comforting her or asking us what the hell had happened, Araminta appeared from the house leading a very chastened-looking Stinky by the hand, like a small child.

They hurried to their Land Rover and drove off without so much as a goodbye.

In the same way that it hadn't spoiled the concert, the bombing didn't spoil the celebrations afterwards. After the initial realisation of what had happened—and what had very nearly happened—had sunk in, everyone stopped discussing it. As if by silent mutual consent they decided to ignore it.

And ignore the fact that whoever had tried to kill the women had failed, and would know it, and would no doubt be getting ready to try again.

Maybe this is the way it works in wartime. Otherwise everybody would just go crazy worrying all the time.

Anyway, as the evening grew colder everyone retired to the house where the champagne flowed in copious quantities. Then Ophelia presented Erik with her copy of the LP, which turned out to be in what we vinyl fanatics would call genuinely near mint condition—which made sense if it had spent its existence sealed in a box, first with Saxon Ghost and then with Fanzine Frank.

Whatever bad blood there had been between Ophelia and Erik was evidently gone now. She even gave him a kiss as she handed him the record.

With the album proudly under his arm, Erik sought me out in the crowd of fairly drunken revellers and said, "We need to talk."

I went into the kitchen with him, followed a moment later by Nevada and Helene, keeping tabs on their men. We all found seats and listened to the party taking place in assorted other rooms of the house as I made coffee for us.

"I asked Derren if he would mind not reporting the bomb to the pigs," said Erik. "And he was only too pleased not to get them involved." Not for the first time I wondered what the hell Derren's deal was. For all his brisk poshness he struck me as more than a little shady.

Helene was studying the LP. She set it aside as I brought the coffee over to the counter where they were all sitting and regarded me rather anxiously. "Now, just because you've found the record for us, that doesn't mean that you're going to…"

"Stop looking for your assailant?" said Nevada. She shook her head. "No. Absolutely not."

"That's good," said Erik. "Because this shit is getting out of hand."

"We would have been… massacred," said Helene. "Fuck, fuck. You were so right when you said someone was trying to kill the whole band. We didn't believe you." She glanced at Erik. I think what she actually meant was that Erik hadn't believed me. "But you were so right. If you hadn't confiscated that amp…"

She seized my hand and squeezed it hard. Apparently I was now believed to have forcibly confiscated the amp from Erik, thereby heroically saving the lives of everyone on stage. Helene was more than a little drunk. Even so, it was impressive how this tale had grown in the last few hours.

If it continued like this, pretty soon I would be believed to have beaten up the bad guys with my shirt off.

I said, "Whoever is doing this, it's the second time they've sabotaged an amp."

"Yeah, I was thinking that," said Erik, never one to concede that somebody else had got there first. And also never one not to labour the obvious. "First the one at the Bull's Head that was supposed to electrocute Hel, and now this."

"So," I said. "Our aspiring killer's begun to repeat himself. Or herself. Or themselves. It feels like they're running out of ideas, running out of steam, growing weaker."

"That's good then, isn't it?" said Helene.

"Not necessarily," said Nevada.

"Not necessarily?"

"They're getting desperate," I said. "Which could make them a lot more dangerous."

There was silence in the kitchen as we all contemplated the possibility of someone who was already insanely dangerous getting more dangerous. Elsewhere in the house the merriment continued.

"This has got to stop," said Erik finally. He sipped his coffee and looked at me. "Do you have any leads?"

"We've got a Christian midget," I said.

Nevada and I explained about Bill Bridenstine and his rather more highly functioning girlfriend. "Fucking Bridenstine," said Erik. "I knew that bastard was behind it." He was more than a little drunk himself.

"Not necessarily, doll," said Helene, still tracking rather better than her paramour. "Mustn't jump to conclusions."

"Exactly right," said Nevada.

Suddenly everyone was very weary. Time for bed. As Helene and Erik wandered deeper into the house, hand in hand, heading for one of the numerous bedrooms, Tinkler came hurrying in to the kitchen.

"There you are! Have you been hiding from me?"

"We would have, if we'd thought of it," said Nevada.

"Listen," said Tinkler excitedly. "Opal is staying here tonight and so am I…"

"Yes?"

"And, well, Opal said she would like to sleep outside, in a tent." He gave us a beseeching look. "Do you guys have a spare tent?"

"We might do. Why?"

"Because if I can find a tent, Opal said we can *share* it."

"Okay, let's say for the sake of the argument that we have a spare tent…"

"Can I borrow it please please please?" The prospect of possibly having sex had profoundly altered Tinkler. He was now almost polite.

"Of course you can," said Nevada, commendably sparing Tinkler any more torment. "But it's the one that had the bottom cut out of it."

"You mean the one we used in Canterbury when we robbed that grave? That's great. That's a plus. That's a bonus. It's a bonus-plus. I can tell Opal all about it. Tell her all about what happened. Spellbind her with the story. When we're in the tent. Alone together. She will be spellbound. Oh, boy. I can't wait to tell her about it. Won't it be great?"

"Sure," said Nevada. "Nothing puts a girl in the mood quicker than an anecdote about grave robbing."

"Really?"

It had been a long, hard day, and the last thing we wanted to do at this late hour was to help Tinkler set up the tent he'd borrowed from us—Tinkler never knowingly doing any form of physical labour himself. In this case, though, he was uniquely willing to give it a try. But what he lacked in reluctance he more than made up for in incompetence, so it was left to Nevada and I—and, in fairness, Opal, who pitched in—to organise everything. The tent itself went up quite quickly, but it had to be positioned over the no-longer integral groundsheet which itself had to be fixed separately to the ground.

But we got it done.

Because we were helping them with the set-up, and for reasons of general inertia—and maybe out of a sense of safety in numbers, after the events of the day—Tinkler and Opal's tent was virtually right next to ours.

It was only as we crawled into our shared sleeping bag that Nevada began to wonder if this was a good idea. "What if they keep us awake?" she said. "With loud sexual cries?"

"This is Tinkler we're talking about here," I said.

"Good point." Nevada kissed me. "Which is a relief because we need to make an early start tomorrow."

Nevada had got a phone call from her mother inviting us to join her the following day on a tour of destruction of the charity shops of the area. It was fairly obviously an olive branch—"My mother has never knowingly set foot in a charity shop before," said Nevada—but nevertheless a very sweet gesture. "She knows about our modus operandi now, so she's contrived a sort of family outing, so to speak, for the three of us. You can look for records, I can look for clothes and she can look for masterpieces of cinema on Blu-ray or DVD. Although there may be ugly scenes if she finds anything really good and I have to fight her for it."

So we were going to set off first thing in the morning on an early-bird raid.

It was an inviting prospect, some downtime after all the recent stress, and we fell asleep to visions of magnificent charity shop discoveries.

Only to be wrenched from sleep by a piercing scream.

"Christ, what's that?"

For a second I thought we might have been wrong about sex cries as a result of Tinkler's prowess, but the sound was repeated and it was horrible, like an infant wailing in pain or—

"Is that a cat?"

"It sounds like a cat."

More accurately, it sounded like a cat in acute distress.

We scrambled out of our sleeping bag. "You take the Taser, I'll take my bow," said Nevada. "I don't think it's a human making that noise. But you never know."

We dressed hurriedly, armed ourselves and emerged from the tent to find that Opal and Tinkler were already there, also dressed but not armed.

"Did you hear—"

"Yes, we're going to investigate," said Nevada.

"It could be a fox," said Opal.

"It's not a fox." As if to hammer this point home, the sound came again. It was both horrible and heart-rending.

"We have to do something about that," I said.

"Come on," said Nevada, and we hurried into the night. Tinkler and Opal hesitated for a second and then followed us. We moved across the dark field with the recently occupied stage now just an abandoned shape in the shadows. We passed Ophelia's caravan, empty for the night because she was, uniquely, sleeping over at Tania's house in one of the numerous spare bedrooms.

"Where are all the goats?"

"Maybe they're not around because Ophelia isn't around?"

"Maybe." Or maybe they'd fled because of that hellish cry.

Which hadn't been repeated since we'd set off.

"Oh, shit," said Nevada. "I forgot the fucking night-vision binoculars." This wasn't surprising. We'd been awoken from a deep drunken sleep and our nerves had been well and truly jangled. Nevertheless…

"That's all right," I said. "I brought them."

Nevada laughed and I felt her relax in the darkness, and she moved close to me and kissed me.

Walking slightly behind us, Tinkler moved closer to Opal. "Don't try to kiss me," she said. "Unless you want to lose some teeth."

"It might still be worth it," said Tinkler. "How many teeth, and which ones?"

Opal giggled and, to my surprise, Tinkler did move in and kiss her. I looked at Nevada to see what she made of this, but she was staring fixedly ahead of us. "Can I have the binoculars, please?" I passed them to her. Behind us there were more giggling and snogging noises.

But they stopped when Nevada said, "What the fuck?"

"What?" I said.

"I can't see anything through these... What... Fuck me..."

"What is it?"

"Somebody's stuck gaffer tape over the lenses," said Nevada. "I'm taking it off..."

Just then a beam of light stabbed out of the darkness into our faces. "Put down the bow and arrow please," said a man's voice off to one side of the light. It sounded rather affected and artificial, the voice of someone trying to sound posh and authoritative at a small public meeting.

Nevada did no such thing. She lifted her bow and notched an arrow to the string, drawing it taut. As she did so, the light swivelled over to shine in the direction where the voice had come from.

It disclosed a man standing there wearing a tartan cap and a raincoat. He was tall, thin and middle-aged with a perfectly ordinary face, red-cheeked and if anything looking rather bored. In one hand he was holding a ginger kitten. Around its head was one of those cones vets use to stop animals licking themselves. In this case it seemed to be there to prevent the kitten from biting the man holding it. The kitten's front paws were bound to each other with some kind of white tape and the same tape held its rear paws together. The little creature had no way of defending itself, but nevertheless it was struggling gamely.

He held it by the scruff of the neck in his left hand.

In his right hand he held a pair of pliers.

"My lovely who is holding that light," he said, "also has a shotgun pointing at you." Nevada's gaze wavered between the man and the unseen person holding the light. "But I understand this might interest you even more than the notion of that," said the man in his pedantic, unctuous voice. He lifted the kitten up high, and it screeched with complaint.

"If you don't put the bow and arrow down I'll get back to work on this little chap with the pliers."

29: DOWN ON THE FARM

We were in the back of a vehicle, evidently one used for transporting animals. It had been modified so that the stalls in it had been subdivided. And before we'd been sealed inside, and thrown into complete darkness, I'd seen that these stalls were walled with some kind of padding, like cushions stuck to the sides. At first I'd thought the purpose of this was to prevent us being injured if we were tossed around in transit. But then I realised it was actually soundproofing, to prevent us communicating with each other.

Because we'd been separated into two groups when we'd been herded into the back of this thing, Tinkler and I were forced into one stall and Opal and Nevada in the other.

Now we were being bounced along a curving country road at high speed. Tinkler was thrown against me in the darkness, and he apologised, a strangely normal act in this vastly aberrant situation. There was a powerful smell of disinfectant in the stall, and in the vehicle generally.

I suspected that this disinfectant had been applied

liberally to get rid of the smell of dead goat. "I think I know who's doing this," I said.

"Well, that's a relief," said Tinkler. "Who?"

"A farmer called Fancher. A fucking fascist farmer."

"Who is he?"

"He stole a bunch of Ophelia's goats."

"And now… what? He's stolen us?"

"It looks like it," I said.

"Why?"

"It's got to be the Helene situation."

"So fucking fascist farmer Fancher is the guy who's been trying to kill Helene?"

"I suppose that's possible," I said.

"But you don't think so?"

I remembered the person who'd been holding the flashlight for Fancher. They'd said nothing, and we had seen nothing more than a shadow. It could have been a man or a woman. But Fancher had called them 'my lovely', which argued for a woman.

"I think he's working for the person who's been trying to kill Helene."

"Oh, great, so now they're subcontracting."

"It looks like it."

"What do we do?"

"Wait until we get to wherever we're going," I said.

We both fell silent, rocking with the motion of the vehicle. Were we slowing down?

"Do you know what the worst thing is about this whole situation?" said Tinkler.

"No." There seemed a wide range of choices.

"If it hadn't happened, I think I was going to get laid."

Our ride was brief. The vehicle turned off to the left, slowed down, rattled over a bumpy stretch of road that eventually smoothed out and then came to a halt. There followed an agonising wait during which there was no sound and nothing happened. We stood in absolute darkness, breathing in the stink of the disinfectant and straining to listen. Eventually there was a muffled sound of a door opening. Then silence. Then what might have been someone shouting.

What might have been Nevada shouting…

My whole body tensed and I lurched towards the area of darkness that was the door of the stall. Tinkler grabbed my arm. "Steady, big fella."

We waited in silence again, for a long time. And then the door of our stall slid open, disappearing to one side and letting in light that was much too bright after being in the dark for so long. We blinked until we could see properly.

Ahead of us was a sort of tunnel or corridor made of sturdy opaque white plastic, very brightly lit from the outside. In cross section it was slightly larger than the open doorway of our stall, to which it was firmly fastened. We advanced like understandably wary livestock and stared out of the stall at the corridor.

It led straight for a short distance and then curved away off to the left. We couldn't see beyond the curve.

And I for one was in no hurry to do so. I backed into

the stall once more, again like reluctant livestock, I couldn't help thinking. "What do we do?" said Tinkler.

"They obviously want us to go down that tunnel, so I suggest we do the opposite."

"Just wait in here?"

"Yes. Wait and see what they do."

"You don't have any other weapons, do you?" said Tinkler. I looked at the Taser, which I had been allowed to keep when Nevada had surrendered her bow. At first I had triumphantly imagined that they didn't know about it.

But then I realised it wasn't working. I didn't know what they had done to it, but I knew *when* they'd done it—at the same time they'd taped up the binoculars, sometime this evening before we'd returned to our tent. I had no idea why I was even clinging to the thing. It was an inert piece of plastic.

And, what's more, it was pink.

"So we just stay in here?" said Tinkler nervously.

I opened my mouth to reply when a wave of sharply burning pain lashed up from my feet, causing me to cry out, and at the same time to understand what had happened to Nevada a few minutes ago.

Tinkler and I were now standing in the white plastic tunnel, staring back at the dark recess of the stall we had just jumped from. We no longer had any desire to go back in there.

"They electrified the floor," said Tinkler.

"Yes," I said. My voice was tight, but I was glad I stopped myself saying the thought that flashed into my mind. Of course—they were good with electricity. They'd tried to kill Helene with it, hadn't they? Which led inexorably to the thought that thank god they hadn't just killed us.

Which is what I stopped myself saying.

I also didn't mention the obvious next thought.

If they were keeping us alive, what for?

Tinkler and I were looking at each other, standing there in the plastic tunnel. "Now what?" said Tinkler.

"They clearly want us to go down this tunnel," I said.

"So we don't do that and stay here instead?"

I hesitated.

"Because that strategy didn't work out so great last time," said Tinkler.

We both looked down. The white plastic that formed the floor of the tunnel had a series of dark squares underneath it, a thin, dark shape snaking beside them.

"Is that—?"

"Yes, I think so," I said. "Metal plates and a power cable."

Tinkler and I started walking before they shocked us again. As we walked towards the bend in the tunnel I was thinking furiously. We were obviously being funnelled towards whatever they had in mind for us, and I was still in no hurry to find out what that was. As we reached the bend I realised it was sharper than I'd thought, more like a corner than a bend, the way that the tunnel had been fashioned. In other words, instead of a gentle curve it had some hard edges, which would be structural weak points.

I touched Tinkler on the shoulder just as we came to the corner. I turned to the tunnel wall, at the angle where one section was joined to the other. "Come on," I whispered, "let's—"

And then the electric shock hit us. We ran around the corner as fast as we could move, down the remaining short length of tunnel and straight through the dark, open doorway that was waiting for us.

A heavy wooden door slid shut behind us. It had a narrow horizontal slit in it, and through the slit we saw the lights in the tunnel go out. Darkness again. But we'd had enough time to register that we were in a large concrete shed with a low tin roof, big shadowy rectangular bales of hay stacked around the walls, the floor covered with a thick coating of straw.

Then sounds began outside. "What's that?" said Tinkler.

I went to the slit in the door. It was set high up, but if I stood on tiptoes it was just about in line with my eyes. I pressed my face against it, trying to peer out into the night. Cool fresh air flowed in and I could smell farmyard smells. They smelled like the freedom that had been so recently stolen from us.

I felt an intense desire to get out of here, followed by a surge of panic. I forced myself to calm down and listen.

"They're dismantling the tunnel," I said.

"So they aren't planning to take us out of here again," said Tinkler.

Something in his voice made me turn towards him. "Not just yet."

"Not ever." Was his voice beginning to shake?

"Don't jump to that conclusion."

"Why not?" Yes, his voice was shaking. Who could blame him?

I said, "Why not is because it will be daylight soon and they may not want anyone to see their creepy little tunnel. For all we know they plan to assemble it again tonight after dark and move us again."

Tinkler thought about this for a moment. "That makes sense," he said. His voice was steadier now. Which just made me feel very alone. Because I actually agreed with his first interpretation of the situation, and now I was carrying the burden of that all on my own.

After the tunnel had been dismantled it fell silent outside. It became maddeningly obvious that Farmer Fancher, assuming that's who it was, and his silent assistant had simply gone away and left us.

"How dare they just abandon us like this?" said Tinkler. "If they're going to kidnap us, you'd think the bastards could at least keep us entertained—with extravagant threats and gloating or something. I'd say it was morally incumbent on them."

Then, a little later, he said, "What happens if we have to go to the loo?"

"That's what the straw is for."

"Oh, great."

Later still we dragged some bales of hay from the walls and heaped up the straw against them to form a kind of bed and pillows. As we did so we made a discovery. There was a package of a dozen litre bottles of water shrink-wrapped amongst the bales, apparently left there for us to find. We ripped it open, took out a bottle each and drank deeply of the warm, plastic-smelling water.

"It's a pity the bottles aren't glass," I said.

"No shit," said Tinkler.

My mind ran wildly on, uselessly elucidating all the possible ways I could have used a glass bottle. Tinkler was lost in his own thoughts. And then, unbelievably, we fell asleep.

When we awoke a bright band of sunlight was coming in through the slit in the door. By the intensity of the light and the angle it was falling I got the impression it was late morning, or perhaps even noon.

I'd been awakened by some kind of sound. I lay there on the straw, listening, trying to identify what it was. Beside me Tinkler was awake, too, and listening tensely.

The sound came again. Like sheep, but lower pitched.

"What's that?"

"Goats," I said.

"Stolen goats?"

"I think so."

And then there was another sound. Someone moving around outside. Then voices.

Or, rather, just one voice…

We moved to the door to listen. I couldn't see anyone through the horizontal slit, but I could hear him quite clearly. It was Farmer Fancher.

"I'm sorry about the radio, my lovely. I know you were listening, but I had to turn it off. It just makes me so flipping angry. We do the most dangerous job in this blooming country, you know that, don't you? More dangerous than the police or the firemen, and do they thank us for it? No, they're busy worrying about brown hares and beavers.

You'd know what to do with a brown hare, my lovely, wouldn't you? Or a beaver."

There was something about his voice that was different from last night. Abruptly I realised what it was. Tinkler realised at more or less the same moment.

"He's drunk," he said.

Fancher was indeed drunk. I was still unsure if it was late morning or just after noon, but either way it was way too early to be drinking. Was this a good thing or a bad thing? From our point of view.

"If he's completely blotto," said Tinkler, "do you think…?"

"I'm just trying to work that out."

"Maybe it will improve our chances."

"Maybe. But that depends on who he's talking to."

"And whether *they're* blotto, too," said Tinkler.

"Something like that."

"So, who is he talking to?"

I stared out of the slit.

"It was only making me angry," said Fancher, his tone indeed taking on an angry, ranting rhythm. "That flaming, filthy radio. I know you like listening. I'm sorry, but it had to go off. I couldn't hear another minute of that bilge. That sodding BBC bias. They're completely in the clutches of those animal rights nutters and those vegan psychopaths. You can even see that in their so-called daily online menu suggestions. Plant-based recipes? Plant-based plonkers."

Fancher had wandered into sight now, so close to the door that I almost jumped back.

What I hadn't registered last night was that he was so very tall, which explained the height of the slit in this door. It had been set at his eye level, so he could comfortably look through it. He wasn't looking through it now, however. He was standing in profile, a short distance away, apparently staring off into the distance.

He was wearing the same green waxed cotton jacket I'd seen him in the other day, with the grubby collar of a red and white checked shirt poking out of it. His face matched the shirt quite well, with blotches of inflamed redness on otherwise dead white skin. Thinning blonde hair stuck messily from under the greenish yellow cap he wore. His eyes were blue and oddly blank.

That was all I could see of him—his head and shoulders. The height of the door slit didn't allow me to look any lower, so I couldn't see who was with him, apparently keeping pace as he strode restlessly back and forth.

"Who else is there?" said Tinkler.

I shook my head as I watched Fancher. "I can't see."

"What do you mean, you can't see?"

"They're below my line of sight."

"Here, let me try." I willingly relinquished my position, giving Tinkler a chance at the slit. Being about the same height as me, he could also look out by standing on tiptoes. But almost immediately he sighed with disgust and sank down on his heels again. "I can't see, either."

"Whoever it is," I said, "they must be considerably shorter than him."

"Right. Exactly. So, do you think it's his wife? The

farmer's wife? Do you think that was her with him last night?"

"Maybe," I said, thinking. "Wait…"

"What?"

"I have an idea."

With Tinkler's help I dragged a bale of hay right up to the door and then I stood on it.

"Ah," said Tinkler. "I see what you're up to now. Very sly."

At this angle, despite the narrow aperture of the slit being rendered narrower still, I could see considerably further down outside. So even a much shorter person would be within my view if they came close enough. I just needed Fancher to walk back this way.

His voice was still audible, though he'd clearly wandered off some distance.

"And their precious buff-tailed bumblebees," he was saying. "So we're supposed to just let the bruchid beetle have its way with our broad beans, are we? I don't think so, my darling. I really don't think so."

His voice was getting steadily louder as he grew nearer.

"Not while we can get our mitts on some chuffing neonicotinoids. It's got to be that, of course it's got to be that. The pyrethroids just don't last in this heat. So, sod the sodding buff-tailed bumblebees."

Now I could see that he had a shotgun tucked under his arm. I hate shotguns. I've had them pointed at me a couple of times.

And then I saw who he was talking to.

"Jesus Christ," I said.

"What is it?" said Tinkler urgently. "Who is he talking to?"

"His dog."

It was a large black and white collie with pale brown fur on either side of the long black streak on its nose. The dog was following closely and eagerly at its master's heels, dodging nimbly from one side to the other whenever he executed one of his erratic changes of direction. The dog's tongue was hanging out and it altogether looked like it was having a fine old time.

"His *dog*?" Tinkler gradually took this in.

I dropped back down off the bale and looked at him.

"So, is that who was with him last night?"

I said, "Only if it's a dog who can operate a torch."

"But he called the torch operator 'my lovely' and he calls the dog 'my lovely'."

"I guess he has a limited range of endearments," I said.

"There is another possibility."

"What?"

"Maybe it's a weredog," said Tinkler. "It's a dog now, but last night it was a man."

"Actually, I think it was a woman," I said.

"Okay, so it's a werebitch. That's even cooler. As a matter of fact, it's a really cool name for a band. Maybe a heavy metal band. Maybe an all-girl heavy metal band."

Tinkler was talking too much—even more than usual. This was because he was scared. Which was all right, because I was scared too. But what he'd said about an all-girl band had got me wondering. The Blue Tits. Tania and Ophelia and Helene—and Monika too, come to think of it (how furious she'd be to know that she remained an afterthought).

They would probably all be waking up about now. Probably with hangovers.

"Do you think they'll miss us?" said Tinkler.

"Not immediately," I said. "Not for quite a while. Maybe not at all." I looked at him. "How did you know what I was thinking?"

Tinkler shrugged. "All-girl band, right? Plus, maybe in situations like this people begin to develop telepathy. As a survival mechanism."

"I don't believe in any of that stuff," I said.

"I know. You're so boring."

"Except for your ability to psychically sense when Clean Head is taking off her clothes..."

"*Agatha*," said Tinkler, as if the solution to all of our problems had suddenly come into view. "Won't she miss us? Won't she know something's wrong?"

"I don't see why," I said, reluctantly. The seriousness of our situation was hammered home to me by the fact that Tinkler hadn't lingered on the prurient aspects of my remark and instead had gone straight for the possibility of rescue.

Which unfortunately didn't really exist. Agatha was staying at our house, looking after our cats when she wasn't busy working. Which is probably what she was doing right now, driving around London in her cab without a care in the world. Except the encroachment of Uber. "She isn't expecting to hear from us and she knows we're busy. She won't think it's strange if she doesn't hear from us for a while."

"How long is a while?"

"I don't know. Maybe a day or so."

"A day or so? Christ."

Fancher was still near the door, and still talking. I wasn't paying much attention.

"Now they're saying we might lose our direct income subsidy payments. So what do they expect? What are we supposed to do? Whose fault is it? It's not our fault. Not with livestock at these prices. Not with those, my beauty. Our meat sale returns make you want to laugh."

The dog, apparently tracking its owner's spiel more closely than I was, made a sympathetic sound.

Fancher chuckled. "No, you're right, my love. They don't make you want to laugh. They make you want to *cry*. That's what they do. They make you want to cry. So what do they expect us to do? How are we supposed to make a living? We have to make a living, we have to open new markets, of course we do. We have to diversify. We have to be creative. To be entrepreneurs. Now, those girls…"

Suddenly I was paying a great deal of attention.

"They should go for a tidy sum. A very tidy sum. Get a camera on them for the online auction, upload a live feed during the bidding so people can see what they're bidding for. Start with a low minimum and that will get them thinking they might get a bargain and that will drive the bidding up. A very tidy sum. Those boys might fetch something too. And if they don't, we'll just dig a pit out back by the old piggery."

At that point he wandered out of earshot again. Tinkler was staring at me with an agonised expression. "We'll dig a *pit*?" he said.

We had already thoroughly explored the building we were in, but now we started in again, decisively energised, scrutinising every inch of the place, looking for something useful. Anything useful.

It wasn't easy, because we were working in virtually total darkness except for the area near the door, which allowed a feeble spread of light through the slit.

We went through everything by feel, searching with our hands. Literally like looking for a needle in a haystack, if the haystack had been dismantled and spread over the floor. Tinkler, it has to be said, performed like a champion considering that any kind of physical labour was pretty much a foreign concept to him.

Even so, the result of all our painstaking work was that we found a lot of hay (in bales), a lot of straw (loose on the floor), and those twelve plastic bottles of water, two now empty.

In other words, nothing we could use.

So we set about examining the door.

It had been retrofitted to the building. A wooden frame had been constructed around the doorway, fitted with metal runners. The door itself was a slab of wood which fit tightly and slid laterally along the runners to block the entrance. Once it was in place it was presumably secured there by some kind of lock on the outside of the door. The inside was flat, featureless wood, and very new by the smell of it.

I was standing on the bale of hay again, staring down through the slit and trying without success to contort myself in such a way that I could see that lock on the outside, when

Fancher and his dog came meandering back towards us.

He was saying, "I've been thinking, we could probably get an even better price on those girls if people can really see what they're getting. You know what I mean. Really see. Take their flipping clothes off. Show everything. Take their knickers and bras off. Their dirty little knickers and their little grey bras. Put everything on display. Yes, that would make for a much better price."

The dog at his heels whined softly.

"But you're right, yes, you're right, my sweet. How do we get their clothes off? They won't be anxious to cooperate, I'm afraid. They won't be wanting to do anything as helpful as that. We'll have to work out a way to get them to do it. Drat, drat, drat. Why did we leave those bottles of water in there?"

The dog gave a little bark.

"Yes, yes, quite right. That's our trouble, all right. Too soft, too kind. That's always been our trouble all up and down the line. We've just been too nice. Too soft. Too accommodating. And now they're telling us any future subsidies will have to demonstrate 'a clear environmental benefit'. Translate that as invite all the brown hares and bumblebees and bruchid beetles into our parlour and make them a nice cup of tea. What mugs we are. Too soft. Too kind, by half."

The dog barked a little louder, as if encouraging him.

"If we hadn't been so nice and kind and left that water in there for them we could give them the water now and give them something *in* the water. Put them to sleep. And then we could take off their clothes, take off their dirty damp little knickers and their tight little bras with their tight little elastic straps. Flipping heck. Why didn't we think of that before?"

The dog whined plaintively in reply.

"Never mind, my girl, we've thought of it now. There must be a way. There always is. We wouldn't have been able to make a go of this place for thirty-odd years if we weren't resourceful, now would we? So we'll just put our thinking caps on and see what we come up with."

At this point man and dog ambled off again.

Tinkler was staring at me. "At least we know Nevada and Opal have water," he said. "Without any drugs in it."

"For now," I said.

I turned around and started searching again, for anything we could use against that fucker and his fucking loyal dog. I knew it was useless, a fool's errand. We'd already examined every grubby inch of this place, cutting our fingers on the straw. So I didn't ask Tinkler to help.

But he did.

And this time we found something.

All the bales of hay in here were bound in the same way, with plastic twine. Try as I might, I couldn't think of any useful application for this. But then we discovered one bale, in a far corner, that was bound differently.

With wire.

It was somewhat rusty on one side of the bale, but otherwise in good shape. The rusty section broke away easily, which helped us get it off the bale. Discarding the rusty fragments, we now had three pieces of stiff, heavy-duty wire which were sharp at the broken ends.

Two of the pieces were short, roughly the same length. The other was much longer. The big piece we folded in the middle, and then folded again and again, working it back and forth until it snapped.

Now we had four pieces of wire of similar lengths. I showed Tinkler what to do. I think it actually speaks well of him that he didn't come up with this idea. But as soon as I saw the sharp edges of those first pieces of the wire I started thinking how good it would be to put them to use.

For example, by inserting them with a no-nonsense speed and firmness into the blank blue eyes of the man outside.

We'd deal with the dog later.

I showed Tinkler how to wrap a length of wire around each of our hands, winding it over the palm and knuckles in a tight circle so we could grip it easily.

The rest of the wire we bent so it jutted out between the second and third fingers of our hands with the sharp point extended in a narrow spike. "When he comes in, use your fists like you're punching him, but drive the wire into his body anywhere it will cause a lot of pain and do a lot of damage."

"What a lovely thought," said Tinkler. "We'll teach that bastard to dig a pit out by the piggery for us... Oh yeah, and attempt to drug and undress and grope our girlfriends and traffic them as sex slaves. Let's not forget that, too." He examined his improvised weapons proudly. "I feel like Wolverine."

And then we waited. And waited. Tinkler had to unwrap the wire from his hands at one point before he went to urinate in the straw. "Otherwise there could be a nasty accident," he said.

He had just put the wire back on when we heard someone moving outside the door.

And then the chunking sound of the lock being released—it sounded like a bolt sliding aside.

And then the lurch and rasp of the door as it slid open, letting in a blinding slab of daylight.

Standing silhouetted against it was not Fancher, but someone much smaller. The dark shape of a woman.

We moved quickly forward, the wire wrapped around our hands.

The woman jerked back, and her face was suddenly in daylight.

Penny—Nevada's mother.

She looked at the vicious makeshift weapons fastened to our hands.

"I've had friendlier greetings," she said.

30: MICKEY SPILLANE

Penny stepped back in surprise as Tinkler and I pelted through the open door and out into the daylight. I suppose, in theory, we could have just walked out, but that wasn't going to happen. We stood blinking in a tarmac square with buildings on two sides. These were sheds and barns, like the one we'd just escaped from. They were placed opposite a low, rambling residence made of grey stone with a green roof, which looked like it had once consisted of two or three separate buildings which had been combined, and clumsily modernised. What might once have been flowerbeds in front of the house were now just rectangles of damp mud.

On the other two sides of the tarmac square there were fields, one of them divided by a narrow access road that entered the square through a white wooden gate. That must have been the way we'd come in. A number of larger vehicles could be glimpsed in an open-sided shed beside the gate.

The whole place was glistening and wet. It had apparently rained heavily in the night while we were asleep.

I could hear the distant low cries of the goats, but other than that, the place was unsettlingly silent.

Penny was standing there looking at us expectantly, and I suppose I should have thanked her, but there was only one thing on my mind.

"We've got to get Nevada," I whispered. And then, as an afterthought, "And Opal."

"I've already done that," she whispered back, and gave me a wry smile just like her daughter's. "Sorry. Releasing you guys was my number two top priority."

"Where is she, then?" I said.

She nodded at the farmhouse. "She went in there with your friend Agatha. Do you really call her Clean Head? Isn't that rather offensive?"

Perhaps reprehensibly, this wasn't my top priority at the moment. "They went in there?"

"Yes."

"In the fucking farmhouse, where he fucking lives?" I forced myself to remember I was supposed to be whispering.

Penny shrugged helplessly. "Yes."

"What are they *doing*?"

"Apparently rescuing a ginger kitten."

"I tried to stop her," said a woman's voice, low and scared, and I turned to see that Opal had come out from behind one of the sheds where she'd been hiding. Sensible girl, I thought, as she and Tinkler embraced furiously and tearfully.

I wish my own true love was equally sensible, I thought—or started to think, because at that instant the door of the farmhouse burst open and Agatha came out at a dead run. She was holding a thick blue towel bundled up in both her arms, clutched tight to her chest, a small furry ginger face staring fearfully out from it.

"*Run.*"

She was yelling at the top of her voice, which took my breath away because it was so insanely dangerous and stupid and reckless. But then I realised that the ferocious barking of a dog had already begun in the farmhouse, so the game was up anyway.

Now Nevada came out of the same door, also running at top speed, also shouting at us.

"*Go.*"

This time we did, turning and fleeing as fast as we could, Penny in the lead, heading towards the access road. It took me a second or so to realise that Nevada wasn't with us. I turned to see what had happened to her.

She was standing in the middle of the tarmac, looking back towards the farmhouse. What was she doing? Why wasn't she running? Any moment now—

Fancher appeared in the doorway of his house. He was trying to run and put on his rubber boots at the same time, which might have been comical in another context. Any chance of comedy was ruined, though, by the presence of the shotgun clutched under his arm.

He got his boots on, started forward, and then froze.

He saw Nevada standing there, looking at him.

I began to run towards her.

Fancher stared at Nevada. Then, casually and with great deliberation, she gave him the finger.

He raised his shotgun and fired.

"Nevada!" My voice was drowned by the shotgun blast—a loud, sharp snapping sound that echoed off the fronts of all the buildings. I closed my eyes so I wouldn't have to see what it would do to her, but I couldn't keep them shut. I had to know.

Nevada was standing exactly where she had been, unharmed, unmoving, staring towards Fancher.

He was lying on the ground, his shotgun a mangled wreck. One of its barrels was swollen and burst, peeled back like some kind of metal flower that had blossomed suddenly and savagely. The back of the gun was blown open, too.

As for Fancher, his face was a red smear and part of his head was gone.

Inside the house the dog stopped barking and began to howl.

By now I was with Nevada, holding her, clutching her fiercely with my arms stuck out awkwardly behind her to keep her safe from the sharp wires I still had wrapped around my hands. She clutched me back, her arms wrapped tightly around me. I could smell her hair, pungent with the scent of straw. We rocked back and forth like two drunks clinging to each other for support. I didn't know what had just happened. I only knew that she was still alive.

"Why didn't you run?" I whispered.

"Because I knew both barrels of his shotgun had about six inches of mud rammed into them." She looked at me, her eyes like a child's searching for reassurance. "Because I did it."

"It was my idea," said Agatha. She and the others had drifted back to join us. She stood there, holding the kitten wrapped in the towel and staring at us.

Opal was gaping at what remained of Mr Fancher. "Don't look," said Penny, and turned her away from the sight. Opal moved obediently. Tinkler didn't stop staring, though. His face was white, but he seemed very calm as he unwrapped the wire from his hands and threw it away. It jangled as it hit the ground.

"It was my idea," said Agatha again. She was staring at the man's body with a stricken look. "I got it from a Mickey Spillane novel I read, *The Girl Hunters*." She turned and looked at me. "An early Corgi edition." Her voice was beginning to tremble.

Nevada let go of me and went and hugged her. "It's not your fault," she said.

"It was my idea."

"But I was the one who *did* it." She released Agatha and turned and looked down at Fancher. "And nothing would have happened to him if he hadn't tried to shoot us."

The dog howled and howled.

In a way, it was thanks to our cat Turk that we had been rescued.

When we didn't turn up for our meeting with Nevada's mother early that morning, and didn't answer our phones, she had tried our landline in London and reached Agatha.

"I was supposed to be out working today," said Agatha. "But last night about three in the morning there was this terrible commotion in your garden so I jumped out of bed to see what was going on. Turk was standing out there with her tail all swollen up…"

"Like a wine bottle?" said Nevada.

"Like a wine bottle," Agatha nodded. "She was staring at the roof of your shed, and standing on it was this *fox*. This full-grown red fox. Turk had chased it out of your garden."

"Was Turk all right?" I said. A man was lying dead and I was worried about my cat.

"She's fine. The fox looked a little freaked out, though."

Nevada tutted. "Honestly. Even so, what a reckless girl. I'm going to have to give her a good talking to."

All of us were standing by Tinkler's car, while we waited for Penny to return from Tania's. Kind of Red was parked on the access road, some considerable distance outside the farm gate. When they'd arrived, Agatha and Penny had stopped at this point and continued on foot so no one could hear them approaching.

We'd left the farmyard and come out here because none of us wanted to be near Fancher's body, or the howling of his dog, which was still audible even at this remove.

"Anyway, I was wide awake after all that," said Agatha.

"I should think so."

"The fox took off, vanishing like a wraith as soon as I opened the back door, but I was still worried about Turk. She wouldn't come back in and insisted on standing guard in the garden. Which meant I was awake for the rest of the night, lying in bed listening in case anything else happened. So the next morning I was completely knackered and decided to take the day off."

"So you were at home when my mum rang."

"Luckily, yes."

"Good old Turk." Nevada looked at me. "That would have been about the time we were getting into trouble. Do you think she sensed something?"

I thought she had sensed something all right, a bloody great fox in our garden. But I wasn't called upon to offer this response because Agatha was continuing with her story.

"Penny and I worked out pretty rapidly that something must be wrong and we rang Tania's house and eventually got an answer. They were all hung-over and pretty pissed off, but they went out and found your tents with your stuff still in them, including your phones."

"We got up in a real hurry," I said. "We hardly had time to grab our clothes."

"And our bow and arrow and Taser," said Nevada. "For all the good they did us."

"So I drove down to Tania's," said Agatha. "And met up with Penny there. By that time Ophelia had had a look around, and she said she'd found some tyre tracks that were exactly the same as when her goats were stolen. In the same place and everything."

Fancher had been a creature of habit, I thought. Past tense.

"And you followed the tyre tracks all the way here?" said Tinkler.

"Of course not, genius," said Agatha. "The tyre tracks were just in that spot. But Ophelia knew it must have been Fancher and she told us where his place was so Penny and

I drove over here." She put her hand on the roof of Kind of Red. "I left my car at Tania's because it's a two-seater and so is Penny's." When she wasn't driving a black cab, Agatha used a Smart City-Coupé.

"I knew we'd need something bigger." She looked at Nevada and me, and Tinkler and Opal, all listening solemnly. "To take four people back with us."

She'd *hoped* they'd need to take four people back, I realised later, with a cold feeling in the pit of my stomach.

"We parked here and walked. It was easy enough to find where you guys were—the only two sheds with specially modified doors. And they didn't need keys to open them from the outside. You just pulled the bolts back." Agatha shrugged. "So that's what we did. We let out Nevada and Opal."

"And, my word, were we glad to see you," said Nevada. "Have I said thank you, by the way?"

"Yes. And you're welcome, by the way. And then Penny went to get the blokes out and Nevada and I went to rescue the kitten." Agatha paused and peered in through the window of Kind of Red. The exhausted kitten in question was dozing on the blue towel on the back seat. "The house was quiet. The farmer and his dog must have been asleep." She hesitated. "We found the kitten as soon as we went in. And we found his shotgun…"

"We thought about using it against him," said Nevada. "Turning his own gun on him. But I had no idea how he'd react, or if he had any other weapons, or even where exactly he was in his house." She shook her head. "Too many variables. So we decided to put the gun out of commission."

"Why didn't you just unload it?" said Opal. "Take the shells out of it."

"He'd have other shells. And we didn't know where he kept them."

"Then just hide the gun," said Opal, as if it was all happening now, in real time, and we could change the way things had turned out.

"Again," said Nevada patiently, "we didn't know if he had other weapons. So long as we left the shotgun where it was, and rendered it unusable in a way that wasn't immediately obvious to him, that was our best bet."

"Which was when I suggested doing the thing with the mud in the barrels," said Agatha. She turned to look back towards the farmhouse where the dog still wailed. Her voice was soft and calm, but tears began to flow freely down her face.

Nevada moved in close to hug her, and so did I.

Tinkler remained where he was beside Opal, but I could tell that he wished he could join us in the group hug.

There was the sound of a car approaching, and Penny's Nissan came bouncing along the road with her and Ophelia in it. They pulled up beside us and got out. "I understand you've found my goats," she said.

"We assume they're yours," I said, and described the building where they were.

"Okay," said Ophelia, looking at our two cars. "We're going to need something else to take them back in."

"There's a lot of big farm vehicles in that shed, just inside the gate."

"I can't drive a big farm vehicle," said Ophelia.

"I can drive anything with wheels," said Agatha, wiping her face.

We drove back to Tania's place in a convoy: Nevada's mum in the Nissan with the kitten, Nevada, Opal and Tinkler in Kind of Red with me driving, and Agatha and Ophelia following us with the goats. When we reached the turn-off for Tania's mansion, Penny kept going, heading for her vet's to get the kitten looked at. The rest of us turned into the driveway and parked.

There was no sign of life for a moment, and then Tania came out, looking warily at our mismatched assortment of vehicles.

In the end, Agatha and Ophelia had opted not for a big farm vehicle but rather a battered old Range Rover with a handy trailer already attached to it. The Range Rover was also a brownish red colour—kind of red, you might say—although I don't think that coincidence influenced her decision. Now Ophelia jumped down from the passenger seat and hurried off towards the stables.

Tania came towards us slowly, tentatively, as though concerned we might be contaminated with something. I wondered how much she knew. I gave her a big smile and she smiled back, relieved.

"Any chance of some coffee?" I said.

"Of course," she said. "And something to eat?"

"Yes, please," said Tinkler.

"You must be famished," said Tania, and rushed off, glad to have a clearly defined task.

Food was apparently also on Ophelia's mind, though food of a different kind. She came back carrying one of those large plastic sacks of grass pellets. She dropped it, split it open and spread the pellets on the ground. Then she opened the back of the trailer and coaxed the goats out. As soon as they saw the pellets they were in business, hurrying over and hungrily beginning to hoover them up.

All except one, a small brown goat with ears like a spaniel. He hung back, staring first at the food on the ground, and then in the direction of the stables.

Agatha had got out of the Range Rover but now she went back to it and opened the door again. "We better return this," she said.

"I'll drive it," said Ophelia.

"All right," said Agatha. "I'll follow and bring you back." She took the keys for Kind of Red from me and started the car.

Ophelia had climbed into the colour-coordinated Range Rover. Now she wound down the window and said, "That's Archibald, by the way." She nodded at the goat with the spaniel ears.

The two red vehicles pulled away and, as if taking this as a sign, Archibald the goat came to a decision. He ignored the food on the ground and set off towards the stables. Nevada and Tinkler and I immediately followed. Opal stared after us for a moment and then, never one to miss out on something, came along too.

As he passed the stables and approached the paddocks, Archibald broke into a run. We ran after him. Standing in the left-hand paddock was Charlie the horse, not wearing his gimp mask today. His big head turned curiously in our direction and then seemed to give a jerk of surprise when he spotted Archibald.

The fence of the paddock was designed to keep horses in, not goats out, and Archibald had no trouble slipping in between the horizontal wooden bars. And then he was in the paddock with Charlie. He ran over to the horse, who was walking rapidly towards him. They met in the middle and stopped, the goat rubbing against the legs of the horse.

Charlie snorted and Archibald gave a low cry, nuzzling up at the huge head pushing down to meet him and rub against his face.

"I still say sex is at the root of it," said Tinkler.

31: GHOULISH NEWS

The first cup of coffee had been pure bliss. The fourth was still pretty good, but I forced myself to put it aside and have a much-needed talk with Tania. I was in the kitchen helping her load the dishwasher while the others, now all having eaten, were outside admiring the horse and goat reunion, which was still continuing over an hour later, after a break for refreshment in the form of hay and grass pellets. No doubt Tinkler was offering a scurrilous commentary.

"You heard what happened to Fancher?" I said. By unspoken agreement we'd studiously avoided this topic all through lunch.

Tania didn't look up from the cabinet under the sink where she was choosing from an impressive assortment of washing powders and liquids. "Yes, I heard."

"We have to tell the police about him."

"They already know," she said.

"What?"

She selected a box of ecologically sound powder and

turned to look at me. "You remember I got a phone call while you were eating?"

"No."

"Well, you were eating, weren't you? Anyway, I took a call from a neighbour. They wanted to pass on the news. Have you ever noticed how eager people are to dish up ghoulish news? It's never anything cheery or positive. So, anyway, apparently they went over to the farm because they heard the dog howling. Actually what they said was that they were sick of the dog howling and they went over to complain to Fancher. And they found him."

"What about Agatha and Ophelia?" I said. "Did they spot them?"

"Don't worry. They were long gone before these people arrived. In fact it was Ophelia who let the dog out of the house into the yard."

"Wasn't that rash?" I said. "Didn't it go for her?"

"Yes, but no."

"So what did these people say when they found the body? About how Fancher died?"

Tania smiled contentedly. "They said he was always drunk and he never cleaned his shotgun. They said they were amazed that something like this hadn't happened before."

"And what was he supposed to have been shooting at?"

"Rats, foxes, pink elephants, flying snakes, flying saucers. He'd been known to shoot at all of those and more before now."

* * *

Later that day I asked everyone who was still at Tania's house to gather for a meeting. We got together in the library, which if I described it as a room full of books would sound redundant—but it really was *full* of books.

It was a big room; my house could easily have fit into it, with a portion of the garden included, perhaps for cats to frolic in. And there were bookshelves filling every wall of the room, running up from the dusty red carpeted floor to the high ceiling, with books packed onto them. The books had come with the house when Tania bought it and she freely admitted she'd never even looked at them and had no idea what was there. She wasn't much of a reader, except for Elizabethan history.

But there weren't any books on the large oak table in the middle of the room, so it was ideal for us all to sit around.

Erik and Helene had gone back to London early that morning, before anyone had become aware of our abduction—which was good, because it exactly suited my purposes.

Present were Agatha, Nevada and myself, Opal and Tinkler, Tania and Derren, Saxon Ghost, Monika, Ophelia and Fanzine Frank. Of these, Derren was the most tetchy, and clearly resented being summoned to a meeting in his own home.

"What exactly are we doing here?" he said.

"We need to talk about what we're going to do next."

"What do you mean, do next? Isn't it all over?"

"Of course it isn't over," I said.

"But Hoyt Fancher's dead," said Derren. So, Hoyt was his first name. With a name like Hoyt Fancher, no wonder he'd turned out to be a psychopath. "Dead in a shooting accident. All done and dusted."

"But he wasn't alone," said Nevada.

"What are you saying?"

"There was someone with him when he abducted us last night."

"That hardly matters, does it?" said Derren stubbornly. "It was probably just some hired hand."

"No," I said. "Fancher was never the one behind the attempts to kill the Blue Tits. It's hard to imagine him having any motive to do so, or even knowing who they are."

"Then why did he come after you lot?"

"Because somebody paid him," I said.

"With the bonus of trafficking us for whatever he could get," said Nevada.

"You and Opal, maybe," said Tinkler. "But he was downright insulting about the prospect of getting any money for me."

"Don't put yourself down," said Agatha. "I'm sure some buggery club somewhere would have had you." But she said it with the strangest, tender smile. And Tinkler was smiling happily back at her.

Opal was attentively following all this and didn't look best pleased.

Neither was Derren, though for different reasons. He was about to say something impatient and conclusive, but I beat him to it.

"Fancher simply wasn't the mastermind."

"Then who is?"

"Okay," I said. "You may want to brace yourselves."

"What the devil are you talking about?"

I looked for a moment at the faces around the table staring at me, then I said, "It's Helene."

There was an impressive silence. Of our party, Tinkler was gaping at me openly, Agatha was staring at me, rather more guardedly but equally surprised, and Opal was just taking it all in, trying to work out what it meant to her personally. Nevada, of course, knew everything I was going to reveal, having discussed it with me earlier.

Tania was the first to speak, in a neutral, give-nothing-away politician's voice. "You're saying Helene is behind this whole thing?"

"Yes."

Saxon Ghost cleared his throat. He looked embarrassed, as you might do if you had to point out that a friend had made a terrible faux pas. "But, mate, the first attempts were all on Helene."

"That's right."

"And why would she try and kill herself?"

"She set it all up as a cover, so she could kill the others without being suspected."

"Nonsense," said Tania. "Helene would never do anything like that. And how many times did someone try and kill her?"

"Think about it," I said. "Let's go through those attempts. No one witnessed that hit and run."

"But she had a photo of the car," said Tinkler.

"That's right."

"A car that turned out to be stolen."

"I imagine it's not too difficult to arrange to have a car stolen and take a picture of it from behind as it is driving away." I looked around the table at my listeners. They were all staring at me. "And it was taking that photo with her phone which tipped me off in the first place. I almost got run over when I was cycling through Richmond Park, and did I think of taking a photograph of the car that had done it? Yes. But about three weeks later."

"You mean she was just too on the ball?" said Agatha.

"Precisely. Like she'd been expecting it to happen. And then there was the attempt with the gas in her kitchen…"

"I suppose all she had to do was turn on the gas herself?" said Tania. It was hard to say if there was caustic sarcasm in her voice, or perhaps the first stirrings of belief.

I shrugged. "Why would she even do that?"

"What do you mean?"

"She just needed to *say* it happened," said Nevada. "It was all just a story she told. There was never any corroboration from anyone."

"And the cocaine spiked with Fentanyl," said Tinkler, getting into the swing of it. "That was just as easy."

"Right," I said. "She would have been in a perfect position to do that. No one had better access than her, except Erik himself. And of course Helene knew all about his little rituals of folding the wraps in a certain way."

"So it was easy for her to make it obvious that someone had tampered with it," said Nevada.

"Exactly. And she could be sure Erik would spot it. But

even if he didn't, she could draw his attention to it."

"Shit…" said Saxon Ghost. But he sounded like he was beginning to be convinced. And his face had a look of deep concentration, as he tried to put all the pieces together.

"Then there was her master stroke," I said. "The killer amp at the Bull's Head. The one supposedly wired to electrocute her. Just as with the drugs cache, she would have been in a perfect position to replace the real amp with the doctored one. She was there at the pub with the band. No one would have questioned her presence. She could come and go as she pleased. All she needed to do was slip out at some point while they were eating before the gig, switch the amps, and rejoin the others.

"Then, when they went back in to get ready to play, all she had to do was the same trick as with the cocaine wrap—make sure that Erik noticed something was wrong with it."

"By using the wrong colour power cable," said Nevada.

"Exactly. And once his suspicions had been aroused and he took a closer look, he saw for certain it wasn't his amp."

"But wasn't she running quite a risk?" said Ophelia. "If something had gone wrong and no one had spotted the amp she could have electrocuted herself."

I said, "Who says the amp was ever actually capable of electrocuting anyone?"

They all looked at me.

"You mean it was just rigged so that it looked like it might be deadly?"

"So that it might have *been* deadly. Past tense. Before the acid hit it. Why not just design it so that it's a convincing dummy, and the only thing that really works is the acid-release mechanism when the power is cut? That was a touch of genius. But she was a little *too* clever. For it to work there had to be enough of the amp left to be examined. So the acid had to be stopped before it was too late."

"By dumping baking powder on it," said Tinkler.

"That's right. And it was Helene who came up with that suggestion. As with the photograph of the hit-and-run car, I always thought that that had shown just a little too much presence of mind."

"She outsmarted herself," said Agatha.

"Right," I said. "But she so very nearly succeeded."

"You see?" said Nevada, to the people sitting around the table. "Who would suspect her if she seemed to be the primary target? And, having established this quite emphatically by making all those fake attempts on her own life, she could then start going after the others."

"When, suddenly," I said, "you'll notice the attempts become deadly effective, like when she moves on to Dylis."

"If we hadn't been there when she drank the juice she would have been dead for sure," said Nevada.

"But what about the second amp?" said Tania. "The exploding one that nearly killed all of us?"

"It was a calculated gamble," I said. "But whatever happened, Helene knew she'd be safe."

"Because the detonator in the amp could only be triggered by a signal she would send," said Nevada. "From her mobile phone."

"I think she planned some kind of diversion to get herself offstage at the critical moment," I said. "Maybe a broken guitar string. She gets out of range of the blast and then sets it off."

"But Erik would have been on stage," said Tinkler. He sounded like a child who'd learned the truth about Santa Claus. I felt sorry for him, but I couldn't stop now.

"You can't make an omelette without breaking eggs," I said.

"Then why did she blow up the amp in the back of my van?" asked Monika, who had remained unusually silent up until now.

"The longer it was lying around after she couldn't use it, the more likely someone was to spot something was wrong with it," I said. "When it was 'confiscated' and put in your van, it was an ideal opportunity to get rid of the evidence. Sorry."

I looked at Nevada. That was about it. She nodded.

"Okay," I said. "We'll just ask you to keep this to yourselves until we work out what to do about Helene."

"And be careful," said Nevada. "The threat level to the former Blue Tits is still high. I'm looking at you Ophelia, Tania."

Nevada and I, and Tinkler and Agatha, were standing in the driveway by our cars, waiting while Opal used the loo before the drive back to London. Inside the house the others were still discussing my bombshell.

Out here, Agatha and Tinkler were both staring at me.

"My god, full marks to you for working that out," said Agatha.

Tinkler was shaking his head disconsolately. "Poor Erik. This is going to destroy him."

"He's better off without her," said Agatha. "She's a fiend in human form."

"She would be," I said, "if anything I just said in there was true."

32: TIME FOR FUN

Silence.

The staring at me that they'd done before in the library was nothing compared to the staring they were doing now.

I said, "No one seems to have noticed that I didn't ascribe any motive to Helene. That's because she didn't have one. Because she didn't do it."

"What the fuck…" said Agatha.

Nevada didn't say anything, but she couldn't keep a mischievous smile from her lips.

Tinkler, however, was shaking his head in a tormented fashion. "Please, please, don't toy with my tiny brain like this."

I patted him on the shoulder, gently, not in Erik's style. "Don't worry, old friend."

"You mean Helene was *not* trying to kill the others?"

"No she wasn't."

"So someone really is trying to kill her?"

"Yes they are."

"Then why…?"

"We needed everyone to think it was Helene," I said. "Or at least to think that's what *we* believe."

"For the love of god, why?"

Agatha was watching me with a level gaze. "Disinformation," she said.

I nodded.

"We want the real culprit to think we're barking up the wrong tree," said Nevada.

"We want them off their guard," I said. "Because if they know we're coming after them, they'll be very dangerous indeed."

After we got home, Tinkler took charge of Kind of Red—a rare example of him driving his own car—and took Opal back to his place. "I think he thinks he's going to get his end away," said Nevada as we walked to our front door.

"I hope so," I said. "He's certainly worked for it. That was his major complaint about our being kidnapped, by the way. Not getting laid in his tent."

"Our tent," said Nevada. "Our *spare* tent." She took out her keys and shook them so they jingled. Fanny promptly emerged from the cat flap and waited while we opened the door, then followed us inside. Turk came bashing in from the back garden through the other cat flap and joined us, the whole family converging together in the sitting room.

We fed the cats, took baths, went to bed and slept a deep, oblivious sleep only occasionally troubled by dreams of farms and shotguns and howling dogs. We woke briefly around noon the following day at the prompting of two hungry cats, fed them, drank some water, took a loo break and collapsed back into bed.

We probably would have slept the clock around if the doorbell hadn't rung.

I opened the door, still groggy and uncoordinated, but I came fully awake fast when I saw how white Tinkler's face was.

"What's wrong?"

"It's Stinky…"

"Oh, Jesus, what now?" said Nevada, knotting the belt of her dressing gown.

Tinkler came in and told us all about it.

"I had to tell him," he said.

"Tell him what?" I said. "This is Stinky we're talking about, right?"

"Yes. I had to tell him that Helene isn't really the culprit."

"Why the fuck would you do that?" hissed Nevada.

"How did Stinky even know about any of this?"

"Because he got it out of Opal," said Tinkler.

"By 'got it out of her' you mean she phoned him and told him."

"Something like that, but—"

"Fucking Opal," said Nevada.

"In fairness," said Tinkler, "you did want the disinformation spread around."

Nevada was implacable. "I'm not interested in fairness. And we only wanted it spread around in Helene's circle."

"Okay, so that's sort of exactly my point," said Tinkler. "Stinky was about to reveal it to the whole world, to blow the story wide open. As soon as I found out what had happened I phoned him and begged him not to. But you know Stinky."

"He scented a scoop," I said.

"Yes. So you see, I had to tell him."

Nevada was gradually calming down. "You did, actually. If word had got out to the general public that Helene was trying to murder her friends, it would have destroyed her."

"Not to mention Erik," said Tinkler.

I nodded. "That's right. We wanted to spread our story. But we didn't want to spread it that far."

"I'm sorry," said Tinkler. "But I had no choice. I had to tell him the truth, to stop him."

"We accept that," said Nevada. "But you see the problem."

"That's why I'm here. To alert you…"

"That blabbermouth Stinky knows what we're up to," I said. "So it's only a matter of time before word gets back to the killer."

"That's right."

"So we've got to act now," I said.

Fanzine Frank's house looked much the same as the last time I'd seen it. I rang the doorbell and electric guitar chords swelled inside. There was no immediate response, but that was nothing new. So I waited, pushed the button, and waited some more.

When it became clear that nobody was coming to let me in, I went around the side of the house where there was a narrow alley leading to a garden gate.

The gate was unlocked but opened with a loud, hellish screech of unoiled hinges, as though announcing me. I stepped through it into the big, chaotic garden, with its high walls and big fruit trees, and its bizarre display of life-sized cut-out Christmas effigies.

I saw with relief that Mindy was there, a good distance from the house and out of earshot of the doorbell. She was busy among Santa and the snowman and the oddly mounted wise men. There was a black and yellow toolbox in the long grass at her feet as she worked on the giant Rudolph the Red-Nosed Reindeer. I saw that some bolts had been removed and were lying on the lid of the box.

When she caught sight of me, Mindy waved and smiled. I went over to join her.

"Looking for Frank?" she said.

"Yes. Any idea where he might be?"

"Haven't a clue, but if you find him, please tell him I'm looking for him, too. And tell him to switch his phone on, the old mug."

I looked at Rudolph. "Finally dismantling the Christmas display?"

Mindy nodded happily. "That's what I want to tell him. By the time he gets back, all this is going to be gone."

There was a long silence as the breeze rustled through the branches of the fruit trees.

"Maybe we should just cut the shit," I said.

Mindy looked at me in puzzlement and then smiled. It was a very different smile. "That would be nice."

"Why did you do it?" I said.

"What makes you think I did anything?"

"Oh," I said. "A whole bunch of stuff. But I guess the standout moments include the coffee machine."

"The coffee machine?" Her puzzled look cleared. "Oh, you mean when I told you I was modifying it." She sighed. "I suppose I shouldn't have mentioned that. I didn't have to. It's just that you got me a bit peeved when you suggested that it was broken. It wasn't broken at all. It was on its way to being better than it was before."

"That's right," I said. "Which got me wondering about what other things you might have modified."

Mindy shrugged. "Only a lazy person accepts factory settings and factory standards."

"And then Tania told us that you'd got a double first class honours degree."

"That's right. From Imperial College."

"Good university," I said.

"A great university."

"So I checked exactly what your double first consisted of. Which turns out to be electrical engineering and chemistry."

"How did you find that out?"

"From your Facebook page."

"Oh. Did you send me a friend request?"

"No," I said. "I guess it's too late now."

"What's wrong with electrical engineering and chemistry?"

"Nothing at all. In fact they're the perfect background for someone who wants to pursue a career in bomb making and poisoning people. And then there was the costume parade."

She quickly glanced at me, as if I'd finally said something of interest.

"What about it?"

"It got me wondering if you had some hospital scrubs in your collection."

"It's entirely possible," said Mindy.

"Like the ones someone wore when they tried to kill Dylis in the hospital."

"It's entirely possible," she repeated.

"So, why did you do it?"

She gave an exasperated sigh. "You just said why."

"What do you mean?"

"The costume parade." She was standing behind Rudolph as she kept working, peering at me over the reindeer's shoulder. She was looking at me as though she was honestly searching for the answer to something.

"Can you imagine what it's like, doing something like that for years and years? Years and years of him fancying them and never me. Or, when he did fancy me it was because I looked like them. Because I made myself look like them. Because that's what he wanted. For years and years and years. He was never really with me. He was with them. He might be near me—in physical proximity to me—but he was really with them, wherever they were. Always keeping track of them, of their lives, whatever was happening to them."

She picked up one of the bolts from the lid of the toolbox.

"So I decided it would be better if they didn't have their lives anymore."

I realised she wasn't taking anything off the figure.

"If nothing was happening to them anymore, and never would again."

She was putting something on.

"You didn't have to do that," I said.

"Didn't I? What else could I do?"

"Just stop doing it," I said.

"Stop doing what? The costume parade?"

"Yes."

She seemed sincerely puzzled. "But why deprive Frank of his pleasure? His pleasure wasn't the problem. The problem was their being alive. That's what I couldn't stand. I just couldn't stand the thought of it. But if they were feeding the worms, or if they were dust, then I really wouldn't mind at all. In fact, it would give *me* a lot of pleasure. Don't you see?"

I think she genuinely wanted me to understand. That wasn't going to happen, so I said, "Okay. But why us? Me and Nevada, and Tinkler and Opal. Why did you set Fancher on us?"

Mindy shook her head. "That wasn't the plan. Not originally. I knew about Hoyt because Tania was always complaining about him. She'd even said he'd stolen some livestock from her land, although she didn't tell us it was goats or that they belonged to Ophelia. I thought he might be a useful man to know, so I got to know him. And he was. When I heard about the concert I put our friendship on a business footing."

"You mean you paid him?"

"Of course I paid him. I needed his help. And with his help I was going to get as many of them as I could. Take them away and either deal with them on the farm, at our leisure, or—as I suggested—sell them to someone who would really teach them a lesson. I introduced him to the dark web and he took to it like a duck to water. But then the opportunity to use the amp presented itself, so I did that instead. That was a much better plan. There was so much less that could go wrong with it."

She gave me a sour smile. "At least, that's what I thought. I should have stuck with my first instinct and gone with my original plan, but I didn't. And look what happened. Thanks to you."

I felt I should point out that I didn't deserve all the credit for impounding the amp, but it didn't seem the right moment.

"But I decided I could still use Fancher," said Mindy. "To put you out of the picture. By the way, are you recording this?" Before I could answer she said, "Of course you are. It doesn't matter."

She suddenly turned and walked away.

I hesitated for a moment and then followed her, stepping carefully through the line of Christmas cut-outs. I almost felt like I should apologise for brushing past them, like people in a crowd. As I headed further down the garden I looked back and confirmed my suspicion that she'd been fitting something to the back of the figures.

There were grey plastic bags resting on metal brackets attached to the flat plywood back of each of them. The bags bulged and wires emerged from them, running through the grass where I was walking, snaking back towards the windowless shed at the bottom of the garden.

Mindy caught me looking back at the figures and she said, "That's right. I had plenty of explosive left."

She was at the shed now, with that big electrical switch mounted on the wall facing us, and the bright painted arrow pointing towards it with the words *TIME FOR FUN!* in their festive colours.

I was right on her heels. She turned to look at me, her face flushed and pink, and her eyes bright. She looked very much alive. Positively exultant.

"No one's going to judge me," said Mindy. "I'm not going to prison. And what's more, I'm finally going to get those Christmas decorations taken down." She laughed. "Or rather taken *up*. And me with them." She gave me a sly look. "And you with me, Mr Nosy Parker."

"Time for fun?" I said.

"That's right. It's the detonator." She reached for the switch.

As she did so, a feathered shaft appeared as if by magic in the back of her hand, pinning it to the wall.

Mindy screamed. She screamed rather a lot.

Behind us, further up the garden, a lithe figure dropped from the branches of one of the apple trees.

Nevada ran towards us, bow in her hand, quiver full of arrows on her back.

The garden gate opened and Tania stepped through, right on cue. The gate probably screeched like hell, but I didn't hear it because of the noise Mindy was making.

I considered telling her that I hadn't just been recording

our conversation, but also transmitting it. But that just seemed pointlessly cruel.

I was standing between Mindy and the switch in case she tried to throw herself on it despite the arrow in her hand. But, to tell the truth, all the fight seemed to have gone out of her.

EPILOGUE

One day I found Nevada watching YouTube videos of shotguns exploding because of blocked barrels. I sat down beside her on the sofa and asked her why.

"Because none of them backfire the way Fancher's did. The barrels blow up, but that's it."

"So why did his gun explode and kill him?"

"I don't know," she said. "Maybe it was an antique, or particularly badly maintained. Damaged or rusty." She closed the laptop and settled back on the sofa with me. I felt her relax and I knew why. She might have been responsible for Fancher's death, but so was he.

"What it all comes down to," I said, "is that he chose to pull the trigger, thinking he was going to kill *you*. It's what you said yourself."

"I know."

"That's what you have to keep in mind, if you ever wake up in the middle of the night remembering it." I took her hand. "You know what? If you do wake up, wake me too. I'll keep you company."

"If I wake up in the middle of the night and remember it," said Nevada, "I'll open a bottle of wine to celebrate."

I kissed her. My savage darling.

"What I keep remembering," I said, "is the way he manipulated us, using the kitten like that. He was so sure that we'd do anything to stop him hurting it. And he was right."

"He used our better nature against us."

"Exactly," I said. "But I don't know what we could have done differently."

She put a hand on my cheek and turned my face to hers, looking me in the eye. "If something like that ever happens again, we're just going to have to harden our hearts."

"Then let's just hope to god nothing like that ever happens again. Because I don't know if I can."

"Neither do I."

"He knew a hell of a lot about us," I said. "He knew exactly how to push our buttons. I mean, a cat in distress? It was tailor made for us."

"Do you think Mindy briefed him?"

"Absolutely. It was easy enough working out that we were cat lovers."

"True," said Nevada. "A quick glance at either of our websites would have told her that."

"How is Almodóvar, by the way?"

Almodóvar was the name Nevada's mother had given the ginger kitten when she adopted him.

"Fully healed and thriving. He's settled in with the Spirit, who's gone from ignoring his presence to tolerating it. Apparently they sit for hours in the garden, side by side, watching the bees."

Elsewhere in the animal kingdom, Archibald the goat and Charlie the horse remained delighted with each other's company. Every morning Archibald would go calling at the stables and they would spend the day together. Despite Tinkler's insistence to the contrary, their attachment was strictly platonic.

Or, to put it more simply, they were just friends.

The way the various human beings fared was a little more variable.

Helene's many near misses with death, followed by the final elimination of that threat, had brought her and Erik even closer. They couldn't quite bring themselves to make the big leap and move in together, but Helene started spending an additional weeknight over at Erik's house. Which made Bong Cha happy, because she got another night off.

Opal did move in with Tinkler, briefly. Just long enough, as Nevada cynically noted, to give her a comfortable base of operations while she was flat hunting. As soon as she found a suitable place of her own, Opal moved out of his house and, very decisively, out of his bed, and didn't return.

In fact, the rumour was that she was seeing Stinky Stanmer.

"Oh well," said Tinkler. "Maybe she can help him change his pants."

So Tinkler was once again the sad singleton clown we knew and loved, though his brief sojourn with Opal had done him a lot of good.

Or, as he put it, "I got my ashes hauled."

On the subject of romance, we discovered to our amazement that Saxon Ghost was seeing Sydney the camerawoman. They'd met when she was filming the Goat Aid gig and had clearly hit it off despite the fact, as Tinkler put it—with a certain degree of accuracy—that he was 'over twice her age and less than half her height'.

Monika the roadie might have taken offence at this new arrangement, since she used to be Saxon's designated booty call. But Monika was fully engaged with other matters.

Dylis had come out of hospital. However, she was still far from fully recovered, and indeed it wasn't clear that she ever would be. So Monika moved into her riverside flat with her as a kind of carer and companion. The arrangement seemed to work and, far from resenting Monika stepping into her shoes as bass player at the goat gig, Dylis bought a second bass guitar and decreed that they should regularly practise together.

We told Erik about this, and mentioned the fact that Monika's bass playing at Goat Aid had been well received by the Blue Tits' fans, many of whom said that she was at least as good as Dylis had been.

"You can't fall off the floor," replied Erik, an unlikely Philip Larkin quote from a retired rock god.

As for the woman who had put Dylis in hospital and so nearly killed her and so many more of us, she was now safely behind bars. On the day of Mindy Fewston's arrest Erik and Helene came over to our place to give us their heartfelt thanks, along with kisses, handshakes, thumps on the back, kind words, bottles of high-end champagne and money. A lot of money.

Indeed, I found myself thinking that things were all going suspiciously smoothly. But just then Erik, with the better part of a bottle of Bollinger in him, insisted on cornering me and giving me a long-delayed lecture about guitar technique.

"Low action means the strings are close to the fretboard," he said. "You have better chord construction that way. Gibson designed its guitars for low action. You go from one note, from one string, to another faster because you don't have any return or release lag to worry about."

And he went on, too.

Mindy Fewston's arrest and prosecution definitely didn't go the way we expected. For a start, the evidence we'd congratulated ourselves on gathering against her proved irrelevant, because she made no attempt to deny anything she'd done in connection with the Blue Tits. Instead her legal team took a very different approach, arguing that she'd been the victim of years of abusive oppression and manipulation by a controlling and obsessive husband.

In fact, Mindy was showing signs of becoming the poster girl for survivors of controlling behaviour. It was a smart move by her lawyers, and they might even have got her off, if Fanzine Frank had been her intended victim.

But the big problem for Mindy's legal defence team was that she hadn't tried to kill the man exerting the controlling behaviour on her. She'd never harmed a hair on Frank's head. Or his face. Instead she had tried to murder a number of perfectly innocent people.

And the element of premeditation was never in question because, when her initial attempt on Dylis hadn't immediately worked, she'd gone into the hospital and cold-bloodedly tried to finish her off.

The jury seemed to get this, and in the end Mindy received the sort of sentence we felt she deserved.

Which left Fanzine Frank devastated.

Because all through the trial, even when he was being presented by the defence as the despicable oppressor who had driven his poor innocent wife to murder, he and Mindy had remained clandestinely in touch. Despite everything, their bond seemed as strong as ever.

The scary thing was that these two loved each other.

When Mindy began to serve her prison sentence it looked entirely possible that Frank would go off the deep end, but Tania intervened. She was virtually his neighbour and almost his friend, so she hired him to take on the gargantuan task of sorting, sequencing and cataloguing the vast collection of books in her library. It was the sort of undertaking that appealed to his compulsive need for order, and gave him a lifeline while he adjusted to an existence without Mindy. Or rather, an existence in which they only communicated by phone call, prison meetings and email.

And, since he was working at the mansion, Ophelia enlisted him in helping her make goat's cheese.

So gradually Fanzine Frank began to live a new life, and things really weren't so bad. After all, he was being bossed around and exploited by two of his goddesses. Just like the good old days.

We knew all this gossip because we remained in touch with Tania. She'd even drop around to see us on her excursions to London.

It was on one of these visits that she made the devastating disclosure that a lot of people hadn't accepted the official explanation for Farmer Fancher's death.

"They're saying it's not an accident," she told us.

"Oh, Christ," I said, my stomach going cold.

"They're saying it's *suicide*."

Nevada and I gave a sigh of relief. "Why suicide?" said Nevada.

"Because they—they're all farmers, these people— they say that he was a poor, hardworking, self-sacrificing, unappreciated farmer driven to despair by cruel economic forces."

"Poor, hardworking, self-sacrificing?" I said. I was thinking of a trailer full of dead goats.

"That's right. Penniless and desperate, they say he took his own life. And now he's being treated as a martyr and they're making him the centre of their rally, More Funds for Farmers."

"For Fucking Filthy Fascist Farmers," said Nevada.

"In any case, they're planning to march on Parliament."

March on Parliament they did, several weeks later. Tania texted us to watch the news and we tuned in to see an impressive crowd carrying banners, the marchers spearheaded by the late Fancher's collie, who looked like he was enjoying all the attention. There were speeches about Fancher, now recast as a noble son of the soil driven to the ultimate, tragic extremity; the victim of vicious government cuts and an uncaring public who didn't understand the vital role that farmers play.

And so on.

There was also a moving account of his faithful canine companion howling over the poor chap's body. Cue a close-up of the collie.

Seeing that dog again gave us a strange feeling, so we switched the broadcast off and resumed doing what we did best—me playing records on my rather lovely hi-fi, and Nevada selling high-end second-hand clothes.

In this case, to Agatha, who had dropped around for specifically this purpose.

She and Nevada were going through my darling's latest acquisitions, which included a vast range of cast-offs from Tania and Helene.

This celebration of fashion had spilled over into the living room. I wasn't complaining, not least because I was allowed to go on listening to my esoteric playlist— Morricone giallo scores, exotica by Johnny Richards, British jazz on Lansdowne—unhindered and unquestioned while this revelry took place. As a matter of fact, the women were enjoying the music.

Nevada had dug out a silk blouse which I recognised as the one Helene had worn under her duster on her first visit. Freshly laundered of course.

"I love this," said Agatha, holding it up in front of her, a spectral apparition in shimmering translucent white, like the top half of a headless ghost.

"I was saving it especially for you," said Nevada with satisfaction that her friend had fallen into her retail trap.

"What do you reckon, bra or no bra?"

"Definitely no bra."

"Tell the boyfriend to look away."

"Look away, boyfriend," said Nevada.

"Was that the doorbell?" I said.

"I didn't hear anything."

"Neither did I."

"Wait for it," I said.

The women shrugged and ignored me, continuing to go about their business, which consisted of Agatha taking off her top while I continued to look away, in the direction of my record shelving. I found myself closely scrutinising the spines of the LPs. Oh, so that was where my copy of *Katanga!* had gone.

The record on the turntable concluded and in the ensuing silence the snap and slither of Agatha's bra removal was followed instantly by the ringing of the doorbell. I trotted down the hall and opened the front door.

Tinkler stood there smiling. He looked cheerful and innocent—if that word could be applied to him.

"Hi," he said. "What's happening?"

The End

ACKNOWLEDGEMENTS

I'd like to thank Matt West of Miwk, for driving me all over Epsom on research trips and sharing his beekeeping expertise, not to mention coining the term "neck bollocks"; Debs Turpin for invaluable help with archery research; Shaun Kelso and his daughter Emily, a big fan of Nevada, for allowing me to appropriate her name for Nevada's old school; Mark Yexley, for taking me to the Chalk Hill Bakery and encouraging me to finally visit Olympic Studio Records in Barnes; to Ben Aaronovitch for suggesting the cameo featuring his character Lady Ty from his Rivers of London novels (if you haven't read them, do check them out, they're fantastic); the late (and very great) Peter O'Donnell who taught me so much about writing; the equally great American novelist Thomas McGuane, who is still very much with us, for nicking one of his lines; to my perceptive new editor George Sandison; to Nick Landau and Vivian Cheung at Titan for their stalwart support of the series; to Lydia Gittins, my wily publicist; and to my agent John Berlyne for helping me to man the barricades.

ABOUT THE AUTHOR

Andrew Cartmel is a novelist and playwright. He is the author of the Vinyl Detective series, which was hailed as "marvellously inventive and endlessly fascinating" by *Publishers Weekly*. His work for television includes commissions for *Midsomer Murders* and *Torchwood*, and a legendary stint as script editor on *Doctor Who*. He has also written plays for the London Fringe, toured as a stand-up comedian, and currently has a play scheduled to open in the West End. He lives in London with too much vinyl and just enough cats. You can find Andrew on Twitter at @andrewcartmel.

THE RUN-OUT GROOVE

A VINYL DETECTIVE NOVEL

ANDREW CARTMEL

His first adventure consisted of the search for a rare record; his second begins with the *discovery* of one. When a mint copy of the final album by Valerian—England's great lost rock band of the 1960s—surfaces in a charity shop, all hell breaks loose. Finding this record triggers a chain of events culminating in our hero learning the true fate of the singer Valerian, who died under equivocal circumstances just after—or was it just before?—the abduction of her two-year-old son.

Along the way, the Vinyl Detective finds himself marked for death, at the wrong end of a shotgun, and unknowingly dosed with LSD as a prelude to being burned alive. And then there's the grave robbing…

"Like an old 45rpm record, this book crackles with brilliance." **David Quantick**

"This tale of crime, cats and rock & roll unfolds with an authentic sense of the music scene then and now – and a mystery that will keep you guessing."
Stephen Gallagher

VICTORY DISC

A VINYL DETECTIVE NOVEL

ANDREW CARTMEL

This time the search for a rare record ensnares our hero in a mystery with its roots stretching back to the Second World War. Three young RAF airmen played in a legendary band called the Flare Path Orchestra. When a precious 78rpm record of their music turns up in the most unexpected place the Vinyl Detective finds himself hired to track down the rest of their highly sought-after recordings.

But, as he does so, he finds that the battles of the war aren't over yet—and can still prove lethal. While fighting for his life, our hero unearths dark secrets of treason and murder, and puts right a tragic miscarriage of justice. If all this sounds simple, it's only because we haven't mentioned drive-by shootings, murderous neo-Nazis, or that body in the beer barrel.

"An enthralling mystery with a wonderful gallery of grotesques." **Ben Aaronovitch**

"One of the most innovative concepts in crime fiction for many years. Once you are hooked into the world of the Vinyl Detective it is very difficult to leave."
Nev Fountain

FLIP BACK

A VINYL DETECTIVE NOVEL

ANDREW CARTMEL

At the height of their success, the electric folk band Black Dog invited journalists to a desolate island for an infamous publicity stunt: the burning of a million dollars. But the stunt backfired and the band split up, increasing the value of their final album vastly. It's this album that Tinkler's got his eye on, and he hires none other than the Vinyl Detective and Nevada to hunt a copy down.

Narrowly avoiding a killing spree, negotiating deranged Black Dog fans, and being pursued by hack celebrity Stinky Stamner and his camera crew, the Vinyl Detective and Nevada discover that perhaps all was not as it seemed on the island—and that in the embers of that fire are clues to a motive for murder…

"Marvelously inventive."
Publishers Weekly

"An irresistible blend of murder, mystery and music."
Ben Aaronovitch

"A quirky mystery of violent death and rare records."
The Sunday Times

For more fantastic fiction, author events,
exclusive excerpts, competitions, limited editions and more

VISIT OUR WEBSITE
titanbooks.com

LIKE US ON FACEBOOK
facebook.com/titanbooks

FOLLOW US ON TWITTER AND INSTAGRAM
@TitanBooks

EMAIL US
readerfeedback@titanemail.com